Cole threw the lamb to the floor as if he were casting away and claim of innocence. He moved to the edge of the bed, right in front of Brooke. He held his hands out, wrists together. Shaking, eyes pleading, he looked at Brooke. "You have to arrest me now, right."

Brooke frowned. "What? Why?"

Cole inched closer, his hands ready to be cuffed. "I let him keep doing it. I'm sorry. I won't run." A shaky sob rippled through his body. "I'm bad and I have to go away."

Torn to Pieces

by

Vincent Morrone

Torn Series, Book Three

Torn to Pieces

Cover Art by *Kristian Norris*

The Wild Rose Press, Inc.
PO Box 708
Adams Basin, NY 14410-0708
Visit us at www.thewildrosepress.com

Publishing History
First Edition, 2023
Trade Paperback ISBN 978-1-5092-5043-1
Digital ISBN 978-1-5092-5044-8

Torn Series, Book Three
Published in the United States of America

Dedication

By the time this book is published, my wife and I will be married for 27 years. We've raised two of the most amazing young women in the world, had a few more children come into our lives who became family, and seen each other through some pretty hard times. Every time I came close to giving up on myself, she pushed me to go further. Inspired me to write to the point where this is my 10th novel. Encouraged me to go back to school so that I graduated and plan on going to get my master's. And we just started over again with three new kids who we love. If that ain't worth a dedication, nothing is.

Rebecca,
I love you. Forever, and always

Chapter One

The Taste of Fear

Alice Mills was already dead, she just didn't know it yet.

She raised a slender hand to signal the bartender. "Hey, Bill, can you give me a refill, and turn that up? I want to hear that newscast."

As she waited, her killer sat nearby, studying this walking corpse wrapped in a dull blue business suit. He licked his lips at the prospect of tasting her.

Her sharp, brown eyes watched the screen for the newscast that had caught her attention a moment ago. How fitting, as the story she was waiting for was the reason behind her untimely demise.

The bartender found the remote and elevated the volume of the TV so that everyone could hear the local weather. It was raining, with a chance of blood on the horizon.

The bartender brought over another tall glass of Guinness and placed it in front of her.

Alice accepted the drink and watched the news channel intently, unaware of the fact that her last meal would consist of the overpriced stout and bad chicken wings. Of course, she had no idea she was just a walking, talking pile of meat, whose expiration date was coming up quickly.

Alice checked her phone and sipped her drink, as she enjoyed the last few heartbeats she'd experience before being in the grip of terror and agony. The man next to her made a passing snide comment about the current news story involving the beginning of the presidential election season.

Just as she was bringing her glass to her lips for another sip, the story she'd been waiting to hear came on. The glass hovered by her mouth for a brief moment before she placed it back down.

As the newscaster introduced the segment from the town of Ember Falls, the man who watched Alice turned his attention away from her to the screen. Vanity meant if Alice left before it was over, she might have a chance of surviving, but this was the story they'd both been waiting for.

The screen flashed to a woman in her mid-fifties, wearing the dress uniform of a police officer. The banner at the bottom of the screen gave her name as Chief Ann Miller. "Nearly a decade ago, the city of Ember Falls tried to hold an innocent man responsible for a reprehensible crime. While we can't go into details without compromising what is now an active FBI investigation, I can tell you that the killer of Molly Winters was also responsible for at least five other murders here in Ember Falls. We also have irrefutable evidence that Drew Duncan, who spent nine months in jail waiting for a trial, did not commit the crime that he was originally accused of. Evidence that was available at the time was ignored for reasons I cannot understand. As the police chief of Ember Falls, I humbly apologize for what was done to Mr. Duncan."

The picture shifted. Another woman filled the

screen. This one may have been the same age as Chief Miller, but she appeared almost ancient. A young man stood next to her, holding her hand. "I always had a difficult time believing that Drew could have hurt Molly. I couldn't believe that the young man who often helped me bring in groceries would do that to my child. And I was right. He risked his own life to save my son. Drew Duncan is a good man, and I'm sorry that he was hurt in my daughter's name."

The son didn't speak, but his face still displayed bruises from whatever ordeal he'd gone through.

The scene changed, and the next image was Drew Duncan. He was much bigger now. His eyes were harder, colder. Before his arrest, he'd been a tough son of a bitch, but now? He looked deadly.

All the better.

"I'd convinced myself that I didn't care anymore if people thought I'd committed this crime. It was a lie I told myself because the weight of the truth was crushing. I've been out of prison now for nearly ten years. But I think, thanks in no small part to Chief Miller and the work of the current Ember Falls PD, I may finally be free."

Duncan's statement was short but effective. So, he felt free? He wouldn't for long. None of them would.

Alice Mills finished her drink and gave Bill the bartender a generous tip. Saying goodbye to a few of the regulars, she headed out.

She only lived three blocks away. It was probably a route she'd walked thousands of times before. The night air was cool and crisp, and the moon was deep blue.

She was FBI, but with less than a year since graduating from the academy. Plus, she'd never done any fieldwork. She was an office rat. The two tall glasses of Guinness wouldn't help her already pathetic instincts. She *should* sense him. He was a predator and she was nothing but his next meal.

Alice saw the door to her walk-in brownstone apartment was left ajar.

She paused, her hand hovering above her holster. It was just a momentary hesitation, one that she would pay for dearly.

She swung the door open. Her small gasp was delectable as she entered her home. The pathetic figure chained to a chair just beyond the door whimpered. Still gazing forward, her eyes glanced. "Who are…?"

From behind, he moved, quick as lightning. Unlike her, he'd been doing this for years. He placed the taser to her neck and sent fifty thousand volts through her. She screamed and fell to the floor.

She glanced up as he slammed the door closed behind them.

The room was dark, but there was just enough light coming through a nearby window for her to see his face. "Y-y-you?"

He stood over her and grinned. He knelt on her back, pulled out a syringe, and pierced her skin with the needle. "We haven't been formally introduced, Alice. My name is Edward Hunter."

Chapter Two

Besties

Special Agent Brooke Madison watched as the sign welcoming him to Ember Falls swished past as he barreled down the highway. The sun dimmed as his mouth went dry, and for the first time in nearly a decade, he felt a craving for a cigarette. "Home sweet home."

"I'm sorry, sir?" Agent Jacob Rivers glanced up from his phone, pulling the right earbud out of his ear. "Did you say something? I was re-watching the news conference from Saturday."

Brooke shook his head, pushing the sense of dread down as best he could. "I just mumbled something to myself."

Jacob pulled out the other earbud, and opened his mouth to say something, but seemed to think better of it after a moment. He glimpsed the passing scenery through the window as he sank slightly down in his seat.

Brooke sent him a sidelong glance. "Something on your mind?"

Jacob's young face turned pink. "I know I wasn't your first choice to come with you, and that you kinda got stuck with me, but I appreciate the chance."

Brooke sighed, as he passed by a slow driver. "That's not exactly true. I didn't ask for Alice. She was assigned. I was fine with her. I'm sure she would have done the job, but she called in with the stomach flu." Brooke shrugged. "They needed a replacement on short notice. I asked for you."

"Really?" Jacob sat up straight, his eyes going wide. "Um…thanks."

"You're welcome." Brooke checked his review mirror as he maneuvered to the right lane. "You've never been out in the field, but you've kept doing your job despite certain *difficulties*. I figured you'd handle yourself out here."

Besides, the kid needed to get away from the idiots back in Quantico.

Still avoiding direct eye contact, Jacob shifted in his seat "I very much appreciate it. And that you don't hold certain…*things* against me."

Brooke frowned as he took the next exit, and headed into town. "What would I hold against you?"

Jacob swallowed hard, his pale white skin burned bright red this time. "You know. When I kinda sorta…" He winced. "Hit on you?"

Doing his best to hide his grin, Brooke glanced at Jacob. "Is that what that was? You were hitting on me?"

Jacob groaned and sank down into his seat again. "I didn't say I was very good at it."

Brooke laughed, recalling his first encounter with Gary Aster and how they'd squared off. Gary saw Brooke as nothing but trailer trash and thought the Bureau should be comprised entirely of straight, white men who came from the equivalent of a Norman Rockwell painting. Brooke's light brown skin didn't fit Gary's vision of how a Special Agent of the FBI's Behavioral Science Unit should look. Things hadn't started well between them, and they'd gone from bad to worse.

"It's not a problem. I've been hit on before. Just because you're not my type, doesn't mean I was upset. And that was Gary's way of winding you up. He does that to nearly all the rookies. Gary is..." Brooke considered his words, warring between a diplomatic response and stark truth. "Gary is a class-A asshole, and that's on a good day. You just need to put him in his place." Well, just fuck diplomacy. Someday, Special Agent Gary Aster will get his. Brooke only hoped he was there to see it.

Brooke took a turn on Route 9, headed toward Broadway. The town seemed both familiar and foreign at the same time.

"I've never been good at that," Jacob said. "That's pretty much why I'll never get to be a field agent."

"Hey," Brooke said, indicating the area around them. "Does this look like the office?"

"No, but..." Jacob shrugged.

Brooke grinned. "Go ahead. Say it."

Jacob took a deep breath and exhaled slowly. "Everyone knows this isn't a real assignment. I mean, they wanted you here because you know the town, and you're good at getting kids to talk. They need you here, but everyone wanted to be on the manhunt. They want to help take down Edward Hunter."

Brooke tried to ignore the sick tightening in his chest as they passed the home of his childhood friend, Drew Duncan. There was a time when the pair of them were inseparable. He thought he knew Drew back when they were kids, but from the reports he'd gotten, he didn't know him as well as he thought.

"Everyone wants to be in on the action. To be a part

of the chase." Brooke took a right and headed towards the police station. "Trust me when I tell you that what we're doing here in Ember Falls is going to be important work. And far more difficult than anything you've ever done before."

"Difficult?" Jacob frowned. "Foster's team is going to be chasing down leads. They say there's a good chance Hunter has gone underground. He'll lay low. Try and disappear. What are *we* doing?"

Brooke pulled the car into the parking lot across the street from the police station and killed the engine. "We're going to try and reconstruct who Edward Hunter is. How he became the monster that killed those people, and probably a lot more. The Foster team is looking forward. We're looking back. Into Hunter's history. Trust me, that's plenty scary."

Brooke gazed at the police station, where he was about to come face to face with his own history, and it was terrifying.

"Part of that," Brooke continued, "is going to be talking to Cole Duncan. You read the file on him?"

Jacob nodded. "I feel bad for the kid. He's been through a lot, but how much do you think we'll learn from him."

Brooke scowled. "I want you to read his file again. Read how the kid reacted to each situation he's been in. Kid has balls, so why is he not talking about what he knows? Our job is to get him to talk. That's not going to be easy. Have you ever dealt with a traumatized child before?"

Jacob shook his head. "I know you have. Everyone was talking about what happened in Somerville. How you…"

"I don't want to talk about Somerville," Brooke snapped, losing his patience for the first time and instantly regretting it as Jacob sank a little lower in his seat. "Sorry. Sore subject. Dealing with a victim is always tough. The raw pain you see in their eyes gnaws at your soul. But kids? Man, they tear you up. Your instinct is to get angry. To curse and yell, and talk about what you're going to do to the son of a bitch who did this to them. You do that, you're just traumatizing them all over again. You have to be in control at all times. You have to read their verbal and non-verbal cues. At some point, he'll talk. And then comes the most difficult thing we'll have to do."

Jacob blinked. "What's that?"

Brooke undid his seat belt. "Listen."

****

Drew Duncan found his nephew Cole sitting in his room. He was staring out the window, stiff as a board, his arms folded as if he were holding himself.

Drew knocked on the open door.

Cole jumped, his eyes going wide and he started to shake. He spun, ready to fight. Once he registered that it was his uncle, he calmed down, although his cheeks turned pink.

While Cole no longer seemed terrified of Drew himself, he was startled easier by anything unexpected. He'd hold his breath if the phone rang, turn white as a sheet if someone came to the door, and he screamed the other day when a car backfired. Drew thought it might get better with time, but it seemed to be getting worse now that the truth was out about his stepfather.

"You ready for school? I'm going to take you in myself."

Cole glanced around absently. "My bookbag. It's um…"

Drew stepped closer and pointed to the corner near his bed, by the trash can. "Right there."

Cole sighed and grabbed the bag, accidentally knocking the trashcan over, its contents spilling out onto the floor.

"Hey." Drew knelt, picking up the trashcan and the homemade comic book that Cole had written. "Why is this in the trash? You and Jay worked hard on it."

Cole refused to look at his uncle or what he was holding. "That's what almost got Aunt Ashley killed. Because I…" Cole closed his eyes. "It's just a stupid story. It doesn't mean anything."

"No, it's not," Drew held up the comic. "Cole, this didn't hurt your aunt. A hired killer named Jericho did."

Cole snatched the comic away and threw it back in the trash. "Because he *saw* this. He thinks I told on Edward. I didn't, it's just a stupid story. It doesn't mean anything."

Drew wanted to pull the kid into a hug, but he'd probably scare him even more. "Cole, it wasn't your fault. If anything, it was mine. I brought that comic to the police station. I showed it to him. He fooled me. He got past me. I'm sorry."

Cole didn't respond. "I need to go to school." He pushed past Drew to head out.

Drew stood up with the comic in his hand. "Cole, you can talk to me. None of this was your fault. You can tell me what he did, and I swear I'll never blame you."

Cole paused at the door, but wouldn't make eye contact. "He'll know."

Before Drew could respond, Cole dashed down the

stairs.

Drew decided that he'd hang onto it himself. Cole would want it back someday. He went downstairs, put the comic in a drawer so Cole wouldn't see it, and found Cole grabbing his lunch that had been lovingly prepared by the woman who loved Cole as if he was hers.

Lilly Danvers fussed over Cole, smoothing his hair and straightening his shirt. "I'll see you after school today. You have a good day. Say hello to Jay for me."

Lilly kissed Cole gently on his cheek.

Drew leaned on the doorway, watching the interaction between his nephew and the woman who had been best friends with both of his sisters for what seemed like a lifetime.

"Your aunt is waiting in the car." Drew saw how Cole stiffened as he spoke. "I'll be there in a minute or two."

Cole headed outside.

Drew made eye contact with Lilly. Something that required looking down. She was a pixie of a girl, with long red hair and a smattering of freckles on her nose.

"He'll be okay," Lilly said. "We'll make sure of it. I'll meet you at the school to pick him up."

Drew stepped closer. "You don't have to go. Ashley and I will be with him the entire time." This time, he wouldn't make the mistake of going off after Hunter and leaving Cole defenseless.

"I'll be there," Lilly insisted. "You told me that Cole is as much mine as he is yours. Did you mean that?"

Drew shoved his hands into his pockets. "Of course. I know how much you love him. That's what Kelli wanted. We've got the paperwork in. In a few months, it'll be official. He *is* yours. And you don't have to be there to prove that to him."

Lilly patted his chest. "Yes, I do. More than ever, Cole needs to have his entire family stand with him. That includes me. He needs to know that we'll be there for him no matter what."

****

After she watched Drew pull away with Cole in the car, Lilly went to work in the kitchen, cleaning the breakfast dishes, scrubbing the counters down, and putting everything just right. How did Ashley manage to get coffee stains on every surface imaginable?

She scrubbed at one, frowning at how the whiteness of the granite seemed to refuse to get clean. Was it really that filthy, or was that just her, seeing dirt and grime where there was none?

She had a few hours to kill before it was time to get Cole from school and take him to the police station.

And see Brooke again.

Not that she hadn't seen him at all since their breakup. For years, he'd haunted her in her dreams. For the last three nights, she'd barely slept because the moment she'd closed her eyes, he was there.

And he wasn't alone.

Wincing at the tightness in her chest, she continued to scrub the counter. The more she scrubbed, the dirtier it seemed. She could feel herself being pulled down, into the filthy darkness of her mind, which made her attack the imaginary grime even more.

Her fingers began to ache, so she bit down on her lips and scoured harder. Her chest tightened, so she sprayed more cleaning solution and hunkered down. The air seemed to be thinning, but that just meant she needed to rinse the sponge and start again.

Her lungs were starting to burn for lack of oxygen as she moved to the sink, passing the fridge where Cole's report card hung for all to see. Everything else in the kitchen was dimmed in shadow, but the white paper report card was like a beacon of light. All As, and enthusiastic comments from the wonderful Mrs. Hanley. A smile tugged at the corner of her mouth, and suddenly, she remembered how to breathe.

Heaving for breath as if she'd just been drowning, Lilly dropped the sponge and wrung her hands. She couldn't fall apart. Cole needed her. Now more than ever.

And if that meant facing Brooke Madison, that's what she would do.

****

Drew stood with his arms crossed, glaring at the door. A private war waged silently in his stomach; butterflies of excitement battled dragons breathing the fire of doubt.

Brooke had been in with the chief, who wanted to speak to both agents alone since Drew arrived, but sooner or later that door would open. How would Brooke view him? As a long-lost brother, or a man who got away with murder?

A shadow appeared at the door and Drew held his breath. His best friend. His oldest buddy. The guy he'd once come close to confiding in.

The door opened and in walked Drew's partner and soon-to-be brother-in-law, Ollie Miller. Dressed in his navy-blue suit, with his detective shield clipped to his black leather belt, Ollie paused as he studied Drew. His face melted into a frown. "Where are you?"

Drew scowled. "I'm right here."

Ollie shook his head as he closed the distance. "That's not what I meant. I can see those wheels turning in your head. You're in a dark place."

When the hell did Ollie get so good at reading him? "Yeah well...I'm about to see my former best friend. Part of me is scared. How do I know if he thinks I'm still guilty?"

Ollie furrowed his brow. "Drew, you've been fully exonerated. You'd have to be an idiot to think you're still guilty, and Brooke was no idiot. I mean, it's not like we were buddies or anything, but you two were like brothers."

Drew inhaled. Brothers. That's how he looked at Ollie now. The guy he tormented for years; Ollie was family.

Another shadow appeared at the door. Drew could hear Ollie's mom, the chief of police in Ember Falls, as he recognized her shape. Her voice was formal and professional.

This was it.

The door opened and Chief Miller came in, followed by Polansky, the desk sergeant with the bulldog face. A young agent carrying a bag with a laptop, with dark hair and a boyish face walked in but barely made eye contact. Whoever he was, he appeared fresh out of the academy.

Brooke Madison didn't appear to be the same skinny kid that Drew grew up with, but neither was Drew. Back in high school, he'd nearly always worn his football jacket, or jeans and a hoody. Now, he wore his dark suit and FBI ID like a second skin.

Brooke had bulked up since Drew had seen him last, but his face was still the same. His light brown skin was offset by deep blue eyes, an attribute Drew always assumed he'd inherited from his unknown father.

Those eyes locked on Drew's for only a moment, before Brooke turned to Ollie. "Congratulations on your promotion Detective Miller. Your detective's shield looks good on you." He briefly glanced at Drew. "It's been a long time Mr. Duncan. We'll need to catch up."

Drew felt his insides freeze. *Mr. Duncan?* Where was his best bud? He didn't want professional courtesy. He wanted the guy who busted his balls and ripped him a new one for kicks. He needed that smirk that Brooke always wore that just let you know you were in for it.

"Allow me to introduce Agent Rivers." Brooke indicated the young, fresh-faced man next to him who quickly shifted his laptop bag and offered his hand to everyone. "He'll be my liaison. If I'm not available, please make any questions or concerns known to Agent Rivers."

Brooke leaned on a small table in the cramped conference room. "As you're aware, there's a manhunt going on for Edward Hunter. I've worked with the agent in charge. She's one of the best out there. I'll be kept in the loop of the progress of the manhunt, and as such, I'll do whatever I can to keep you in that same loop, but I can't do anything that could jeopardize the investigation."

"Why would telling us where you think that punk is jeopardize anything?" Polansky crossed his arms and glared, his face as sour as ever. "We dealt with Jericho on our own. We're not some redneck bunch of yahoos that don't know dick."

A glimmer of amusement flickered over Brooke's face. "I'm not suggesting otherwise, but Chief Miller has acknowledged, openly and on the air, that there's been corruption within the department. We need to be careful. I can only give you my word that I'll keep you in the know as much as I can."

His tone made it clear that he considered the matter closed.

Polansky pointed a finger to put in his two cents again when Ann held her hand up to silence him. "I understand your need for discretion, and the last thing we would want is to do is jeopardize your manhunt into Edward Hunter. We all want him caught, but let me be clear. If you have any reason to believe he might return here to Ember Falls, I must insist you tell us. Hunter's presence in Ember Falls would put our community in extreme danger, now more than ever. If that happens, and you didn't warn us, I will hold both the FBI and you personally responsible. Are we understood?"

"Crystal." Brooke's tone was all business. "I can assure you, the last thing I want is Edward Hunter to kill again, here or anywhere else."

Ann nodded. "What's our next step?"

Brooke casually looked at his watch. "I'll want to read all files regarding Hunter. I'll need to debrief all personnel who have had any involvement. I'm not trying to cause trouble for your people. If I have reason to believe that anyone has had anything to do with it, I'll make sure you know right away. This is your house."

"Damn right it is," Polansky muttered.

This time, Brooke did grin. He was still avoiding most eye contact with Drew and hadn't spoken to him since first coming into the room. "I'll need to also interview non-Ember Falls witnesses. That would include any members from McAlister Security that have been involved. If they're not available to speak in person,

Jacob can arrange video interviews. I'll need to speak with anyone that came in contact with Jericho or his alter ego of Ian Corvidae."

Drew pictured the hired killer who'd come into Ember Falls and nearly killed his sister. He'd formed some sort of strange attachment to Cole and had even expressed feelings of protectiveness over Drew's nephew, but that hadn't stopped the Picasso of hitmen from kidnapping him.

Brooke reached into his bag and pulled out a vanilla folder. "This is what we know of Jerry Bushfield, Jericho's real name. He murdered his parents. And we believe he may have had his first kill when an old man across the street died in a fire. Jericho would have been ten at the time."

Polanski snatched the file, opened it up, put his glasses on, and quickly scanned the information. "Psycho. Old man across the street was terrorizing Jericho's best buddy. Blamed the other kid for his mutt getting out. Bet Jericho was responsible for letting the dog escape."

"*If* he did escape," Ollie put in. "Jericho may have taken and killed the dog. It would fit the profile of a serial killer. Wouldn't be surprised if he wet his bed too."

Brooke gave Ollie an impressive nod. "The Macdonald triad and we've examined his medical records. Bedwetting was present until at least age twelve. Very good."

Ollie beamed as if he'd just earned a gold star.

"I'll also need to go to the dump site where the bodies were located." Brooke glanced towards Polanski. "I know you've been over that, and with the assistance of McAlister, but I'd still like to see it for myself. I'll also be going to where he lived while here in Ember Falls and traveling to his residence in Cheyanne. Agent Rivers will stay in Ember Falls while I do, but if you'd like to have someone from your department accompany me, I'd be open to the idea."

Ann had taken the file on Jericho from Polansky. "I would, yes. We'll also need to discuss the cover-up of Molly Winter's murder."

Brooke glanced down to the ground, an obvious sign that he was deliberately avoiding eye contact with Drew. The sense of dread was starting to be washed away by anger. They were talking about things that nearly destroyed him. Brooke at least owed him the courtesy of looking him in the eye.

"We'll get into that soon, but I want to get my bearings first." Brooke glanced at his watch. "One of the first people I'll want to meet will be Edward's stepson, Cole Duncan. I understand he'll be brought here today."

Like it or not, Brooke was going to have to deal with Drew now. "I'll be leaving soon to get him. Brooke," Drew used his friend's first name, not his title, very much on purpose. He waited until Brooke finally made eye contact. "You need to understand how fragile Cole is. When I first met Cole, he trembled when I walked into the room. He scurried away from me on more than one occasion if I got up too fast. Just the thought of anyone speaking Hunter's name, he turns white as a sheet. You need to be careful."

Brooke held Drew's gaze for a moment. "I've dealt with traumatized children before. I can't promise it'll be easy on him, but I'll be gentle. You have my word."

Drew felt a small knot unravel in his gut. Whatever issues he had with Brooke; he knew what the man's word meant.

Slowly, everyone headed out, but Brooke stayed put. "Can you spare a moment Mr. Duncan?"

Drew felt his back stiffen.

He stopped in place and waited until the others left. Agent Rivers was the last to leave, getting instructions from Brooke to set up someplace at the Chief's discretion. Brooke closed the door, turned around, and made eye contact. "It's been a long time."

Drew refused to blink, but he could barely breathe as he waited. "It has."

"I'm going to need to interact with you and your nephew," Brooke said, "so we need to deal with a few things first. If that's okay?"

Drew stepped forward. "Yeah, we should. Look, Brooke, I—"

Brooke's fist flashed out and slammed into Drew's face, knocking his childhood best friend on his ass.

Chapter Three

Pleased to Meet You

"I owed you that from the last time we saw each other. Not get up here and hug me, brother." Brooke held his hand out for Drew.

Grinning like an idiot, Drew took the offered hand and let Brooke pull him up. The two men embraced, and suddenly the world felt a little more right.

"Jesus, I missed you," Brooke said. "I tried to see you in prison, but they were having none of it."

Drew sighed. "I know. Same with my sisters. I was pretty much cut off."

Brooke folded his arms and leaned against the wall. "This goes deeper than one psycho. Someone has a stake in keeping all of this buried. You know that, right?"

"Yeah, I do." Drew closed his eyes, and the image of his father helping to plot his frame-up filled his mind. "I've got a few thoughts, but I'll have to lay it out for you. I don't think I have the time now. There's a USB drive they found at my place," Drew winced. "Sorry, my dad's place."

Brooke nodded. "I still think of Four Foxglove Way at the trailer park as my place, even though I haven't stepped foot in there in a decade."

Drew felt more of the anxiety within him melt away. Brooke understood, better than most. "You should have

Chief Miller show it to you. I haven't seen it, but it shows there was a conspiracy."

Brooke glanced towards the door. "Miller wasn't Ember Falls Chief at the time, but she was a ranking cop in Albany. This might reach there. I need to be careful with what I tell her. I know she was forced to clear you, but what's your read of her?"

Drew waited until Brooke was looking him in the eye again. "Ann Miller was in no way, shape, or form *forced* to clear me. She has done everything in her power to stand by me, starting with the moment she took over here in Ember Falls. I didn't know it until a couple of months ago, but I might never have gotten out of that fucking prison if not for her. That press conference was *her* idea. Those were her words. I'm here at her invitation. Ember Falls PD was one of the most corrupt forces in the nation when I was arrested. I've worked with dozens of departments over the years with McAlister. Some of the best. None of them have the integrity of today's Ember Falls PD, and the credit for that belongs entirely to Ann Miller. I trust her with my life."

Brooke's eyebrows shot up. "Okay. I was going to be stingy with what I share, but if you're sure…"

"I am," Drew insisted. "She's family. And that's going to be official. Ollie and Ashley are engaged."

"Really?" Brook raised his eyebrows. "And you're okay with your sister marrying Elephant Boy?"

Drew jabbed a finger in Brooke's face. "Shut up about Ollie. He's been here for my sister when I ran. He's put himself on the line for Cole in every way possible."

Brooke held up his hands. "Whoa. That was your name for him, not mine. I used to tell *you* to lay off him."

Drew glared at Brooke, unblinking for a moment before he stalked away. The shame of how he'd treated Ollie made his face burn. "When I came back, Ollie reminded me of how I treated him. He was worried I'd bully Cole, and he made it clear he wouldn't stand for it. Got right in my face. He's not the timid kid he used to be. He's a damn fine cop and an even better man. I apologized to him. I asked him to help me keep Ashley and Cole safe."

Drew turned to face Brooke. "Ollie had no reason to let go of the years of abuse, but he not only forgave me but he's also become a better friend to me than I have any right to expect. He's been loyal to Ash and Cole to the point of being willing to give up his shield to protect them. We're partners. So, am I okay that he's engaged to Ash? I'm thrilled. I couldn't ask for a better brother."

Brooke studied Drew but his face remained impassive. "I think I've got a lot of catching up to do."

Drew folded his arms. "You haven't asked about Lilly."

For the first time since he'd arrived, Brooke's professional detachment was washed away by stunned angst. The pain on his face was clear as he turned away. "I know she probably hates me, and I don't want to make her uncomfortable. I'll respect her space. She won't have to see me if she doesn't want to."

Drew glanced at the clock on the wall. He needed to leave soon, but he could spare a few more moments. "You're going to have to see her. She's not going to let him come here for an interview with the FBI without his full family by his side. I tried to tell her she didn't have to come, but she wouldn't hear of it."

Brooke kept his eyes on his own feet. "I wasn't sure

if she was involved more because of her friendship with Ashley, or if it went deeper. The last thing I want to do is hurt her." He fidgeted with his tie. "Is she… happy?"

Drew shrugged. "She's Lilly. She's still the same sweet girl we knew growing up, but we haven't had a lot of happy since I've been back. My sister's murder, Cole being kidnapped twice. But she's been solid and steady as always."

Brooke shifted uncomfortably but remained quiet.

Drew inhaled and glanced at the clock. "I do want to catch up, but I've got to get to Cole's school. I'll be back soon."

Drew headed for the door but stopped when Brooke put his hand on Drew's shoulder. "The FBI thinks he'll try and put as much space between himself and Ember Falls as possible. That's not just the official line, that's their *belief*. Drew, I've profiled Hunter. He'll run, but he intends to come back. I'm sure of it. That's *my* belief. He'll come for Cole, and he'll target your sister and Lilly. I can't have that. I'll stay away from Lilly if she wants, but I'm sticking close. I won't let him near her."

Locking eyes with Brooke, Drew realized that for the first time in over a decade, he and his best friend were ready to fight on the same side. And instead of feeling like a powerless eight-year-old with a broken arm and fresh burns on his skin, he was a warrior with a powerful army behind him as he charged into battle. "Hunter comes near any of them, we end him."

With one final nod to each other, Drew headed out to get his nephew.

****

Lilly watched Ashley pacing in front of the administration office of the school, impatiently waiting for Cole to come down the hall. They were pulling him out early today to take him to talk to Brooke.

Her Brooke.

Only he hadn't been her Brooke in a very long time. And she knew there was no way he would ever be hers again. She had no business missing him. No right to want a life back that she'd once dreamed of, knowing she could never have.

Lilly shook her head and put those thoughts away in a box. Her focus was on getting Cole through the day. And maybe Ashley too.

"Why do they need Cole? He's just a little boy."

Lilly frowned. "They want to understand as much about Hunter as possible. The more they know, the faster they'll catch him. And besides, it may be good for Cole."

"Bullshit. What would be good for Cole is if they found Hunter and killed him so Cole won't have to be afraid. Brooke shouldn't be making an eight-year-old boy do this." Ashley stopped dead in her tracks. "And *you* shouldn't be there. Brooke doesn't deserve to see you again."

Lilly struggled for patience. Ashley meant well, even if she wasn't making this any easier. "Cole is going to be nine in less than two weeks. And Brooke didn't do anything to not deserve me. You don't know what happened."

Ashley scowled. "Because you won't tell me. And don't bullshit me. I saw how heartbroken you were. He fucking destroyed you."

Lilly's eyes grew wide as she glanced around. "Ashley, this is a school. Watch your language."

Ashley appeared ready to let loose with another verbal volley of adult words when the front door to the school opened. A dark-skinned woman entered, and her eyes settled on Ashley. Wearing a smart grey suit and a grimace as if she were about to deliver bad news, the woman approached them.

"Jeannette, hi," Ashley said. "Lilly, this is Jay's aunt."

Jay was Cole's first, and so far, only friend. The pair had bonded over superheroes, zombies, and monsters. Each, having lost their mothers, had found kindred spirits in each other.

"I'm here to pick up some work for Jay," Jeanette said, indicating the front office. "I kept him home today."

Ashley frowned. "Oh, I'm sorry. Is Jay not feeling okay?"

Jeannette shifted uncomfortably. "Well, that's the thing. Jay was fine, but I kept him home anyway. I knew Cole was coming back today and well…" She glanced away. "I'm sorry, but I don't think it's a good idea for Jay and Cole to spend time together. Your nephew is very sweet and polite, don't get me wrong, but you brought a killer to our home."

Ashley stepped back as if she'd been slapped. "Jeanette, I'm sorry. None of us knew… That wasn't Cole's fault. You shouldn't punish him for my mistake."

Jeanette closed her eyes. "I'm not blaming Cole. Or you for that matter. I can't tell you how bad I feel. I know he's been through a lot, but I'm doing this to protect Jay. You should know that this isn't coming from Jay. He's fiercely loyal and very concerned over Cole, but until his father comes back later this week, he's my responsibility. I've got to put him first."

Ashley shook in rage. Lilly, knowing her best friend was only mute because of the utter shock, stepped forward.

"Jeanette, we would never want to put Jay in harm's way. I can promise you we'd never leave them unattended, but I'm begging you to reconsider. You don't understand how much Jay's friendship means to Cole."

Jeannette wiped a tear away from her eye. "I'm sorry. I know Jay is one of Cole's closest friends, but…"

"Jay is Cole's *only* friend," Ashley said. "He wasn't allowed any when he lived with his stepfather. Cole has gone through…" Ashley paused, wiping away her own tears. "Is *still* going through so much more than you can understand. If you take Jay away, you'll destroy what little happiness he has. *Please*."

Jeannette shook her head. "I'm sorry. I lost my sister to cancer. I can't lose him too. They'll see each other at school. We can pretend like Jay is just too busy to come over, but I can't take any chances."

Jeannette turned away to retreat into the administrative office when Lilly stopped her. "Would you consider at least allowing Jay to attend Cole's birthday party in two weeks? It's his first one ever and it won't be the same without Jay. It'll be perfectly safe. Cole's uncle is an ex-marine who works with a security company, and his fiancé is a cop. So is Ashley's fiancé. They'll be at least a dozen police and ex-military personnel there. It'll probably be the safest place on the planet."

Jeannette shook her head. "I don't think it'll be a good idea. I'll make sure Cole gets the present Jay has been working on, but I don't think a party out in the open is a good idea. And um…" She leaned a little closer. "You may want to think of something else for his birthday. A family day. I know I'm not alone. It might be better to cancel than have nobody show up. Once his father is home, it'll be his decision, but I'm sure James will back me. Please, I hope you understand. And I'll pray for Cole. He *is* a sweet boy."

Jeanette quickly turned and went into the administrative office before either woman could say anything else.

Lilly turned to Ashley. Both of them were in shock, but Lilly could see the utter disappointment in her friend's eyes turning to anger. "Don't. I know you want to go in there and scream, but that'll only make things worse."

Ashley's lip curled. "She just took away Cole's only friend."

"No, she didn't," Lilly said. "She just doesn't want them spending time together outside of school. She's scared for Jay, and who can blame her? Maybe once they catch Hunter, she'll be okay. Or maybe his father will feel differently. Let's just..." Lilly glanced around Ashley. "It's Cole. Don't mention this to him. Not now."

Ashley quickly wiped away her tears as she spun around.

Cole was coming down the hallway, escorted by Mrs. Hanley. As always, his teacher with the pale red, frizzy hair had been incredibly supportive and kind. Lilly wasn't surprised to find Mrs. Hanley bringing him down personally. She was talking to Cole, but from the look on the boy's face, Lilly didn't think he was hearing a single thing she was saying.

Mrs. Hanley handed a paper to Ashley. "I wanted to give you Cole's test that I just graded today. It was a hard subject and Cole missed a lot of the work while he was out, but he still managed to get a perfect score."

Ashley accepted the paper with a smile. A large 100% was written on the top, along with three giant star stickers and hand-drawn hearts. "That's wonderful Cole. He kept up with all of his work. He didn't want to disappoint you."

Mrs. Hanley beamed. "Never."

Cole wasn't listening, instead, he was searching the hallway. "Where's Uncle Drew? He said he'd be here."

Just as Lilly started to say something, Drew came running in. "Sorry, I'm late. Got hung up at work and there's an accident on Broadway. We'll use the back streets."

Ashley handed Drew the test paper. As Drew fawned over it, Mrs. Hanley pulled Cole over to the side where there was a bench. She sat so she was eye to eye with her student.

"I'm sure today will be nothing to worry about," Mrs. Hanley said. "But just think of this as story research. Imagine how you'd describe it if you wrote it as a scene in your comic. Okay?"

Cole gave an absent shrug. "Do you think Jay will be back tomorrow?"

Lilly took his hand. "I don't know, but why don't we go and get this over with."

She quickly steered Cole outside, before Jeanette could come out of the office.

****

Cole sat in the back seat of his aunt's car as she followed his uncle to the police station. He tried to think about what he could say to the FBI to make them not want to talk about anything, but all he could think about was how Edward would know.

He always knows.

Cole knew Lilly and Aunt Ash were talking to him, but he couldn't hear them over the pounding of his heart. Their faces were no longer in focus. He gripped the seatbelt, and desperately tried to breathe.

When his uncle opened the back door, Cole humiliated himself by screaming.

I'll know. I'll always know.

Uncle Drew was there, saying something, but Cole couldn't hear the words.

"It's okay, buddy." Drew knelt so he was lower than Cole, keeping his voice calm. "Nothing bad is going to happen to you. The agent you're going to talk to is an old friend of mine. He'll be very understanding. You've done nothing wrong, you know that, right?"

Cole picked up bits and pieces of what was being said. His uncle, promising not to leave him. His aunt urged them to just go home. Eventually, it was Lilly's voice that he focused on. "Cole, just stay here. I'm getting Brooke."

Cole felt hot and cold at the same time. He couldn't see. He could barely breathe. Was he drowning in a car?

A door opened, and somebody got in the car beside him.

"Okay, buddy, just breathe. You're not going into the police station today. Okay. Just breathe for me. In and out. You got this. Don't think of anything. Just breathe."

It was a gentle voice that Cole didn't recognize, but he understood what he was being told. He didn't have to go in. He didn't have to talk to them. Suddenly, there was air. He felt himself begin to surface.

"You don't have to talk if you're not ready. I

promise. Just breathe. That's it. Connect with the seat beneath you. Feel the fabric of the seatbelt. You got this. We're just gonna sit here for a little bit. Breathe in through your nose, out through your mouth. Let's do it together."

Cole sensed the person breathing, slowly, steadily. He was shaking but managed to breathe with him.

"That's it, you got this. You don't have to say anything. I promise. Just breathe and know you're safe. When you can, look at me. That's all I'm asking for the day. Just look at me."

Cole loosened his grip on his seatbelt. Slowly, his breathing became more controlled. The odd shapes in front of him started to coalesce into recognizable images. The back of the seat in front of him. The steering wheel. His uncle's face. The tears in Aunt Ashley's eyes. Tears he was responsible for.

Cole closed his eyes, not wanting to see the pain he caused.

"You're okay buddy. Everyone is okay. And when you're ready, maybe not today, but when you are, I'm here to show you how you can keep them safe."

Cole knew that was a lie, because he was small and weak, and could never keep anyone he loved safe. But he so wanted to believe it possible, he turned towards the voice that he didn't recognize.

A face slowly came into focus. The light brown skin, the deep blue eyes. Something about those eyes made Cole want to scream, but his patient voice and kind face were enough to offset that. When the face clicked, Cole found his voice. "You're the guy in Lilly's box that Uncle Drew punched for hurting her."

Brooke smiled. "Yeah, I'm the one he punched. You

want to punch me too?"

Cole's eyes searched out Lilly. She was watching Cole, her eyes full of tears. "I will if you hurt her again."

Lilly started to say something, but Brooke shook his head. "I promise you, that's the last thing I want to do. And if I do, you have my permission to belt me. You know how to throw a punch?"

Cole swallowed hard. "Uncle Drew showed me. He lets me use his punching bag."

"Well then." Amusement danced in Brooke's eyes. "I'd better be very careful with her. Cole, I'm going to show you something." He reached onto his belt and pulled something off. "Do you know what this is?"

Cole took the item that was offered to him. He knew right away what it was. Ollie and Sam each had one, although neither like this. "A badge."

"A shield," Brooke said. "Some of the old-timers call it a tin. But what it means is that it's my job to stop the bad guys and protect the innocent. I'm very good at my job. And what I need to do today, is just to let you know I'm here to listen when you're ready to talk. I'd also like to get to know you because I've got a feeling that you're a pretty amazing kid. And maybe I can talk to you about what I do. Would you like that? I heard you like to write stories. I'd think learning what an FBI profiler does would be cool. When you're ready. Okay?"

Cole used his finger to trace the pattern on the shield he held. "I like Ollie's better."

Brooke laughed. "His *is* pretty cool. Cole, let's have an agreement. No lies between us. I won't lie to you, and you don't lie to me. If I ever ask you a question and you don't want to answer, just say that. Don't lie. I'll respect that and I'll do the same. Can we agree to that?"

Brooke held out his hand. Cole stared at it a long moment before he took it and shrugged. "Okay."

"Great," Brooke said. "Why don't you hold onto that for a little bit? I'm going to talk to your family. Is that okay with you?"

Cole stared at the shield in his hand. "What are you going to talk about?"

Brooke smiled. "I'm going to tell them how impressed I am with you, ask them a few questions, and try and figure out when I can spend time with you. I don't want to interfere with any of your social plans. I heard you have a birthday coming up. Turning nine, right?"

"Yeah," Cole said. "It's not a big number like ten."

"Nine's pretty big. If you let me come, I'll get you a cool present, but I'll have to get to know you so I know what to get. So, is it okay if I talk to your family for a few minutes?"

Finally, Cole shrugged.

Brooke sent Cole a lopsided grin before he got out of the car.

Cole watched as Brooke spoke to everyone. Brooke spoke too quietly for Cole to hear, and the conversation was over in a few minutes. Uncle Drew came back and told him he was going to follow them home. Aunt Ash got in the backseat with Cole, and took his hand. Lilly promised to make him his favorite dinner, but the thought of food turned his stomach.

Brooke had lied. There was no way Cole could protect his family from Edward. He was too small, too weak.

Too scared.

As they drove away, Cole kept his eyes on Brooke, trying to figure him out.

But Brooke's eyes were on Lilly.

Chapter Four

Making Deals

"He looked good, didn't he?" Lilly asked as she laid out the ingredients for Sloppy Joes, one of Cole's favorite meals. She had a feeling that Cole would barely eat, but she had to try.

"Don't." Ashley stood by the counter, her arms folded and a snarl fixed on her face. "Don't go getting ideas about Brooke Madison. He blew it with you. I get we have to deal with him for Cole, and he did good today, but I'm not letting him do what he did to you again. And I can't believe you invited him to stay in the garage apartment!"

Lilly pulled out a sharp knife. "It makes perfect sense for Brooke to stay close. It will help Cole get used to him, and it gives us extra protection. He's FBI and right in our backyard." She felt the stinging in her eyes as she sliced, but convinced herself it was just the onion. "Besides, I broke up with him. Not the other way around."

"With good reason." Ashley took a drink of water.

Lilly stopped her preparations and arched an eyebrow at her.

"Don't give me that look," Ashley said. "You don't do anything without a good reason. I remember how much of a wreck you were. Maybe you've forgotten that night here in your kitchen, but I haven't. I thought I was going to have to drag you to the hospital."

Lilly closed her eyes, trying to block the memory out. It didn't work. The memory of utter desperation to scrub the floor flooded her mind, along with a fresh wave of humiliation.

She shook her head and got back to work on dinner, ignoring the emptiness she felt from her core. "That wasn't what you think it was. I was having a bad time. I broke it off with Brooke because it was the right thing to do, not because he did anything. He deserved better."

Ashley scowled. "Bullshit."

A speck of onion flicked off the cutting board, onto the floor. Lilly used a paper towel to pick it up. Opened the cabinet for a Clorox wipe, pulled one out, and cleaned the spot on the floor. Standing up, she glanced at the rest of the floor.

"No," Ashley said.

Lilly blinked. "No what?"

Ashley placed her glass down on the counter. "No, you're not going into cleaning overdrive."

Lilly closed her eyes and took a deep cleansing breath. She placed a hand over her stomach and knew there was no way to get back what she'd lost. "I haven't had an episode like that in years." This morning didn't count, because she'd talked herself through it.

Ashley pulled Lilly into a hug. "You scared the hell out of me."

Lilly returned the embrace. "I'm sorry."

Ashley stepped back. "Don't be sorry. Just don't let him do that to you again."

Lilly shook her head and returned to chopping. "You're so loyal, you took my side instantly, but really

Brooke didn't hurt me."

"Bullshit," Ashley said. "You adored him. I thought out of anyone in high school, you two would be married with kids now."

Lilly winced as she poured a little oil into a skillet and put the heat on. "Well, it didn't work out that way. What matters now is Cole. Brooke is clearly good at working with children. If he can help Cole, even just a little, we need to let him. Nothing comes before that. I'll be fine."

Ashely grabbed her glass. "I know, but if he hurts you again, I swear I'll…"

"He won't." Lilly picked up the cutting board and used the knife to push the diced peppers and onions into the skillet where they began to sizzle. "Brooke being here brings back memories of what might have been, but the fact is he can't hurt me. What happened wasn't his fault. Just please, leave it at that."

The unspoken question was if, in the end, she'd end up hurting him again.

****

Sam heard a strange but wonderful sound emanating from the conference room. It was something she didn't hear very often. Drew was laughing.

Sam had heard him laugh on more than one occasion, but it was rare. Usually, it was a short snort of amusement, but this was carefree, happy laughter that was music to her ears. She knocked and waited.

A moment later, Ollie opened the door and invited her in. Drew was leaning on the back wall, amusement in his eyes. Brooke sat in the chair next to him, his friendly smile was instantly contagious.

Ashley had given her the lowdown on Brooke

Madison. He'd dated Lilly, and things ended badly although neither told anyone what had happened. The pair hadn't spoken since.

Right now, they were like two kids who had been playing games together all afternoon.

Drew's eyes locked onto hers, and she felt that familiar quiver in her belly. That jolt of excitement shot through her when she realized that he was hers. He was her schoolgirl crush and the bravest man she'd ever known. They'd just moved in with each other in their house. Drew had insisted it be in both of their names even though he'd been the one to purchase it. They were living out of boxes, with a mattress on the floor and the entire place in disarray, but it was heaven.

Brooke stood and walked over, offering his hand. "I wanted to offer my condolences."

Sam frowned and blinked in confusion. "I'm sorry. For what?"

Brooke pointed toward Drew. "I heard you got roped into marrying this bozo. Y'know I'm FBI. I've got some pull with the witness protection people." He leaned closer. "Blink twice if you need help."

Sam saw the amused scowl on Drew, letting her know this was typical banter between old buddies.

She laughed. "Drew doesn't scare me, although if he doesn't learn how to pick up his socks, he's gonna be the one blinking for help."

Brooke threw his head back and laughed again. Sam couldn't help it, she instantly liked him. He held his hand out to a young agent sitting in the corner, working on a laptop. "This is my partner, Agent Jacob Rivers."

"Pleased to meet you." Jacob rose to say hello.

Another knock at the door had Sam answering. She

found her young partner Brandon Burr on the other side. He was built like a college football player with bulky arms and a muscular chest, offset by a young face. "Chief said we were on special assignment tomorrow. What's up?"

"That's my doing." Brooke quickly introduced himself and Jacob, as Sam introduced her partner. "I'll need some uniforms for some of what we'll be doing. I asked for you, as I'll be interacting with Cole Duncan and he knows you. We'll be here tomorrow going over things for the first half of the day, reviewing files, but tomorrow I'm going to take Cole somewhere. I want him to see the police. Know he's safe." He turned to Brandon. "You ever meet him?"

Brandon nodded. "Couple of times. Quiet kid, but I got to read a story he wrote. Better than most fan fiction these days."

Drew beamed with pride. "Cole's going to be a novelist."

Brooke leaned back against the desk. "I might like to read some of his stories, but let me get them from him. Anyway, you guys are with me or Agent Rivers until further notice. Hope that works for you."

Brandon shrugged and pointed to Sam. "I go where she tells me to go."

Sam grinned. "Anything to help Cole. Have you met him?"

The smiles faded and eyes closed. Sam felt her heart tighten. "What happened?"

Drew's eyes grew dark as he walked over. "Panic attack. He couldn't get out of the car. We were this close to rushing him to the hospital. I don't know if he can handle this."

Sam pulled him into a hug. "We'll get him through it."

"Yes, we will." Brooke folded his arms. The friendly, approachable buddy was gone, and in his place stood a professional with a quiet and gentle authority. "I've got a good read on him. I can help him. He's not just going to handle it, he'll come out of it stronger. I give you my word."

Sam watched as Drew locked eyes with Brooke, an unspoken vow between them. It was clear, these men were brothers reunited.

Jacob stood up and started to pack up his things. "I should go back to the hotel. You're sure you're not coming?"

Brooke shook his head. "Lilly offered to let me stay in the garage apartment, and that sounds best to get him to trust me. I'd offer to have you join me, but I hear the garage apartment is small. Get some food, and a decent night's sleep, and be here tomorrow at seven. We've got a meeting with the chief."

"Will do." Jacob tossed his computer bag over his shoulder. "Where's a good place to grab something and take back it to the hotel? I still need to get through some things."

Brooke considered. "Maria's would be closed at this hour, but there's always Roscoe's Pizza. That's near the hotel."

Drew shook his head. "They went out of business. So's the Dumpster. Great tacos, horrible name, which is why they probably went under."

Brandon stepped forward. "You like Sushi?"

Jacob smiled shyly. "Love it."

"Taste of Japan," Brandon said. "Two blocks over

from the hotel, best Sushi in town. I was thinking about hitting there myself."

Jacob held Brandon's gaze for a few moments before saying goodbye to everyone one last time.

"Agent Rivers," Brooke called just as the young agent was following Brandon out. "You did good work today."

Jacob reddened and flushed with pride as he pulled the door closed.

Sam turned towards Brooke. "You're staying in the garage apartment at Lilly's? Whose idea was that?"

"I was going to ask that too." Ollie crossed his arms. "After how things ended between you two. I'm not judging or asking you to defend what happened, but she was pretty broken up."

Brooke's face remained passive. "She offered and I accepted. I can tell you I have no intention of bothering her, but I want to get to know Cole someplace where he's comfortable and feels safe. And..." He trailed off, glancing at Drew.

"Tell them," Drew instructed. "They need to know your take."

Brooke sighed and lowered himself into a chair. Slowly, he started to explain the FBI theories on Edward Hunter and how his opinion differed. He was breaking protocol by talking to them about this, but he trusted Drew, and Drew had wanted Sam and Ollie read in. Agent Rivers was unaware of any of this.

"I've been spending my nights mostly at Ashley's anyway," Ollie said. "My place has more privacy, but she prefers being close to Cole, now more than ever. I can easily tell her that it'll be good for Cole to have us all close by until this is over. It wouldn't be a lie."

Sam folded her arms and leaned her butt on the table. "And I'm staying with Drew. You plan on reading the General into this?"

Drew nodded. "Already done. He'll be here by Wednesday. Said he'll bring a few McAlister peeps. Hunter is used to going after teenage girls, taking them by surprise. He's gonna have to get past us to get to our family."

Brooke stood up and gathered his things. "Tomorrow, we'll get started on learning everything we can about Edward Hunter and who was willing to kill to keep him a secret. The more we know, the closer we get to putting him in a cell for the rest of his miserable life. And when we do, Cole will feel as if he's the one turning the key."

Sam studied Brooke as he made his pronouncement. It sounded good and Brooke had gone out on a limb telling them his thoughts. She knew his bosses at the Bureau wouldn't be happy, and it was clear he was being very protective. Of both Cole *and* Lilly, which Sam found rather interesting.

But there was just something in Brooke's eyes that told Sam he wasn't being as open as he appeared. He was holding something back, and Sam wanted to know what it was.

****

Cole finished his latest polish of the story as his phone buzzed. He grabbed it and opened the text app.

—*Sorry I didn't see you today. B there tomorrow. Can't hang. Aunt says stuff to do. KMN.*—

Cole snickered and replied.

—*It's ok, cant hang tomorrow got stuff. But soon. I got new story idea. U like zombies?*—

41

Cole's eyes scanned the last few paragraphs again, picking out any errors. He hit print just as his phone buzzed.

—Whats not to love? Aunt is being weird but Dad coming home Wednesday so I'll be busy with him but I wanna hear bout zombies—

Cole sent a last good night message, ran downstairs, and arrived at the worst moment. Uncle Drew came in with Sam, Ollie, and Brooke. All eyes were on him. "What?"

Brooke offered a friendly smile and walked over. "Nothing. We just got here when you came pouncing down the stairs."

Cole took a step back. "I didn't do anything wrong. The printer is down here."

Brooke held up his hands. "I didn't say you did. Homework?"

Cole didn't answer.

Instead, Lilly came into the living room, holding some papers. "Oh, Brooke." She stopped in her tracks, but she quickly recovered. "I'll get the key in a moment. Cole, I assume you were coming down for this? It printed in the office while I was doing some paperwork. I want to read this new version."

Cole eyed Brooke again but didn't take the pages. "You want that? I could print another for myself."

Lilly beamed and this time the smile she wore didn't seem forced at all. "I'd love to. Thank you." She held up the pages to Brooke. "Cole is a very talented writer and I can't wait to have his books in my store."

"I've heard," Brooke sat down without invitation. He was closer to Cole but didn't seem as scary when he wasn't towering over him. "Your uncle was telling me about the stuff you've written. I'd love to read some of it."

Cole scowled. "Why?"

Brooke sat back casually as if this were a normal conversation. "I'm a fan of stories. Lilly and I used to love sitting for hours under a tree and just reading." He scooted forward. "Can I tell you something about myself? It's a little embarrassing." He paused, his eyes going to Lilly. "When I was young, I had a problem learning how to read. I'd fake it in school. It didn't come easily to me. Your uncle used to throw me hints, help me hide it. I didn't even realize it at first. I was pretty embarrassed whenever someone found out. But Lilly here, she figured it out next. She'd sit with me at lunch when we were nine and teach me. I fell in love with stories because of her, and now I read whenever I can. When I was in the academy, I was top of my class and a big reason was that I was able to read, understand and remember everything quickly. So yeah, I love reading."

Lilly was blushing and avoiding eye contact. She had a weird look in her eyes like she was proud and ready to cry at the same time. Cole wasn't sure what to make of it.

"You should say thank you to Lilly." Cole felt his face burn and wished he had kept his mouth shut.

Brooke stood up. "You're right. I'd never have become an agent if she hadn't helped me." He turned to Lilly and gave a small bow of the head. "Thank you. Really."

Lilly's face turned red. "I always enjoyed reading with you, but you're welcome."

She went to a drawer nearby and pulled out a key which she handed to Brooke. "Cole, is it okay if I give this to Brooke? You can print me out another one, and maybe a few more. Everyone likes to read your stuff."

Cole didn't know if he wanted Brooke to read his story, but he didn't know a way to say no without it becoming a *thing*. After a moment, he nodded.

Lilly handed Brooke the pages. "Great. I understand you have a half-day tomorrow. I'd like to take you somewhere. It'll be fun. Maybe the entire family will come."

Cole scowled, ready to rip the pages away from him. "What do I have to do?"

Brooke shook his head as if to say nothing. "It'll be like a game, but one designed for cops. You ever play cops and robbers?"

The fact was, Cole never really did much playing. He'd seen movies where kids his age ran through the house, yelling and screaming for no reason other than it was fun. When he did it, it was because he was terrified. Until Jay, he'd never had a friend to play with.

Cole shook his head but didn't say anything. A wave of heat spread through his face. There was something about the way the FBI agent watched him that was too...*understanding*.

"Well, that's what we're going to do," Brooke said as he stood up. "We'll play cops and robbers."

Cole frowned. There was a catch. What would he have to do?

Brooke gave him and understanding look. "You want to know what happens after? What I expect from you?"

Instinctively, Cole stepped away from Brooke. It was as if Brooke could see into his head. He felt naked as Edward's words echoed in his mind.

I'll know, because I always know.

"There is something I do want," Brooke admitted.

Cole retreated another step, backing into Lilly who placed a calming hand on his shoulder.

Brooke backed up a step. "Here's what I want. Something you can think about until tomorrow. Cole, I would like to earn your trust. I know that's not easy, but I'm willing to put in the work. What I'm asking for tomorrow is for you to just *consider* trusting me. I know you can't trust me because I ask you to, and you won't trust me tomorrow. All I'm asking for is that you consider that you can. You can ask me any question you like. I'll answer as best I can. I give you my word, I'm not going to ask about anything tomorrow that makes you uncomfortable. Okay?"

Cole felt himself relax a little, but not all the way. He glanced up and saw Lilly's smiling face. Lilly trusted Brooke. Cole trusted Lilly. "But you want me to talk about stuff."

"Yes, I do. But not tomorrow." Brooke held out his hand. "Deal?"

Cole glanced over to his Uncle who was watching. "Uncle Drew will be there?"

Brooke nodded. "Yes, so will Sam and a few other people you know."

Cole took a breath. Uncle Drew would punch Brooke if he broke his word, so Cole reached out his hand. "Okay, I guess."

Brooke smiled and Cole knew it was because he saw this as a victory. Cole studied Brooke's eyes. They seemed kind and gentle and understanding. And yet something about Brooke's eyes scared Cole. He just wasn't sure why.

****

Brooke took stock of the small apartment. To call it cramped would be an understatement, but it would do. All he needed was a bed, a desk and to be someplace close to Lilly and Cole. And he would be willing to sacrifice the first two for the third.

Cole was going to be his biggest challenge. It wasn't that he hadn't dealt with children as traumatized as this boy was. And Cole, unlike some of the other kids he dealt with, had an excellent support system. Every single person that was connected to this family was committed to the kid. He had already learned to trust them, which was huge. Children like Cole Duncan knew nothing about trust.

Brooke opened the file that contained the contents of the USB drive found at the home of Frank Duncan and began to read. As he went page by page, Brooke felt his professional detachment slip away. He'd known things were bad at the Duncan home but never imagined it was nearly this bad.

A video file contained the walkthrough of the Duncan house the day after Frank had been killed. Brooke watched as both Ashley and her brother went from room to room. Heard the recollections of the horrific abuse. Brooke scowled, clenching his fist and wishing Frank Duncan was still alive so he could kill him with his bare hands. Witnessing the moment when Ashley confronted the closet where Drew had hidden his sisters while being tortured by their father made Brooke snap the laptop closed.

"Bastard."

A knock sounded on the door. Pushing aside his rage, Brooke quickly rose to answer. He expected it to be Drew, looking to hang out and catch up.

As the door opened, he saw he had the wrong Duncan.

"Ashley, come on in."

He stepped back and let her enter. He wanted to pull her into a hug, beg her to forgive him for not knowing, not doing more to protect her and Kelli. But that wouldn't help her. She was here on a mission.

Her arms were folded, and she stalked in as if she owned the place. She was at war with herself, wanting to both scream and cry. Brooke made an internal wager that he knew which side would win out.

"I need to set a few ground rules with you Madison." Ashley's eyes were narrow slits and her sneer was firmly in place.

Brooke just won an imaginary bet with himself. If he was correct, Ashley would warn him, then thank him, then threaten. He sat down, spread his hands, and smiled. "Please."

"You need to stay away from Lilly as much as possible." Ashley stood, tapping her foot and sneering. "I know there's going to be some contact, but it needs to be kept professional. Act like you're a monk. I mean it, Brooke."

Brooke folded his hands on the table, his fingers interlocked. "I understand."

Ashley began to pace. "You were wonderful with Cole. What happened today in the car..." She stopped, closed her eyes, and took a deep breath before she began to pace again. "It scared the hell out of me. There are times I feel so useless. I want to help him. I love that boy more than I ever thought possible, but there are times I think my sister was crazy to leave him with me."

She stopped short and stared at him. "Thank you for today. I mean that in the sincerest way. I'm going to be honest with you. I'm scared. I'm terrified not only that Hunter is going to come back, but that even if he doesn't, Cole will never heal enough to be truly happy. We get glimpses of it here or there, but seeing him smile, that's rare. He's going to be nine. Nine-year-olds should laugh and joke and act like little loons, not have escape plans in place so his stepfather can't hurt us to get to him. You get that, right?"

Brooke sat forward. "Yes, very much so. I know how much he means to you. Ash, you guys were once family to me. I promise you; I'll treat Cole like he *is* my family."

Ashely tilted her head back and closed her eyes, clearly trying to fight the tears threatening to spill over. She won the battle, but not without one stray sliding down her cheek.

She wiped it away, and her face went from weepy to warrior in less than a second.

"Drew believes in you," Ashley said. "And Lilly keeps telling me I should trust you, so I will, but I swear to God if you hurt Lilly you will answer to me."

Brooke ignored the tightening in his chest. "The last thing I want to do, that I *ever* wanted to do, was hurt Lilly. I don't know what she told you I did, but however I lost her, it's my greatest regret."

Ashley glared at him for a solid minute before turning away. "I'm choosing to believe that because I have no choice." She gave him a humorless laugh. "Can I tell you a secret?"

Brooke nodded, unsure for the first time where Ashley was going.

"You know damn well that Drew and I didn't grow up in a happy home," Ashley said. "I had no reason to believe in true love. It took me until just recently to believe I could have that. Ollie and I are engaged, by the way." She held up her hand with the ring. "I'm pregnant too."

Brooke's eyebrows went up. "Drew mentioned the engagement, not the pregnancy. Congratulations."

"Thank you." Ashley lowered her hand. "Lilly always believed in true love. And growing up, seeing the two of you together, was the best example of what true love *could* be. Maybe when it ended, it didn't just hurt Lilly, but me as well."

Brooke frowned as he stood up. Was he supposed to apologize to Ashley for the worst moment of his life? Yet oddly, he not only felt the need to offer one, but he was also touched. "Ashley, I'm sorry that the breakup was rough on you. I was heartbroken."

Ashley studied his face. "I guess you were. I know Drew was pissed."

Brooke rubbed his chin. "Yeah, he found me and expressed that displeasure."

That earned a chuckle from Ashley. "I'm surprised you didn't punch him back."

Brooke grinned as he stepped closer. "I did, it just took me until this morning. I figured that made us even and neither of us would feel the need to apologize for the missing decade." Brooke shrugged. "It's a guy thing."

Ashley shook her head. "I don't doubt it. Why did it take so long?"

Brooke shrugged and walked to the window where he could see the house. The kitchen light was on. Was Lilly aware Ashley was up here? Or was she scrubbing the floor?

"At the time, I figured I deserved it, even if I didn't know why."

Ashley's frown deepened.

"What?"

Ashley signed but didn't answer right away. She seemed to be waging an internal war from within. "Lilly never told me what happened between you two. I assumed you'd screwed up, hurt her and she gave you the boot. I didn't want to think you cheated on her, and if you ever raised your hand to her, Drew would have killed you."

Brooke knew it was true, but any amusement was short-lived as he recalled the life-altering event that changed everything for them. "Lilly never told you what was going on at the time?"

Ashley shook her head. "No. I don't suppose you want to."

Brooke shook his head. "You should hear it from her if she wants to tell."

He remained silent as Ashley continued to study him. "Fine, I'll leave that alone. And I'm not stupid enough to think this is easy on you. You lost one of the most awesome people in the world."

Brooke scowled, and couldn't keep the resentment out of his voice. "I know how wonderful Lilly is. And how close she is to both you and your nephew."

Ashley blew out a breath. "I'm not sure you do. The moment Lilly moved out of her mom's house, she gave me a home. My grades in school were shit, but she let me buy into the book store, to make it ours. My sister left paperwork that she put together in case Hunter tried to come back. If anything happened to her, she wanted Cole raised by the three of us. Me, Drew, and Lilly. Cole is as much hers as he is mine. I believe you when you tell me you don't want to hurt her, but you need to be careful because she's already hurting. And you need to treat Cole as if he's her only child because he is."

Brooke's deep blue eyes bore into Ashley's. "What do you mean she's already hurting? Drew said she hasn't had a panic attack since he's been back."

Ashley's eyebrows went up. "Checking up on how she's doing?"

Brooke ignored the question. "Is she okay?"

Ashely shrugged. "She's holding it together, but you being back is twisting her up. Part of me wants to tell you to stay away, but that's impossible with Cole. The other half wants you to see if maybe she can get some closure. I don't know, and maybe I'm not the one to be telling you considering how badly I screwed things up with Drew."

Brooke frowned, replaying the afternoon's interactions back in his head. Searching for something he missed. "I don't understand. You two seemed solid today. You were always close."

Ashley folded her arms and looked at her feet. "When Drew didn't come back, didn't even call, I started to hate him. I felt as if he was telling me I was worthless. For a time, I thought I was. Lilly and Ollie were the only ones that kept me sane. Then when Kelli died and he came home, I was completely shitty to him. He let me rip at him because he believed he deserved it. I found out Dad had threatened us if he had any contact. He was protecting me the whole time."

She turned away, but not before Brooke could see the tears begin to cascade down her face. "Every time I felt close to forgiving him, I felt a rush of anger and hatred for him. I was fucking cruel to him. And he let me be. But I'm a bitch and you were always one of the most patient guys I know. So hopefully, you'll do better."

Brooke put his arms around Ashley and turned her to face him. "You were never the bitch you thought you were. Do you remember Brad Liverman?"

Ashley snarled. "How could I forget the bastard? Why?"

Brooke grinned. "You think I don't know you ripped him a new asshole because he gave me a hard time about my reading when he caught me and Lilly trying to make it through Lord of the Flies at lunch? You scared the crap out of him so much, he begged me to have you lay off."

Ashley snorted out a laugh. "I wasn't afraid of him. I could take him in a fight and he knew it. Plus, if he tried to hit me, he knew Drew would have murdered him. He picked on Kelli once and regretted it."

"Sounds like Brad," Brooke said. "Ashley, if he hurt you, Drew wouldn't have been alone. I would have pounded him too. I will take care with Lilly. Maybe we'll have that closure you talked about. And I swear I'll take care of Cole. I like him. I want to help." He paused, wondering what he could tell her to put her at ease. "Last big case I worked on, I got reprimanded because I made a case personal. It involved kids too. And I get why we're supposed to stay professionally detached, but this one is already personal. I'll treat Cole like he's my own family."

Ashley leaned in and kissed his cheek. "Thank you."

She said goodnight and left. Brooke sat down at the computer to finish what he started, but he had a hard time concentrating. Ashley's little visit had him thinking about Lilly. About what could have been, and the one thing he didn't want to ever consider.

Could she ever forgive him?

Chapter Five

The More Things Change…

"Bob Reynolds." Ann Miller tossed a file down in front of Brooke the moment he sat down.

Brooke chanced a glance towards Jacob who had his face hidden behind his laptop. "Bob Reynolds?"

Ann sat across from him, folded her hands, and arched an eyebrow. "I think you know who that is."

Feeling a mix of amusement and annoyance, Brooke placed his hand on the file but didn't open it. "Former DA of Ember Falls Robert Reynolds. Married Stacia Cook, now Stacia Cook-Reynolds. Old money. They have three children. Samuel, the oldest son. Went to school with Drew and I. Ethan who would have been a freshman my senior year at Ember Fall's High. And their youngest. Tiffany who should be a college freshman. DA Reynolds had a very high conviction rate. In fact, the one major case that he failed to get a conviction on was the disappearance and murder of Molly Winters. He has said that if he hadn't left to work for the Governor's office, he would have found a way to make the case against Drew. I think we can all agree, he's full of shit, but beyond that…?" Brooke shrugged.

Anne took a moment to study Brooke, before turning to her right where Sargent Polansky sat. His bulldog face was one step away from snarling, which

Brooke figured was normal for the rotund officer

"We know that someone powerful was protecting Hunter," Polansky said. "Someone went to an awful lot of trouble to hide evidence that would have cleared Duncan. Someone sent a hitman to this town, not to take out Duncan, but to make sure we didn't hear what Diana had to say. Which means she had much more to say than just 'I know who the killer was.' Hunter didn't have deep enough pockets to pull this off. Jericho was working for someone with money and brains, but no balls. Reynolds fits that bill."

Brooke matched Polansky's glare for a good five seconds before opening the file and flipping through it. He skimmed it more out of courtesy, as he was fairly sure there was nothing in here he didn't know. "There are a lot of people who came from Ember Falls who have money and could have afforded to hire Jericho." Brooke closed the file and pushed it an inch away. "I'm not sure I understand why you're focused on Bob Reynolds."

Polansky pushed the folder back towards Brooke. "He's got more than the deep pockets. He's connected up the wazoo. He's got motive. We think he was a part of the underage sex ring we had going on here. Plus, his son Sam was a dealer."

Brooke reopened the folder and flipped until he found that information documented. It was all suspicions, but Brooke knew it was true. "You've known this and can prove it?"

"We know it now," Polansky said. "Working on the proof thing."

Brooke closed the file, and slid it to Jacob who accepted it and put it in a bag for later scrutiny. "As an agent of the Bureau, I can't confirm what you've told me without hard evidence, but it's a valid theory. As Sam's former schoolmate, I can assure you the dealer part is correct. He did get busted in college two times, both times the charges were dismissed and ignored by his school. Then there was what happened with Ethan."

Polansky scowled. "Younger brother get into trouble himself?"

Pulling out a folder from his briefcase, he slid it across the table to Ann and Polansky. "Of a sort. Someone stole from the suppliers. People pointed the finger at the Reynolds kid from U of S, where both Sam and Ethan went. Nobody bothered to tell them it was the college senior Reynolds that was in the drug trade, not the incoming freshman brother. There's nothing to suggest Ethan ever knew what his brother was up to, or had a hand in it, but they grabbed him and worked him over pretty good for three days."

Ann opened the folder and started to read, flipping pages as she listened. Brooke knew she'd gotten to the pictures when Ann's eyes widened. "Worked him over? That's what you'd call this? Can he even walk?"

Brooke folded his hands. "He's going through physical therapy, recovering. His brother managed to skate, *again*. But it caused political trouble for the father."

Ann closed the file, and pulled it closer, making it clear she wasn't done with it. "You've already come to the same conclusion as us. Someone who came from Ember Falls is behind all of this. Kelli Duncan was murdered by two of my detectives because she was asking questions about her brother. They didn't want anyone to disrupt the narrative that Mr. Duncan had killed Molly and hidden the body. As long as he stayed away, he'd just be 'that guy' that got away with murder. If he returned, people might see he's not the type of person capable of just murdering someone. Killing in self-defense, or defense of another, yes, but Drew Duncan is simply not capable of killing a defenseless teen girl. Anyone who knows him knows that."

Brooke read the flush of anger on Chief Miller's face. The inflection in her voice told him she was ready to defend Drew. This wasn't a case to her, it was personal.

"We're looking at someone who had a lot to lose," Polansky said, bringing Brooke's focus back to him. Brooke understood the dynamic. Polansky was playing attack dog, while she mostly watched. "We think Molly Winters was blackmailing Reynolds. We're pretty sure she was a part of this ring."

Brooke glanced toward Jacob. He had thought the Ember Falls PD would be several steps behind and not eager to catch up. Instead, they were a dog, hot on the trail of someone they wanted to bite and they weren't going to be dissuaded by offering them a bone.

"Yes," Brooke said. "The FBI is already thinking along the same lines. We're considering Reynolds as a possibility, but I'm not willing to say he's the one. Not until we've identified everyone who might have been a part of that ring."

"Is that right?" Polansky scoffed. "And how do *we* do that?"

Brooke did his best to appear casual. "I need to look into the background of anyone who was a member of the EFPD, DA's office, and other parts of your local government and start connecting the dots. We just need to identify *just* one. Then we apply pressure and they'll point to the others. I'll be taking lead on that. It would be difficult for you to maintain professional integrity in that aspect of the investigation."

Polansky jabbed a thumb toward Brooke. "Listen to this guy. Maintain professional integrity. These punks put a stain on this house and in this town. You think we can't play it straight and flush them out?"

"What I think Agent Madison is saying is that politically it might be seen as being career suicide for us to be a part of an arrest that brings down the current State Attorney General, or anyone else." Ann's voice was calm, steady, and resolute. "I can assure you, this department will not hesitate to bring anyone to justice. Be they a State Attorney General, someone from the Governor's staff, or even our former Mayor, now US Senator Brooks. Do I make myself clear?"

Brooke ignored the tightness in his chest and held her gaze for a solid five seconds, doing his best to keep his breathing under control. "Crystal. I'll have to report this and see where we should proceed. Chief Miller, I'm not trying to freeze your department out, but we have to be very careful about this."

Ann sat back. "I agree. I've asked General McAlister to assist. I offered to pay him personally, but as he saw this as a part of the investigation he'd already committed to, he refused payment. Nevertheless, I assume General McAlister will find whatever I missed."

Brooke had never personally worked with McAlister Securities, but the reputation of both the firm and the man was beyond reproach.

Feeling his phone vibrate, Brooke pulled it out and saw the display. Abbie was texting again. "I have to make a phone call, but I'll keep you as apprised as possible. Let's keep Drew out of this part. I trust him, but it'll just look better."

Ann pulled out another folder. "We've held this part back. Jericho liked to play games. I think this will explain why we're focused on Reynolds."

Brooke accepted the folder but didn't open it. "I'll review it today, but I'm also going to be spending some time with Cole Duncan."

Ann stood up. "I expect you to be gentle with Cole. He's been through a lot."

Brooke gathered his things. "It's going to be rough for him, no way around that. But I've had experience with traumatized children. I'll get him through it."

Ann came around her desk. "How much experience, because I can't imagine a child more traumatized than that poor boy."

Brooke sighed as he hesitated by the door. "A lot of experience. And unfortunately, I can."

****

As the excited rumble of schoolchildren getting ready to go to lunch filled the air, Cole packed up his bookbag, hoping nobody would notice he wasn't coming down with them. Jay was the only one he'd told, who had given him his most sacred vow to keep it to himself.

Jay leaned over, a big grin plastered over his face. "I may not be in tomorrow. Dad's getting in really late, and he told me I could be there when he gets home. My aunt told me not to plan on it, but I bet Dad lets me stay home tomorrow. This way, I can spend a lot of time with him. I can't wait to show him all my drawings. Especially that new story we started on."

Mrs. Hanley started to call everyone's attention. It was time for lunch. "Jay, can you and Cole hang back a moment."

As Jay started to talk to Cole about all the things he was planning on doing with his dad once he was back, Mrs. Hanley got the kids into a line and sent them down to the cafeteria, following the class from across the hall.

Mrs. Hanley pushed strands of her pale frizzy red hair out of her face as she waved at the other teacher taking the class downstairs. She closed the door and walked over. "Your family is downstairs. They told me Jay knew the reason why you were leaving early. I thought maybe you'd like to have Jay walk out with you."

"That'd be great!" Jay slid out of his seat, excited to see Cole's Aunt Ash.

Cole slowly followed. He didn't want to go. Despite promises, he knew it was going to be awful. Brooke would want him to talk about his stepfather, and he couldn't do that. He'd never do that. They should just leave him alone.

Or maybe he should leave.

Mrs. Hanley held a hand out to Cole. "Let's go."

Cole let Mrs. Hanley take his hand and escort him down. He would be nine in a week, so he shouldn't need his teacher to hold his hand, but the fact was, there was a part of him that worried he'd run off, so he allowed himself to be humiliated by being tethered to his teacher until they reached the front steps.

Stepping out into the midafternoon air, Cole found the faces of his family. Right there were his aunt and uncle, with Lilly by their side. Ollie and Sam were there too. In the distance, Cole could see a cop car, where Sam's partner sat and waited. Someone else was at the bottom of the steps. A woman standing with a man. "Jay, is that your aunt? What's she doing here? Who's that with her?"

Jay, whose attention had been solely focused on Ashley, glanced in the direction that Cole had pointed to. His arm raised to wave, but froze halfway up. His eyes glistened as his mouth dropped open.

Instinct had Cole stepping closer to his friend. "What's wrong?"

Tears rolled down Jay's cheeks.

"*Dad!*"

Jay launched himself down the school steps and crashed into the arms of his father. Jay's father lifted his son into the air, swinging him around. Jay kept begging his father never to go away again.

Cole looked away as images of his mom flooded his head.

Mrs. Hanley knelt by his side. "Cole, I know you're scared, but you're going to be fine. Your family is going to be with you the entire time." She smoothed his hair down. "I've never known a child as brave as you. I know you'll be okay."

Cole forced himself to nod. He should say something, but he didn't want to think about what Brooke was going to ask him to do.

Cole was thankful for the distraction when Jay dragged his father up the stairs to introduce everyone. "Dad, this is my best buddy Cole. He and I are doing that comic together. I gotta show you the new story we're working on. Cole, this is my dad."

"Pleased to meet you Mr. Lancaster." Cole held his hand out.

It was taken and given a hearty shake by a hand the size of Cole's face. "Please, call me Robert."

"New story?" Jeanette's eyes were worried and they examined Cole in a way that had him squirm.

"Yeah," Jay exclaimed. "I'll tell you all about it. It's great. And this is Cole's family. Cole's Aunt Ashley, Uncle Drew, Lilly, Detective Miller, Officer Rossi, and Aunt Ashley," Jay continued.

"You already introduced Ashley, Jay." Robert turned to face everyone. "I feel like I know all of you. Jay talks about Cole and his family all the time. Some more than others." He laughed in Ashley's direction.

Mrs. Hanley stepped forward. "Welcome home, and thank you for your service. Would you like to come in and see Jay's classroom? I've got some of his artwork displayed. Jay is very talented. Jay can grab his books. I'm sure you'd like to pull your son early today."

"I'd like that very much." Robert turned to Cole. "I'm sorry, but you might not see Jay as often as you're used to. He and I have a lot of catching up to do."

Mrs. Hanley opened up the door and Jay pulled his father in, giving Cole one last wave goodbye. Jeanette slowly followed. "I'm sure you'll have a wonderful birthday even though Jay can't make it."

Aunt Ash quickly steered a frowning Cole to the car, as he replayed what Jay's aunt had said. He climbed into Uncle Drew's car and snapped his seatbelt into place. "Do you really think Jay might not make my party?" He caught the glance from Aunt Ash to Uncle Drew, to Lilly, and back again. "What?"

Drew sighed as he pulled out. "Jay's aunt is just worried because of what happened with Jericho."

Ashley smacked her brother's arm hard. "*Drew.*"

"No lying," Drew said as he followed Sam's patrol car. "I promised Cole I'd never lie and I meant it. It's normal to be worried. She's not mad at you, but it's been her job to protect Jay. I'll talk to Robert after he's had a day or so to adjust to being home. If I have to, I'll hire McAlister Security to guard your party. So don't give up yet."

Cole crossed his arms. "If Jay's not there, I don't want a stupid party."

Lilly reached over and took his hand, but Cole pulled away. "Cole, she's just worried. Hopefully, by then the FBI will catch Edward and it won't matter anymore."

Cole turned to face the window.

His eyes burned, and he could feel the tears wanting to come, but Cole refused to cry. Tears didn't matter either. So in the end, he'd end up without any friends again. He'd be alone. It was nothing new for Cole.

Nothing ever changed.

Chapter Six

Target Practice

Drew entered the darkened room, his gun drawn, and his senses on high alert. He couldn't see more than a few feet in front of him, but he could hear. Three, maybe four targets. He crouched down and tried to sense their movements. Footfalls from down the hall told him he had seconds to act. There would be a light switch on the far wall, but that would expose him. And they were just waiting for their shot.

He reached into his pocket, pulled out a flashlight, placed it on a table, turned it on, and quickly rolled away.

Shots rang on, aimed directly at the light. Drew returned fire, and heard the curses as he hit his mark. Like lighting, Drew crossed the room, while more gunfire erupted, aimed at where he'd been moments ago. He hit the lights and surveyed the room. Two gunmen stood by a far door searching for him, while a third held a hostage.

Drew shot the two by the sides of the room, then fired at the door he'd come in from moments ago, taking out his pursuer. Now it was him, the hostage, and the last of the gunmen.

"Let her go," Drew said.

The gunman hesitated, surveying the room. "Okay, I'm going to let her go. Hold your fire."

Drew's scowled. Too easy.

The hostage came forward, slowly. She shifted to the left as if heading for the door. Her hand was by her side.

Drew readjusted his aim. "On your knees. Hands in the air."

The hostage froze, locked eyes with Drew, and reached for her back.

Drew opened fire, putting a solid four rounds in her chest, before turning the gun on the last terrorist. "Where?"

The gunman rolled his eyes. "Over there."

"Face the wall, and…"

The man tried to fire, but Drew was faster. Deadlier.

He crumpled to the floor with a pained curse. "Son of a bitch, that hurts."

Drew grinned. I just bet it does buddy. Drew raced for the door, checking it for wires. Satisfied, he swung it open and went in low. The real hostage was bound and gagged, flanked by two last gunmen who cried expletives before Drew shot them. They never had a chance to pull their weapons.

Sweeping the room for safety, Drew stormed over and pulled the pillowcase off of the head of the hostage. A young man blinked as his eyes adjusted and then whistled. "Jesus. This never happens."

Drew offered his hand to one of the gunmen who he'd shot in the chest a moment ago.

The lights came on full, revealing an undecorated, plain room with old, dinged furniture and walls filled with spackled areas where holes had been repaired. Drew followed the hostage and one of the gunmen, both of who talked amiably about which football team stood the best shot in the next season. Drew made his way out of the house, over to a table where he handed in his weapons, ammo, and other equipment to an older man in an FBI baseball cap and a grey mustache. "I think I left the flashlight in there."

The man in the cap shrugged. "We'll send one of the yahoos in there for it. Nice job. You can head over to the green door over there. They're waiting for you."

Drew nodded. "Thanks."

He exchanged a few pleasantries with the men he'd just shot and killed before heading over to the green door. Opening it up, he found the room filled with four large monitors. Everyone from his family was present, with Sam, Ollie, Agent Rivers, and Sam's partner Brandon Burr all decked out as if they'd gone through the course themselves.

Brooke sat in front of the main screen, with Cole by his side. The kid wore a grin a mile wide, which Drew took as a good sign.

"How'd I do?" Drew asked.

Brooke shook his head. "I'm waiting on the official report, but damn Drew. That was impressive. I've seen people run these courses before. It gets harder and harder with each level. Most don't make it to the end."

Brandon rubbed the back of his neck. "I sure didn't. I made it to level five, and I took out an innocent old lady to get there. She reminded me of my Gram. I'm going to have to send her muffins or something."

Jacob groaned. "At least you made it to level five. I got taken out by level four. I hesitated with that first hostage."

"Those were hard." Ollie rubbed his chest as if it still hurt. "I made it to the last level, fell for that fake hostage.

Thought I was free and clear. I was about to dance a little jig when she started to come towards me, then bam. I'm dead." Ollie shook his head.

Sam pointed to her shoulder. "I realized she was up to no good, but too late. We shot each other."

"Okay people, the results are in." Brooke swerved his chair around. "As none of you have been tested here, they tabulated your results based on first-timers. The course is usually run by experienced officers and agents with experience in the field who are here for advanced training for their agency or department. Often the first time is sort of rough. Keeping that in mind, Rivers."

Jacob moaned.

Brooke showed the screen to Cole, pointed to the iPad, and urged Cole to read it. "Four point three. Pass."

Brooke sent Jacob an encouraging smile. "That's on the average side for first-timers. And yes, they gigged you on the hesitation. They give you three shots to hit a four or you're out of the program, so you'd make it to the next level, but you'd be on close watch."

Jacob put his fists in the air. "Yay, I'm barely adequate." He rolled his eyes and sank back in the chair.

Cole snickered, enjoying himself as Brooke showed him the next screen. "Burr. Three-point seven."

"What?" Burr put his hands on his hips. "I got one level higher than Jacob. No offense, but how'd I score lower."

"Easy." Brooke took the iPad back. "You called it earlier. You killed grandma. You also got very lucky at level two. Missed that gunman in the corner. He just happened to miss you. You'd have two more takes to get that up, and each time the scenario changes and the scoring gets tougher. Because you and Rivers are considered rookies, the panel said that they still felt you both showed high potential. So don't be so hard on yourself. Although, in my professional opinion, I'd ditch the muffins and take your grandma out to brunch. They still do a nice one down at the Tomato Barn on Sunday mornings?"

"Sure do," Ashley put in. "I'd bring her flowers too. Like the kind you'd put on her grave."

Brandon put his face in his hands. "Great."

Cole giggled as Brooke showed him the iPad again. "Rossi. Eight point one."

Brooke scanned the screen. "That's a very good score, well above the average of anyone's first time. Average newbie gets 4 or under. You lost a few points of time, but not much. Better to do it slow than do it wrong. However, you lost big points since, in the end, you died. Still, you would be a clear pass, especially since this was your first go. You'd get the gold star. The downside is because you did so well, they'd expect you to improve from there. Still, nicely done."

Sam gave a fist pump which had Cole laughing as he took the pad again. "Miller. seven point nine."

Ollie seemed to consider his score a moment and then shrugged. "All in all, I guess that's okay."

Brooke nodded. "It's very much okay. Again, well above average for a newbie. High marks, and again, the biggest loss for dying."

"Understandable," Ollie said. "Although it's not a nice thing to say to the dearly departed. Don't they have any respect for the dead?"

Cole snorted.

Brooke rolled his eyes. "Walk it off, Miller. You and Rossi both placed in the top twenty for first-timers. A very good showing. All of you will get official write-ups to add to your folders at EFPD."

Sam rolled her eyes. "Great. They can add it to the plaques they give officers when they've been killed in the line of duty."

Brooke handed the iPad back to Cole. "And last but not least. Duncan."

Cole read the screen and smirked. "Nine point nine." He offered his fist for Drew to bump.

Brooke took the iPad back. "Drew, this really impressed them. I told them that you probably ran similar courses through McAlister. Was I right?"

Drew nodded. "Yes, quite a few. Not this one. I'd bet the general would like to get his hands on that one, it was a challenge."

"Based on that," Brooke continued. "Yours was the only one they graded as an experienced agent. Therefore, they were stricter. You officially have the best time for any person navigating that course to completion. If you had been a rookie, you'd have gotten an even ten, which is as high of a rank as they come. As it is, they were thoroughly impressed. They were trying to find ways to take points off, but couldn't find anything except that you missed one shot. You scored better than most of the instructors who know what to expect. I've run this course, five times. Beat my time and score by a decent margin." Brooke scowled. "I'm going to have to have another go sometime."

Drew laughed. "Bring it, Madison."

Cole laughed again as Brooke turned to him. "So, now for the final judge. What did you think, Cole? They all did pretty well, right?"

Cole chuckled. "Yeah, it was awesome. It was like

seeing you guys in an action film. Do those things hurt?"

Sam raised her eyebrows and pointed to her shoulder where she'd taken a round. "You mean the simunitions? The fake bullets? Yeah, and this one is going to leave a bruise."

Brooke reached into a drawer, pulled out a box, and placed it in front of Cole. Opening it, he pulled out a few wax bullets with plastic tops of various bright colors. Pink, blue, green, orange, and yellow. "Simunitions are non-lethal ammo that's designed specifically for these courses. Without the padding, you could still hurt someone, which is why they have to wear headgear. You wouldn't want to take one to the eye. I've been hit myself, and yes, they hurt."

Cole took one and studied it. "Wow."

"Wow is right." Brooke stood up, inviting Cole to do the same. "So now we've seen what these yahoos do with fake ammo. Let's see how they handle real ones."

Cole sat up. "Really? Like real guns and bullets? Man, I wish I could shoot one."

Brooke glanced at Drew first, then Ashley, and finally at Lilly. "Maybe we can arrange that."

****

Cole stood on a chair, wearing a pair of cool-looking plastic goggles to protect his eyes and thick headphones that kept his ears safe from the loud bangs. This was one of the coolest things he'd ever done. While he doubted they'd let him actually shoot a gun, he wondered if he could at least hold one.

Cole tried to absorb the experience with every sense he had. The rich smell of the gunpowder, the loudness of the bangs that he could feel in his feet.

"You got a good view there?" Brooke asked.

Cole gave a thumbs up.

Brooke pointed to the paper outline of a man that hung far away. "That's about ten yards away."

In one fluid motion, Brooke pulled his gun, aimed, and fired once. He re-holstered his sidearm and hit a switch that brought the paper target closer. As it reeled in, it was clear that he'd hit the target dead center of the head. He pulled off the protective gear from his ears. "You aim, take a deep breath, and pull the trigger."

Over the next several minutes, Cole watched as the others each took their turn. Brooke explained how they stood, aimed, and fired. He talked about breathing, the protection of the weapon, and how to keep your finger off the trigger until you're ready to fire. He spoke a lot about gun safety, telling Cole since he lived with so many people who used them for work, it was important he understood they weren't a toy.

He called Ashley over and handed her his weapon. Showed both Ashley and Cole how they should check to see if it's loaded, no matter the circumstances. Helped her get into a stance and fire.

Ashley fired five times. One hit the target paper, but outside the lines that would have been the target head. She screamed each time she pulled the trigger, and nearly dropped the gun twice. Brooke remained calm but seemed relieved when he took the firearm back from her.

Lilly came up next, taking the gun from Brooke. She checked the chamber to verify it was loaded without being told.

"It's been a while," Brooke said. "You remember how?"

Lilly raised an eyebrow and made a flicking motion with her fingers. "I remember the first time we went to a range together with my grandfather. You'd never shot a gun before. *I* showed you."

Brooke backed away, holding his hands up.

Lilly took her stance and studied the fresh paper target as casually as she might choose a wooden spoon for cooking, and pulled the trigger seven times. When the target came back, there was a perfect grouping of six holes dead center in the chest, where Brooke had told everyone to aim for. There was one shot right in the blank figure's forehead.

Lilly put the safety on and handed the weapon back to Brooke. "I'm still a solid shot, Madison."

Brooke's smile faltered. "No doubt little princess. No doubt."

They held each other's gaze for a good thirty seconds before Brooke shook his head as if coming out of a trance.

He turned to Cole. "Your turn, Cole. Um…Lilly?"

Lilly turned around. "Yes?"

Brooke gave Cole a knowing look. "Maybe Cole might feel more comfortable with you doing the hands-on part here. You remember? Like you did for me years ago."

Lilly smiled. "That was much more awkward as you were taller. I've still got a few inches on Cole. For now, anyway."

Brooke showed Cole the weapon in his hands. "So, a gun is never a toy. It's a weapon, and you have to remember that it can easily kill you or someone you care about. You never want to be that kid that showed his friend the gun to be cool and accidentally kills his best buddy."

Cole shook his head. "There's a thing on here to

make it so it doesn't shoot, right?"

"Yes, right here." Brooke pointed to a small switch. "You should never take that off unless you intend to shoot, and even then, you don't put your finger on the trigger unless you're positive. There are no accidental discharges. Just *negligent* ones. Do you understand what I'm saying?"

Cole studied the gun. "If you're careful, if you do it right, the gun shouldn't hurt anyone by accident."

Brooke smiled. "Smart kid. There are four rules of gun safety. One, you always treat the gun as if it's loaded. *Always.* So you never point a gun at yourself or anyone else. Got it?"

"Yes." Cole knew even an unloaded gun was scary as hell when it was pointed at you, and the trigger was being pulled.

"Two, never point it at anyone or anything unless you're ready to kill or destroy them or it. You need to always be aware of which way the business end of this is pointing. And it should never be at another living thing unless you intend to kill them."

With an impassive face, Cole listened intently. He was still suspicious of Brooke, knowing that the agent wanted him to talk about things Cole could never talk about, but he wanted to understand this.

"Number three," Brooke continued. "Always be aware of your target, and what's behind it. We're at a range. You should be able to just fire, but you look. You make sure that somebody didn't run out toward your target. You think, if I miss, who could I hit? Always."

Cole glanced up. "But what if it's an emergency? I mean, you have to shoot when a bad guy is coming at you, right? You can't wait."

Brooke gave a reluctant nod. "That can be true. If your life is in immediate danger, you have a fraction of a second to decide. That's why you have to practice these skills, so they're second nature. And there are plenty of times when cops have fired because they're afraid for their lives, and afterward they wished they hadn't."

"Have you?" Cole asked. "Wished you hadn't?"

Brooke absently rubbed his shoulder.

Cole instantly regretted the question. "I'm sorry."

Brooke's shook his head. "No need to be. You can ask anything you want Cole. And the answer is no, I haven't ever regretted pulling the trigger, but you know most cops and agents don't ever shoot their guns except on the range."

Uncle Drew and Ollie had both told him the same thing. "Have you...ever shot anyone?"

Brooke hesitated before he moved in closer. "I did, yes. And I did kill him. He was a bad man who had hurt a lot of people. I don't regret pulling the trigger. What I regret is..." Brooke sighed, "*having* to pull it. I don't celebrate it."

Cole studied Brooke's eyes, even though something about his eyes scared him. There was something more to whatever story Brooke was telling, something he didn't want to finish.

"Last of the big four rules," Brooke said, getting back into the lesson. "You don't ever touch the trigger until you're ready to shoot." He took the gun, held it in his hand, and pointed it to the floor. His finger was outside the trigger guard and along the side. "Got it?"

Cole nodded.

Lilly ran her hand over Cole's shoulder as she leaned over him. It was a gentle reminder that she was there, so Cole wouldn't be surprised.

Brooke checked the chamber and popped out the magazine. "Here."

Hesitating, Cole glanced around at Lilly. He saw Aunt Ash and Uncle Drew watching while trying not to appear like they were watching. Slowly, he turned back to Brooke, held out his hand, and took the gun.

Even though he knew it had no bullets, he wanted to check. Careful to keep the muzzle pointed down, away from everyone, mindful of people's feet, Cole tried to figure out how to pull the chamber open.

Lilly reached down. "Like this." She guided his hands, showing him how to pull the chamber back. "See, it's empty."

Cole let the chamber slip back into place.

"Show him how to stand with it." Brooke indicated an area to stand to shoot at the target. "Get him into the right stance."

"Like this?" Cole moved into position. He'd been watching, studying how they stood, both hands on the gun.

Brooke's eyebrows went up. "You pick things up fast. Pull the trigger. It won't fire."

Doing his best to aim the gun toward the target, Cole checked to make sure there was nobody who had wandered onto the range. He studied the target, an outline of a man's body. Circular lines were drawn on the torso, with a red spot in the middle. "Am I supposed to aim for the middle of the body?"

"That's right." Brooke pointed ahead. "Center mass."

Cole lowered the gun. "But if I hit the head they're dead, right?"

Brooke leaned down close to Cole, who made sure the empty gun was still pointed at the floor. "If someone is coming at you, your goal isn't to kill them, it's to stop them. Heads are smaller and harder to hit. In a life-and-death situation, you're not playing for points. You're shooting for one reason only. To stop someone from killing you or someone you love."

Brooke reached out and pressed two fingers into the center of Cole's chest. "Center mass. That will give you the best shot of stopping them. You can't stop them if you don't hit them."

Cole thought about that a moment before turning around, and re-aiming the gun at the target. He closed one eye, tilted his head, and pulled the trigger.

Nothing happened except for an unsatisfying click, but Cole imagined the bullet flying out of the barrel and piecing the target right in the red center. He pulled the trigger several more times. Each time, his fictional bullet was dead center. How hard could this be?

Lilly leaned in, gently putting her hands on him. Cole stiffened, his face burning red from the fear he felt from being touched by Lilly. He knew he was safe here. He breathed in, forcing himself to relax.

"But keep your arm like this." Lilly repositioned his arms so his right one was fully extended, and his left bent at the elbow. "Look down the sights of the barrel." She tapped the top. "Good, like that."

Cole pulled the trigger again.

Brooke held his hand out. "You ready to shoot for real?"

Cole's eyes widened. He was really going to shoot a gun? Desperate to hide his grin, Cole nodded.

Brooke took the gun, inserted the magazine, and

pulled back the muzzle. "There's a bullet in the chamber now, so be careful." He handed the weapon back to Cole with the safety on.

Cole felt the weight of it. It was heavier. It felt more deadly. He kept the gun aimed at the ground as he went through the check as he'd been instructed. Cole planted his feet, took aim, imagined the bullet hitting the target, and fired.

The explosion of force from the gun recoil surprised Cole, but not nearly as much as the appearance of the unblemished target sign. Brooke kept it at five meters, and he'd missed. "Shit."

"*Cole*," admonished Lilly.

"*What?*"

Brooke smiled. "Aim again, don't pull the trigger."

Cole did as he was told. As he got back into position, he felt Lilly press her body against him from behind.

Gently, Lilly helped him aim as Brooke gave him further instructions. The scent of Lilly's perfume mixed with the gunpowder. Cole concentrated on the faceless target.

Someday, it might have a face. It could be Edward's, his eyes staring at Cole as he began to hurt his family.

Brooke's voice sounded more distant as the empty face filled with Edward Hunter's. Cole took a deep breath and pulled the trigger.

Bang. Cole hit the target, outside the lines, but it was close. That would make his stepfather think twice.

Bang. A hit on the shoulder. That'd hurt the son of a bitch. Make him bleed. He liked pain.

Bang. Better. He'd be scared now. *How do you like it?*

Cole slowly fired over and over again. Each shot

getting closer. Each bullet tore through the target. Each one would stop Edward Hunter from hurting anyone he loved.

When the gun was empty, Cole pointed it down, went through his safety check, and handed it back to Brooke who was pressing the button to recall the target.

"That's very good, Cole." Brook pulled the punctured paper target down and showed it to Cole. "You got closer each time. These shots," Brooke pointed to ones near the right side of the upper chest. "They're great shots. You got better with each trigger pull."

Cole scowled as he studied the blank man. "I missed the red."

Brooke knelt down and studied the picture himself. "You stopped him. If this were someone trying to hurt Lilly, he would be down. These shots would have probably killed him, but even if not, all of these…" He indicated a cluster of holes near the right armpit. "You stopped him, Cole."

Cole took the target and felt a lifting of an invisible weight from his chest. He'd stopped him.

Chapter Seven

Finger-Lickin' Good

Lilly wiped down the counters for the fifth time that morning. It wasn't obsessive, she told herself over and over again. She was aware everything was clean, she just needed to keep busy as she tried to get the courage up to do something she needed to do.

Ringing out the sponge, Lilly peeked out through the kitchen window where she could glimpse Brooke as he paced back and forth by the window. He was on the phone. Brooke always paced back and forth when he spoke on the phone.

She had dreaded seeing Brooke again. Assumed he'd look at her with hatred and scorn, but he hadn't. He'd avoided being alone with her, and she couldn't blame him for that. When they were together, he was friendly. He'd asked her to work with Cole at the range, not Drew. And more than once, she'd caught him glancing at her.

Maybe she could make things right with him. Lilly knew she'd never repair what they had, what she'd lost forever, but maybe she could at least get him to forgive her.

Lilly surveyed the kitchen. She could mop, again. Or just go to the store. It was bound to be a quiet day, but there was work to be done. She still needed to arrange for their monthly book club, place orders for some of their titles, and speak to a couple of local authors about book signings.

Or she could bite the bullet and go talk to Brooke. That's what she wanted to do. She wanted to be alone with him to see if he was okay. She'd missed him. She'd nearly forgotten how desperate that need to be with Brooke was.

Hell, if she was being honest, she wanted more than a few minutes of conversation with Brooke. She wanted him. To have him touch her in that way that only he ever could. For a moment, Lilly remembered what he felt like, his weight on top of her. His musky scent as he tasted her, his fingers teasing every inch of her skin.

Closing her eyes, Lilly took a slow, deep cleansing breath. For now, maybe she should start small.

She went out through the back door and headed to the garage apartment. She refused to pause at the door and went in. She pep-talked herself as she climbed the stairs.

You can do this, and keep it casual. He used to touch every part of you and fill you full of ecstasy, maybe he won't hate being alone with you.

Ugh, worst pep-talk ever.

He needs to get Cole to trust him, and I can help with that.

Lilly ignored the pang of the guilt of using the guise of helping Cole to spend time with Brooke as she knocked on the door to the apartment.

She nearly gave into fear and ran when he opened the door.

Brooke was still on the phone, but his eyes widened at the sight of her. He froze, the other person on the phone continuing to talk.

"Hello? Sir, are you still there?"

Brooke held up a finger to Lilly as he blinked. "Um, yeah sorry, Peters. I've got to go, but get me those files as soon as possible." He scowled. "Peters, I don't want to hear about the backlog, find me the information. Goodbye."

Brooke ended the call and placed the phone down on the counter. He gazed at her, those deep blue eyes of his that saw right through her. "You probably saw me pacing by the window, huh?"

Lilly gave him a sheepish grin. "Guilty. It's nice to know some things don't change."

Brooke rubbed the back of his neck. "Thank you for letting me stay here. I know you'd rather I didn't, but I think my being here will help Cole."

"Nonsense," Lilly said. "I'm fine with you being here. I'm okay Brooke."

Brooke narrowed his eyes. He reached down and took her hand. Traced her palm with his fingers. "Dishpan hands. You were cleaning, weren't you?"

Lilly's face flushed red but didn't move. She liked the feeling of his touch. "I'm not *over*-cleaning. I promise. I just was…" She pulled her hand away. "Trying to get the courage to come up here."

Brooke took a step back. "You've never been shy or timid. What's the matter?"

This wasn't going as she'd hoped. "Nothing, I just wanted to ask if you'd be able to have dinner with us tonight."

His eyebrows raised. "Dinner?"

Lilly felt her face grow warm. "For Cole. You told us that you need him to get comfortable with you. So if you had dinner with us tonight…" She shrugged. "I don't know…I thought it'd help and…" She avoided eye contact, shrugging. "I'll be making Chicken Marsala."

It was one of Brooke's favorite dishes and she could see the hint of a smile form at the corner of his lips.

"I'd be a fool to turn down an invitation to a dinner you're cooking," Brooke said. "Especially for your Chicken Marsala. If you're sure you don't mind, I'd love it."

Lilly forced herself not to smile. "Anything that helps, Cole."

Brooke gave a bow of his head. "That's why I'm here."

His eyes studied her, and she was sure he was reading her mind. He'd always been good at reading people, and that was before he became an agent for the FBI.

Don't look him in the eyes. Those beautiful eyes.

Lilly began to walk around the apartment. "How is it up here? I know it's cramped. You can bring your laundry in. Or just, y'know…" she shrugged as she examined his laptop on the table, next to his gun, shield, and his cell. "If you need to stretch out or… something?" She winced at her lameness.

Doing her best to smile as if she wasn't ready to smack herself on the back of the head, Lilly turned to face Brooke who was still watching her intently. "I'm just saying, you don't have to avoid me. We're…okay. I mean if you're okay."

Brooke folded his arms and gave her that lopsided grin. "Do you have a few minutes? I'd like to ask you some questions."

All the air was sucked out of the room, and the

pounding of Lilly's heartbeat was so loud she was surprised Brooke didn't hear it. "Questions?"

Brooke offered her a seat at the small table. "Yes, about Cole. It might be better if we talk while he's not here."

Lilly administered another mental head slap as she forced herself to breathe. "Yes, of course. What would you like to know? I'm sure you've seen for yourself what a smart boy Cole is. Have you had a chance to read that short story?"

"I did." Brooke reached over to a folder and pulled it out. "Have you?"

"Of course." Lilly felt a surge of pride as she recalled the story of an astronaut named Drake who had crashed on an alien planet. "I thought it was very creative and well written. Not *just* well written for a boy his age. I spoke to Mrs. Hanley, that's Cole's teacher. She told me that Cole is writing well above his grade level."

Brooke studied the paper. "I'd agree with all of that, and he's got an awful lot of talent, but that's not what concerns me. It's the undercurrents of the story.

Lilly shrugged. "It's just a story about a space monster. Boys love that sort of thing."

Brooke pushed the paper towards her. "In the story, Drake is stranded on this planet where it's always cold, and he's always afraid. He survives day by day, knowing that the creature can kill him whenever it wants. Drake sets a distress beacon, and when his friends come to save him, the monster kills them but leaves Drake alive. Drake accepts that the monster thinks of Drake as a pet, and the monster terrifies Drake for its amusement. He shuts off the beacon, and resigns to live the rest of his life in captivity so as not to let anyone else get hurt by this monster that is always there, always knowing, always seeing."

Lilly knew the story as she'd read it more than once, but the way Brooke explained it had Lilly shivering. She rubbed her arms and felt a wave of nausea. "What are you saying? I don't...I know Cole channeled some of what he saw into their comic, but this story? How?"

Brooke reached for his laptop. He opened it, keyed in a long password, and waited as the screen came to life. "I understand Cole has a friend named Jay. His first friend?"

Lilly was unsure where this was going but was sure she wasn't going to like it. "Jay's a sweet boy. The two of them are such good friends. They remind me a little of you and Drew."

Brooke moved the laptop so Lilly could see it. "This is Cole's report card from when he was in first grade. Pretty decent grades, especially when you consider what a living hell his home life was, but they mention his need to make friends. They called him shy. Would you say Cole is shy?"

Lilly frowned as she considered the question. "He's quiet. Reserved. He's not shy around Jay. But really, can you blame him? You said it yourself, his home life was hard."

Brooke pulled the laptop back to him and began tapping. "I called the school, spoke to his former teachers. They told me Cole was well behaved, did his work, just didn't interact. If there was a party that the entire class went to, he didn't. They tried to help him make friends. His second-grade teacher saw him interact with another boy named Jake Garrett. Thought maybe, with time, Cole might have a buddy. It didn't work out."

Lilly folded her hands. "Cole may have just not been ready for a friend. It's not his fault."

Brooke reached out, putting his hand on hers. She'd hoped for physical contact since she first came up, but her heart was filled with too much dread to enjoy it. "*None* of this is his fault. But the reason it didn't work out was that Jake had to move. Parents were divorced, father lived just a town over. Different school districts. Jake had to move in with his father when his mother Olivia disappeared. She's never been seen again."

He turned the laptop so Lilly could see the picture of a woman around her own age, smiling as she held a child of six.

Lilly pulled her hand away and pressed it against her chest. "You think Edward took her?"

Brooke held her gaze. "Do I have proof? No. But yeah, he took her. And I wouldn't be surprised if he let Cole know afterward?" Gently, Brooke closed the lid on the laptop and pushed it away. "Hunter might have just alluded to her so Cole knew. Or he might have been more direct."

Lilly swallowed hard. "Direct?"

Brooke held her gaze. "Maybe Hunter told Cole straight out. Killers like Hunter keep trophies. Perhaps a picture. Something fed the idea of Cole's comic where he had those women chained up, with the lock crisscrossed over their hearts. I'm thinking this was it. A picture on his phone of Jake's mom, tied up and bound."

"No." Lilly got up from the table and walked to the window. "Why would Hunter do that?"

Brooke rose and went to her side. "Hunter gets off on their fear. He gets a sexual release from terrifying these women. He tortured them, slowly. It wasn't just the pain he inflicted, it was the sheer panic. Their fear, *his* pleasure. My opinion is that Hunter has a difficult time achieving release if he wasn't hurting and scaring someone. With Cole, he got more of that. He kept Cole in a constant state of fear. If Cole said anything, his stepfather would do this horrible thing to his mother. Now, he's afraid Hunter will do those things to you."

Lilly's hand went to her face. "Oh God, my poor baby."

Brooke closed his eyes. "I'm sorry. I know how much you love him. I shouldn't have laid this on you, I just thought…"

"That because I'm not related by blood it wouldn't be as hard on me?" Lilly asked. "I love that child with all of my heart. I'd hope that you can understand that just because he's not blood, doesn't mean he's not family."

Brooke put his hands on her arms. He seemed to consider his words carefully. "I do. Trust me, I get that. You always loved so deeply. Lilly, I promise, I'll do right by him. I give you my word. I don't know how much that's worth to you, but…"

Lilly shook her head. "Your word is everything. Thank you."

Brooke reached up and gently wiped away a tear from Lilly's cheek.

They stared at each other. She wanted him to hold her but knew he wouldn't, so slowly she stepped back. "I should go. I've got to get to the bookstore. Dinner is usually at six."

Brooke frowned, and she wondered if he were searching for a way to back out. "I'll be there. Can I bring anything?"

"Just your appetite." Lilly opened the door when

Brooke called her.

"Lilly, I've missed talking to you." Brooke ran his hand over his head. "I'm sorry that we had to have our first private conversation like this, but I've missed you."

Lilly allowed herself to smile. "Me too. I'll see you tonight."

She slipped out before she could beg him to take her back.

****

Jay hadn't gotten his wish, which had been to stay home with his dad all day, but he figured his dad just might sleep most of the day anyway, so it was okay. Besides, the school was closed tomorrow, so they would get plenty of time together. What was annoying him was his best buddy Cole who seemed quiet.

It had been a busy day at school, with a math test and a review for the upcoming state tests, but during lunch, Cole had just sat and read while Jay tried to talk with him. He knew Cole had gone through some bad things recently, but still, they were supposed to be talking about their comic and Cole didn't want to do more than just offer grunts and shrugs.

Toward the end of the day, they had an art project to do. Mrs. Hanley had told them they could talk amongst themselves as long as they didn't get too loud. Jay figured maybe Cole was just having a bad day, so he'd just talk about things other than their comic for now.

"We went out to Dad's favorite restaurant last night." Jay drew on the paper before him. They were supposed to be drawing an animal, so Jay was drawing a dragon. Mrs. Hanley had never said it had to be a real animal. "He's got a job training program in a few weeks, going to work as an engineer right outside town."

Cole stopped drawing but kept his eyes on his paper. "So…you're moving?"

Jay shook his head, thinking that maybe that was what had his friend upset. "No, I asked him. Dad said it's a twenty-minute drive. We're not going to move."

Cole stared ahead for a few moments, then went back to drawing.

Jay frowned. Something was wrong, but if Cole didn't want to tell him that was fine. "I'm not going to be able to come over today. Dad wants to go visit Mom. And well…"

Cole turned in his chair. "Uncle Drew took me last week to visit my mom's grave too. I get it."

After an awkward pause, both boys returned to drawing. "You'll love my dad when you come over."

Cole didn't respond. He just continued to butcher the drawing of a baby deer.

Jay put his crayon down. "Dude, what's up?"

Cole shrugged. "Nothing."

Jay scowled. "You're not talking to me."

Cole spun. "Get used to it. Your aunt says we shouldn't be friends anymore, so just forget about the comic. Okay."

Jay goggled as Cole turned back and tried to save his deer which looked like spilled brown soup with white specks in it. "Bullshit. Aunt Jeannette likes you."

Cole placed his crayon down but didn't turn to face Jay. "That was before I was nearly killed. Now I'm dangerous. You probably shouldn't even be sitting this close to me. My baby deer might attack you."

With a curled lip, Jay tossed his crayon down. It left a smudge on his paper that he'd have to fix, even though he knew Mrs. Hanley wouldn't care. It would matter to him. "Bullshit. My aunt was nice to you. I don't know what your problem is…"

Cole spun around. "My problem is that I don't need you to be my friend. If you're scared of me, just go away."

Jay jutted out his chin. "I ain't scared of you or nobody else. What I should do is…"

"What's happening here?" Mrs. Hanley seemed to appear out of nowhere. Jay and Cole crossed their arms, each staring away from the other, and neither looking directly at their teacher. "Don't make me ask again."

Cole was the first to speak. "I don't feel good. Can I go to the nurse's office?"

Mrs. Hanley studied them, clearly aware that there was a problem. "Get your things together."

Cole shoved everything into his backpack without care, ripping the picture. Getting up, he slung his backpack over his shoulder and headed for the door. He never said goodbye to Jay.

****

Brooke reread the text that had come over the last few minutes while Ollie guided the car off of the highway. Sighing, he sent a response to Abbie. This wasn't the first time he'd been away on assignment, and it wouldn't be the last. She needed to learn to deal with it.

"Everything okay?" Ollie asked.

Brooke sent another promise to call soon and put his phone away. "Yeah, it's nothing. There's the house."

Ollie pulled into the driveway. "He's expecting us? You think he'll cooperate?"

Brooke studied the three-story Victorian house. DA Reynolds lived well, with the top-of-the-line Lexus in the driveway, the perfectly manicured lawn, and trimmed bushes, even the statue of a blindfolded woman holding out scales of justice said whoever lived here was important and you'd better remember that if you rang the doorbell to deliver a pizza. "No, but he'll want to appear as if he's cooperating. He'll play it off as he can't believe some underlings hid evidence. Be sympathetic towards Drew. He'll know we're here to explore the Edward Hunter angle, but he'll concentrate on Drew. So we let him. Play into that. The more he talks, the more he'll tell us, even if he's lying."

Ollie killed the engine. "Ego. He'll want to show how much he understands. We play like he's explaining it to us, gently steering him here or there. Get him on record."

Brooke smiled, confident that Ollie would do fine. "Drew told me how you impressed General McAlister with your ability to profile Jericho, and from what I've heard, he's not easy to impress. You've got a mind for this. Ever think of joining the FBI?"

Ollie flushed with pleasure at the compliment but shook his head. "No, I don't want to be taken that far away from Ashley, Cole, and the baby. I'm happy being a detective here in Ember Falls. I may not take down drug lords, but we can help people here. This is my home."

The man was living his best life, getting married to the woman who held his heart, and about to start a family. It was what a man like Ollie was built for.

Together, they got out of the car and approached the house. "You still think Reynolds isn't good for framing Drew and sending Jericho?"

Brooke thought about lying, telling him they'll see

what they see, but he respected Ollie too much to lie any more than he had to. Besides, Ollie may have the heart and soul of a small-town detective, but he had the instincts of a seasoned agent. "No, I don't. I think he's knee-deep in the reasons for it, but he's not the center."

Ollie shrugged as he rang the doorbell. "I guess we'll see. Cop face on."

Brooke allowed himself a small grin and quickly wiped it away as the door opened.

Mrs. Reynolds answered the door. She was dressed in her Sunday best, a conservative, yet classy periwinkle dress with little flowers on it, a white sweater, and matching pearls. She offered a small, polite smile. Immediately in host mode, her eyes glanced past Brooke and Ollie, searching the road. Probably worried the neighbors would be snooping. "Agent Madison? Please, come in. My husband is expecting you."

"Thank you," Brooke said. "This is Detective Miller, from the Ember Falls PD."

Mrs. Reynolds stepped back to allow them to enter. Brooke caught her staring outside again before she slowly closed the door. "Can I get you something? Coffee? Tea?"

Ollie smiled and shook his head. "No, thank you. Is Mr. Reynolds available? We appreciate him being willing to help us with this and we don't want to take any more of his time than necessary."

Brooke admired Ollie's tone and wording. It was perfect. We're here to get help, and your husband is so kind to take the time for us. Ollie had the act of nonthreatening down pat. He was friendly and approachable, but nothing he was saying was putting her at ease. Despite her skillfully trying to hide it, she was clearly on edge.

Two men entered the room. One was tall and built like a linebacker and the other walked with a painful limp. Both boys kept their distance from each other, each was scared to death, which meant Reynolds has told his family the FBI wanted to pin this on him.

Brooke recognized both men, not just from their files, but from their time together in school. Sam Reynolds was still solid as a rock, with a square jaw and a pretty face that made it easy to forget he used to strut around and peddle garbage to high school students. Brooke had decked him twice and would love the chance to do it again, but instead of strutting in, he slinked, avoiding eye contact with everyone. He glanced at Brooke and Ollie just long enough for the flicker of recognition to cross his face, and then he studied his shoes.

Someone had taken him down a peg or two. Brooke would love to know who and buy that person a beer.

Sam's younger brother Ethan used a pair of crutches, and each step was excruciating. He held eye contact but didn't seem to remember Brooke or Ollie. He wasn't steady on his feet, and there was a sheen of sweat on his forehead. Was it just from the pain or something else? He seemed to almost stumble and Sam moved in to quickly help, only to have Ethan jerk irritably away from his brother. Sam's face went pale and Ethan closed his eyes.

To Brooke, the dynamic was clear. Sam was desperate to earn his brother's forgiveness, and Ethan was struggling to give it to him, but couldn't get there.

"Agent Madison and Detective Miller are here to speak with your father." Mrs. Reynolds' voice trembled slightly as she spoke. "Is he ready?"

Sam flinched as Ethan answered with a slightly curled lip. "Dad said he'd be ready soon. He'll let us know."

Ethan and his mother held an uncomfortable gaze for a good ten seconds. Brooke glanced at Ollie trying to gauge if he was picking up on the stress signs, but Ollie was doing too good of a job as appearing unthreatening.

It was time to try a different track. "Ethan, I don't know if you remember me. I was a senior when you started at Ember Falls High. I'm very sorry for what happened."

A spark of panic crossed Ethan's face. "What do... oh." He glanced down at the crutches, then at his brother who seemed to shrink. "Yeah, well. I'm fine."

A moment of painful silence followed, broken by Ollie. "That's a wonderful portrait of the family. Your daughter's at college now, right? What's she studying?"

Mrs. Reynolds' face grew paler as her eyes widened. "I'm sorry, but—"

A gunshot exploded from down the same hallway where the boys had just come from.

Pulling out his sidearm, Brooke raced towards the sound of the blast, Ollie right beside him. Mrs. Reynolds' screams echoed behind them as they closed in on the office. Brooke positioned himself on the far side of the door.

"Dad!" Sam came running down the hallway but stopped with a warning glance from Ollie. He instead held onto his mother.

With silent cues, Brooke and Ollie entered the study, fast and hard. Brooke went low while Ollie went high.

State District Attorney Robert Reynolds couldn't

hear his family sob as he lay face down on his desk, the back of his head splattered on the wall behind him. A forty-five was in his right hand. The smell of gunpowder lingered in the air as Brooke pulled the weapon out of his grip, and felt the sweat on the grip left by Reynolds.

Ollie was herding the family back down the hall, no easy task as both Mrs. Reynolds and Sam had collapsed, rocking back and forth as Mrs. Reynolds' grief-filled wails echoed through the house. Only Ethan remained on his feet as he glared at the heap that had once been his father. "Bastard," he said with a glare before he turned away to tend to both his mother and sibling.

Brooke examined the desk. The former prosecutor had left a note, hastily scribbled and sprinkled with blood. Clenching his fist, Brooke had to resist beating the dead man as he read the words.

My family doesn't deserve the shame I brought on them by having affairs with underage girls while DA of Ember Falls. I couldn't stand to be blackmailed by Molly Winters, and when Edward Hunter offered to deal with it for me, I never realized what he meant. In a panic, I decided to try and pin her murder on an innocent kid. I'm sorry for all the pain I've caused.

Stacia, Sam, Ethan, and especially Tiffany... please forgive me.

****

Lilly reread the same email three times before she typed out her answer.

Yes.

An employee had asked if it was okay to leave an hour early for a doctor's appointment the following day. They had plenty of coverage, so it wouldn't be a problem. But Lilly had to read and reread the email before the understanding of the request sank in.

Ashley came in carrying a box of bookmarks which she placed on her desk opposite Lilly. "These are cute, did you see them?" She tossed a few to Lilly.

Lilly examined the bookmarks with felt-tip animal faces on top. Place it in a book, and it appeared as if the dog or cat's front paws were holding the page for you.

Ashley sat down and started to go through the mail. "Also, I got a text from Ollie. He and you-know-who ran into an issue of some sort today. He didn't go into details, but long story short, they'll be a while, but Ollie said they'd be there for dinner. Might be a little late, but hopefully not. Why'd you invite Madison?" Ashley picked up her bottle of water to take a sip.

"For dinner?" Lilly continued to struggle her way through emails, each one making less sense than the last. "Because it'll be good for Cole. He needs to learn to trust Brooke. Besides, I think maybe I might sleep with Brooke."

Water spurted out of Ashley's mouth as she started to choke, and her face turned red. She grabbed tissues and began to sop up the mess. "Are you insane?"

Lilly leaned back in her chair and glanced around the room as she carefully considered the question. "No, I don't think so. Ashley, I told you Brooke never hurt me. I was devastated when it ended because he was the best thing that ever happened to me. We were good together." She grinned. "*Really* good."

Ashly rolled her eyes. "I get that you need to get laid. I've been telling you that for nearly a decade now. It's been so long for you, I'm pretty sure your hymen has grown back."

Lilly's mouth dropped open in amused outrage.

"Ashley!"

Ashley shrugged. "My point is, you could use a good lay, but not Brooke. You're not capable of having a roll in the hay, letting him ring your bell, slapping his ass, and sending him on his way after he makes you a sandwich. You'll spoon him all night and have thoughts of forever."

Lilly's smile faded. "I destroyed any chance I had at a forever with Brooke years ago. And I'm not even sure he'd want me after all this time. I just always assumed…" She stared off into space.

"What?" Ashley prompted.

Lilly glanced at her best friend. She'd avoided this for so long. Every time Ashley asked what had happened, Lilly had just begun to cry and walked off. She still didn't want to think about it, to remember what she'd lost, but if she was considering taking Brooke to her bed, she should be able to talk to her best friend about this. "I always thought he'd just hate me. *I* ruined what we had." She crossed her arms, feeling a need to clean off her desk, the office, and the entire bookstore. Anything to ward off the feeling of how *unclean* she felt. "I ruined us. I don't want to talk about what happened, but it was never his fault. And I probably shouldn't think about being with Brooke. It's selfish, but today when I was talking with him, I didn't feel as if he hated me. So maybe we could be…friends."

Ashley cocked an eyebrow. "Friends? I have plenty of old boy toys who would be more than willing to be that sort of friend with you. I even have one who asked if I'd be willing to have you join us once."

Lilly's eyes widened. "What? Who?" She shook her head and closed her eyes. "Never mind, don't answer that, I don't want to know. God, I'm so happy you're with Ollie now."

Ashley leaned back in her chair, smirking. "Yeah, so am I. I woke up this morning with flowers on my bed from him. He's just so stinking sweet."

Lilly inhaled a breath of joy and happiness that her best friend had found love. "Aw, that's cute."

"No, cute was last night in bed when we pretended to—"

"All right," Lilly interrupted. "That's enough. Why do you do that?"

With a shrug, Ashley picked her water bottle up. "Your squeamishness amuses me. Besides, you're the one who said you wanted to bounce on Brooke."

Shaking her head, Lilly gave in and started to straighten her desk, which amounted to little more than shuffling papers and dusting off trinkets. "I didn't say that. I certainly didn't mean it that way, but I'm a healthy young woman. If I want to allow a man into my bed, there's nothing wrong with that."

Ashley leaned forward. "Of course not, and I'm the last person who would say there was. But this is you. You haven't been with someone that way in…" She glanced up as if the name of Lilly's last lover would be written on the ceiling. "Who *was* the last guy you were with?"

Lilly shifted her chair, so she was facing the far wall of their office. "Brooke."

Ashley's eyes went wide. "Holy crap, how have you not gone insane? Never mind." Ashley waved her hands as Lilly buried her head in her hands. "Lilly you're one of those people that can't do the deed with someone without that deep, personal connection. I get it and there's certainly nothing wrong with that. Hell, I don't think if anything ever, God forbid, happened to Ollie, that I'd be able to just be with someone for a quick bang. Not now that I know what it's like to have someone touch you that lives and breathes to make me happy. But you're asking for trouble if you open that door with Brooke."

Lilly rolled that around in her head. Would it be asking for trouble, or would it give them closure? "Maybe I can handle it. Have you considered that?"

Ashley rose from her desk. "Sure, and only you can decide that, but consider this. You keep telling me whatever the hell happened between you two wasn't his fault. I know you didn't cheat on him or do anything intentionally to hurt him because that's just not you. But let's say I take your word for it, that it wasn't his fault."

Lilly turned to face Ashley. "It *wasn't*."

Ashley held up a hand. "Fine. Then have you asked yourself, is this fair to Brooke? That man was head over heels in love with you. If his heart has started to heal, the last thing he needs is for you to open old wounds. I can't believe I'm the one saying this, but maybe you need to think about *him* before you go get you some."

Ashley left Lilly alone to ponder if she was being fair to Brooke. It wasn't like she was going to just rip his clothes off, throw him on the bed and have her way with him.

Maybe it would be a wonderful moment of healing and forgiveness.

Or maybe, it would bring all the pain back, not just for her, but for him as well.

****

Edward Hunter watched the house. The woman was

98

dealing with a couple of kids. It was almost time for dinner, as evidenced by the mom holding a bucket of chicken in one hand, and a small one-year-old in the other. Mom also had a young girl a little older than Cole, bouncing a soccer ball on her knees. She was talking a mile a minute, God only knows about what. She was a pretty thing, with her hair pulled back into a ponytail, and her pink gym shorts. As she spoke, a little boy climbed out of the back seat. He watched in awe as his sister bounced the ball, and hung close to his mother's side. The girl grabbed the chicken and with the boy right behind her, they ran for the door, beating the mother there. Now, they had to wait for her as she was the only one with a key.

Edward pulled the van he was driving up near the curb and casually got out. The scent of the chicken had his mouth-watering as the woman spotted him walking up to their front porch steps.

She shifted the weight of the one-year-old, another girl now that Edward was closer to see the teeny, tiny pigtails. "Hi, can I help you?"

Edward flashed his best smile. He was aware of the fact that he was a handsome guy, with a friendly and disarming face. It had gotten him closer to his prey in the past on many occasions, but he'd always done it in private, never leaving witnesses.

That didn't matter anymore. The audience added an extra layer of excitement to this. He was ready to explode in his pants, he only hoped the woman wouldn't realize he was already hard and ready.

"I sure hope so, ma'am," Edward said as he pulled out a piece of paper. "I'm a little lost and I hope you could point me in the right direction. Any idea where this is?"

He held out the paper with an address on it, wondered if the attention to detail would, in the end, be worth the effort, and waited for her to take it.

She frowned as she read it. Did she realize that the address went to a local Ben's Big Boy Burgers? Probably not in the brief second she had before he pressed the taser to her gut and shocked her so she collapsed to the ground.

"Mommie!" The little boy charged forward and Edwards swatted him away with the back of his left hand, sending him flying into the porch steps.

As his sister rushed to his side, Edward pulled out a gun. The woman was stirring as he hadn't used that high of a setting. The baby hit the dirt in front of their house and was wailing. Edward grabbed the woman by her hair. "Leave the brat, your kid can take her."

He pulled the woman up, reveling in the surge of power as he realized how terrified she was, not just for her own life, but for her stupid spawn.

"Please don't hurt my babies," she begged.

The boy was fighting to get up and come to his mother's rescue, but he was being held back by his sister.

Edward grabbed her by the throat. "I've got no interest in them. Tell your girl to get the screaming brat. Have her bring the chicken."

"Olivia, give the man the bag. Take your sister."

The girl, shaking like a leaf and telling her brother to stay on the porch step, walked forward and slowly held the bag out. Edwards snatched it from her and started to drag the woman back to the van.

As the girl gathered her sibling in her arms, Edward gave the mother another quick jolt. He laughed as she screamed and the boy came running to save his mother once again.

Olivia managed to snag him while not dropping the baby who was shrieking. Edward aimed the gun at them and Olivia gasped, shoving her brother behind her.

It reminded him of Cole and his feeble attempts to protect, filling Edward with an almost irresistible urge to blow the girl's head off.

Instead, he flung the mother's limp into the back of the van and got in the driver's seat. "Tell Drew Duncan I said hi." He laughed as he left the kids holding onto each other, their image growing smaller in his rearview mirror while he reached into the bag, grabbed a drumstick, and used his teeth to rip meat off the bone.

Chapter Eight

Saying I Love You

Brooke stepped into the kitchen, closed his eyes, and inhaled the smell of heaven. The rich scent of Marsala wine wafted through the air, triggering the memory of Lilly once cooking it for him here at her grandmother's home. It happened while Grandma Danvers was away on a cruise with some of her friends and she'd asked Lilly to house-sit. It was the summer before their senior year of high school before everything had gone to hell. For those two weeks, they played house. It was the closest thing to perfection that Brooke had ever known.

He could still recall seeing her make dinner for them that night, wearing a white apron and nothing else. She would glide from one side of the kitchen to the other, whisking the liquid into a pan, and adding butter and flour to the mix. He could still see the curve of her breasts, and feel the softness of her skin as he pressed himself against her.

This time, Lilly was dressed. It was unfortunate, but probably for the best as a young boy was sitting at the table working on homework. Effortlessly, she tended to the simmering pots and pans as she helped Cole with his long division. The nurturing smile displayed on her face as she leaned over the boy. Cole didn't stiffen despite her closeness. Lilly was in her element. This was her place in the world, and Brooke couldn't help but be awestruck at how beautiful she was.

Brooke did his best to ignore the bitter heaviness in his heart as thoughts of the future they should have shared swirled in his mind.

Clearing his throat to announce his presence, Lilly's smile widened while Cole's faded. The child's face went white and his eyes darted around to plot out his escape, yet he didn't move.

"Dinner will be ready in about fifteen minutes," Lilly said, both to him and to Cole. "Why don't you put your homework away and go clean up."

Cole eyed Brooke suspiciously. "I can stay here if you want and read."

Brooke kept his distance. Cole was still wary of him, even after the day at the range. Brooke was an unknown quantity and the kid didn't like that. Who could blame him? But he was intent on protecting Lilly.

"God that smells amazing." Brooke inched closer to the stove. She'd just removed the chicken from the pans and there was a large Dutch oven filled with green beans, slowly simmering in garlic and a touch of olive oil. Lilly started to prepare the mashed potatoes. "Can I help with anything? Set the table?"

Lilly glanced over her shoulder. "That'd be lovely. Cole can show you where things are, won't you Cole?"

Warily, Cole shoved his things into his bag and rose from the table. It was Lilly's way of trying to get him and Cole to spend time together. The more they interacted, the more comfortable Cole would get with him. Brooke followed Cole into the dining area.

Pulling open a drawer, Cole pulled out a white lace tablecloth. Brooke took one end and they spread it out together. Once it was smoothed out, Cole scowled at Brooke. "I can't reach the plates." He pointed to the top of the china closet. "She'll want the nice ones."

Brooke opened the cabinet and picked up the stack of plates, while Cole disappeared. Counting out seven plate settings, Brooke began to put them around the table, wondering if he'd seen the last of Cole until dinner. A moment later, Cole came in holding a tray of silverware that he put next to the plates Brooke was setting out.

"How was your day at school?"

The corners of Cole's mouth downturned and his lower lip pulled in a touch. He shrugged but made a concentrated effort to avoid eye contact. "Fine."

Brooke placed the last plate down. "What happened?"

Cole studied a fork for a long moment before putting it down. "Nothing."

Pulling out a chair, Brooke sat so he wasn't so much taller than Cole. "Something's upsetting you. Talk to me."

Cole placed the last fork and knife down, but his eyes remained on the silverware.

"I know you think of me as an FBI agent here to talk about your stepfather, but I'm also your uncle's oldest friend. I've known your family for a long time. And tonight, I'm not here as an agent, I'm here as a friend of the family."

Cole sat as well, but while he didn't have his back to Brooke, he was mostly facing away from him. "It's nothing."

Brooke studied Cole, the stiffness of his back, contrasted by the turning of his head. He was defensive and closed off, but he was hurting and wanted to talk about it.

"Was it something to do with your teacher?" Cole kept quiet and still. "Or did someone tease you?" No reaction, just a deep breath. "Or did you argue with a friend?"

By just the smallest fraction of an inch, he turned away even more.

"So what happened between you and your buddy?"

Cole folded his arms. "Nothing, and he's not my friend."

Brooke got up and moved closer, sitting next to Cole. "Sure he is. You wouldn't be upset if you and he weren't pals. I can tell you that your Uncle Drew and I pissed each other off plenty, but we always came around. Often, we never apologized, we just made a few bad jokes about each other's manhood and we were friends again."

Despite his sour mood, the corner of Cole's mouth twitched, but it was short-lived. "His aunt's afraid of me. You saw him the other day, the kid whose dad just came home? His aunt was there and ever since she found out Jericho kidnapped me, she hates me."

Brooke recalled the scene. He'd sensed something then. Remembered the way the woman watched Cole. "No, she doesn't."

Cole turned all the way around, away from Brooke. "You don't know."

Brooke smiled. "Sure I do. That's what I do. Look out the window."

Slowly, Cole did. Through the window, Ashley could be seen going out to greet Ollie. "So? She almost always goes out when he gets here."

"Just watch. You can't hear them, right?"

Cole shook his head, his face softening as he became interested in Brooke's game.

"So watch them," Brooke said. "Tell me what they're saying, what they're feeling, just by what they do."

The first thing Ashley did was pull Ollie into an embrace, which she held for several moments. Ollie buried his face in her hair. "She's hugging him."

"Aren't they hugging each other?"

Cole tilted his head, considered. "No, she hugged him. Like he's upset and she's trying to make him better."

Brooke moved closer. "See the way he's got his face in her hair? Why?"

Cole shrugged. "He does that, sometimes."

"Right, but why?" Brooke leaned closer. "Your aunt's perfume. Scent is a strong sense. He doesn't realize it, but that familiar smell, the smell of Ashley, gives him comfort. It centers him. Watch."

Cole did. "They're gonna…Oh yuck." He scrunched his nose as they kissed.

"How did you know they were going to kiss?"

Cole shrugged. "They always kiss. And it was the way she looked at him. She touched his face and…I don't know, but I knew it was going to happen. Why?"

Brooke pointed towards the window. "Ashley and Ollie locked eyes for a moment. She was touching his face. There were physical signs. You don't recognize them all enough to know what they are, but you're still reading them. Keep watching."

The kiss ended, and Ollie touched her stomach, where their baby grew.

A flash of Brooke touching Lilly like that flooded Brooke's mind, but Brooke pushed it away.

Ollie said something, and Ashley rolled her eyes.

"She's gonna swat at him…"

Brooke watched closer. "Really, why…"

Ashley laughed and gave Ollie a playful smack with her hand, which Ollie caught and kissed before they walked to the door and out of view of the window.

"Well, there you go. How'd you know that?"

Cole shrugged. "Just the goofy look on his face. Ollie made a joke or something. She does that all the time." Cole sat back in his chair, still not looking directly at Brooke, but not avoiding him altogether.

"So Ollie had a goofy grin on his face, and I saw that too, but because you know him, and you know your aunt. You could predict that she'd react that way. Now part of that is the fact that they're family. You know them well. But you also read their faces, their movements. Have you ever seen your uncle angry, but where he's not yelling? He's not doing anything specific that tells you he's angry, but you know he is."

Cole folded his arms and pursed his lips. "Yeah, I guess. So?"

"It's called body language, and reading it is something I'm very good at. I've had a lot of training and education in reading people, but I've always had a knack for it. It's something I imagine you'd be good at as you're very observant and you pick up on subtle cues. That comes naturally to people like you and me because of how we grew up."

Cole frowned, shifting in his seat. Slowly, he turned around in his chair so he was face to face with Brooke and studied the agent's face. "What do you mean?"

Brooke decided to break one of the rules that had been drilled into him. Don't get personal. It nearly cost him his job. Hell, last time he got personal, it nearly cost him his life, but if it weren't for that "error in judgment" as the bureau had termed it, he wouldn't have Abbie in his life.

Cole was his oldest friend's nephew, and he'd seen the way Lilly loved the boy. It was already personal.

"Growing up in a home where you have a parent who is quick to hit," Brooke explained. "Where mood changes could mean being left alone or having a nightmare of a night. You haven't talked to me about what happened to you because you're not ready, and I respect that. But I know at least a part of it because that's how I grew up."

The young boy searched Brooke's face, trying to decide if he was being lied to. Brooke waited, knowing that the kid would make up his mind. Brooke could read Cole. He was still wary of Brooke, but the boy's curiosity was piqued, and more importantly, his compassion had kicked in. "You're dad hit you?"

Brooke shook his head. "I was brought up by a single mom. My father wanted nothing to do with me. My mom, however, was a piece of work."

"How?" Cole bit his lip the moment the word was out of his mouth. "I'm sorry, I…"

"It's okay," Brooke said. "I told you, I'm not here as an agent tonight. I'm a family friend. Hell, Drew, Lilly, and Ash were like family to me when I was a kid."

Brooke leaned back. He didn't like going down memory lane, but Cole needed to understand who he was and where he came from. Besides, there was something about the kid's kind eyes that made Brooke want to open up.

"My mother was a wreck," Brooke said, closing his eyes. He could still smell the scent of pot, crack, or whatever other poison his mom had gotten a hold of. On a good day, their trailer home reeked of cheap beer and cheaper sex. Brooke never knew who was going to be with his mother, or how interested they'd be in him. Sometimes he'd be an annoyance, someone to be thrown out so they wouldn't have an audience. Other times, they'd be very friendly to Brooke.

Too friendly.

While he didn't think it was wise to tell Cole all of that, he didn't want to lie. "My mom was an addict. She could be violent one moment and hold onto me for dear life the next. There were always strange men there, and if one of them took a dislike to me and decided to kick me around, she'd usually find it funny as hell. She was no slouch in the hitting department. Slapping my face, throwing things at me." Brooke winced, his hand rubbing his side. "She came at me once with a knife."

Cole's eyes widened. "Like…She was trying to kill you?"

Brooke huffed out a hollow-sounding laugh. "It wasn't planned. She was in a rage, after the first time I fought back against one of her 'guests' who thought I was just an amusing punching bag. I hit back, and he grabbed his party favors and left."

Cole's lip curled. "You mean drugs."

Brooke had to remind himself, he may be talking to a child, but Cole was hardly a naïve little kid. Cole had seen far more than most adults had or ever will. "I do. I didn't grow up with a great life. It wasn't as bad as what happened to your aunt and uncle. I'm sure it's nowhere near as bad as what happened to you and your mom, but you and I have a lot more in common than you realize."

A noise came from the hall, and Brooke could picture Lilly ready to serve, but holding things up because she'd know somehow he and Cole were making progress in here.

"And that's how I know your friend's aunt doesn't hate you," Brooke explained. "I watched her. It's automatic for me. I saw her, watching you. She's probably scared for….*Jay* was it?"

Cole nodded. "He's my best friend. Or…at least he was."

Brooke smiled. "Don't write him off just yet. I'll bet it'll work out. If your friendship means to him half of what it does to you, the two of you will find a way to work it out."

Concentrating very hard on the plate before him, Cole didn't react with more than a subtle shrug. Moments later, when Lilly started to bring the trays of food in, he stayed in the same chair for dinner, next to Brooke.

****

Lilly was pleased with herself. Dinner had come out perfectly. The chicken was tender, the gravy was smooth, and everyone came back for seconds. The food wasn't the only thing that turned out well.

Cole seemed to be a little more at ease with Brooke, which was huge. He laughed at some of the stories Brooke and Drew told from their youth, and even asked him a few questions about working with the FBI.

They spent a lot of time talking about the upcoming double wedding. Lilly had it all planned out. Sam would stay in the back while Drew would escort Ashley down the aisle. Then Nana would do the same for Sam. "We've still got to go dress shopping. That's this weekend."

Cole squirmed in his seat. "Ugh, sounds super boring. Do I have to go?"

Drew shook his head. "No, you can hang with Ollie and me."

Cole sat up, his face brightening.

"We've got an appointment for all three of us to get fitted for tuxedos." Drew waited for a beat so Cole's smile could fade. "And for that matter, so do you."

Cole groaned and dropped his head down on the table, causing a ripple of laughter to cascade around the table.

"Don't worry," Ollie said. "Our part is easy. It's just getting ones that fit, we're not trying on fifty million dresses to find the right one. We'll be done before lunch and then we'll come back and do something fun."

Cole groaned, but he picked his head up.

Lilly rose from the table. "I'm going to get coffee and cake."

"Cake?" Brooke said. "What kind of cake?"

Lilly grinned. "You remember my carrot cake?"

Brooke put his hand over his heart. "With the cream cheese frosting?"

Lilly ignored the warning glance Ashley was sending her. "Maybe. Feel like giving me a hand?"

Brooke got up from the table and followed Lilly into the kitchen.

Lilly immediately went to the cabinet and started to pull out coffee mugs. She arranged them on a platter, along with a small bowl of sugar and a carton of milk. She pulled over a plastic cake platter that was in the refrigerator. "Can you grab the tray and I'll bring this and the coffee?"

Brooke frowned. "Why don't you leave the coffee? It's hot. I'll come back for it."

Lilly smiled. "Are you starting to worry about me?"

Brooke leaned on the counter. "I never stopped."

She studied him, seeing the differences that the last years had brought on. His chest was bigger and his face seemed more defined, but those beautiful blue eyes set in that majestic and kind face were the same.

She stood on opposite sides of the kitchen, nothing between them but the hurt that she'd caused, and the platter with the carrot cake.

Brooke shifted, rubbing the back of his neck. "It's been a little strange, being back here. Seeing you. But it's nice."

Lilly took a step closer, keeping the cake between them. "It has been. Things didn't end well with us." She studied the top of her cake and noticed one of the frosted carrots on top wasn't lined up perfectly. "I know I hurt you. I'm sorry."

Brooke took a deep breath. "You don't owe me an apology. If it wasn't what you wanted…"

Lilly continued to examine the cake in her hands. Seeing each tiny imperfection, every little smudge. Was it too late to redo the entire thing? "You deserved better than that."

The weight of the cake disappeared as Brooke took the platter from her and put it on the counter. He gently put his fingers under her chin so she lifted her head and her gaze met his.

"Why would you say that?" He caressed her face, and she placed her hand on top of his.

She closed her eyes and for a moment they were

teenagers again.

Opening her eyes, she saw his face, so full of kindness.

Ashley had been right. If she went through with this, she wouldn't be able to just walk away without her heart being shattered.

But she also didn't care.

"What's going on?"

Lilly took a quick step back, turned, and saw Cole standing by the doorway, eyeing them suspiciously. "Brooke and I were just talking."

With narrowed eyes, Cole walked into the room and stood between them. "About what?"

Brooke reached over for the cake. "A few things, one was that she shouldn't carry the tray and the coffee. Why don't you take the cake in, I'll grab the coffee."

He held out the platter for Cole, who hesitated before grabbing it. With one glance over his shoulder to Lilly, they headed back into the dining room.

As Lilly handed out plates, she couldn't keep her eyes off Brooke. If Cole hadn't walked in right then, would Brooke have kissed her? Was he open to starting again? Would it be fair for her to do that to him?

She was still just as damaged as before.

Just as she cut a piece of cake for Brooke, a buzz sounded from his pocket. Pulling out his cell, Brooke scowled at the screen, then tapped the answer button. "Agent Madison."

Lilly watched him. Saw his eyebrows draw in and his lower lip thin. Something was wrong.

Brooke stood up, his face a mask of fury. He gripped the back of Cole's chair as if to steady himself. Something he was being told made him wince.

"Yes, sir." Brooke ended the call and glanced toward Lilly. "I'm sorry, I have to go."

Lilly stood as well. "What's happened?"

Brooke's eyes darted toward Cole, who was watching him warily. "FBI related. I'm sorry. I need to go."

Shell-shocked, Brooke quickly left. Lilly followed to the window, watched him race to his car, and peel away.

****

Brooke pulled into the driveway of the Hamilton and pulled out the keycard Jacob had given him. He slammed the door to his car closed and rushed in. He'd called three times, but Jacob hadn't answered. Brooke prayed that the kid was all right, so he could kill him for not answering the damn phone.

Although he was staying above the garage apartment at Lilly's, he had kept the room here in case he needed the space. It made more sense to meet there with Jacob when they needed to talk in private. They hadn't used it much since their arrival, but he'd kept the key card.

He also had one for the adjacent room where Jacob was staying.

Running down the hall, Brooke put his hand on his gun, stood on the side of the door, and banged. "Agent Rivers." He waited. Listened. "Jacob."

To hell with privacy.

Brooke pulled out the second keycard, moved it over the door pad until it flashed green, and went in. He swept the room, his eyes absorbing everything he saw. The bed was rumpled, but empty. Clothes were scattered on the floor. Dinner sat on a table, uneaten and getting cold.

A cold stab of panic hit him as he realized there were two glasses of wine.

The bathroom door opened behind him and Jacob came out, wearing a huge smile and nothing else. He held hands with Sam's partner Brandon. "Agent Madison?" The young FBI analyst glanced down at himself, realized he was naked, and dashed back into the bathroom.

Brooke heaved a sigh of relief as Brandon, unconcerned with his own lack of clothing, laughed.

"I'll be next door." Brooke pointed to the door that joined the two rooms. "Get dressed and come over."

Brooke headed for the door, but Brandon stepped forward. "You're not gonna jam him up, are you? He's off duty."

Brooke scowled and put his weapon away. "I'm sorry for barging in. That's not what this is about."

Jacob emerged from the bathroom, this time with a white terrycloth robe wrapped around his waist. He tossed another to Brandon who used it to cover himself. "Then what is it about?"

Brooke turned on Jacob. "Why didn't you answer your phone? I called three times."

Jacob's face turned red. "Because it was out here charging and I was…" He winced. "In the shower."

Brooke pressed a finger to his temple. "Alice Mills. The analyst that dropped out of the op because of the stomach flu? She's dead. So is her husband."

Jacob blinked in surprise. "Dead? An accident?" He shook his head. "You wouldn't come rushing over if it was an accident."

Brooke pushed past Brandon and reached for the door. "Get dressed and meet me in my room. I'll unlock it from my side."

Brooke's phone buzzed and he glanced at the screen. "Drew Duncan is here. He brought Sam and Ollie." He looked at Brandon and Jacob, their skin still glistening from their shower. He didn't know how Brandon would feel about his coworkers knowing he was here. "You wanted to slip out the back or something?"

Brandon shook his head. "I'm fine hanging if you're okay with my being here."

Brooke nodded. "Get dressed and go meet them at the front. Bring them to my room. I've got to call and get more information."

Jacob was sitting on the side of the bed, his head in his hands. As Brandon searched for his clothes, Brooke walked over and put his hand on Jacob's moist shoulder. "You okay?"

Jacob took a deep breath. "I was thrilled that she called in sick. I got to go on assignment, and I was happy that she wasn't."

Brooke and Brandon exchanged glances. "You didn't know," Brooke told him as he headed for the door. "Neither of us did."

****

When Drew led the others in, they found Brooke sitting at the desk with the phone held to his ear in one hand and a pen in the other. He glanced up for a brief second to lock eyes with Drew, and the gaze spoke volumes.

With that glimpse, it was back. That sick heaviness in the center of his chest, telling him that something was very wrong.

Sam stood against the wall next to her partner Brandon. Ollie took a spot on the foot of the bed, while Jacob sat opposite Brooke, working furiously on his laptop.

"Yes, sir, I agree that's heading away, but I still think…" Brooke scowled as whoever was on the other line interrupted. "Yes, sir. I will."

Brooke ended the call and sighed.

Drew walked over. "How bad is it?"

Brooke sat back, rubbed the bridge of his nose, and shook his head. "Bad. Originally, the Bureau assigned an analyst named Alice Mills to this job, but she called in sick last minute. At least, we thought she did."

Brooke stood, crossed his arms, and paced to the other side of the room. "When you're sick, you've got to call in every day for the first three days. She sent emails, which is acceptable. On day four, if you're not better you have to see the department physician. When she didn't call on day four or show up, they called. When she didn't answer all day, they sent someone. That person found her and her husband."

Sam shifted off the wall. "Dead?"

Brooke continued to pace. "Very. Both were tortured. He was tied up to a chair, forced to watch. He didn't sexually assault Ben Mills, but he went to town on him." He paused mid-pace and glared. "It was Edward Hunter. Her computer was open to the files on him. He left plenty of fingerprints.

"He wants us to know he's out there, and he can hurt us." Brooke stopped pacing and sank into the chair. "Last time I talked to Alice, she told me she and Ben were thinking about starting a family."

Drew ran his hand over his head. "I'm sorry."

Sam closed her eyes. "What else?"

Brooke leaned forward in the chair. "He took a woman. From the sound of it, he tased her in front of her kids."

Brandon frowned. "Are we sure it's him?"

Brooke gave a curt nod. "Description fits. And he told the kids to say hi to Drew Duncan."

"What?" Drew's eyes widened and his head snapped up. "Why would he…"

Brooke shook his head. "He's calling you out. He wants to strike at you without coming directly at you."

Drew stalked to the other end of the room. "Fucking chicken shit little bastard. Let him come at me. I'll take him apart for what he did to Cole and Kelli. I'm not a terrified little boy and he knows it."

Sam went over and rubbed his arm. "We'll get him."

Ollie crossed his arms. "Great. He's going from serial killer to spree killer."

Brooke stood up. "The woman was grabbed in Pennsylvania. Bureau asked me to check it out." He looked at Drew. "General McAlister has been making inquiries. He wants to have his people involved. My director is an old friend of the General's and decided you'd be the best candidate as you do still work for McAlister and you're familiar with the case. Makes sense."

Drew clenched his jaw. He wanted to go. He wanted the chance to get his hands on Edward Hunter, but the idea left him feeling queasy. "Last time Ollie and I went up to Cheyanne halfcocked, Jericho managed to get his hands on Cole and Ashley."

"That was different," Sam said. "We didn't know Jericho was posing as Corvidae. We didn't know who to look out for. This time we do. I'll stick close to them."

"Count me in partner," Brandon said. "I'll hang with Sam off duty. Nobody's getting near the kid."

Drew reached out and pulled Sam into a hug, feeling more solid with her close.

"I've been able to hack into traffic cams," Jacob said. "The van entered PA 39 North. He could be heading towards Mexico."

"Away from Ember Falls," Ollie said. "Good."

Drew glanced at Brooke and saw the doubt in his eyes. "He's managed to stay hidden all these years. Why is he this sloppy now?"

Ollie shrugged. "Maybe because he's out and knows his days are numbered. Didn't Ted Bundy do this after he was caught? He escaped and killed those sorority girls. We should warn all states between Pennsylvania and the Mexican border that he might come their way. Circulate his picture, the van."

Brooke went to the window. "I'm not buying the Mexico angle. And I don't think he's on a stampede to get from here to there."

"So what *is* his play?" Drew asked.

Slowly, Brooke turned back to face him. "Not sure, but I'm damned well going to find out."

****

Lilly made her way up the stairs to the garage apartment. She took a deep breath and knocked.

"It's open."

Steeling herself one last time, she entered to see Brooke packing his things. Her heart tightened as she watched him shove his belongings into a bag. "Ollie told me that you were going, but he wasn't sure how long you'd be away."

Or if you're coming back.

Brooke paused. "Not long. He's probably not there. We're not in on the search for the woman, just to tell

119

them what we know and see if there's any reason why she was targeted. Sam said you'd be okay if she stayed in the house."

He glanced to Lilly who nodded.

"Good." Brooke took a deep breath. "Ollie called his mother. She's authorizing her and her partner to stay in plain clothes for a few days, however long we're gone at least. Keep close to Cole." He turned and looked at Lilly. "And you."

"I can take care of myself," Lilly assured him.

"I know you can," Brooke said as he zipped up the bag. "But Hunter is dangerous. I don't want him near you."

Lilly felt a rush of hope, buoyed by the fact that he was still protective of her.

"We'll be okay," Lilly said, taking a step closer. "You made progress with Cole tonight. The fact that he was sitting next to you was huge for him. It took him a while before he'd be comfortable sitting next to Drew for dinner."

Brooke turned to face her. "He's a really smart kid."

Beaming with pride, Lilly took another step forward. "He is. Just like you were. I haven't told you, but I'm proud of you. Special Agent Brooke Madison. You've overcome so much. I'm sorry that I wasn't there to celebrate when you got your shield."

Brooke fidgeted. "I thought about you. When they handed it to me, I looked out and thought, 'Lilly should be here.' I wouldn't have made it if you didn't believe in me." He closed his eyes for a moment. "All these years, I still don't know what went wrong. Whatever it was, however I hurt you…" He opened his eyes and stared into her soul. "I'm sorry."

Lilly placed her hand on his chest. "You never did anything. I know you think you did, but it was not something you did. It was me."

Brooke reached out, putting his hand on the side of her face. "How can that be true? You were always perfect." His fingers trailed softly down her face. "You still are."

Gazing into his soft-blue eyes, ripples of excitement washed over her. How easy would it be to pull him into a kiss? It was a moment where their history and everything she'd lost seemed so far away. Lilly was afraid to breathe, wishing to live in the moment forever.

But the moment was broken by the buzz of Brooke's cell.

Pulling it out, he sighed. "I've got to take this."

Taking a step back, Lilly bit her lower lip. "I'll see you soon."

Turning, she walked out to leave him to his phone call. She started down the stairs and paused. What the hell had she done? She'd gone up there because Ollie had come in to let Ashley know he'd be leaving for a day or so. Once she'd heard Brooke was leaving, she thought this might be her last chance to see him. Her last chance for forgiveness.

Still, there was that moment, right before his damn cell buzzed, that she thought he was going to kiss her. Now she'd have to wait a day or two to see if it would happen again.

Or did she?

Climbing the stairs, she went back to the door. She could go in and kiss him herself, tell him it was for good luck. It didn't have to be a major lip-lock, curling her toes, seeing fireworks sort of kiss. Although those were the kind Brooke always excelled at.

Lilly just needed that small, physical connection.

She started to open the door and paused. She didn't want to walk in on a confidential conversation and get Brooke in trouble. She listened with the door ajar, hearing Brooke's voice carry.

"Abbie, I promise it won't be long." Brooke's voice was soft. "You know that's not true. I miss you too. I'm coming back, I just need to do this."

Lilly looked through the window of the door, where she could see Brooke's feet as he paced.

"I promise you, I'm never leaving you, Abbie," Brooke said. "I love you."

A cold hand reached into her chest and twisted her at her heart. She nearly stumbled down the stairs as she turned to retreat. She'd lost everything. Again.

Desperate to escape, she stumbled down the stairs and made her way to the house. The night air was warm, but she was shaking as she went inside, made her way to her room, and collapsed on the floor.

Lilly rocked herself, realizing that somehow she'd started to believe she might have even a little piece of her soul back. She hadn't lost him again.

This time, she never had him.

Chapter Nine

The General

Brooke was used to local law enforcement not always being welcoming to a Federal agent butting their nose into what they considered to be a local matter. He tried not to take it personally himself when most of the local PD from Milford showed Drew more professional courtesy than they did him. McAlister had worked once with the police in this town, and that thirty-two-day investigation that resulted in the rescue of a small child had made an impression. So had the fact that, in news conferences, McAlister spokespeople made sure to lavish praise on the officers. The impression most had gotten was that McAlister had been there to give support, not run the op.

When General McAlister himself walked into the precinct, he was treated as royalty.

Brooke might have felt downright annoyed if the dynamic weren't so fascinating to watch. Captain Mastronardi came out of his office and shook the General's hand, welcoming him back to his house. Officers young and old went out of their way to have any sort of interaction with the man. Drew instantly fell in step alongside the General, anticipating his every need, request, and question.

Brooke could tell his friend was struggling

internally and although he performed professionally, Brooke knew Drew was in a dark place mentally.

The presence of the General gave Drew a degree of solace that was visible. Drew seemed more in control, more confident standing by the General's side.

Everything about General McAlister, from his hawk-like face to his sharp grey eyes, and even the way he stood as if he were casually inspecting the troops, spoke of authority and being in control. Several police chiefs came in, each deferring to him, calling him sir, and listening to every word he said.

When Drew got around to introducing him to the General, Brooke was eager to shake the man's hand. "I've heard a lot about you, sir. Both from my superiors and Drew himself."

The General took Brooke's hand firmly and held it as he made direct eye contact. "Agent Burkhart spoke well of you and your work in the Atlanta case. I understand you've worked well with children. I trust you're taking care of Cole."

Brooke didn't blink. "I've made good progress with Cole. He's been through a terrible ordeal, but he's a strong, extraordinary young man. Very protective of his family, which is what Hunter has exploited to keep Cole from talking. I also believe that in the end, the love of his family will be what will allow Cole to heal and to help us."

The General still held Brooke's hand. "I consider Cole to be my grandson, and I understand that feeling of being willing to do anything to protect your family. I'll be back in Ember Falls very shortly and I'm very much looking forward to seeing Cole."

Finally, the General let go of Brooke's hand but held

his gaze. Brooke understood what was being implied. *Screw with Cole, you'll answer to me.*

"What can you tell me?"

Brooke pulled out a small notebook. "Hunter abducted the woman, Laura Grant, in front of her children. Used a ruse of needing directions to get close. Didn't need to keep it up very long. He wasn't interested in the kids. Said as much, but mentioned Drew's name. To me, that indicates he wanted people to know he was here." Brooke paused, figuring that for now, he'd go with the official line. "The indications are that he's heading south."

The General's eyes narrowed. "That's what your boss Agent Burkhart tells me. He's on a rampage as he puts as much distance between him and Ember Falls."

Brooke pursed his lips. "Yes, sir. My analyst was able to hack into traffic cams, track them as far as I-84 West. Most probable route to go to Mexico."

The General pulled out a seat at the conference table and sat down. He folded his hands and fixed a casual expression on his face. "In your estimation, how long until he makes a move on Cole?"

Brooke started to answer but caught himself. He glanced toward Drew, who didn't seem surprised. "I'm sorry?"

The General's eyes flashed between the pair. "I asked a simple enough question, agent. That task force is too big of an opportunity to pass up without so much as an objection. You didn't want to go. You wanted to stand between Hunter and Lilly. I'm aware that you used to date her. Don't glare at Drew. He didn't tell me anything. You did."

"Did I?" Brooke thought back over his words since

meeting the General. "How did I do that?"

"For one, by not denying it." The General motioned to a seat.

Brooke, understanding that he was now being invited to sit down, did. Watched as Drew did the same. "I told you the indications are he's heading south."

"But not that *you* think that," the General pointed out. "I also saw the way you looked at Drew. You wanted to know if he'd told me. But the fact is that you told Drew what you think. I'm guessing supervisors disagree and told you to keep your theory to yourself. Despite that, you told Drew that Hunter will come for Cole. That tells me what I need to know about you. So let's drop the bullshit song and dance and figure out how to stop this son of a bitch before he hurts anyone else."

The corner of Brooke's mouth quirked. The General, who as far as Brooke knew had never studied behavioral sciences, had just read him as well as the best of any member of the Behavioral Analysis Unit within seconds. No wonder Drew had once called him a mind reader.

"I don't know his plan yet," Brooke said. "But yes, his end game, and he very much sees this as his end game, is in Ember Falls. There's certainly a possibility that he'll make a mistake, slip up and the Task Force will capture him. He's not infallible. But he's stayed hidden for over a decade."

The General frowned. "I get why he targeted Agent Mills, but how does this woman's abduction fit in?"

"She might not," Brooke said. "Right now, Hunter is under a tremendous amount of stress. He *could* try and escape, and all evidence is that's what he's trying to do. Agent Mills can make sense because of her connection.

He may have thought she could give him information on the Task Force. Something that would help him evade them. But this victim almost seems random."

The General's eyebrows went up. "Almost. Traditionally, prostitutes or hitchhikers, women who would willingly get into your car with you, are the preferred targets for creatures like Hunter. A mother in full sight of her children, one old enough to give a detailed description, a partial plate. That suggests this woman was a target. Why?"

Drew leaned forward. "I've been wracking my brain to try and see if I recognize the name, Laura Shaw. I've known a few Shaws. A few cops, a Marine that was KIA. A family from the neighborhood when I was young." He reached into his pocket and produced a cell. He thumbed at the screen. "I can't recall a Laura, and she doesn't seem familiar."

Brooke leaned back in his chair. "He appears to be headed away from Ember Falls. Abducts a woman and makes it certain that we'll know it's him. In my opinion, he wants us to chase him."

"The question is," the General said. "Will we be chasing our tails? How long does this woman have?"

Brooke scowled as he recalled what they knew of Hunter's victims. "He likes to spend a few days with them. We believe he killed women after he left Ember Falls."

"I'd bet money on that if it weren't such a morbid wager," the General added.

"So would I," Brooke agreed. "A lot will depend on how much the victim can take. The more she fights, the longer she'll live. She'll have already been raped. Hurt in ways that will leave scars." Brooke glanced at Drew, whose face had gone white. "Drew, could you go find the lead detective? Anderson, I think his name is. Let's see if he's got any background on our VIC."

At first Drew didn't respond, he just concentrated on his knuckles, which he slowly rubbed.

"Drew, I think Detective Sanders is in the bullpen," Brooke said.

Drew snapped out of his trance and rose. "I'll be back."

Drew crossed the room, sent the General one last look, and exited.

"He's shaken," the General said.

Brooke studied the door where his friend had just disappeared. "He's never had to deal with it knowing the man we're chasing was once in bed with his sister. He's blaming himself. For Kelli, and Laura."

"He's got no reason the blame himself for either," the General barked. "He knows that."

Brooke shook his head. "He understands that, here." Brooke tapped his temple. "Logically, there was nothing he could have done to help Kelli without crossing the deal he'd made with his father. Come back in town, he'd have his sisters raped and murdered. Drew would have done anything to have them be a part of his life, but he couldn't without putting them at risk. So he stayed away, and Kelli suffered and eventually died. Cole is suffering. In his mind, if Drew had come back he would have stopped Hunter back then. How many women would be alive? Laura Shaw wouldn't have been abducted. Logically, he knows that's not his fault, but he'll never accept it in his heart."

The General narrowed his eyes. "I'll just order him to accept it."

Brooke considered that. "While that won't be enough, it *will* help. Most people who went through what Drew has would have spiraled out of control. Turned to drugs and alcohol to numb themselves. Lost their way." Brooke paused, saying the thing he didn't want to. "Taken their own lives. I've read a lot of the reports on Drew. He was cited for bravery dozens of times. Risked his life over and over again. It wasn't direct suicide, but…"

"It was extreme risk-taking," the General said. "Suicide by proxy. When he started with McAlister, I made sure he understood that if he got hurt, our client, an innocent person, would also suffer. He chose ops where he knew people needed help. I encouraged that. And I made sure to order him not to get dead."

Brooke imagined those conversations. "You came to this understanding a long time ago. If there's any single reason why Drew is alive today, I'm sitting across the table from him,"

The General scowled. "Bull crap. There's one reason why Drew didn't give in to his demons, and that's Drew. He's the strongest man I've known. Maybe he needs reminding now and then, but he'll make it through this."

Brooke disagreed with the former, but not the latter. Still, there was no reason to point that out. "He's in a different place now. He doesn't want to die, because he's got so much to live for, and too many people that need him. He and Ashley have repaired their relationship. He's engaged to a woman that loves, supports, and understands him. His sister is about to marry a man he calls a friend, a man who has earned his respect. And Cole. Drew would do anything for that boy, even living with whatever pain he was in. But this is taking a toll on him."

"He'll stand," the General said. "In the end, there's nobody more solid and steady than Drew Duncan, and if he needs…"

The General trailed off at the sounds of raised voices and scraping chairs. He and Brooke exchanged confused frowns as they went to investigate. Brooke was closer and far younger than the General, but Paul McAlister still beat him through the door.

From around the corner, a pained voice screamed out obscenities as calmer voices tried to get control of the situation. Brooke and the General entered the bullpen and found overturned chairs, and papers strewn across the floor. Drew stood alone in the center of the room, a small trickle of blood dripping from the corner of his mouth. He was facing a man being held back by two officers.

The man's face was red as he struggled to attack Drew. The receding hair on his head was ragged and his eyes bloodshot, not from overindulgence of drink or drugs, but grief and anger. He wept as he jabbed an angry finger at Drew.

"You keep ruining my fucking family!" He tried to burst free, but the officers held him back. "Why are you doing this to me? What the fuck did I do? What did my children do?"

At the mention of children, Brooke noticed three of them standing in the corner. A girl of ten, holding a one-year-old. Tears streamed down her face as her lip trembled. Their brother, who couldn't be more than six, had his face buried in his sister's chest, unable to look at what was happening.

"It's your fucking fault my father's dead," their father continued to scream. "And now Laura…" He stopped, his sobs taking control. "What the hell am I supposed to do?"

Drew started to step forward, but that just enraged the man again, so Brooke stepped in between them. "Mr. Shaw, I'm Special Agent Madison from the FBI's Behavioral Analysis Unit. I can't imagine what you're going through, but we're doing everything we can to locate your wife. Right now, you need to take care of your children. They're scared and they need their father."

Mr. Shaw winced as he glanced over to his children. The little boy peeked out at his father. "Daddy?"

Brooke stepped closer. "They're terrified right now. They need you to find the strength to be strong for them. Let us help you."

Mr. Shaw closed his eyes, sobbing. The officers relaxed their grip, and he heaved out a breath filled with pain.

Brooke directed the officers to bring the family into a private room, telling them he'd be in there soon.

As the family disappeared, most of the remaining police officers went back to work. Some picked up chairs and papers, while others stood in groups, having muted conversations. All of them glanced toward Drew who stood unmoving.

Brooke turned towards his friend. "What happened? What was he talking about with his father?"

Drew didn't answer. He seemed almost in shock.

The General stepped up, getting in Drew's face. "Agent Madison asked a question, Marine. Report."

Drew's head jerked, but he snapped out of his trance. "I didn't put it together. His name is Jeff Shaw.

131

He used to live behind us. His father called the cops when he heard…" Drew paused and placed his hand over his chest where his black phoenix tattoo hid under his clothing. "My father hurting me."

Brooke scowled, the picture coming together. "So Jeff's father called the police when your father was burning you with cigarettes. And what happened?"

Drew shook his head. "Nothing. The police showed but didn't come in. The next time, they talked to my father. I could see them from where I was. I was still on the floor. They saw me. Didn't care. Dad said he'd take care of it. Two days later, Jeff yelled at me at school. Dad had gone over, beat the crap out of Jeff's father in front of him."

Drew stared at the door where Jeff Shaw had disappeared with his children. "By the following week, I saw moving trucks. I never saw them again. I never thought…He targeted that woman because of me. Because of what I did…"

"You didn't do anything," the General snapped, pointing at the room where the Shaws were. "Any more than those children did anything. You were a child being tortured. His father tried to help. The asshole then was your father. The asshole tonight is Edward Hunter, not you. Now help us to figure out what this means because it's not a coincidence."

Drew shook his head. "I don't know."

Brooke scowled as the pieces fell into place. The General was correct, this wasn't a coincidence. "This is all a distraction, but it's a deadly one. We need to figure out who else Edward Hunter might target. People who are connected to Drew either from his childhood or someone he helped as part of McAlister. He's searching for connections. There could be a lot of innocent people he attacks because of it."

The General glowered. "That would be a lot of people."

"Oh, God." Drew put his hand to his head as if it ached. "Jen. The girl we rescued right before I found out about Kelli. Her name, her parents' names. They'd have been in that file you gave Wilson to establish I was nowhere near Ember Falls when Kelli was killed."

The General pulled out a cell. "She's a day or two away. I'll have her and her family completely covered within the hour. We protect what's ours. Hunter won't touch anyone connected to McAllister."

Chapter Ten

Guess Who Just Dropped By

The sunlight broke through the blinds, creating lines of yellow over the bedroom wall where Cole had a poster of a golden dragon. Cole liked the way it made it appear as if the majestic beast was flying through the air.

Cole was still tired. Sleep hadn't come easy knowing Uncle Drew wasn't there. They had spoken by phone last night, and Uncle Drew had said he'd be home today. School was out today, so he could go back to sleep, but he was worried about the dreams he might have. Now that he was awake, his mind was already going.

Cole jumped at the sound of someone knocking on his window.

He spun and was shocked to see Jay waving at him from outside his window to let him in. With wide eyes, Cole ran over and opened the window. "What are you doing here?"

Jay pulled himself in, bookbag and all, and placed his big feet on the floor, and grinned. "I had to come. We're leaving buddy."

Instinctively, Cole took a step backward. His eyes and mouth were wide as he studied his best friend's face. He wanted to ask Jay questions, like why he was here or what he was talking about, but Cole had lost the capacity to form words.

Jay, however, stood, ready to go. He was still by the window, waving for Cole to get a move on. "C'mon. We've got to hurry."

Despite an urge to follow Jay out through the window, Cole finally found his voice. "I can't go. I'm in my pajamas."

Jay frowned and looked Cole up and down. "Oh, yeah. Cool PJs. I've got the same ones. Why don't you get dressed and we can…"

"Wait." Cole pointed a finger at Jay, suddenly remembering that the two of them were still angry at each other. "Why should I go anywhere with you?"

Jay offered a sheepish grin. "Because I'm your bestest friend in the whole wide world?"

Cole crossed his arms and scowled.

"Okay, okay." Jay held up his hands. "I'm sorry. I should have listened to you. I asked Aunt Jeanette about what you said. She told me some garbage about how it was for my own good. Next thing I know, I was grounded for life."

"Grounded?" Cole asked. "For what?"

Jay sat down heavily on the chest near the window. "I may have called my aunt a Nazi bent on destroying my life and anything good in the world like friendship, dragons, and pancakes. And someone gave someone the finger, but I can't swear it was me."

Cole found himself going into blink overdrive. Jay was in huge trouble, not just for what he said, but for the fact that he'd run away. Still, Cole couldn't keep himself from grinning ear to ear. Jay was in trouble, more and more trouble by the moment because he valued his friendship with Cole.

"I can't believe you." Cole sat down next to Jay. "Aunt Jeanette must have been so angry."

Jay's smile faded. "She wasn't angry as much as hurt, but I don't care. She can't keep us away from each other. It's not like being near you is dangerous."

Cole's grin melted into a frown and he studied the foot of his bed. "It can be." His eyes sprang up to Jay's. "It's not my fault that I was kidnapped though."

Now it was Jay's turn to blink. "You were kidnapped? All I heard is something bad happened and we weren't supposed to ask you. Wait, were you kidnapped back before we met? I remember hearing something had happened that involved the police. Or was it just recently when you were out for a week."

Cole folded his arms. "Both times. The first time, it was the men who killed my mom. The second time, it was because well…" Cole winced. He wished that an Earthquake would come and tear the house apart so he didn't have to tell Jay this part. "Because of our comic."

"Our comic? The first one with Captain Nova?" Jay's mouth dropped open. "Was it Galactor?"

Cole shook his head. It wasn't Galactor of course, yet oddly, it was. He owed Jay the truth, but he couldn't tell.

"I can't talk about it. I can't tell you what I did."

Jay frowned. "I don't understand."

Cole was having trouble hearing Jay but tried to stay focused. "I didn't…It was…" He swallowed so hard it hurt. Cole glanced around, looking to make sure they were alone. "I-I-I can't talk about it. He'll know. He *always* knows. And if I tell anyone, he'll c-c-come. He'll come and hurt Aunt Ash and Lilly. Ollie, Sam, and Uncle Drew." Cole slid to the ground, closed his eyes, and wept. "You."

The air was becoming thin, and there was a sound in the distance that only Cole could hear. "I didn't realize I was making you draw stuff…" Cole winced, shaking his head. It was getting darker, and the air was being squeezed out of his lungs. They were no longer alone in the room. Edward must be close by. In the closet, under the bed. He was listening. He would know. "I can't tell you. I'm sorry, *don't make me.*"

Cole desperately sucked in a breath. His eyes opened wide as he searched the room, not seeing Jay, just Edward's eyes. Cole scrambled back, making Jay gasp. He couldn't breathe, he could barely see. He struggled to fill his lungs, gasping as he drowned in his own tears.

Someone screamed for help, but Cole couldn't tell who it was. Only that it was too late. Only that he was powerless to help them.

Footsteps thundered closer and Cole prepared himself to die. It was going to happen, and there was nothing he could do to stop it.

"Cole, you're safe. You're okay. Listen to my voice."

That wasn't Edward. The voice was soft and kind, two things Edward never was.

"Just listen to my voice. You're safe. *I'm* safe."

Cole shook his head. They had to get away from him. *He* was no good. He was dangerous. It was his fault.

"Cole, I need you to hear my voice. Just listen and hear me. He can't hurt us, but I need you to breathe. Can you do that? Please, just breathe."

In the haze of panic and despair, Cole recognized Lilly's voice. She was safe. They were all safe. For now.

Slowly, Cole's lungs started to work again. The

room came back into focus. The first face he saw was Lilly's, calm and concerned. She was kneeling beside him, her patient eyes watching.

Jay watched him, his eyes full of panic. Cole wanted to run, but he knew his legs wouldn't carry him anywhere. He'd just gotten his best friend back, and now Jay would be terrified of him forever.

Jay pulled away from Sam and sat next to Cole, putting his arm around his friend. "Don't worry buddy. Ain't nobody getting near you. I got your back."

****

Delivering a profile to a squad room of cops was nothing new for Brooke. He fielded the usual questions and drew a sharp picture of what everyone knew of Edward Hunter. The fact was if you believed the official line on Hunter, he was heading south. If you believed what Brooke did, he wanted to get to Cole. Either way, he wouldn't be in this town for long. When he was done, he went searching for the General and Drew and found them in a small office.

Drew was still shaken from earlier, but he was keeping it together. He stood in a corner, his face hidden by shadows. The General was sitting in a chair by the far end of the room scowling as he spoke on the phone.

"Drew…"

Brooke stopped the moment Drew glanced at him.

"I don't want to talk about it." Drew's eyes went back to the General. Before he could counter, the General ended the call and stood up.

The General held up his phone as if it contained a transcript of the phone conversation. "We need to wrap this up. Hunter is not in town anymore and the Task Force has sent someone after him. We've been summoned."

Brooke grimaced, not liking the way that sounded. "By whom?"

The General put his phone away. "Tom Brook, the former Mayor of Ember Falls, current US Senator, and now a candidate for the White House. Has his name been connected to the sex ring?"

Brooke tried to concentrate over the thundering beat of his heart, which he was positive the entire room could hear. "No, but he's not excluded. Frank Duncan coded everyone's names. There are a few that could be him. He probably wants to make sure we're not connecting the dots to him."

The General raised an eyebrow. "Probably. He wants us back in Ember Falls pronto. We need to hit the road."

Brooke leaned against the wall, trying to appear casual. "And he called you personally?"

Drew gave a curt nod. "Yeah, I noticed that too. Why not go down the chain of command to Brooke?"

"Good question," the General said. "We'll make sure to ask him that."

Brooke tried to swallow, but his mouth was dry. "Let me finish up around here, then we'll get going."

Brooke quickly walked away, but not before he caught the General's narrowing eyes assessing him.

This wasn't going to end well.

****

Cole had watched from the top of the stairs as Lilly had spoken to Jay's father and Aunt Jeanette. Jay sat beside him, having not left his side since Cole's breakdown, waiting for that moment when he'd have to go face the music.

Jeanette seemed far more upset than angry. She wiped away a stray tear, but Cole was certain they were not on his behalf, but because her feelings had been hurt. Jay's dad was stoic. His face remained passive, and he listened patiently as Lilly explained whatever it was she was explaining.

Finally, Jay's dad turned towards the stairs. "Jay, come down here now."

Jay and Cole exchanged worried glances as they got up and walked down the stairs together. If Mr. Lancaster was disturbed to see his son next to Cole, he didn't show it. "Jay, you and I need to talk, but first, apologize to your aunt. You may not agree with her, but you will respect her. She came in to care for you because I had to do my job. She loves you, and she deserves better than that."

With downcast eyes, Jay nodded. "Yes, sir." He turned ever so slightly to Jeanette but didn't lift his eyes to meet hers. "Sorry, Aunt Jeanette."

Mr. Lancaster turned to Lilly. "Is there someplace private I could have a conversation with Jay before we go home? I promise to not be long."

Lilly pointed towards a side room. "I've got an office back there. It's not much, but it should be fine. Would you like a cup of coffee? Jeanette?"

Both declined, and Mr. Lancaster pointed a finger toward Lilly's office.

Jay shot one last, desperate look at Cole before he marched off with a groan.

Cole sat down at the bottom of the stairs, avoiding eye contact with Jeanette. He was worried about Jay. He didn't want to lose his friend now that he got him back.

"Are you sure I can't get you anything? Coffee or tea?" Lilly asked. "It's not a bother."

Once again, Jeanette shook her head. "I'm sorry that Jay intruded on you. He's normally so well-behaved."

"Jay is never a bother," Lilly said. "And it meant the world to Cole that he came."

Cole caught Jeanette studying him.

"I take it Cole is aware…" Jeanette searched for the right words, "of what I said?"

Lilly placed her hand gently on Cole's shoulder. "You need to understand how much Jay means to Cole. He's never had a friend. Jay coming here, the way he helped Cole."

Jeanette frowned. "Cole, I like you. I'm just worried about Jay. The idea of him being put in danger… I'm sorry, but I just can't stand it. I hope you understand."

Cole wanted to scream at her, but the sad fact was, he did understand. "Jay's probably safer staying away." He shifted, turning away from everyone. "Everyone is."

Jay and Mr. Lancaster chose that moment to come back into the room. Cole saw their feet as they approached. Mr. Lancaster took a seat next to him. "How are you doing tonight, Cole? Jay tells me you had a rough moment. A panic attack?"

Cole pulled his knees up to his chest, as his face burned, and his gut twisted.

Mr. Lancaster let out a tired breath. "You feel like you're underwater. Can't breathe. You get that heavy, sick feeling right here." He tapped the center of his chest. "It's like there's a house parked right on you and you're in a nightmare, only it isn't a nightmare 'cause it did happen. For me, it was this time I was in Afghanistan. Me and my buddy Mike had a pair of IEDs to defuse, about fifteen feet from each other. I had just finished with mine and looked over to Mike. Gave him a thumbs up. He did the same, then he exploded."

Cole gasped.

"It was pretty bad," Mr. Lancaster said. "The wires on his were crossed weirdly, so even though he thought he'd diffused it…Well." He shrugged. "You know how we decided who got which IED? We had a little round of rock, papers, scissors, shoot and he won, so he got to choose which bomb to diffuse. If he had chosen the other one, I wouldn't be here right now. Sometimes, I think that's the hardest part."

Cole listened intently, shocked that someone else could understand that feeling.

"It's called Post Traumatic Stress Disorder," Mr. Lancaster explained. "PTSD for short. And it's rough. *Very* rough. It did a number on me. I was a grown man, who had fought for his country and I had one moment of horror."

Mr. Lancaster's eyes were full of sympathy and compassion. "I can't even begin to imagine what it is you've been through. You're about to turn nine, and you've been living with this for your entire life, haven't you?"

Cole wiped the tears away from his eyes. "Yeah."

"It can help to talk about it," Mr. Lancaster said. "The first time I did, it felt like my world was about to end, but it didn't."

Cole moved away, just a few inches. "I can't talk about it. He'll know."

Mr. Lancaster lifted his chin. "Who'll know? You're stepfather?"

Cole somehow managed to nod. "He will."

"Maybe," Mr. Lancaster said. "Maybe not. But if he does, he'll be dealt with. You've got two cops in the house. I understand your uncle is going to be one. Works for someplace called McAlister Security? I checked them out when I heard Jay was spending time here. He's an ex-marine too, right?"

Cole didn't answer. None of them were Edward.

Uncle Drew was a hero.

Edward was a monster.

Cole stifled a sob. "You should keep Jay away from me."

Mr. Lancaster held out his hand for his son. "Nothing in this world comes before my son Cole. You know that, right? You understand that I can't have anything happen. He's my boy."

Cole used the heel of his hand to push the tears away. "Yeah. I get it."

"Good," Mr. Lancaster said. "So you'll understand when I tell you that I'll be there, keeping an eye on the pair of you this weekend when you turn nine."

Slowly, Cole's head came up. "Jay can come?"

Mr. Lancaster pulled his son to his side. "My son told me in no uncertain terms that he needs to stand by your side. I made sure he understood there is a risk. Jay understands that some things are worth that risk. He told me just like a marine doesn't leave a man behind, neither does a friend. That's my boy. If he's going to stand by your side, so will I. As far as Edward Hunter is concerned..." Mr. Lancaster leaned in. "Let him come. You may just find that when he's not facing a small child, he's not as bad as you think he is."

Cole shook his head. "You don't know what he'll do."

Mr. Lancaster raised his eyebrows as he considered this. "No, I don't. I *do* know what I'll do. What Detective

Miller and Officer Rossi will do. What your uncle will do. You need to think of that. I'm not telling you to talk to me, but you need to take away his power. And that starts by standing up to him. I'm not going to lie. That first time, you'll feel as if he's right there, breathing over your shoulder. The next time, it'll be like he's across the room. The time after that, as if he's outside the window. Eventually, you'll beat him."

Mr. Lancaster stood up. "Jay is going to be grounded this week, for the way he spoke to his aunt and for running away. But for that, we'll take away his TV time and no computer or drawing, except for school. What he did was wrong. But the reason why he did it? I couldn't be prouder. He'll be at your party. And you can spend time together as long as I'm there. He'll stand for you. So maybe it's time to consider standing for yourself."

Mr. Lancaster held out his hand to Cole, who stared at it for a long time before taking it and giving it a shake.

"Say goodbye to Cole," Mr. Lancaster said.

Jay went over and grinned. "My dad's the coolest."

Somehow, Cole managed to return the smile. "So are you."

After a few more goodbyes, Lilly showed them out. "I suppose I should get dinner started." The doorbell rang. "I guess Jay must have forgotten something."

Cole stood up and raced to her side. "He didn't bring anything."

Lilly shrugged. "Maybe they just wanted to say something more." She went to the door and pulled it open. She looked straight ahead, saw nothing, but heard someone clear their throat. She glanced down. "Oh."

Cole stepped around, ready to protect Lilly no matter what. But he didn't find his stepfather. Instead, he saw a girl about his age, with dark skin and wild hair, with her arms crossed and her eyebrow arched. While she was smaller than Cole, she appeared ready to fight anyone who got in her way.

Lilly stepped forward. "Hello. How can I help you?"

She stepped inside without invitation, tossed the overstuffed backpack she carried over her shoulder, and scowled. "I'm here for my dad."

Lilly frowned. "I'm sorry sweetie. What's your name and who's your father?"

The girl's scowl deepened as she rolled her eyes. "My name is Abbie and my dad is Agent Brooke Madison, FBI."

****

The Mayor's office in Ember Falls was physically part of the same building as City Hall. It was an old brick structure that was over a hundred years old. Three stories high, it wasn't the most impressive Mayors office that the General had ever been in, but it was a strong, sturdy building, with a rich history and proud tradition.

The General hadn't met Mayor Charlene Ybos, but she had a good reputation. She'd also given the green light for Chief Miller to give the press conference exonerating Drew. The General was pretty sure Chief Miller would have done so with or without the mayor's approval, but they had to know they were opening the city up for a major lawsuit. So far, the mayor had stayed out of the way, which was just the way the General liked his politicians.

The doors opened and Mayor Ybos walked in. She was younger than the General imagined, but something about the way the small-framed woman carried herself in her blue blazer spoke of her ability to hold her own.

She offered her hand to the General. "General McAlister, it's a pleasure to meet you. Chief Miller has spoken highly of you." She turned to Drew next. "And you as well. I understand that McAlister's loss will be Ember Falls's gain very shortly."

Drew took her hand and smiled. "Thank you for the opportunity. Especially since you cleared it before there was definitive proof of my innocence. You believed in me."

Mayor Ybos returned the smile. "I want to be honest. Ann believed in you, I believed in her. She came to me and made the case for hiring you. She was very convincing and I take what Ann says very seriously."

"Sounds like a smart idea," the General said. "This is Special Agent Brooke Madison."

Mayor Ybos's eyebrows went up as she took Brooke's hand. "I wasn't aware that you were coming. I offered to reach out to you for the Senator, but he requested to just speak to General McAlister."

"Really?" Brooke turned to the General. "Is that so?"

The General shrugged. "He may have mentioned to me that he wanted me to come in, without any FBI in attendance. I told him I understood."

Brooke arched an eyebrow. "Then why am I here?"

The General shrugged. "I said I understood, I never said I agreed."

Mayor Ybos held her hand out, indicating for them to follow. "He's waiting in my office. Shall we?"

Drew followed her, while the General studied Brooke. The man had an internal battle of anger, fear, and insecurity raging behind his eyes. The General was curious to see which one would win.

Outside the Mayor's office were two large men, each in a dark suit, each packing. Both took a step closer to each other intending to block the Mayor from entering her own office.

Mayor Ybos drew herself up as much as a woman of five foot three could and smiled in a way that was anything but friendly. "Is there a problem gentlemen?"

The two men glanced at each other, then back at the Mayor. One of them, the taller white male, cleared his throat. "The Senator requested privacy."

Mayor Ybos blinked once in astonishment, and the two men tried to stare her down. Appearing more annoyed than intimidated, she stepped forward, causing both large men to quickly glance at each other again. "The Senator can have all the privacy he likes, but not in my office. Step out of my way."

After a few more worried glances, the pair of guards stepped away from the door. Mayor Ybos entered her office.

Senator Brook sat with his polished shoes perched on the edge of Mayor Ybos's desk, as he spoke on his cell and glanced out through the window at the view of the magnificent gardens. He held a pen which he put in his mouth like a smoker used to holding a cigarette. Even from his profile, he had the appearance of a movie star playing the part of a politician. Dark hair with a hint of grey, and an impressive physique.

The General knew he was being groomed to run in the next presidential election. The scuttle bug was that the plan among the party elite was that he would run for the top spot to make a name for himself, and if he placed well in the primaries then the frontrunner would choose him for their running mate. The General had sources that he trusted that told him Senator Brook would play that game but was ready to go hardcore if he had a chance of winning the top ticket, even if it meant releasing damaging Op Research on the presumed front-runner.

They fanned out, with Drew standing directly in front of the Mayor's desk, while Brooke moved to the right, well out of the Senator's line of sight. Mayor Ybos went around her desk and stood directly in the Senator's view, in front of the window. She crossed her arms and arched her eyebrow. "I see you've made yourself at home."

Senator Brook grinned. "I'll have to call you back." He ended the call, put the phone in his pocket, and spread his hands. "I apologize Charlene. This used to be my desk, although it seems much smaller than it did back then."

Mayor Ybos ran her fingers over the wood of her desk. "Actually, I had the desk replaced. Something about it didn't suit me. I brought my own which I used when I was a teacher. Not as Brobdingnagian, but it worked for me."

Senator Brook frowned. "Not as…What?"

"*Brobdingnagian.*" The General stepped up beside the Mayor. "It means big, or gigantic. Usually excessively so."

Senator Brook raised his eyebrows, and absently chewed on a black pen again. "Interesting word. I'll have to work it into a speech one day. You must be Paul McAlister. Please, sit down Paul."

"I'll stand, thank you, Thomas."

The Senator's friendly facade faded. "Usually, people call me Senator Brook."

"Is that right?" The General shrugged. "Usually

people call me General McAlister or sir. Either will do. Now, what can I do for you?"

Senator Brook stood up and drew himself up to his full height. At six foot three, he was two inches taller than the General and he towered over the Mayor, but neither seemed to notice. "I wanted to talk to you about dealing with the inconvenient investigation into your man."

"Indeed?" The General held his hand out. "I brought my man, who was *inconvenienced* by nine months in prison, and was effectively banished from his sister's lives because they were threatened if he ever came back, with me."

The senator frowned and turned to Drew. For the briefest of moments, annoyance flickered on his face before he went back into full politician mode. Instantly, the smile was back in place and he offered his hand to Drew. "Mr. Duncan. I'm sorry for what you've been through. And if he were still alive, of course, we'd prosecute him for his role in attempting to frame you. However, since he's passed, there seems to be little point. Except to bring pain to his family. I just spoke with his widow as well as his sons. They're beside themselves in grief over losing the father they loved and respected. They did want me to apologize directly to you. Of course, they understand that after everything you've been through you'll want and deserve more than just an apology. They've asked that I talk to you about such things. Stacia is an old friend, and she's very fragile right now. Having to deal with her grieving sons is hard enough, but the scandal may be too much for her."

Releasing his grip, Drew folded his arms. "To be honest, I haven't even thought of any legal action. My focus right now is keeping Cole safe and that means finding Edward Hunter. But with all due respect, this doesn't end there. Someone knew about Hunter all these years. My father knew about him. I'm willing to bet others did as well."

Senator Brook nodded as if he was considering. "Of course, your focus needs to be on your family. And you would be doing so by considering litigation so you have the means to provide for your nephew. Nobody would blame you for wanting to provide for that."

Drew held up his hand. "I'm not ready to even think about that right now."

Senator Brook bowed his head solemnly. "I understand, and I also get that you probably don't have much sympathy for his family, but his wife and sons are suffering right now. Taking this off of their plates would go a long way to healing."

The General stepped forward. "Perhaps Drew could think about it. In the meanwhile, would you like to discuss the rest of the investigation? We brought Special Agent Madison with us."

The senator narrowed his eyes as he turned to find Brooke standing to his left. He seemed unsteady for just a moment, as he dropped the pen onto the Mayor's desk.

The General studied the reactions of both men. The statesmen's veneer fell off of the Senator's face as Brooke moved out of the far corner of the room. His mouth parted, and his blue eyes examined Brooke as if he were trying to decipher a puzzle.

Brooke seemed to wait, his face impassive, but his hands slowly clenched into fists.

"I uh…" Senator Brooke gripped the armrests tightly as he lowered himself into the Mayor's chair.

"I'm sorry, I wasn't expecting to speak to Agent Madison today. I um…" His gaze slowly moved away from Brooke to the General, back again. He sat up straight and suddenly the mask of a dedicated public servant was back in place. "I believe I asked you to come alone."

The General shrugged. "Oops."

The senator rose, fixed his tie, and started to come around the desk. "I would have thought that you'd have been willing to meet alone with a US Senator. McAlister has a lot of interests that require congressional approval."

The General bared his teeth as he leaned in. "I don't take kindly to threats, Senator. You want to get into a pissing contest with me? I've got a lot less to lose than you do."

The two men stared at each other unblinking for a solid ten seconds before the Senator broke contact and moved around the General, sending one last look at Drew. "You let me know if you're willing to deal with the family. I'll make sure you're well taken care of."

Drew stepped to his right, placing himself right behind the General's right side.

Understanding the gesture, Senator Brook headed for the door but was intercepted as Brooke stepped in front of him. "Do you have any questions for me?"

The two men stood eye to eye.

"I would assume you couldn't talk to me about the manhunt, or am I wrong?"

Brooke's face remained passive. "You wouldn't be wrong. I'm not part of the Task Force, but I thought maybe there were other questions you might have. I'd be willing to speak with you in private."

Once again, they stared at each other. And again, the senator was the first to turn away. "No thank you. I'll be awaiting your call, Mr. Duncan. Remember, a widow and her two innocent sons are suffering."

Without another glance at anyone, Senator Brook left.

Brooke's fists were clenched, and his lip was curled in disgust. He didn't answer as he walked out.

Drew turned to the General. "What the hell was that?"

The General scowled, hating the fact that he'd been right. "The missing pieces of the puzzle falling into place."

****

Lilly carried the tray of cookies over to the table and placed it near the mug of hot cocoa she'd made. So far, the young girl with the light brown frizzy hair hadn't even noticed it. Her eyes hadn't stopped watching Lilly from the moment she'd arrived, except for the several moments when it appeared as if she might fall asleep.

Abbie tapped her fingers on the table, waiting.

"I called your father, but it went to voicemail." Lilly sat down, picked up her mug of hot cocoa, and took a sip. "Your cocoa is probably cool enough to drink."

For a brief moment, Abbie's eyes moved to the floating marshmallows before returning to Lilly. "Did you tell him I was here?"

Lilly shook her head. "Of course. Won't your mom be worried?"

Abbie folded her arms. "She's dead."

Lilly's hand went to her heart. "Oh, I'm sorry."

Abbie shrugged. "Shit happens.

Cole placed his mug down. "I lost my mom too. It

sucks."

Abbie responded with a yawn so long it seemed almost painful.

Lilly reached for her mug. "So who was supposed to be watching you?"

Abbie crossed her arms. "Sandy. Her husband works with Dad and she's watched me here and there. She's okay for an old person."

Picturing the wife of one of the senior agents, she wondered what would happen when Abbie was discovered missing. "Why don't we call her?"

Annie rolled her eyes. "Please no. I can't stand to be dragged to any more yoga classes or watch her sit on those big balls."

Lilly frowned. "How old is Sandra?"

Abbie shrugged. "Not as old as you, but still old. Something's wrong with Dad, and I have a right to know what it is."

Lilly exchanged a bewildered glance with Cole who was sitting next to Abbie, nibbling on his cookie.

"Why don't we just call her?" Lilly said. "What's her number?"

Abbie reached into her bag and pulled out her cell from the bag she had by her feet. It was heavily bejeweled and powered down. She turned it on and saw a dozen messages. "Shit."

Abbie hit her screen and the phone instantly rang.

"Abigale?"

Abbie rolled her eyes. "Hey, Sandra! I was going to call you." Her voice went up several octaves and suddenly she sounded as sweet as a box of chocolates. "I had to make a little trip to see Dad and make sure he's okay, but it was great staying with you and…"

"Don't you try and pull that innocent act with me, you had me worried sick. Your father is going to kill you and then he's going to kill me. When he finds out…"

The back door opened and Brooke came in, an impressive scowl on his face.

"I'm pretty sure he already has," Abbie managed to say before Brooke snatched the phone away from her, and took it off speaker.

"I'm here. I'm very sorry. I'll deal with Abbie." Brooke closed his eyes "I understand. Again, I'm very sorry."

A moment later, he put Abbie's phone into his pocket. "I think we can forget about having Sandra watch you ever again."

Abbie smiled. "Well, that's good news."

Brooke raised a finger, narrowed his eyes, and breathed in slowly. "Abbie, you know I can't be with you all the time. I've got an important job to do."

Abbie attempted to appear as innocent as possible. "I know how important your job is, but I had to come."

"Why?" Brooke asked. "Sandra is perfectly nice and she takes good care of you."

Abbie slouched back in her chair and rolled her eyes. "*Puh*-leeze. She tries to get me to wear matching clothes with her and do everything she does. I don't want to do Pilates or wear yoga pants. The woman spends more time at the gym than the entire lineup of the Giants."

"That's not the point."

"And she drinks all these health drinks," Abbie continued. "Green ones. Ew. At least Lilly made me hot chocolate like a normal person would."

"And that's another thing." Brooke began to pace.

"You can't just intrude on Lilly here in her home."

Abbie rubbed her eyes. "She doesn't mind." She held up her mug. "Hot cocoa and cookies."

Lilly smiled at Brooke. "I really don't."

"That's not the point," Brooke said. "You can't just run away like that. Anything could have happened to you."

"Why do you think I came here?" Abbie jumped out of her chair, her eyes filling with tears. She shifted her gaze to Lilly. "You could have decided not to come back."

"Hey," Brooke got down on one knee. "You know I'd never do that. I promised—"

"People lie all the time." Abbie pulled away.

Brooke reached for her hand. "I've never lied to you. I never will."

"You said you'd never leave, and now you're here." She glanced toward Lilly.

"Abbie…"

The small girl pulled away and headed towards the kitchen door, then paused. Her shoulders slumped. "Shit, I can't storm off to my room." She turned around. As she did, she stumbled and almost fell. Both Brooke and Lilly raced over.

Brooke took her in his arms and felt her forehead. "Abbie, are you okay?"

Abbie leaned against the wall. "I'm fine. I just haven't slept."

Brooke felt her forehead. "Since when?"

Abbie's eye's fluttered, as she struggled to stay awake. "Since you left."

"She's been yawning and nearly falling asleep since she showed up. She's exhausted." Lilly knelt by Abbie's side. "We've got an empty bedroom. We can put you in there for now while your father and I talk. Maybe take a little nap? Is that okay?"

Abbie yawned again. "I'm sorry. I really wanted to meet you."

Lilly held out her hand. "I'm glad I got to meet you. C'mon."

"Lilly," Brooke stepped forward but stopped short when Lilly held up a finger as he had earlier.

"You and I need to have a conversation, Brooke. One that's long overdue."

****

Lilly came downstairs and found the kitchen empty just as Ashley walked in the back door. "Did you see Brooke? He was just in here with Drew and the General."

Ashley gestured behind her toward the yard. "I just saw them heading up to the garage apartment. They didn't look happy." She folded her arms. "I got your text. Brooke has a kid?"

Lilly headed for the back door. "Yes. Poor thing was exhausted. She's upstairs now taking a nap and Cole is in his room doing homework. I need to go see Brooke, can you stay with them?"

Helping herself to three of the untouched cookies, Ashley nodded. "Yep."

Without further comment, Lilly made her way outside and headed to the door that led to the small apartment in the garage. The moment she opened the door, she could hear Drew's muffled voice tinged with anger as he berated Brooke. She quickly ascended and let herself in. Drew was by the punching bag, glaring at Brooke, while the General sat at the tiny table with his hands neatly folded in front of him. Brooke stood in the center of the room. Conversation stopped as she entered, and everyone turned to her. "Ashley's in the house. Could you guys give us a moment alone?"

Drew started to leave, but Brooke stopped him.

"No, wait. You might as well hear this." Brooke sat down heavily. "It's about time I told you some things." He grimaced and glanced toward the General. "I don't know how much you know about my past here in Ember Falls, but I'm guessing you've done your homework on me."

The General leaned forward. "Yes. Your mother has numerous arrests for solicitation, drug possession, and other petty offenses. With her record, you should have been removed from her care before you were six. Despite your home life, you still did well enough in school. You went to New York City and graduated valedictorian at John Jay College. You applied and were accepted to the FBI. One of their youngest recruits. You excelled. So much so that Agent Burkhart pulled you for a special assignment. The Graceland killings. You were supposed to be there to learn, but you came up with the profile that led to the apprehension of serial killer Andrew E. Moore. Your supervisors all noted that you refused to take special credit, but they were impressed. The agent in charge of that case, Agent Foster, made it clear you picked up on clues nobody else did. Including that the killer would likely have a stutter. I don't mind admitting that I would have missed that."

Lilly beamed, happy and proud of Brooke.

"You quickly made a name for yourself," the General continued. "And were highly sought after for many cases. You were assigned to the Sommerville murders where…" The General hesitated, his eyes going to Lilly. "You had dealt with three children who had been kidnapped and managed to escape. Your job was to help them through their trauma and get them to tell you something that would lead to the person behind the kidnappings. Four dead bodies, all young children, had already been found. The Special Agent in charge, Gary Astor, thought your theory was wrong. You disagreed. So much so that you checked out a lead on your own. You were right, but instead of waiting for backup, you went in and were nearly killed because of it."

Lilly's eyes widened in alarm. "What happened? Are you okay?"

"I'm fine," Brooke said. "It was nothing."

"Nothing?" The General raised an eyebrow. "You were shot. Tortured for about three hours, until you saw an opportunity and took it. Saved your own life and the lives of seven kids. Mostly kids the town of Somerville had forgotten about. But you were in trouble as you'd broken protocol."

"I didn't have a choice," Brooke said. "The UNSUB knew we were on to him. He would have killed those kids and fled. I had to move." Brooke took a deep breath. "But they were right. I broke protocol. And if I'd been killed, I wouldn't have been able to help those kids."

"Your bosses at the FBI decided you'd become too emotionally attached to the victims," the General said. "Based on what I know, I'd say that's a good description. However, since you did save lives, the backlash wasn't that bad. Foster pushed for you to go on the Edward Hunter Task Force, but the brass decided to send you here instead. You came up with a profile of Hunter that differed from what the FBI heads believed. They predicted he'd try to go underground. You believed he would circle back to come here. You were certain he'd target the people close to Cole. Especially Ashley and Lilly. You weren't going to let that happen."

Brooke glared at the General. "You're damn right I'm not. I screwed up and hurt Lilly years ago. I'm not about to let that bastard get anyway near her."

The General arched an eyebrow. "Son, I believe that's your big reason for being here. I do, but let's not bullshit here. She's not the only reason. Your father played a big role in coming back here."

Lilly moved closer. "Your father? I didn't know you had any idea you knew who your father was. Your mom didn't have…" She searched for the most sensitive way to phrase things. "She didn't have a steady boyfriend."

Brooke scowled. "Mom didn't *have* boyfriends. She had guys she partied with and customers." Brooke turned his head away from Lilly. "The ones Mom brought home were the low lives. Fifty dollars and score a dime bag, she'd entertain them for the night. Or give them a chance to get at me. But the big scores were the ones I never met. The ones that kept the lights on, the rent paid, and put food on the table."

Brooke rubbed his face. "Our house was shit, but there was usually food, always electricity. She never worked, yet somehow there was money. Not a lot, because the majority of it went up her nose, but it was there." He turned to face Drew. "There were times she'd say something like, 'I had to give your daddy a call.' I figured she was just bullshitting me. What were the chances she even had the faintest idea who my biological father was? But now and then, she'd say something that made me think she did."

Brooke started to pace, as though if he kept moving,

the truth wouldn't catch up with him. But he knew that was impossible. "She'd caress my face and tell me I had my daddy's eyes. Or slap me, telling me she ought to drop me off at the mansion where my father lived."

"Mansion?" Drew exchanged bewildered glances with Lilly.

Brooke stopped dead but avoided eye contact. "When I was thirteen years old, she'd disappeared for over a week. You remember that, right?"

Drew frowned as he searched his memory. "You were going nuts, thinking something happened to her."

Brooke winced at the memory. "I knew you thought I was crazy, because why would I care, but I didn't want anything to happen to her. There were days when I wished I'd never see her again, but I still wanted to know she was all right." He shrugged. "I *still* want to know she's okay, but I don't see her. I just know she's cashing the checks."

"Brooke," Lilly said. "Nobody faults you for still loving your mother."

Brooke backed up from her. "Drew and I searched. We found her lost, high. She slapped me. Remember?"

Drew scowled. "How could I forget? She was rambling. Talking about how you were the only reason she was stuck in this town. She should have aborted you like she did the others, but she couldn't because you were too important. That's why she…" Drew's eyes widened, and his head tilted as the memory came back to him. "You fucking son of a bitch. You should have told me."

Drew moved towards Brooke, who made no move to block him.

Lilly, however, did, placing herself between the two of them. "Stop it now and tell me what you're talking about."

Drew jabbed a finger toward Brooke's face. "His mom said that's why she named him after his father. I had no idea what the hell she was talking about then, but..." Drew stepped back, his balled-up fists to his sides. "Tell me I'm wrong."

Brooke shook his head. "No, I don't think you are. She gave me my father's last name as my first as a middle finger to him. Mayor Thomas Brook."

Lilly gasped. "Are you sure?"

Brooke rubbed the back of his head. "She never confirmed, and today was the first time I was in the same room with the man. It's not like I can run a DNA test to verify, but you saw the way he reacted to me. He knew who I was."

The General rose. "I did see it. He thinks you're his, which means, based on your mother's current age, he was part of that little underage sex circus. As far as the DNA goes." The General reached into his pocket and pulled out a plastic bag containing a black pen with teeth marks on it. "I can find out."

Brooke gazed at the pen. He wanted to take it, but he was too far away and he was quite certain his legs couldn't carry him across the room. "How did you...?"

The General held the pen out to Brooke. "I could have taken Senator Brook's wallet, watch, and shoes the moment he saw you and he wouldn't have noticed. Grabbing this off the desk was child's play."

Brooke reached his hand out for the bag, but couldn't quite get himself to take it. "I can't ask for a DNA analysis of that. They'll pull me off this case."

The General's eyebrows went up. "Is that more important than finding out the truth, once and for all?"

Once again, he offered the pen to Brooke who scowled at it.

"I'm not leaving. Not until…" Brooke folded his arms to keep himself from taking the pen. "If you want to send that to Director Burke, fine. I can't stop you and I won't try. Just give me the time I need to see this through."

The General folded his arms. "That son of a bitch is about to launch a campaign to become President of the United States. That's got to burn your ass."

Brooke scowled. "I don't give a shit about him. He's nothing to me, but I'll tell you this. That's one hell of a motive."

Drew's eyes went wide. "You think the senator is the one who framed me? Reynolds confessed before he blew his brains out."

"Let's just say I'm not convinced." Brooke's eyes were fixated on the pen. "Reynolds didn't have as much to lose. After one of his sons got kidnapped and tortured because the other one dealt drugs his political career was effectively over. I'm sure he didn't want anyone to know he had a hand in a teen sex ring, but would he hire someone like Jericho to kill to cover it? I've profiled Reynolds. He had a hand in it, but he didn't have the balls to have Molly or your sister killed. I think there's more to this."

Drew shook his head. "Do you? Or are you just so pissed off at him that you're seeing him as being guilty? He's an ass, there's no doubt, but Reynolds framed me. He took his own life so he wouldn't have to face up to it. Do you think an innocent man would do that?"

"I don't know," Brooke replied. "Drew, I'm telling you that the senator is in this up to his eyeballs."

"You *want* him to be," Drew snapped back. "Jesus Christ, Brooke, nobody understands hating your father more than I do, but I also know what it's like to be presumed guilty of something I didn't do. You're letting your hatred for a father who never wanted you cloud your judgment. We need to be focused on Hunter, not your father."

"I *am* focused on Hunter!" Brooke jabbed a finger in Drew's face. "I'm here because I plan on stopping him. He'll come. And I'm not letting him get near Lilly. Nothing is more important than that."

The General stepped between the pair. He sent Drew a glance, which had Drew backing away. The General turned towards Brooke. "You're right. Hunter is going to come. Unless someone stops him before he gets here, he's going to come. That's what's important."

Brooke clenched his fists. "I don't give a shit what Senator Brook thinks of me or if he ever acknowledges who I am."

The Genera's eyebrows went up as he considered Brooke. "We don't need to go through the FBI. I can get the DNA run if you want."

Brooke folded his arms and scowled.

"I know it's a big step." The General put the plastic bag with the pen into his pocket. "It's one thing to think it's true, it's another thing to know it. Let me know what you decide. If we do it, I'll give you the results privately."

Brooke exhaled. "Thank you. I'll let you know."

Drew stepped forward to say something, but Lilly held her hand out to stop him. "I think we've covered this enough. I need to speak to Brooke." She signaled to the door. "Alone please."

The General headed out. Drew hesitated only a moment before following. "Brooke. I'm sorry that you've got a shitty dad. I know this isn't easy on you."

Brooke managed a nod.

The General and Drew left the apartment, and Lilly closed the door behind them.

"First things first." Lilly faced him, her emerald eyes piercing his soul. "Who is Abbie's mother?

Chapter Eleven

Reconnecting

Brooke ran his hand over his head. "Her name was Destiny Fairchild. She was in and out of trouble for years. I believe she loved Abbie as much as she was capable of loving anyone besides herself, but she was too much like my mom. Couldn't kick the habit."

Lilly frowned. Brooke had always been extreme in his dislike of drugs, coming from a mother who was a junkie. It seemed unlikely that he'd hook up with someone so much like her.

"How did you meet her?" Lilly asked.

Brooke took a deep breath and walked over to the window where he peered through the blinds at the house. "I didn't. By the time I came into the picture, Destiny was already dead."

Lilly gasped as she pictured the young girl fast asleep in the guest bedroom. "I'm sorry. How?"

Brooke shook his head. "A man named Jeffrey Jones killed her. His MO was to target moms who were junkies, kill them and take their children to slowly torture. He was a throwaway kid himself."

Lilly nodded as the memory of a news report surfaced. "I remember hearing about that. I didn't know you were involved in..." Her eyes narrowed. Lilly moved toward Brooke, glancing out the window. "Oh my God, was Abbie…"

Brooke closed his eyes. "She escaped. Got a couple of other kids out of there. They were younger and practically catatonic, but I was able to get through to Abbie. She helped me understand Jones. His obsession with water, how he was punishing the children because of his hatred of himself. I was able to determine his signature. His need to keep them alive for weeks. The key was he wanted them to watch whenever he killed one of them."

Tears streamed down her eyes as she pictured the sweet young girl who had rung her doorbell earlier that afternoon. "Oh no. Abbie watched other children be killed?"

Brooke huffed out a breath. "I was a junior agent, and I was convinced I was right. Hell, I *was* right. Agent Astor told me if I thought the lead was worth more than a phone call, I could drive two towns over in the middle of a nor'easter, or I could man the phones for a real tip," Brooke laughed. "I knew he meant for me to sit down, shut up, and mind my place, but I slipped out when he wasn't watching and did just that. When I was in front of the conduct board, I used his words to say I had permission. It was bullshit. I knew it. They knew it. But since I was right, they balanced it out. I was considered on probation for another six months and barred from fieldwork. Which was no big deal as it took me nearly that long to recover, but while I did, I was also taken to task for adopting Abbie."

Lilly found a chair and sat. "Why? That sounds like a beautiful thing to do. It's something I would expect of you."

Brooke leaned on the wall next to the window. "I got

personally involved. That's a big problem. Imagine if a surgeon were to adopt a child when their single parent died on the operating table. Or a social worker adopts a kid after they're removed from their home. And they're correct. You can't get so close to the victims that you can't move on, but Abbie had nobody and I know what that's like. I've been that kid who grew up in a home where there were always drugs and the ugly sounds of sex. I've known what it's like to be ignored because you were just disposable. I was just the junkie's kid. Why bother rocking the boat for me?"

Brooke turned to gaze out the window. "I looked into Abbie's eyes I just saw myself. If I hadn't stepped in, she would have been put into foster care. A nearly seven-year-old black girl with a traumatic past would have been shuffled back and forth until she aged out. Most of the others had blood relatives. Not Abbie. Besides, there was just something about her." Brooke turned and showed the faintest hint of a smile. "When she was in the hospital, one of the lab technicians was not too gentle taking blood from another of the victims. He was a little boy named Victor. I walked in and watched Abbie tear into the lab tech. I remember thinking how she was around the same age…"

Lilly knew what he didn't want to say. That thing that they had never spoken of. "I know. She looks like she could be ours. Please, go on."

Brooke made eye contact and she could see the flash of pain. "As an agent of the FBI, I'm supposed to maintain an emotional detachment. The fact is, I didn't. I became emotionally involved in that case. I made it personal. And I nearly got myself, and by extension, those kids killed. And then I followed up by adopting

Abbie. Brass wasn't happy, but they couldn't fire me for that. They will when they find out how I've crossed that line here. With you."

Lilly stood and crossed the room. "Have you? Crossed the line?"

Brooke turned toward her. "How can you ask that? Lilly, there was talk of me being put on the manhunt. Agent Foster felt I was ready, but she also saw right through me when I told her that I'd be better being here, interviewing Cole. I wasn't letting that bastard come near you. I may not have been good enough to have you, but I'll never let that bastard touch you."

Lilly's breath caught in her throat. "Is that what you think? That you somehow weren't good for me?"

Brooke scowled, but his silence spoke volumes to Lilly, and it was as if Brooke had reached into her chest and pulled her heart out.

"That was never the case." Lilly ignored the tears that she felt running down her face. "I just couldn't have you stuck with me. Not after what happened. Most guys would have been looking to run out the door if they found out their high school girlfriend was pregnant, but you didn't. I know how much you wanted that baby. We were both terrified, but you were so thrilled."

Brooke closed his eyes. "You don't need to do this. You don't need to justify…I have no right…"

"No, I need to," Lilly said. "Please let me. I was too scared to do this years ago, but I need you to understand. Brooke, you didn't throw anything away, I did. I broke us because I'm broken."

Brooke's eyes snapped open. "Why would you say that? Lilly, you're not broken."

Lilly inhaled sharply, and she wiped at her face.

"After I lost our baby, I was so scared and alone. My mother found me and took me to the hospital. You were away. God, you were all I wanted. I felt so alone." She placed her hand on her stomach. "So empty."

Brooke narrowed his eyes, and Lilly could see the flash of anger that he quickly tried to bury, but she needed to go on.

"There were tumors and fibroids." Tears rolled down her cheeks, but Lilly did not attempt to hide them. She needed to shed this truth that she'd kept walled up inside herself for years. "They told me that I couldn't ever have babies. I had to have a partial hysterectomy. I'd lost our family and lost the ability to give you the family you wanted. How could I face you after that?"

Brooke put his hands on Lilly's shoulders. "My God, Lilly. Don't you understand? You *were* my family. You were all I ever wanted."

He pulled her into an embrace and she melted into his arms. His touch filled her with a sense of belonging, easing the guilt and loneliness she had endured for a decade since she'd lost him. "I couldn't face you. I felt like I failed you. Failed us."

Brooke caressed her face, stroking his finger gently over her cheek, drying her tears. "I would have grieved with you. I would have held you in my arms when you cried and I would have broken down myself, but I would still have had you. As long as I had you, I had everything. You didn't fail us. *I did* because I didn't keep fighting. I should have found a way to keep you. God, I'm sorry."

"Maybe we both failed each other." Lilly shrugged. "We failed us. When I heard you were coming, I was so afraid I'd see hate in your eyes. I should have talked to you when I lost the baby. I owed it to you. I owed it to us."

Brooke took a deep breath. "We were kids, and we were both grieving. We should have taken comfort in each other. I never hated you. I hated myself for losing you and I let myself believe I never deserved you."

Lilly gazed into his deep blue eyes, those same eyes she loved when she was a teen girl giddy with love. Ever since Brooke returned to town, Lilly would look in those eyes and see her past, everything she'd lost. For the first time, she saw the potential of building a future.

She reached up, placed her hand behind his head, and pulled him into a kiss.

His lips tasted like heaven, and the smell of him filled her with a sense of being where she belonged. "Do you think there's a chance for us? A chance to rebuild what we had?"

He rested his forehead on hers. "You have no idea how much I'd love that, but I'm not the person you knew back when we were kids. Lilly..." He closed his eyes and took a deep breath. "There are parts of me that you don't know about. Things I've discovered since I left Ember Falls. I'm not what you think I am."

She ran her hands up his broad chest and felt his heart slamming. "Neither of us is who we were in high school. What I know is this. I never stopped loving you. I never got over you. And I haven't felt whole since you left." Lilly took his hand and pulled him towards the small bed.

He hesitated a moment and a flicker of doubt flashed across his eyes.

She turned away, the heat of embarrassment flushing her face. "If you don't want me..."

Brooke gently touched her face, nudging her so she

would look at him again. "Want isn't strong enough of a word for it, Little Princess. I'm no good for you."

Lilly jutted her chin up. "I'm not an innocent little lamb. I'm a big girl. I know what I want. I know what I need. I need you to make me whole again." She intertwined her fingers with his. "Please."

Brooke closed his eyes for the briefest of moments, and when they opened, the doubt and hesitation were washed away.

His lips met hers, and waves of desire flooded through her. His hands, ever so gently, began to roam her body. Quickly, they began to undress each other. She yanked at his tie, throwing it aside. He pulled his shirt open, causing a button to fly across the room. They laughed as he pulled the shirt off, tossing it on the floor.

Lilly studied his bare chest. So familiar, yet so different. The light brown skin felt the same under her fingers, but he was even more muscular. She traced the lines of his ribs, and it felt as natural as pulling on an old comfortable sweater. Her eyes found a patch of roughness by his shoulder. A deep mostly healed scar.

Brooke froze as she touched it.

Lilly pulled her eyes away from the wound and gazed into his eyes. "We've both got scars, even if you can't see mine." She pulled him down into a deep, long kiss. "I want you. Scars and all."

Brooke's hand made quick work of pulling Lilly's clothes off, as Lilly undid his belt. His lips explored her body starting with her neck and traveling lower. His hand held onto hers as his mouth sent shivers through her skin. Her eyes closed, and Lilly saw splashes of bright colors as her body racked with ecstasy.

Brooke's fingers danced across her skin, knowing all the places she loved to be touched.

Lilly sat up, pushed him so he was flat on the bed, and worked his pants off. She let her hands wander over his body before she slowly lowered herself onto him. For the first time in nearly a decade, she felt complete.

They moved together as one. It was as if they'd never been apart. He knew where to touch, how to caress her. She felt steady and sure, and truly happy.

They shifted, and he was on her. In her. A part of her. She bit her lower lip as he locked eyes with her. His muscles tensed, and she could feel him ready to explode.

She felt the rising wave of her pleasure, the frenzy of him driving her over the edge, into a bliss she hadn't experienced since she was a teenager in love. The intensity made her cry out, as he emptied himself in her.

His breath heaved as he lay beside her, pulling her into him. They lay together, tingling from the thrill of what they'd done, at home in each other's arms.

Lilly understood, she'd been only half a soul for the last decade. Now, she was complete.

Chapter Twelve

And It Feels So Good

Lilly allowed the sensation of contentment to wash over her as she snuggled into Brooke. She enjoyed having her head on his chest, feeling the steady rise and fall of his breathing, accompanied by the strong thump of his heart.

Lilly wasn't sure what this meant. She wasn't naïve enough to think that because they'd managed to find their way back into each other's arms that meant they could just pick up where they left off. It'd been nearly a decade since she'd last touched him like this. He had a daughter and a career.

She had Cole.

"I like Abbie." Lilly recalled the small girl now sleeping in the guest room of the house. "She's got a great sense of humor."

Brooke traced her skin with his fingers. "Yeah, she's kept my life interesting. I still can't believe she came all the way here by bus, although I shouldn't be surprised. That girl practically raised herself from the age of six. Her mom lived with their grandmother, but she had a heart attack. From what I've been told, her mom kept it together for a few months but ended up going right back to shooting up. Abbie had to make food for them to eat, make sure money got to the landlord. In many ways, she's the most responsible ten-year-old I've ever met. Not that running away and taking a bus to Ember Falls was responsible."

He closed his eyes. "Sometimes I think that girl will be the death of me. I know she used to have problems sleeping when I wasn't home. She was always afraid, always waking from nightmares, but she hasn't had one in months. It was different when I was not allowed in the field. I'd be late sometimes, but she could see me before she went to sleep." He shook his head. "Sometimes I think it was stupid of me to adopt her. She needs more time than I can give, but the fact is, it's hard for children her age to be adopted. And I can't imagine my life without her."

Lilly kissed him gently. "I think it's wonderful that you took her. And clearly, she loves you. She's lucky to have you."

Brooke beamed. "Truth is, I feel lucky to have her. She filled a void in my life that I hadn't realized was there. I like taking care of her. Hearing about her day at school. I like being her dad and…" The expression on his face faded into a frown. "Oh Lilly. I'm sorry. I shouldn't have…"

"What?" Lilly sat up, frowning. "Why? Brooke, I'm thrilled that you have Abbie. I understand all too well about the hole in your heart because you just have so much love to give that you're bursting. Do you know that before Cole came, I was thinking about fostering a child, with the intent of adopting? I'd even spoken to Ashley about it."

Brooke shook his head. "No. Why didn't you?"

Lilly rolled to her side so she was facing Brooke as she recalled those nights when she and Ashley had those discussions. She'd spent a lot of time on the internet, searching different foster groups, trying to talk herself into it. "We might have if Kelli hadn't arrived with Cole. Ashley was afraid she'd make a horrible mom. I was just afraid."

Brooke moved so his position matched hers. "Of what?"

Lilly took a deep breath, her hand flat on his chest. "Of losing them. Foster kids sometimes go back to their parents, even when they shouldn't. You know that. You were placed twice. Pulled out both times and returned to your mom."

His face hardened, his lips becoming a thin line. "I've wondered whatever happened to those families. They were good to me."

Lilly caressed his arm. She still remembered when Brooke was young, struggling with reading and writing. Just struggling with life. As a little girl, she hadn't understood why. Now, she understood all too well. "I don't know if I would have been able to handle that. Then Kelli arrived with Cole. I knew he wasn't mine, but it felt like he was. I love him as if he came from me. And Kelli named me as one of his guardians, along with both Ashley and Drew. That counts, doesn't it?"

Brooke placed his hand on her heart. "He is yours. The other night, in the kitchen, he didn't want to leave us alone. I can see just how he looks at you. At *all* of you. He feels safe here. Loved here. For a kid like Cole, who's been through what he has, that's huge. I imagine he wasn't so secure when he first arrived."

Lilly closed her eyes to fight the memory of Cole jumping in terror every time she'd entered the room. The white-knuckled fear and wide-eyed panic would take over. "No. He was like a ghost for the first few weeks. He was terrified if you did more than a whisper. And God forbid we mentioned his stepfather. It was as if he expected him to jump out at any moment. Like he believed Hunter was hearing and seeing everything. Kellie wouldn't talk about what he did to them, but knowing now that he killed Molly and those other poor girls…" An ice-cold shudder ricocheted down her spine. "Do you really think he told Cole what he did?"

Brooke inhaled deeply. "There are…" A chirp from Brooke's cell interrupted. With a scowl, Brooke stood up and retrieved his pants that he'd discarded on the floor earlier. He fished his phone out of his pocket and answered the call. "Madison."

His face grew darker and his grimace deepened as he listened. "Where?" Brooke's tone was business, but the intensity in his narrowed eyes was frightening. "Understood. I'll be there soon."

Lilly sat up. "What happened?"

Brooke stared down at his phone. "They found what was left of Laura Shaw and Hunter made a play on someone else. I've got to go." His eyes drifted towards the window. "Shit. Abbie. If she wakes up…"

Lilly went to him and placed her hand on his chest. "Go. I'll take care of her."

He kissed her. Together, they quickly got dressed. "If she's been having nightmares again, she might be scared to wake up in an unfamiliar place."

Lilly helped straighten his tie. "Just go and deal with this. Leave her to me. I promise I'll watch after her as if she's my own."

Chapter Thirteen

Four Foxglove Way

Brooke had every intention of heading back to Lilly's after spending the last few hours at the Ember Fall's precinct. They had gone over the preliminary findings from Laura Shaw. The pattern of torture and death was consistent with Hunter's past kills, with one notable exception. She had been killed within hours and left where she would quickly be found. The Bureau believed it was because Hunter was stressed, devolving under the pressure of being hunted. It was further proof that he was trying to escape. Making a desperate attempt to flee, he was going to stick to backroads, off major highways, and only surfaced long enough to kill. It was a deadly attempt to center himself.

Brooke had disagreed. He pointed out that although he hadn't held Laura Shaw alive for long, there was no evidence of a frenzied attack. The burns, lacerations, and bite marks were slow and deliberate. It was the calling out of Drew that bothered Brooke the most. Hunter was doing everything to say "here I am, come and get me." Wanted Drew to personally go after him. Why?

Did he just want to draw Drew away from Cole, leaving him with less protection, or did he have another reason? It was that other possibility that made Brooke's blood run cold.

Once they called it a night, Brooke knew he should go back and work his way through the reports coming in. That was the professional thing to do. He should also speak to Lilly about what had happened between them. That was the proper thing to do. At the very least, he should be there in case Abbie woke up, that was the fatherly thing to do.

Instead, he went to take care of personal business.

Brooke heard the familiar sound of gravel under his tires. The roughness of driving this road was like hearing a song from your childhood that you hated. The hint of the melody ushered in a symphony of bad memories. Suddenly he was a kid again, heading to the place he was forced to call home. A sense of dread took over as he entered West Side Trailer Park. He passed the lot where his old buddy Jarbar had lived before he'd ODed in his freshman year of high school. The blue and white trailer that belonged to Mrs. Gibson was gone, her having passed years ago. He spotted a group of teens walking by, the scent of pot permeating through his car's air system as they passed.

He wasn't the only one in the park who'd gotten out. Melissa Hopkins graduated top of their Ember Falls class, went on to score a full ride to college, and was now a surgeon at Albany Medical. Joe Perkins got into college on a football scholarship, but he never went pro. Instead, he studied law and was on the fast track to make partner in the firm that took him on. Some went on to more modest achievements, but they escaped. They succeeded. Brooke had talked to a few of them, here and there and for the most part, they were happy.

Not all trailer parks were as bad as West Side. He'd been to a few. Many were nice, modest homes for good people with low incomes. Others were the places you avoided unless you were looking to score. By age six, Brooke knew where he could get a hit of anything from pot to cocaine to heroin. He'd been dragged off more than once by his mother when he was too little to leave alone. He was sure he'd been at least a little high as a kid from his mom blowing smoke at him. She'd laughed, thinking it was funny. He'd gotten sick and puked.

Brooke made a right off of Oleander Road, and headed down the close-ended road he grew up on until he pulled into the driveway of Four Foxglove Way.

Seeing the old, pink trailer home he'd been raised in, he had to swallow hard and fight the urge to retch. He gripped the steering wheel tightly as his eyes scanned the debilitated trailer home. The familiar dirt stains were all there, covered by new patterns of mud. The screen on his bedroom window was still loose. How many times did he crawl out of there to escape the grabby hands of whoever his mother had brought home? When he was little, his quick feet were the only things that kept him safe. As he got older, he learned to fight back with a quicker fist.

Brooke stayed in the car for a good twenty minutes, concentrating on his breathing, trying to stop his body from vibrating from anger. He knew coming back to Ember Falls was going to be hard, but this was worse. It was hard enough to pal around with Drew again, knowing before long the man would loathe him, but he'd gotten used to the idea that Lilly hated him.

He wished he didn't know she was still in love with him.

Brooke could continue the lie. If Hunter was caught, especially if he were killed, the truth would never need to come out.

No. It had to come out. It was time for everything to be put on the table.

And he'd accept the hatred that came with it.

With one final deep breath, Brooke killed the engine and headed for the door. Should he knock? Or just go in?

Brooke pounded on the door. "I'm coming in." He swung it open and was greeted by the stench of crack and stale cigarettes. His mother lay on the sofa, barely dressed, covered mostly by a guy who Brooke didn't recognize. It was his sophomore year of high school, all over again.

Brooke grabbed a pair of trousers lying on the floor, assumed it belonged to the guy who was stirring and tossed them at him. "Get dressed and get out, I need to speak with her."

The man, wiry, six feet tall, and with ghostly pale skin, slipped out of bed. His stubbly face scowled at Brooke. "Who the fuck are you?" He shoved his hairy legs into his jeans and pulled them up to his beanpole waist. "My times not up."

The man who had the body of an eighty-year-old, but was probably in his forties, gestured towards Brooke. "Destiny, who is this asshole."

Destiny Madison opened her bloodshot eyes for the first time since Brooke had entered. It took a moment for them to focus, and another few seconds for her to recognize her son. She rolled her eyes as she pulled the sheet to cover herself. "Harvey, that's my baby boy."

Brooke clenched his fists at the sound of her voice.

Harvey reached for a pack of cigarettes and shook it until one slipped out. Pulling it out with his lips, he attempted to light it. "I don't care if he's the fucking queen of England, I plan on bending you over one more time. If 'Junior' wants to take a turn—"

Snarling, Brooke knocked the cigarette out of Harvey's mouth and slammed the addict against the wall. The trailer home vibrated from the impact. "Listen up, because I'm going to say this one time." He pulled out his shield. "You don't need to worry about the fact that I'm her son. I'm fucking FBI. I can bust you for about a dozen felonies right now. Have you remanded into federal custody, and shoved into prison with very dangerous people while you wait a year for a trial. Or you can take your party favors..." Brooke kicked the nearby coffee table which was covered with a pair of ashtrays overflowing with old, various cigarettes, crack pipes, a pair of very well-used bongs, and three twenties. Everything went flying. "And get the fuck out of here."

He let Harvey go, who scampered out as he was, barefoot and bare-chested. A moment later, the roar of a motorcycle mixed with Destiny's laughter. "You know how to ruin a party."

Brooke kept his back turned to give his mother a chance to get up and dressed. The scent of a freshly lit Marlboro filled the air first, followed by the swish of a robe being pulled on.

"Well, I wondered if you'd ever come visit your mom." Destiny blew out smoke. "If you'd called first, I would have made sure I didn't have a date tonight."

Hearing her calling the men she fucked for money and drugs "dates" always made Brooke sick to his stomach. He found a chair, moved a pile of dirty clothes to the floor, and forced himself to sit. "I need to talk to you."

Destiny's hands fidgeted as they always did.

Running through her hair, brushing against the skin of her thin arms. Always moving. "About what? And where the hell is my money? You here, you might as well pay up now and not wait to the beginning of the month." Her words were fast, slurred, and sloppy.

Brooke ignored her question. "Do you know why I'm in town?"

Destiny took a long drag as she waved her hand. "What do I care what you do?"

Brooke tried to see this as himself speaking to another junkie, not his mother. "I'm here because my best friend's sister married a serial killer. Kelli Duncan is dead. Her son is being raised by her brother and sister, and Kelli's childhood friend. Lilly." He leaned forward. "You remember Lilly, right?"

She froze, still for the first time since she'd rolled out of bed. His eyes moved to the right, searching for details. Her finger absently brushed her nose. "Wasn't she that girl you fucked a few times?"

Brooke's jaw clenched. "She was the girl I wanted to marry. She was pregnant with my baby. Do you remember that?"

She sat back on the couch, frowning. Her hand rubbed her mouth, hiding it from view. "Yeah, I remember you knocked her up." She spoke slowly. "You got lucky she decided to get rid of the l'il bastard."

Brooke clenched his fist. "That's what you told me. She decided to get an abortion, and she didn't want to see me because it was too much."

Her eyes narrowed, and her head gave a small shake. "Yeah, yeah." Her body was very still, except for her eyes, looking up to the right.

He stayed silent, studying her sudden stillness. The

way her speech pattern had changed. Practiced, measured words.

"How exactly did you find out she had an abortion?"

Destiny started to respond but paused. Her eyes narrowed as her mind tried to remember the script.

"Didn't you tell me you spoke with Lilly's mother?"

She gave a nod, stopped shook her head, and took a drag. "Yeah, yeah that's it. Her hoity toity mamma told me."

Brooke forced himself to sit back. "You told me she sat right there and had a heart-to-heart with you. Said some nice things about me, but how it was over." Brooke nearly laughed. As if Lilly's mother would be caught dead anywhere in the trailer park, let alone talking to his mother. The woman had always ignored Brooke.

But after a few moments of concentrated thought, broken only by her shaking hands bringing the cigarette to her lip, nodded at Brooke. "Yeah. She was really sweet about it. Knew how upset you'd be, but that girl was just not ready to be a mamma. I told her that was smart. Don't bring a baby into this world if you can't handle it. I had a few abortions too." She shrugged, smoked. Surer of herself as she was back on solid ground. "Nearly got rid of you too."

That was something he'd heard his entire life. Now he knew why she hadn't.

"You're better off anyhow." She stubbed out her cigarette and immediately reached for another. "Girl like that, from her fancy house and uppity attitude, she never would have wanted to admit you were the one that put a baby in her. You know, I don't think that girl ever liked me."

Lilly hated Destiny, but she'd never have said that

to Brooke, and she'd never treated Destiny with anything less than kindness and respect. Had called her Ms. Madison. Brought her flowers the few times she came to visit. Drove her to the hospital when she'd found her passed out and barely breathing.

Destiny lit the cigarette. "Yeah, we're trailer trash, you and I. We're everyone's throwaways. Good for a fuck, but not for much else." Her hands were a jumble of motion again. These were her words. "We do what we have to do to get by. Never get nothin' handed to us."

This time, Brooke did laugh. "Is that what you were doing when you brought home one guy after another to fuck? Fighting to get by? You spent your life getting high."

Destiny scowled as she blew out smoke through her nose. "You watch your mouth boy. You ain't so old I can't whup your sorry ass."

A big part of Brooke would like to see her try.

"I did what needed to be done. Put food in your damn belly and a roof over your ungrateful head, didn't I?"

"And how many times did you pass out too early from the party favors they brought, and your dates tried to have me finish up? I ran from here more times than you'll ever know. And I came back because it was the only home I knew. You were the only family I had. Did you ever care that those assholes tried to put their meaty hands on me?"

She gave a double shrug while she sucked in more smoke. "You got away. Big deal. Like I never had someone put their hands on me when I didn't want them to. You do what you need to. Ain't no big deal."

Brooke's eyes narrowed. He wanted to tear the room

apart, but couldn't. He was allowing himself to get distracted. He was here for a reason.

She's not your mom. She's just another junkie with a secret to hide.

Brooke leaned back, forced himself to relax. "What exactly did Mrs. Danvers say when she spoke with you on the phone that day?"

Destiny considered the question as she tugged the dirty white robe on her shoulder which had been starting to slip off. "Oh, how you were such a nice young man, and how she knew you'd be upset, but that it'd be best for both of you in the long run, not having a baby ruin your lives."

Brooke nodded, so she would see him agreeing with her. "And she wasn't angry? Because in all my dealings with her, she was pretty damn pissed that I'd put my hands on her daughter. A punk from the hood had no business being with her daughter. You sure she didn't say any of that?"

Destiny blinked, staring off to the far-right corner again.

"That's what you told me, right?"

She paused as if she was frozen. Her hand went to her mouth. "That's right. I sat across from her, and she told me that you were just a thug that got her girl knocked up. That you was lucky that she didn't have you thrown in jail."

Brooke narrowed his eyes. She was back to a face-to-face meeting, without being prompted.

Brooke gripped the armrests tightly. *There had been a face-to-face meeting, but not here and not with Lilly's mother.* A new picture started to form, and it made Brooke want to tear the place apart.

With every ounce of self-restraint "Do you know what I do? What I am?"

Her hands, back in motion, gave him a dismissive wave. "You work for the feds. And what you are is an unwanted bastard."

That much was accurate.

"I'm a special agent for the FBI."

Destiny scoffed. "What makes you special?"

With a deep scowl, Brooke did what he would do with any perp. After all, that was probably all Destiny was at this point to him. He stood up, pulled out his badge, and threw it down on the table in front of her. "That does. I work for the Behavioral Science Unit. I walk into a room, see a crime scene, and I interpret it. I look at a dead body, and I interpret what the killer was thinking." He took a step closer. "I sit across from stone-cold killers, psychopaths, and sociopaths, who have sliced children up with as much care as someone would use to cut off a piece of meat, and I read them. Their choice of words, what they say and omit from saying. Their movements, their sweat, or lack thereof. I'm damn good at my job. I was always good at reading people."

He stalked away and glanced down the hall to where his old room was. "By the time I was twelve, I could usually tell which of your 'dates' might make a go at me if given the chance. A few of them watched me so intently, I knew they were hoping you'd pass out so they could try. That was their real reason for being here, but I haven't been in the same room as you in years. I wasn't able to read you as easily, because I didn't want to see it. Now I need to." He turned back to her. "You're lying."

She jutted her chin out. "You watch your mouth."

Brooke shook his head. "I'd rather watch yours. And

your eyes. And your hands." He bent down, grabbed his badge, and clipped it back to his belt. "You cover your mouth when you lie. Common enough. You glance to the right as if you're trying to remember what you're supposed to say. You're always moving, fidgeting, except when you freeze up to try and stay on script. Someone *else's* script."

He leaned down, close to her face. His nostrils flared at the scent of cigarettes and stale sex. "You're not even able to keep your fake stories straight. It wasn't Mrs. Danvers. She would rather have died than set foot in here. No, there was a meeting, but not here. Not with her. Someone told you to make me believe that Lilly had an abortion."

Destiny shook her head. Rubbed her nose. "I don't know what you mean. Baby, I'd never lie to you about that."

Brooke walked away, into the kitchen. He found a stack of dishes higher than his mother was right now, and trash all over the counters. He pulled open a drawer and found a large, black trash bag.

Pulling it out, he headed back in.

"What you doin' with that?" she asked.

Brooke sneered. "Cleaning up."

Opening the bag, he used his arm to swipe the bongs, glasses, ashtrays, and pot into the bag.

"Stop that! That's my stuff."

She started to rise but sank back down when Brooke jabbed a finger at her. "Paid for by my misery. It's all going."

He grabbed everything he could find, everything she'd use to smoke, snort, inhale, and shoot poison into her body. He poured every bottle of whisky out, threw in every ashtray, every stub of a cigarette, and left-over joint. Within minutes, the bag was full. He tied it up, brought it into the living room, and smashed it on the floor.

Destiny jumped. "You breaking my shit!"

Brooke glared, his eyes full of rage boiling from years of neglect and abuse. "You bet your ass I am. You never loved me. *This* is what you loved." He swung the bag and smashed it again.

"Stop!" Destiny began to cry. "I need that."

He knew she did, as he smashed the bag again. He could hear the pieces break, and the shards of glass rattle. "Well, you can't have it. And you won't be able to get any more. I'm on very good terms with local law enforcement. I'm going to have them station a cop outside of your place. Just to keep an eye on you. A killer is coming to town, and maybe he'll make a play for you. They'll search you, so if you try and get more shit, they'll take it. Arrest you."

With one final smash, he took the bag to the door and threw it outside. He'd toss it in his car and throw it away somewhere else when he left.

Staring down at his hands, he saw they were covered in ash and grime. His lip curled and he swallowed the bile rising in his throat at the sight of them. He would wash it later, but he'd always be disgusting.

Brooke returned to his mother who was watching him with wide eyes. "I know you think that you can get any police report squashed, but not with this chief, and not from your old friend. He's going to want to sever contact with you."

She beat on the couch like a child having a tantrum. "No, you can't do that. I *need* him."

"You need to get clean. I don't know if there's any part of you that ever really loved me, but if you can get clean, stay clean for a year, I'll come back. Until then, no money from me. I'll help you get into rehab. That much I'll do. I'll try to protect you from the shitshow that's about to rain down, but I need something that you've never been able to give me. Honesty. Who told you to convince me Lilly had an abortion?"

She stomped her feet. "Who cares? She did it. Cut that little bastard seed out of her, didn't she?"

Brooke shook his head. "No, she didn't. She lost the baby. Found out she had tumors and cists and had to have a hysterectomy. She can't get pregnant."

Destiny threw her hands up. "I didn't know that. Alls I knew is that he told me the baby was gone. Why you care? She's damaged goods now anyway."

Brooke stepped forward, his hand clenched into a fist. For the first time in his life, he found he was tempted to use it on her, and the thought shamed him. He'd never be able to face either Lilly or Abbie again.

He was so enraged by his mother's words, calling Lilly "Damaged Goods" that he nearly missed it.

He replayed her words in his head. Studied it, like it was a film in slow motion. Her direct eye contact, the lack of hesitation. It was a truth. A cold horrible truth that had him take a staggering step back, and nearly vomit.

He glared at his mother, who he decided probably wouldn't know. "Who was it? Tell me who it was that you met with. I bet everything I already know, but I need to hear you say it."

Destiny froze again, her eyes in that far corner searching for the script. This time, the page was blank, and for her, this was the final act.

"It's going to come out." Brooke knew it was needed. "My career with the FBI might be over because of it, but it *will* come out. Everything about what he did. As an agent, I have what I need. I can leave and never come back. As your son, I *want* you to say it. I know who it is. I need you to admit what he did, and who he is."

Destiny pouted for a long moment before she launched into another tantrum. Her feet pounded the floor, her hands slapped at the sofa for a solid two minutes. Then she threw herself back hard. With tears of exhaustion and frustration in her eyes, Brooke cursed that part of him that wanted to comfort her nearly as much as he was responsible for the emotional attack he'd lodged against his mother.

Destiny made wild gestures with her hands. "It was your daddy. He was still mayor of this damn town at the time. Tom Brook. He paid me to tell you. Alls I know is she was going to be away for a while, and you were to be told she was home, but wouldn't see you. They just didn't want you fucking her again. Any girl outside of Ember Falls was fine, or even some piece of trailer trash. Who'd care then? But a girl with a hoity-toity mother?"

Brooke shook with rage. "They didn't want any chance of someone discovering that Thomas Brook was my biological father."

Destiny winced at the truth coming out. "Yeah, he always wanted to make sure his bastard children were kept hidden. Made deals with some. You, he never bothered with."

Brooke scowled. "Because he made his deal with you."

Destiny shrugged. "And I took care of you. All them

dirty old men were desperate to keep their secrets. Never wanting to own up to any kids they had falling out of us. I got screwed. I ended up here in this damn trailer park, while some got taken care of. Even gots themselves a sucker to be their husband."

A cold understanding washed over him, like ice water. Painfully, the picture of the puzzle came into view.

"I'm leaving." He headed to the door. "I wouldn't count on the former mayor to take care of you. He's about to find himself in a real shitstorm, and if you try and warn him, I will personally put you in a cage for the rest of your life. That's assuming he doesn't have you killed first. My guess is that he's done with you."

He grabbed the handle to the front door and swung it open. With one last glance over his shoulder, he studied how his mother sat shell-shocked. "I know I am."

He left, not bothering to close the door. Grabbing the trash bag, he tossed it in the back seat and climbed into the driver's seat. The sound of gravel mixed with a frightening howl of despair from his mother as Brooke drove away.

This time, he promised himself he'd never return.

Chapter Fourteen

Nuisance Call

The General pulled up in the parking lot inside the park, rolled down his window, killed the engine, and waited. He felt confident he knew why he was here, and what would be asked of him. The General prided himself on his ability to know what people were going to do before they did. Brooke Madison had a great poker face, but it slipped big time today. The General was confident that he knew exactly what the young man wanted.

The General spotted the headlights. He waited until the dark car pulled alongside him, facing the opposite direction. The driver rolled down his window.

Brooke Madison was exhausted. He didn't make eye contact but sat there in silence.

The hair on the back of the General's neck stood up. Something had happened.

Finally, Brooke turned to the General. His face was calm, but the agent's eyes were windows to a storm. The man was barely holding on.

"You okay, Madison?"

Brooke paused. "I need you to run DNA tests. You said you could do that right?"

Didn't answer the question, which was all the answer the General needed. "I have the Senator's DNA from that pen. I've got yours. It's on file with the

Bureau."

Brooke frowned. "You requested my DNA from the Bureau?"

The General sent Brooke a withering stare. "No, but we have it nonetheless. I assumed you'd want to keep this private."

Brooke shook his head. "You're one impressive son of a bitch, General McAlister. And a little scary. Run it like that for now. We'll do it official later. It's going to come out."

The General's eyebrows went up. "That would derail his political plans, but it could hurt your career as well."

Brooke shook his head. "None of that matters. Do we have Hunter's DNA?"

The General frowned. "Yes. Why?"

Brooke broke eye contact, hesitating for a brief moment. "Run it too."

That the General didn't see coming, and it pissed him off. "Okay. Is this a wild guess?"

Brooke shook his head. "I'm putting together the pieces. My mother supplied a few missing ones. I need you to also run a few more."

More surprises. The General found himself both intrigued and annoyed at himself. "Such as?"

Brooke inhaled deeply. "I'm putting you in a bad position if you do this."

The General cocked an eyebrow. "You think I can't take the heat from that asshole? He may be a senator, but he's got skeletons."

Brooke ground his jaw. "That's not what I mean. Drew may get angry. He'll probably never forgive me at this point, and I deserve it. He needs you."

"What does Drew have to do with this?" Realizing he was most definitely surprised, the General was becoming pissed.

"Maybe nothing." Brooke glanced away. "But I'm guessing this goes back farther than any of us realized." He took a deep breath, held it a moment, and exhaled.

The General studied him. The man was struggling, shifting in his seat and avoiding eye contact. "Brooke."

He waited until the young agent's eyes met his own. The General could not only see the emotional exhaustion but the bone-crushing sadness. When the General got the call from Brooke earlier, his voice was rife with anger. In the twenty minutes since, the heat of rage had cooled down and left behind a man who was broken.

"What happened tonight?"

Brooke stared at him blankly. "This needs to be done."

Whatever it was the agent was about to ask of him, it was costing him. "Tell me what you need."

As Brooke explained his thoughts, impressions, and what he needed, the General started to understand what was going on behind those eyes.

"I'll get it done. One day. Two at the most."

Brooke closed his eyes. "Then that's how long I have."

"For what?" The General frowned, trying to read the man in front of him. "Until the FBI pulls you? We don't need to tell them."

Brooke shook his head. "Yes, we do. He can't get away with this. I can deal with losing my badge if I have to. As long as Lilly is kept safe."

The General narrowed his eyes. "You think she's going to turn on you? I've seen the way she looks at you.

The woman is stronger than you think. She can handle this."

Brooke's face softened. "Lilly can handle anything, but once she understands, she's not going to want me anywhere around her. Or Cole." He turned away as he shifted the car into gear, but not before the General saw his eyes glisten. "I wouldn't blame her."

Before the General could respond, Brooke drove off into the night.

****

Lilly hummed as she cleaned up the kitchen one last time. She'd hoped Brooke would come by before it was time for bed. Maybe she should wait for him in the apartment over the garage. Part of her wanted to let him find her in bed, naked and ready but decided that might not be good.

Was she about to get a real second chance with Brooke? She wasn't naïve enough to think it would be simple. He had his own life with Abbie and the Bureau, and she had Cole and the bookstore. Still, maybe there was a way to make it work.

She enjoyed spending time with Abbie. She was a smart, confident little girl who spoke her mind and made Lilly laugh. She'd found her and Cole together, and the two of them somehow had managed to bond. That was huge.

The house phone rang, interrupting the images of her and Brooke raising the kids together. She grabbed it and answered as she wiped down the kitchen. "Hello."

"Hello there." The male voice was pleasant but oddly familiar. "How are you this evening?"

Lilly paused in front of the sink. "I'm very good. How can I help you?"

"Oh, in so many ways," the man responded. "Let's start with Cole. How is my stepson doing these days?"

A cold shiver ran down her spine as Lilly's lip curled. "I'm not discussing anything to do with Cole. He's none of your business."

She scanned the living room, but everyone had gone to bed. Where did she leave her cell?

"Oh, I disagree. Cole is very much my business. I spent so much time with the boy. Showing him the ropes of being a man. Well, I don't *use* ropes." His cold, dark laughter made her cringe like fingernails down a chalkboard. "I prefer chains."

Calmly, but quickly, Lilly walked through the house, checking the doors and windows to make sure they were locked. "Really? What does someone like you know about being a man? You terrorized teen girls, broken people like Kelli who didn't know how to stand up for herself, and little boys like Cole. If you're stupid enough to come back to Ember Falls, I think you'd find Cole is surrounded by people who aren't the same type of person you're used to dealing with."

He laughed again, but this time it was harder. More mocking. "You think you can hide behind Duncan? Or that FBI Agent, Madison? How is Brooke?"

Lilly paused. How did he know Brooke's name?

It didn't matter. This was a game to him. She wasn't going to play by his rules.

"Why don't you come and see for yourself? He'd love the chance to meet you I'm sure. I can set it up. Tell me where you are, I'll send him to you."

Lilly spotted her purse sitting on the back of a chair in the kitchen. She dashed for it, retrieving her cell. She sent a text to Brooke.

Hunter calling on house phone.

She quickly copied it and sent it to Drew, Ashley, Ollie, and Sam.

"Ooh, you're a feisty one. Maybe I'll come see you instead."

Lilly reached into her purse again, pulled out her Glock 43, and ejected the clip. She checked the chamber, and reclipped the black gun with the pink grip, before shoving it in the small of her back.

"Fine. I'm happy to meet you face-to-face Hunter. I'm not Kelli. I haven't been conditioned since I was a small child to take a beating. You come at me, you better be sure you know what you're doing."

The laughter died on the other end of the phone as footsteps pounded on the stairs. Ollie was the first to arrive, followed by Ashley.

"You fucking bitch." His voice was low, cold, and cruel. "You think you won't bleed? You think I won't make you beg for me to kill you just to stop the pain?"

Drew burst in the back door with Sam right behind him.

"I think you'll try." Lilly turned as Ashley and Ollie came thundering down the stairs. She was surrounded by her family as she spoke. "But you just might be the one who ends up begging at the end. Begging for your mother. Do you still have a mother?"

Tires squealed from the driveway. Seconds later, Brooke came through the door. He walked over to Lilly. "Are you okay?" he mouthed.

Lilly nodded.

In Brooke's hand, he had his cell, he spoke quietly into it. "She's still on with him. Get the trace going." Held up a pair of fingers. "Two minutes" he mouthed.

"My mother was a fucking whore. All the women in that town are sluts and whores." Hunter was screaming now. "Brooke knows how that is." His voice gained a touch of control when he shifted to Brooke. "Why don't you ask him?"

"Maybe *you* should." Lilly didn't want him calm. She wanted to push his buttons. "Oh, that's right. He's a big bad, Federal agent. You don't deal with those unless you sneak up behind them. Why don't you try Drew? He's just a former marine? Maybe because you know he'd wipe the floor with you? How about Ollie? Local police detective. He took out a hired assassin. Someone that made you look like an amateur." Lilly shrugged. "I guess that leaves me. So, bring it on, you pathetic son of a bitch."

"*Lilly*," Brooke warned.

The laugh was back. "Is that Brooke? Why don't you put him on?"

Lilly moved away. "Because I'm not done with you. I want to know why you do this. Can't you get it up when you're not hurting a girl or child? Or maybe you just know nobody would touch you otherwise. I'm told I should be terrified of you, but quite frankly, I find you pathetic. You're a joke. You think you frighten me? Please. You know where I am. Come and get me."

Tiny feet thudded down the stairs.

"No!"

Cole came running in. Pushing past everyone, his beat red face begging her. His eyes swam in tears. "I didn't tell. You don't need to hurt them. Please just leave them alone. *I didn't tell.*"

Ollie grabbed him, tried to drag the screaming boy out, but Cole squirmed away.

With a hoarse voice and trembling upper lip, Cole fell onto the floor. Landing on his knees hard, he continued to plead. He crawled forward and insisted over and over again that he hadn't told. Ashley sat on the floor and pulled him in her arms.

Making a rolling motion with his fingers, Brooke indicated that Lilly should keep going.

"Let him talk," Brooke mouthed.

As Hunter was ranting, that didn't seem to be a problem.

"I hear the little punk. Why don't you put him on? I'll make him piss himself."

"No, you deal with me you son of a bitch."

Cole was sobbing, rocking back and forth in Ashley's arms.

Brooke knelt before Cole and put his hand on his shoulder. "Lilly put Hunter on speaker."

Lilly's eyes went wide. *Was Brooke crazy?*

Brooke gestured her to come closer. "Cole, you're safe. He can't hurt you." He turned to Lilly. "Trust me."

Because she did, Lilly took a deep breath and stepped forward. She held the phone out and pressed the speaker button.

Brooke took the phone. "You're here with your family, Cole. You can tell us anything. Why don't we talk about what life was really like with Edward?"

"Because he knows what that means." Hunter's voice was a low, menacing growl. "Don't you, Cole? You hearing me boy? I'll know. I'll *always* know."

"And then what?" Brooke asked. "You'll come back to town if he talks? I think we both know you're coming back anyway. Sooner or later, you're going to come into Ember Falls. And when you do, we'll be waiting."

Hunter laughed. "You think you can stop me? I'm like a demon. I see everything!"

Brooke glanced at Cole. "You don't have this place wired up like you did with the home that you burned to the ground. Cameras in every room. Listening devices so you can monitor everything that was said. There's none of that here. I'm curious though. We all know you're a killer. There's no point in hiding it now. Why do you care if Cole talks? Maybe, it's just because you can't stand the thought of him not being under your spell."

"Shut up, Brooke," Hunter screamed. "Cole won't tell because he knows what happens when he tells. And I'll know if he talks. And when he does, I'm going to gut that little redheaded bitch, slowly."

"Leave her alone!" Cole pushed off of Ashley. "You leave my family alone!"

"Or what Cole? What are you going to do?" Hunter's voice was deep, but it cracked just a bit. "You can't do anything to me."

Brooke leaned closer to Cole. "He can't hurt you. We won't let him. It's time to take away his power."

Cole's shaking subsided, but he was still trembling. Only now, his eyes were full of rage, not fear. "I can. I can hurt you. I'm going to tell them. Do you hear me?" He stepped forward. "I'm going to tell all of your secrets. And they'll know. *I'm going to tell!*"

The words echoed through the kitchen as the meaning reverberated to them all. Cole was ready to talk. Edward Hunter had lost control of his youngest victim.

Chapter Fifteen

Cole's Confession

It had taken hours to calm Cole down, and he only slept for a few hours with Drew standing guard in his room. Brooke spent the rest of the night on the phone with Director Burke, detailing the interaction with Hunter, and how he hadn't denied his intent to come back. Burke insisted that Hunter was still making a run for the border.

"I think he'll try to sneak back into the US at some point. Go after the kid. Might even try to make him a willing partner if he can. But right now, his need for self-preservation is driving him. Besides, the kid is well covered between you and the locals. Just let the kid get a little rest and get him on camera talking about Hunter. See if the kid has anything of value to add."

Brooke was frustrated, but not surprised. By this point, everyone was so invested in their own theory about Hunter that they weren't willing to consider anything else. In truth, the same thing could be said about Brooke himself. He was simply the only one thinking he would return.

When Cole finally emerged from his room with Drew, his face was pale, and he had bags under his eyes. What little sleep he'd gotten was interrupted by one nightmare after another. He was resigned to the fact that today he would talk to Brooke about Edward Hunter.

And to the fact that Hunter would know.

Brooke slowly sat down on the small chair that was strategically placed near Cole's bed. It was short and uncomfortable, but it allowed him to stay lower than Cole.

They were in his bedroom, a place where Cole could feel safe. Sam's partner Brandon was off duty, but he and about a dozen other officers were outside in uniform, all visible from the small window in Cole's room. All to give Cole a sense of safety.

Cole had watched them, not glancing back once as Jacob had set up a small video camera at the foot of the bed to record their conversation. It was the only thing that seemed out of place, except for Brooke. As Cole came to sit on his bed, his eyes darted at the camera once but avoided eye contact with Brooke.

"We're just going to talk. If you need a break, you tell me. Are you okay to talk with just the two of us, or do you want someone from your family up here?"

Cole shook his head. "I don't want them here."

Brooke didn't push. Cole had insisted on his family not being in the room.

Brooke recognized the small, yellow stuffed lamb that Cole carried. Brooke had bought that for Lilly when she told him she was pregnant. The first present for their child that would never be born. It was as if that innocent soul was now Cole's guardian angel.

Cole held the stuffed lamb to his chest like a talisman. His chin rested on the soft, yellow fur as his glassy eyes stared straight ahead. He appeared so small at the head of his bed, but at least so far, he wasn't shaking.

"Okay, but if you change your mind, just tell me." Brooke kept his voice gentle, but firm. "Can you tell me about Edward Hunter? Did he ever hurt you or your mother?"

Cole gripped the lamb tighter. He held his breath and gave a small nod.

"Can you tell me about that?"

Cole glanced around the room. "He didn't like it if Mom left the house. He wanted her inside. That's where she belonged."

Brooke leaned forward. "What happened when your mom went outside?"

Closing his eyes, a tear rolled down his cheek. "He'd get mad."

"Did he hit her?"

He stared at the wall, a vacant look in his eyes. "Yeah, sometimes he just hit her, if he wasn't too angry."

Brooke frowned. "What happened if he *was* really angry."

That was met with a shrug. "I was locked away. When he was done, he'd walk out and leave her. She'd be crying when she got dressed."

Brooke took a moment. That confirmed a theory. No wonder Cole didn't want Drew here. Cole probably believed his uncle would blame him for not protecting Kelli. "How often did she go out?"

"Not often, but he always knew." His glance darted around the room. The trembling was starting.

Cole's face went white. "He'll still know."

He was losing the kid. Time to switch tactics. "Whether he knows or not probably isn't important. He's going to come back. That was his plan from the moment we knew he killed those girls. You know that, right? And that we're all here to protect you."

Cole focused on Brooke, his wet eyes pleading. "You'll stay and protect her until he's gone?"

Brooke held Cole's eyes. If only the kid knew how much he planned on that himself. "I'm not going anywhere until he's caught. You have my word. The better I understand him, the better I can stop him. That's what I need you to help me with."

A heavy silence filled the room as Cole studied Brooke, trying to decide if he believed what he was being told. Children like Cole had sharper instincts about people than most, so let the kid read him.

Finally, Cole nodded, but he still didn't speak.

Brooke inched forward. "Cole, has anyone ever talked to you about trauma, and how it affects our brain? Ever heard of fight or flight?"

Cole shook his head.

"When a person sees something that is scary, their brain reacts in a certain way. Imagine nearly getting hit by a car."

Cole seemed to somewhat relax. The idea of being run over was far less terrifying than Hunter. "That happened to me. I was crossing the street, and a car like almost hit me."

"But what was your reaction at that moment? Did you freeze? Run? What did you do?"

Cole frowned as he tried to remember. "I think both. I mean, I froze at first, then I ran as fast I could."

"What do you think would happen to someone if they were nearly hit by a car nearly every day?"

Cole narrowed his eyes. "I think someone would need to teach them how to cross the street." He shifted in his spot, getting into the lesson. "I guess you'd either get used to it, or you'd get scared of cars."

"Exactly. When you're scared, your brain reacts to that fear." Brooke gestured with his hands as he spoke. "Your brain sends a signal to the rest of your body. Like if you walk into the house, and you smell something Lilly is cooking. Your nose sniffs the air, and your brain tells your mouth to water. You may not have been hungry a moment ago, but you are now."

Cole smirked. "Or if I realize Aunt Ash was cooking, then I want to run back out again."

Together, they shared a laugh. Apparently, Ashley's cooking skills were still the stuff of legend. "Well, I suppose that brings us back to the fight or flight. Your body reacts to danger. If it happens often enough, you either become numb to it, or your brain starts to react that way more often. Cole, you grew up in a state of constant fear. In a world where the only male figure was someone who represented pain, humiliation, and terror. There are certain chemicals that your brain produces. If you're always afraid, it keeps producing them."

Cole frowned. "So…I'll always be afraid? I'm just a coward."

"No, just the opposite." Brooke paused, waiting for the meaning of his words to register. "Cole, it's normal for you to have been afraid. Do you think I'm not scared at times? Or your uncle?"

The child glanced away. "You work for the FBI. You fight bad guys. Scary ones. Uncle Drew was a marine. I saw him fight Wilson. He's never afraid. I'm afraid all the time."

"You go to school every day, right?"

Taken aback, Cole nodded.

"You went to a convention recently. You hang out

with your buddy Jay. You're doing well in school. You're making friends. Living your life." Brooke held up a finger to stop Cole from arguing. "Remember our example of someone who nearly gets hit by a car? Imagine someone who got hit and hurt badly. A couple of years later, they were crossing the street and it happened again. Now they're afraid to cross the street, but they have to. They need to walk a few blocks to go to work. So, they do. They cross the street, each and every day. They face that fear. That's not cowardice. That's bravery. I was nearly killed in the line of duty. I'm afraid it can happen again, but I face it and move on. Do you think your uncle wasn't afraid to come back to Ember Falls? Last time he was here, he was thrown in prison for something he didn't do for months. He got hurt in there. He was told his sisters would be killed if he came back. I know Drew. I'd bet he was scared to death to come home, but he came."

Brooke paused, gave Cole a chance to absorb what he was saying. He could tell the boy was considering his words. "Being brave isn't about not feeling fear, it's doing what you need to do despite it. I listened to the recording of when Harrington had you and Samantha's grandmother, Rose Henry. You were facing a man with a gun. One who could kill you. You kept your cool. Tricked him into activating your phone with the dummy code to alert McAlister. You fed details to McAlister without Harrington knowing. Do you realize that Drew and Ollie were closing in on you before they locked in on your phone? You were kidnapped by Jericho, a hired hitman who was a serial killer for hire. He gave you the chance to run at least twice, but you stayed to protect your aunt. Cole, you *are* brave. You're brave *because* you're afraid, but you face your fear. You're doing it right here. Right now. Talking to me. I know Edward told you never to talk about it. He conditioned you to believe he was always aware of what you were doing. Did you hear what I said to him on the phone last night? About him having your house wired?"

Cole tilted his head. "What does that mean?"

"He had cameras in areas of your house. We found one by the front door and another near on the back porch." Brooke pulled something out of his shirt pocket. It was a black device, small enough to fit on the tip of Brooke's finger. "This is similar to what we found. We're guessing he had these all over your house. That's how he knew if your mom even stepped near the door. Or if she was snooping around. He watched you."

He handed the tiny camera to Cole, who examined it. Brooke could see the shift. His eyes narrowed, and his lips drew together. Anger was working its way into Cole, and pushing out the terror.

Cole's eyes wandered the room, once again looking for Hunter, but he wasn't trembling as he'd been earlier. "He likes people being afraid."

Back on track. This was what Brooke needed. "Can you explain how he liked to make someone afraid?"

Shivering as if he was cold, Cole pulled his knees up to his chin. "He liked to play a game. I don't remember what he called it. He'd…" He narrowed his eyes. "He'd put a gun to your head. You wouldn't know if there was a bullet. Sometimes there was."

Brooke stiffened. "Russian Roulette?"

Cole closed his eyes. "Yeah. He had an old gun. It had this piece that spun. He'd point it at you, laugh if it didn't go off." He hugged the lamb tighter. "Laugh if it did."

"That must have been terrifying. Did he do this to your mother? Or you?"

The room was silent as Cole stroked the stuffed lamb. "Yeah."

"Did he only play the game with you and your mom?"

Cole became very still, except for the trembling of his bottom lip. Brooke waited, knowing the kid was ready.

Cole shook his head, crossing the line. It was like a small crack in the wall, with a slow leak at first. Just a trickle of water like the tear running down his cheek. Any moment, that dam was going to burst.

"He'd have them tied up in a bunker." Cole's eyes became distant. "He had chains on them. Heavy ones. Sometimes he played the game with them. He'd put the gun in their mouth or under their chin. They always thought they were about to die." He wiped away a pair of tears. "Sometimes they did."

With a wince as if hearing a loud noise echo in the silent room, Cole closed his eyes. "It was so loud. I thought when someone dies, their eyes close, but they don't a lot."

Brooke tensed. There had to be pictures. Maybe even video. "Cole, do you have any idea where he might have kept the recordings? Or where the bunker is?"

Cole was starting to breathe heavily. His eyes remained tightly shut. "It was close to home. There's a big building that's right there. He owns it, although it's empty. Has the word Tice on the side."

Frowning, Brooke recalled the report he'd read on Edward Hunter. Except for his house, it didn't mention any other real estate holdings, or the Bureau would have found them. While it's possible the kid may be wrong, or Hunter lied, Brooke was guessing that it was owned by Hunter, under another name.

Tice? Could that be his real name?

But now wasn't the time to distract Cole, who was getting closer to the full truth.

"I don't know if he kept recordings." Cole glanced down at the small camera that was on his mattress next to him. "He wasn't holding one, but maybe he had things like this around."

Brooke reached out and picked up the small device. It was possible, even probable that he had the place covered by these small devices.

Something occurred to Brooke that made him frown. "Cole, how do you know the gun was really loud? Did he show you a video?"

Cole shut his eyes again, but the tears began to well up. "Those chains were so heavy. And cold. He always kept that room so cold. I hated waking up like that. I'd hear him laughing, and some girl crying."

With a clenched fist, Brooke trembled with anger. Brooke took a moment to maintain his calm. "You were there? In that room? He had you chained up?"

Cole was frozen. The only movement was from the tears running down his face. For several seconds, it didn't appear as if he was even breathing. Finally, a muffled whimper escaped. "I'm sorry. I'm sorry. I'm sorry. I tried to fight. I yelled at him to stop. But he just laughed. I didn't want to see, but he took me to the Tice place and made me. He made me watch." His voice was a strained whisper, as if there was still a part of him that was terrified Hunter would hear him.

A strangled sob mixed with Cole's gasps for air. "He told me if I said anything, he'd do that to mom. He had ways of disappearing, and he'd know if I ever told. He'd know because he always knew. So, I had to watch. The gun game was scary. So were his other games."

Cole's voice became louder, desperate to be heard. Brooke saw the shift. Cole wasn't just telling a story.

He was confessing.

"He liked to burn them. Or cut them. Sometimes, he'd hook them up to wires. Flip a switch. You'd hear a low sound and they'd scream. Those hurt bad, but they never left marks on us. Some stuff he wouldn't do to me, 'cause he didn't want anyone to see it, but other stuff…"

Shaking his head and shutting his eyes to the memory, Cole wept. "I begged him to stop, but the only way it was over was when h-he…" Cole swallowed hard. "He killed them. That was the only time they stopped screaming or crying. And sometimes they wanted it. They'd just want it over. They were empty. Like they were dead already inside. And some even told him to leave me alone, yet I couldn't do anything…"

Finally, Cole's wet eyes opened. They locked onto Brooke's. "I could have told, but he would have hurt Mom. Sometimes, he took me to look at a girl and I'd beg him to leave her alone and he did. But I could have yelled and screamed and…" He rocked back and forth. "I'm sorry! I should have done something more. I should have…"

He bowed his head, and the sobbing began to subside. "It was my fault. I'm not good. I should have been brave. I'm sorry."

Cole threw the lamb to the floor as if he were casting away any claim of innocence. He moved to the edge of the bed, right in front of Brooke. He held his hands out, wrists together. Shaking, eyes pleading, he looked at Brooke. "You have to arrest me now, right."

Brooke frowned. "What? Why?"

Cole inched closer, his hands ready to be cuffed. "I let him keep doing it. I'm sorry. I won't run." A shaky sob rippled through his body. "I'm bad and I have to go away."

Brooke's eyes widened in shock. He reached forward and pushed Cole's hands down. "Cole, nobody is going to want to put you away. You were terrified of him. You were a child. You've been with Lilly and Ashley for nearly a year, so this was from when you were eight? Maybe younger? Nobody is going to want you punished for this."

Brooke slid off the chair and knelt in front of the bed. "Listen to me, Cole. You're not bad. You're not a coward. Nobody is taking you away. Not the police. Not the FBI. And not Edward Hunter. You're not in any trouble. And together, we're going to make sure that Edward can't keep hurting people. Do you understand me?"

Cole sat in stunned silence.

"I want you to say it." Brooke put his hand on Cole's arm, grateful the kid didn't pull away. "It wasn't my fault. Say it."

Cole took a deep breath. "It wasn't my fault." His voice was a timid whisper, but he managed to get them out.

"Say it again. Louder."

Cole locked eyes with Brooke. "It wasn't my fault."

"Good. Again. Louder. Scream it if you have to. Say it until you believe it in your core because everyone I know; your uncle, your aunt. Lilly. The cops in this town, the FBI. All of them will tell you the same thing. Edward is the monster. It wasn't your fault."

An involuntary shudder rippled through Cole at the mention of Hunter's name, but he didn't close his eyes.

"It's not my fault. It's not my fault." Cole repeated it. Each time, it was louder. The tears were coming again, but Brooke was certain these tears represented not guilt, or shame, but the acceptance of the fact that he'd been abused. "It's not my fault."

"That's right. It's normal to blame yourself. To think you should have been able to stop the unstoppable, but this wasn't your fault. It was his. Say it."

Cole breathed in sharply. *"It's not my fault!"*

Brooke pulled him close and let the child weep. He repeated the mantra over and over again until all that was left was a whisper.

"It's not my fault."

Chapter Sixteen

Let's Go For A Drive

Brooke made his way through the kitchen and to the small room which was Lilly's office. He entered and quickly closed the door behind him. Jacob, who was busy working on his laptop, quickly looked up. "Jesus."

A wave of exhaustion washed over him. Brooke sat down heavily in a second chair, ran his hand over his face, and sighed. "I didn't expect that. I knew Hunter threatened him. Figured he showed him pictures. Maybe a video. Cole knew too many details, but I never realized he witnessed Hunter torturing and murdering women."

"When he held out his hands for you to cuff him? That destroyed me." Jacob sat back in his chair. "But did we learn much? I mean, we already knew Hunter is a sadistic killer, who enjoyed terrifying his victims. We didn't know about the Russian Roulette, but I don't know if that detail adds much."

"Yes, it did." Brooke leaned forward, resting his hands on his knees. "One big thing is not what Cole saw, but the fact that he saw it. Why would Hunter bring Cole and make him watch? He had Cole convinced he had some sort of supernatural ability to *know* if Cole spoke about it, but why expose himself to that risk? Profiling 101. Anything that an UNSUB does that increases the chance of being caught is essential to his signature. He got off on the horror that Cole experienced when he witnessed these acts. He wanted to terrify him. The fact that Cole has stayed quiet so long was in and of itself empowering to him."

Brooke rose and began to pace in the tiny office. "Some killers stumble upon parts of their ritual. A guy breaks into homes, thinking they're empty. One day, he finds someone there. Decides 'why not.' Rapes and kills her. Finds he loves that. It grows. Soon, he's breaking in searching for victims. Sometimes, rapists kill a victim accidentally but enjoy it. There was this guy who used to rob banks and stores. Had the people inside strip. Figured while they were naked, they wouldn't look up, they'd be too embarrassed, and when he left they'd be grabbing their clothes to get dressed. Turns out, he got off on it. Started to make them pose and do things. Extending the time he was in the bank, and someone might pass by and catch them."

Jacob considered it. "Okay, so he didn't anticipate Cole finding out? But he took him to his second location to watch. That wasn't by accident."

"No, it was Kelli Duncan. She was the key." Brooke sat back down. "Hunter married her more for cover. She was someone he could control. Put on the face of a normal man, while he continued his activities, but he couldn't pull it off. Even with someone as passive as Kelli. Someone that violent and controlling would have wanted their wife to do as they were told when they were told. But maybe Kelli pushed back?"

Once again, Brooke got up and paced. "No, that's not right. Kelli didn't push."

Jacob stood as well. "Maybe she learned to. She'd changed. She had a son. That changes you, right? That's what everyone tells me."

How true was that? The moment when he'd realized Lilly was pregnant, he'd been overcome with joy. Somehow, that piece of his soul that had never seemed whole was now complete. Even though Lilly loved him, or said she did, he remained, in his mind, unlovable. A bastard of a child from a whore of a mother. There was always a part of him that believed that Lilly would someday realize she could do so much better than him.

But that child would be a part of him. Every decent thing he was capable of, every little bit of goodness would be filtered into that baby.

That was why he was able to believe that Lilly had chosen to end that pregnancy, and in doing so, ripped away that part of him that had finally felt whole.

"It does change you." Brooke studied a picture on Lilly's desk of Cole clutching a book in the corner of her shop. "I need to go Cheyanne. I want to find this place with the name Tice. I want to lay eyes on where this happened."

Jacob started to fiddle on his computer. As he did, Brooke pulled out his cell, and checked messages. Agent Foster was looking forward to seeing the interview with the "minor child" witness. They had what she considered a solid lead. She was hoping to have him before the end of the week.

"Here, show this to Cole." Jacob pointed to his screen where a picture of an old, run-down warehouse was displayed. Its grey tin siding was streaked with rust stains as if the building was bleeding. There was a row of box-shaped windows, many broken with jagged glass. A huge sign with the name "Tice" was hanging with its left side barely holding on. "It's less than five miles from where they lived, but it's down a road that nobody would probably go down anymore. It was family-owned. Handed down until Howard Tice died and wrote his family out of the will. His son Andrew was a lawyer but didn't contest. His daughter filed a caveat but never followed up on it. The warehouse had already been closed and was just collecting debt. Eventually, it was bought by APEX corp."

He tapped at the keyboard furiously, his eyes never leaving the screen as a dozen different windows popped up. He minimized most, closed a few, and shook his head. "The company was formed one month before the purchase. Closed six months later. No other acquisitions or attempts to sell the property. It's a shell company. One that came from Ambire LLC. That one has a little more activity including…" Jacob frowned. "Son of a bitch."

Brooke sat down next to Jacob and leaned in. "What?"

Jacob's fingers danced across the keyboard. Screens flashed by, documents displayed, and bank statements appeared. "I need to dig into this to make sure this is legit, but this shows political donations, being funneled through what's probably other shell companies. Plus, these." He pointed to a series of numbers that made little sense to Brooke. "Cash payouts." He brought up another document, that showed regular cash deposits of twenty thousand dollars every three months. "Blackmail. No, I can't prove it. Yet. You need to give me time." He shrugged. "Might need a warrant."

Brooke clenched a fist and nearly snarled. "Whose campaign?"

Jacob continued to work for a few moments, whether to be sure or to avoid saying it out loud, Brooke didn't know.

"What campaign did Ambire contribute to?"

With one last keystroke, the banner of the Brook for US Senate displayed on the screen. "Tom Brook." Jacob turned to face Brooke. "I'm sorry. I can only go so far with this unofficially. I'm going to have to make this official if you want to nail him. I can try and do it through back channels, but he might slip through…"

"No." Brooke stood up. "Everything above board. Do what you can to shore up your info to get that warrant. We may have more soon. The General is running DNA. When that comes back, I think we'll have what we need. Jacob, cover yourself. When this blows up, and it will, you need to be seen as being righteous on this."

Jacob crossed his arms. "I can take a little heat."

"This is going to blow like Mount Vesuvius. You can't get burned, because I don't want you pulled. I can resign if I need to stick close to Lilly and Cole, but I need you to stay on this. Senator Brook has a lot of political favors to pull in. He can bribe, cajole, and threaten if he has to. I need someone who can't be bought or scared off. That's you."

Jacob huffed out a breath but nodded.

"Pack it up here." Brooke headed towards the door. "I'm going to see if Drew wants to come with me to knock on some doors in Cheyanne. Keep on this."

Jacob started to save files. "I'll keep digging."

Brooke opened the door and glanced back. "Agent Rivers." He waited until Jacob looked in his direction. "Very good work today."

Brooke shut the door just as Jacob smiled.

He found the General waiting for him. "Please tell me you got something from what Cole went through.

Brooke hesitated. "I'm on my way to check out a lead.

The General crossed his arms. "You can fill me in on the way. I'll drive. Let's go." He turned and headed down the stairs.

The man had no authority to give Brooke an order, but that's exactly what that was. And Brooke didn't even want to imagine what would happen if he'd try to disobey. "Yes, sir."

Chapter Seventeen

Personal Detachment

The black SUV drove through the small development in Cheyanne where the small homes were far apart, the lawns were unkempt, and there wasn't a car less than ten years old, except the one they were driving.

The General grunted as they passed a sign welcoming them to Dante's Kill. A small subdivision of Cheyanne. "You think Hunter picked this place because of the ironic name?"

Brooke had considered the same thing. "It may have factored in, but this area is low key where people minded their business and the houses were far enough apart from each other to prevent anyone from hearing Kelli or Cole scream. He couldn't guarantee police ambivalence here, but he would have researched that too. They don't have a stellar record when it comes to investigating domestic violence or sex crimes. Still, there weren't many missing person reports from here. An older lady wandered off and was picked up three days later, walking down the street naked. A few teens, mostly boys, but some girls. Written off as runaways. Most turned up alive, but even the ones who were found dead it was an OD or a car accident. One suicide. That's spanning back seven years. Might be more. People who go missing don't always get reported as such."

The General nodded. "People aren't reported missing unless there's someone who gives a shit enough to report them."

"And if the cops gave a shit enough to take the report. I tried to report my mom missing once. EFPD said she'd turn up eventually. *Probably* alive." He swallowed the bitter memory. If the situation had been reversed, he doubted his mom would have tried to find him. He suspected as much back then as he and Drew rode their bikes to every drug hangout in Ember Falls. He was certain now.

Fuck it. It didn't matter anymore.

"You okay, son?" The General glanced over as they passed by a group of young kids on bikes who eyed the black SUV with suspicion.

Brooke forced himself back to the here and now. "I'm fine. Just taking a bad trip down memory lane. This town feels too much like Ember Falls when I was a kid. Being here, after being there." Brooke shook his head. "New mayor and Chief Miller? You realize how much they've done to turn that town around?"

The General didn't answer as he continued to drive.

Brooke watched the review mirror and saw the kids starting to peddle behind them. An unfamiliar car brings out curiosity? Before long, the kids faded into the background, unable to keep up.

"There should be an offshoot road coming up." Brooke studied his phone, tracking the GPS Jacob had sent. "Right after that bend."

They passed a water bottling plant that appeared to be abandoned, followed by a field of undeveloped land. An overpass was ahead, but the General was headed to a small dirt road that would take them to the old building.

Cole had given them a few details of the landscape, all of which were spot on.

Brooke noticed one of the kids from earlier coming across the top of the road. He might have taken a shortcut or just finally caught up. The other kids hadn't come all the way here.

The kid stopped at the top of the hill. Sitting on his bike, with one foot on the ground as the SUV made a turn around a corner where they were now hidden from view.

Brooke frowned and wondered if the kid was just curious, or something else.

The SUV rumbled down a gravel road, where an empty warehouse waited for them. The thick steel gates were chained shut. They came to a stop, dirt billowing up around them.

With a scowl, Brooke turned to the General. "Crap. I don't suppose you got a bolt cutter to get that off."

The General grinned. "McAlister is like the boy scouts. We're always prepared. I'll get it."

They both got out. Brooke went to examine the chain while the General went to the back of the SUV. Using his phone, Brooke pulled out a picture of the chain and lock that was used on Agent Mills and compared them.

The General carried a pair of bolt cutters with a red handle over.

Brooke pointed to the chain and lock. "If there was any doubt that this was the right place, I think we can eliminate it. Same lock that was used on Alice Mills and her husband."

With a grimace of utter disgust, the General cut the chain. "I didn't have any doubt. This is the right place. I can feel it in my bones."

As the chain fell away with a rattle, Brooke decided he agreed with the sentiment. The place felt like death. They walked a few feet to the front door. The sour-smelling air seemed very still, like that moment of silence in a horror movie right before the monster leaped out to devour its prey. Neither man spoke, out of respect for however many souls lost their lives here.

Stepping onto the cement steps, Brooke scanned the area. He nudged the General and jutted his chin towards the right of the door where a lone camera sat hidden. "Doesn't appear to be on."

The General pointed to the door. "We're going to have issues getting through that."

The door had a silver panel, with a digital keypad on it. Brooke pressed it, and the display came to life. "Shit. No reason to have this kind of security on a building this old."

Both Brooke and the General reached for their phones at the same time.

With raised eyebrows, the General held his up higher. "I can get my man out here in two hours. He'll make short work of it. Your man is busy."

Brooke grinned. "My man can multitask." Without waiting, he contacted Jacob via video chat.

It took less than two full rings before Jacob's young face came on screen. "What's up?"

Brooke turned the phone to show the panel to Jacob. "We need to get past this. Any ideas?"

There was a short silence for a moment, as Brooke imagined Jacob studying the panel. "I'm going to try and hack in, keep your phone within a few feet. I don't need to see the panel."

Brooke liked the tone of confidence that was slowly

edging its way into Jacob's voice, Brooke turned the phone back to himself. The sound of his fingers dancing along his laptop, entering hundreds of keystrokes broke the still air. "When you're done, I want you to casually see if you can find any local reports on this address. Or anything reported anywhere in town that involved a child around Cole's age that might stand out."

Jacob glanced over briefly as he continued to work. "Funny you should say that. I took the liberty of peeking at the local files. They close things out as unfounded nearly seventy percent of the time, which is way higher than the national average for a town that size. There were a couple of reports to check that place out, but they were ignored since the reports all came from a kid. The recording of the last call stood out. You wanna listen?"

Brooke glanced at the General. His hawk-like face remained impassive, but he nodded. "Let's hear it."

The video shifted to a black screen. Three beeps sounded, and a soft background noise came on, followed by voices.

"Officer Kinney. What can I help you with?" The officer's voice was dull and bored as if answering the call was a bother.

"My friend. His name is Cameron. He's gone. His foster family won't talk to me. I think something bad happened."

A groan from Officer Kinney. "Is this Tommy?"

There was a pause. "Tyler."

"Whatever." Officer Kinney's voice had gone from bored to pissed in less than ten seconds. "We don't have time for this."

"But you hafta look."

"You stupid kid. If you call here one more time, I'm

going put you in a cage until your fifty. I know your father, and he's going to hear from me."

"He's not my father." Tyler's tone was a mix of fear, and defiance.

"Who gives a shit, he'll still tan your hide if I tell him to. Don't call again."

The line went dead.

The General set his jaw. "I'm wanting to have a conversation with Officer Kinney. Maybe we should do that and call my man. He can be here in two hours, and get us in."

Jacob's face came back on screen. "Why wait? Door should be unlocked now."

Brooke tried the door and found the lock disengaged. "Good work, Jacob. Be ready. I may need some help depending on what we find."

"Will do. I'll keep digging from here."

With an impressed nod, the General entered. "He's good."

Brooke searched for the lights. "The FBI may not be McAlister Security, but we get by."

Finding a switch, Brooke flipped it. Nothing happened. Both he and the General used their phones to light the way. "Jacob said there was still power here. Let's find the basement. That's where Hunter would work."

The illumination from their cells found a large metal sign on the wall. Giant letters displayed the name TICE. "Just like Cole said. I'm going to say we're in the right place."

The General nudged Brooke. He motioned towards the floor where a dark stain was visible. "I'd say you're right. We follow that blood, we'll find his new dumpsite."

The image of the Ember Falls dumpsite formed in Brooke's mind. Drew had rightly guessed that the killer had gone there to sit and spend time with his victims and trophies, back when Hunter was more of a fledgling killer. It was a secluded, but still semi-public place.

"It won't be far." Brooke pointed to another part of the wall. The faint imprint of a bloody handprint was visible. "Hunter didn't bother to clean up. This place is private. He would have buried them to avoid the stink, but he had no reason to hide them here. He'll have kept them close. Someplace where he can sit, reminisce." Brooke scowled as he moved down the hallway.

He turned when the General didn't respond and found the man crouched by a second handprint. He held his hand in front of it, comparing. "This isn't a man's handprint. Or a woman's, is it?"

Brooke leaned down to examine it himself. It was way too small for a grown person, male or female. "Could be a teen girl, one on the small side."

The General stood up, hatred etched on his face. It was difficult to tell, but Brooke was pretty sure the man was vibrating in rage. "Don't bullshit me. That print is from a small boy. That bastard had Cole help him bury them."

Brooke didn't answer, which was all the answer the General needed. "You already knew that coming in here, didn't you?"

Brooke started down the long hallway, which he assumed would lead to a door in the back. "I suspected. Hunter discovered when he beat Kelli in front of Cole a new sort of excitement in terrifying a child. We're going to find that Hunter's mother was beaten in front of him by his father or stepfather. He should have been terrified but found the violence exciting. He learned to devalue women. When he did the same in front of Cole, he would have been disgusted at what he saw as Cole's weakness, but excited for the terror he inflicted on Cole. The more powerless Cole felt, the more powerful it made Hunter feel."

They found a back door. A cinderblock sat in a nearby corner. Scuffmarks told the tale of it being used to prop the door open. Brooke pushed open the door, moved the cinderblock over, and stepped outside, knowing what he'd find.

Stepping outside, he and the General surveyed the scene. It was an empty lot, with a few piles of grey gravel in the far corners. A tall fence, with a second building on the back end, gave the area perfect coverage.

It might have been a lunch area once upon a time, but any benches and tables were gone. If there had been grass, it was dead now, although a few weeds popped through the dark earth here and there.

Brooke counted the mounds of disturbed dirt. Matted down from the elements, the ground hid thirty-seven poorly dug graves, side by side, in nice even rows. Brooke pointed to the back. "Those won't be from town. He probably started to go out of state. Early ones from before he started to bring Cole. He might have kept grabbing up runaways and streetwalkers from other counties, brought them here, chained them, cut off their clothes, and made them sit in the cold, waiting for him to return with Cole to watch."

Brooke crouched down to be closer to the dirt that held the remains of Hunter's victims. "When we go downstairs, we'll find his 'playroom.' It'll be cold, cemented in. We'll probably see both blood and urine stains on the ground. He'd have left them chained up for hours. Brought Cole, chained him up too. Made him watch. Made him a part of it."

The General glared. "Cole wasn't a part of this. He's a child. He had no control."

Brooke studied the General. The man was the most disciplined man he'd ever met, but he was close to the edge. Cole had become a surrogate grandchild to him. It was going to get worse before it got better.

"Excuse me, I should have said, 'to make Cole a part of it in Hunter's mind.' Of course, Cole had no control. That was the point for Hunter."

The General paused, his jaw set in hatred for the scene before them. His eyes were slits of fury as he studied the graveyard.

"Let's find where he killed those poor women." Without waiting for a reply, the General turned and headed inside. Brooke followed in silence.

The dark stains of blood that Hunter had never bothered to clean led the way to a service elevator. Using a pen to avoid leaving prints, Brooke pressed the button. The creaking of gears made it sound as if the entire building was being tortured and begging for death.

The shadow within the crack of the elevator doors shifted, but the doors took their time opening. Old, weary machinery that was badly in need of maintenance gave a long dramatic pause before opening up. Brooke wondered if they should find the stairs, but the General stepped on, ready to go. He was pissed, but back in control for now.

They rode down in silence, listening to the wailing echo from the elevator shaft.

The door opened to a long hallway, stained with more blood.

Neither man got off right away.

"He'd let them see this." Brooke wasn't sure why he felt the need to narrate what he saw in his mind out loud. "He'd pause right here. Let them see where they were going. See the trail of blood. They'd know that unless someone came to save them, they were going to die a slow and painful death."

Although there were a few doors along the way that Brooke checked for form, he knew they were headed to the end of the hall. A maintenance closet had a pile of clothes that appeared to have been cut off victims. Piles of shoes, purses, and other various items were in the far corner. There was a small folding chair, and Brooke imagined Hunter spending time here, *enjoying* the sight of the items when he had no warm body to torture for pleasure.

A green door, with a rusted brass handle, waited for them at the end. Using a glove, Brooke opened it.

His nose recoiled at the stench. The pungent scent of rotting meat mixed with death hit Brooke so hard that his eyes watered. The General grimaced with a curled lip.

"You want something to cover the smell."

With a glare of disgust, the General ignored the offer and stepped into the room. "I've smelt worse."

Brooke didn't argue. He found the switch on the wall. The lights flickered on, and Brooke felt as if the floor had dropped out from under him.

This was it. Edward Hunter's playroom. A metal table was situated on the right, where Edward would have laid out his instruments. Most were gone, but he'd left behind a small, well-used Butane torch, which was scarred from burnt flesh. Metal collars with sharp, jagged edges. A large battery with black wires protruding out.

A few cushioned office chairs with wheels sat near the table. Brooke wondered if Hunter had a partner, but realized that they were all set to different heights. All for his comfort, depending on the type of torture he was planning to inflict.

A makeshift table was made from sex swing toys, with metal clamps for the feet, thighs, arms, torso, and neck. Although the table had been scrubbed, bits of flesh and blood were stuck within the joints. Discoloration showed where the blood, urine, and feces had pooled. Nearby there was a pair of chains hanging from the ceiling, with a metal bar on the end.

Death may have come often into the room, but it never came easy.

Near the table was a metal chair, bolted to the floor. Another one by the head of the bed. Brooke bent down to examine the armrests. Scratch marks etched in terror told Brooke what he'd suspected. Whoever sat there hadn't done so willingly, but the marks weren't located where he'd expect to see them if an adult or even a teenager were strapped in.

Brooke ignored the General's cursing and tried to envision the room as it had appeared while there was someone strapped on the table.

Angles. Viewpoints. It was like a stage that was pre-set.

Glancing to the right, he saw one. He went to the bed and checked out the wall at the foot. Another. Light fixtures, but more. He checked each one, including the ones above each location.

"This isn't just a torture chamber." With a pen, Brooke pointed out a small camera, similar to the one he'd shown Cole. "It's a filming set."

The General came closer to examine what Brooke had indicated. "Why? Just so he could relive it? Get his jollies off without having another poor soul in here?"

Brooke searched for the wires, which he found led to a conduit. "We still have no idea how he got his money. According to the notes, he never mentioned what he did for a living to either Cole or Kelli, but there was money for food. Powering this place wasn't cheap." Brooke followed the conduit, back to the door. The General followed.

"My guess is in part, he was getting money from the same people who hired Jericho to keep this buried, but he also knew if he pushed too much there, he risked drying the well. There are people out there who share in Hunter's perversions but didn't have the balls to do the deed themselves."

He found the conduit ran to a door they'd passed earlier. "Why not supplement your income with your hobby."

Brooke opened the back door.

The setup seemed innocent enough. A pair of large monitors, their screens black and empty sat in the center. A mouse, sitting on a rubber pad. A charging station for a cell that is attached for easy uploading of videos, and a laptop with its mouse. A coffee mug that said World's Best Stepdad, a few empty bottles of water with dozens of bottle caps that hadn't been thrown away, and a box of tissues.

On the floor was a half-filled trash can, and a bank of processors behind the table, lined up side by side.

Plenty of power.

It would be a dream setup for a teen gamer. Only he didn't expect to find Legend of Zelda or World War II loaded up. The games Hunter played were far more sadistic.

Brooke sat at the console, booting up the computer as he called Jacob.

The young agent answered within seconds. "I've got a little bit of info on that kid who called in the missing persons who got ignored. And I think I know who his friend might be. You want me to shoot it to you."

He didn't need the distraction, not now, but maybe a distraction wasn't a bad idea. "Yes, but send it to General McAlister as well when you can. I've got Hunter's computer booted up. I want to keep this clean. We had a warrant for the location, not electronics. They wouldn't sign off until we confirmed we had the right place. Get someone to sign off on one, then what do we need to do to hack in."

Jacob grinned. "Info sent to you and the General. I anticipated the need to extend the warrant. That door security was high-tech enough to push the federal judge. I um…" Jacob blushed, his eyes shifting to the General who stood behind Brooke. "I took the liberty of name-dropping General McAlister with Judge Evans. He seemed hesitant until he heard the General was invested directly in this case. Hope that's okay, but the warrant is good and transmitting. Sorry."

The General leaned in. "Son, never waste my time apologizing for being two steps ahead of the game. Can you get into this setup?"

Jacob nodded. "Yeah, Agent Madison needs to put in that USB I gave him earlier. Hunter uses fancy toys, but he's not as smart as his tech. He's using an old method to hide his tracks, but he's not clever about it. I'll get you in. Ten minutes."

Brooke pushed the USB into the hard drive.

Pulling over a second chair, the General sat and pulled out his phone. "You've got five, then I'm calling my man. Don't try that doubling your ETA bullshit with me. Get it done."

Jacob's grin faded. "Yes sir."

Brooke disconnected. "Jacob can handle this."

Folding his arms, the General sat back in his chair. "No doubt. You've been building his confidence up."

Brooke watched the lights on the computer come to life. Jacob was working his magic. "He'll get it done in five."

The General watched the screen intently. "No, he'll have it done in three. He's needed you telling him he's good, but he also needs to be challenged so he can meet that challenge head-on. He told us ten so when he got it done sooner, we'd be impressed."

The screen came to life before them, washing their faces in an eerie light.

"Two minutes, forty-three seconds. Like you said, he's good. Now you can be impressed."

Brooke was already opening files. "I'll be impressed later. Let's see what Hunter has been up to."

Scanning the files, Brooke read the file names.

Lists. Names, emails, and payment info. These were the people who Hunter somehow found out liked seeing videos of women being raped and murdered. Pay for one, he had you. You couldn't refuse to purchase more without Hunter exposing you.

Another list was marked Security. More names,

dates, and video files. He'd send the names to Jacob and have him track them. Brooke knew Hunter had the dirtiest of dirt on them, forcing them to look the other way should anything ever come up. "Hunter was arrested for assault on both Kellie, Cole, and an officer. She had left in the middle of the night, but Hunter found them at the bus station. Grabbed them and tried to drag them back to the car. Report says Hunter slapped Kelli and knocked Cole to the ground as an Officer Leighton Miles came around the corner. A rookie, six months out. He arrested Hunter himself and got a bloody nose for his trouble."

With a grunt, the General moved closer to the screen. "I spoke to Officer Miles. He got a lot of flak for his arrest. Was told to cut Hunter loose. He refused, but someone used Kelli's murder to justify that since the victim was dead, there was no case. He wanted to push the case against Hunter for Cole but was told that Hunter had no interest in the boy. It was taken out of his hands."

The General's frown deepened, and his eyes narrowed. "I can see the names you're focusing on. His Lieutenant, and one of the ADA's. Hunter had something on them."

Brooke highlighted the files. Decided it was something to worry about another time. The why they sold out wasn't important now, but they'd get theirs. "Officer Mills should probably consider leaving Cheyanne PD. When this breaks, it'll hit them pretty hard. Every officer is going to get tarnished to a certain extent, even if they don't deserve it."

Standing up, the General started to pace. "You're behind the times. Officer Miles had already put his papers in by the time I spoke with him. He realized CPD wasn't one he wanted to be associated with." Pausing, a small grin appeared for the briefest of moments. "He started working for McAlister three weeks ago."

With an odd sense of satisfaction, Brooke moved on to other files. Scanning the names, he found the one labeled Ember Falls. Glancing over his shoulder, the General moved closer. "You want me to read that one?"

Brooke's only answer was to click the file open. New folders displayed, with many familiar names. Brooke noticed Mayor Brooks was prominent on top. Judging from the file size, it was the biggest file. Brooke hesitated.

The General sat down next to him. "Nobody is going to think badly of you if you don't want to see what he had on your father."

The words of his mentor and Supervising Agent echoed in his brain. *You became personally involved. A good agent has to be detached.*

Brooke's lip curled, knowing what he'd find. "I don't give a shit what that test says, he's not my father."

Before the General could say anything else, or he had a chance to reconsider, Brooke opened the file.

A list of subfolders existed. Hunter was a sadistic bastard, but he was an organized one. Brooke started with the financials. Dear old dad had been paying him for years. Small amounts. Don't bleed the well dry. Money was coming from the shell companies that helped get Senator Brook into office. Same shell company that bought this place. Larger payments here or there. Biggest payday came three weeks after the dance where Molly Winter's had disappeared.

Hitting the back button, he went to the notes. Hunter had documented everything. Brooke opened the one marked Molly Winters.

Several notes were indexed. Videos too. Brooke clicked on the top note, and read aloud.

"So this is the bitch that has the great man in such a fucking vice. She was a decent enough fuck. Almost worth the money I had to spend. I just wanted to taste what Mayor Brook can't say no to."

Brooke continued to scan the files. Then he hit the jackpot. "Well, shit."

Leaning in, the General scowled. "You find something that *is* a surprise?"

Brooke read and reread the note. The date, the time, and the reason for a meeting. "Perhaps Victim number one. And a crap ton of answers."

He made the note larger. "I was pissed when Tom called me, but I gotta say, cleaning up his mess was a lot of fun. And now the old man owes me big. Stupid fool just has to keep going back."

The General frowned. "I'm not getting it. What mess?"

Brooke opened the video file. A young Tom Brook paced back and forth. His hand shook as he brought a cigarette to his mouth to take a long drag. It was clear he had no idea he was being filmed as he continued to pace and smoke. He was stubbing out his cigarette when the door opened.

Hunter walked in and grinned as he slapped Tom on his back as if they were best friends. Pulling out a pack of cigarettes for himself, he offered one to Tom who accepted it with a trembling hand. Hunter lit it for him.

"I can't deal with this now. I've got a real chance at being elected Mayor." Tom Brook took a long drag, rubbed his eyes, and paced again. "It was just a stupid fight. Your mother knows I've got to keep up appearances. Maybe *someday…*"

Hunter rolled his eyes. "Oh please. We both know even if your political career tanked, you're never going to make an honest woman out of Mom. Or Destiny. Or Racheal. Or whatever other sluts you've got on the side." He smoked and shrugged. "They all know what they're getting with you."

Tom straightened his tie, and a bit of the politician came through. The veneer of decency crossed his face. "Ed, you know that I care about your mom. She's a wonderful woman. My wife is what I need for my public face, but that doesn't mean I don't care."

Hunter waved him off. "Relax. I don't give a shit. Mom is taken care of."

Tom breathed a sigh of relief. "Thank God you got her to see reason. Let her know I'll pay for the medical bills. I shouldn't have gotten that angry. She just took me by surprise, and with the pressures of the campaign."

"Fuck that." Hunter scowled. "It's about fucking time you put that bitch in her place. She knew her worth, and it wasn't much. And you won't have to worry about medical bills."

The hairs on the back of Brooke's neck tingled as he noted Hunter's use of past tense, something the future US Senator hadn't seemed to notice.

Tom reached for his wallet. "No, no, I insist. Plus, some extra for the time off of work. And for you. She'll need help with a broken arm."

Hunter laughed as he invited Tom Brook to step closer. He pulled out an old flip phone that was probably top-of-the-line at the time. "I don't think she's going to be complaining about a broken arm."

He tapped at the phone, then held it out. Tom took it and studied the image. His narrowed eyes began to widen. His body stiffened, almost as if he were afraid to move.

What were you seeing on that phone? Just how bad was his first kill?

"You don't have to worry about anyone finding her. She's buried deep where nobody can get to her easily. It was a pain in the ass to get her there. About two miles past the cut-off on Gazelle Road. Nobody goes there. I kind of feel bad that I won't be able to visit Mom, but I guess it works better this way."

Hunter held his hand out for the phone. "You did say you wanted me to take care of her so she'd stop bitching, right?"

By now, Tom's face was passive again. The shock was gone, but his posture was more relaxed. The panicked pacing didn't return as he handed the phone back. "I honestly wasn't sure how you'd deal with that, but I guess this is fine. Thank you." He watched Hunter, shrewdly. He now knew he occupied the room with a killer, yet he didn't seem frightened of a person who would slaughter their own, wounded mother.

Snapping the phone closed, Hunter put it away. "Oh, it was no trouble. I can't stay here of course. It'll cause questions. I've been working on moving. I was thinking of somewhere closer to you."

Tom Brook froze, clearly measuring his response. It was the first sign of fear since finding out Hunter had killed that Tom displayed.

Hunter was enjoying seeing Tom squirm.

Finally, Hunter laughed. "Oh, don't get me wrong. I don't expect you to come and hang out to watch the game. I know your position would make that awkward, but this way if you *do* want to see me, I'd be closer. I just need a little help getting a new identity set up. I don't want to be Edward Tice anymore. He needs to disappear. My mom's idiot family will reach out. I'm not interested in coming over for Thanksgiving dinner. Besides, you never know. You might need my help again. I heard a few of your little club members are having issues. How is Frank Duncan doing? We hung out. He's pretty pissed with your arrangement."

Tom Brook entered politician mode. He smiled like a statesman. He raised his hands to gently gesture as he spoke like he was giving a speech before an adoring crowd. "Frank is well compensated. He wanted Linda."

Linda Duncan, Drew's mother.

Hunter scowled, not liking the way he was being spoken to. For a moment, Brooke wondered if he was thinking about killing Tom Brook on the spot. The way the future Mayor of Ember Falls studied the future serial killer, Brooke was certain Tom Brook wondered that too.

But the moment passed, and Edward Hunter's humor. "It's your ballgame. I'll be in touch. And don't worry about your little messes. I can clean any of them up if needed. Just let me know."

Hunter held his hand out. Tom stared at it, knowing he might as well shake the hand of the devil himself, but not seeing a way out.

They shook hands, and a moment later the video ended.

"Well, won't that play well on the campaign trail?" The General crossed his arms and scowled. "Shaking hands with a man who just killed his own mother. You think it was a quick kill?"

Brooke considered the question as he fished through the files. He wanted something from when Hunter was living with Kelli and Cole. "I wouldn't be surprised if she was his first kill. We'll look at Edward Tice, now that we know it's his real name. We'll probably find some quashed sex complaints there. More minor charges. Maybe Peeping Tom stuff from when he was thirteen or fourteen if he got caught. I don't think he would have raped her, but he would have gotten sexually excited by her pain and fear. It was the trigger, and Tom Brook pulled it. He probably would have gone that way eventually, but killing his mom? He liked it. It shaped what was to come."

Finding a file from two years ago, Brooke opened it. Hit play on the video.

A young woman lay strapped to the chair. Shivering from the cold, she wore only the heavy chains that Hunter liked to use on all of his victims. She was bleeding and whimpering in the dark. It was hard to make out much detail in the dark, grainy video, but she was young.

How young, Brooke didn't realize until the lights in the room came on. She couldn't have been older than sixteen, at most. She began to sob, shaking uncontrollably. "N-n-no, no," she repeated as she shook her head. Her eyes were shut tight, unwilling to see who she knew was coming.

Edward Hunter entered the room, dragging a kicking and screaming young boy with him.

Brooke clenched his fist as he saw a six-year-old Cole thrown into the room, landing with a hard smack on the floor. The girl was screaming as Hunter grabbed Cole by the hair, pulled him up, and made him stare at the teenager in chains.

"She's pretty hot." Hunter let Cole go, who fell to his knees.

Cole crawled up, his tiny hands gripping the chains that held the young captive in place. *"Let her go!"*

Hunter laughed, smacking Cole on the back of his head. "Not a chance, but it's always funny how you think begging for their lives will make a difference." He kicked the back of Cole's leg, toppling him once again. "Now, go take your spot, or we'll leave Amy here until later and go play the game with your mom. You want that?"

Cole was shaking his head. *"P-p-please…"*

Hunter leaned into Cole's ear. "Go. *Now.*"

His body convulsing with sobs, Cole crawled over to the small chair, climbed up, and waited as Hunter pulled out a second set of heavy chains. This set was designed for Cole.

"Son of a—"

Brooke turned to watch as a chair went flying across the room, smashing across the wall.

General Paul McAlister stood, fury etched on his face. His narrow eyes were windows to the hell he wanted to visit on Hunter, and he trembled with rage. The General bared his teeth at the image that was frozen on-screen of Hunter chaining Cole to the chair to make him helplessly watch the slaughter of a young girl.

"I'm going to fucking find that son of a bitch. I will rip his fucking heart out and shove it up his God-damn ass." His seething gaze shifted to Brooke. "You're going to fucking sit there and watch that little boy be terrified? You can sit there and watch a poor girl be tortured and an *innocent child tormented?"*

Slowly, Brooke stood. He hated himself for the answer he was going to give. "Yes."

The General's chest heaved as he fought for control. "You say you love Lilly. That boy is hers as much as he is Drew's and Ashley's."

Brooke knew that. "And I'll have nightmares for months. I'll wake up in a pool of sweat, and I may not make it out of here without vomiting, but I'll watch. I'll learn. I'll analyze. *Because* he is Lilly's as much as he's Drew, and Ashley's. And I'll fucking torture myself if I have to if it gives me any insight into how to fucking stop him."

The General's eyes shifted back to the screen. He winced and looked away.

Brooke knew those eyes had seen bodies of men he'd led into battle, blown to bits. He probably hadn't flinched then because it would have gotten in the way of the mission and protecting those who were still alive.

But this was too much.

Brooke moved to the door. "Did you see that kid that followed us?"

Standing in the doorway, his face covered by shadows, the General nodded.

"I think he knows something. We could save time if you could go talk to him. Record everything."

With his breathing coming back under control, General McAlister glanced back over his shoulder at the screen. "You think I can't handle this?"

Brooke forced himself to remain passive. "I think you shouldn't have to. And I need to know why that kid followed us. Let *me* do this."

The struggle was clear on the General's face. He wanted to storm off, kick down every door, and find

Hunter. Kill him, slowly. Brooke did not doubt if McAlister had his way, there would be nothing left of Hunter by the time the Bureau got to him.

Finally, the General nodded. "I'll be back." Paul McAlister stalked out of the underground chamber of horrors.

Brooke closed his eyes, willing himself to remember his training. *How the fuck am I going to look Lilly in the eye again?*

Personal detachment. It was needed for this job.

With a heaviness in his heart that broke his soul, Brooke turned around and got back to work.

Chapter Eighteen

The Boy on the Bike

Tyler Reed studied the black SUV. He'd known in his gut that a car like this didn't belong in a shit town like this. The vehicle screamed authority.

For some reason, Tyler had a gut feeling that it would be worth following. And when they came here, to the Tice Plant, he *knew* it was important.

The worn tires on Tyler's hand-me-down bike skidded to a stop. He slid off, letting the bike fall to the ground. His ripped sneakers stepped up onto the running board so he could try and peek into the window, but the tint was too dark for him to make out anything.

"You trying to boost our ride?"

Gasping, Tyler's arms pinwheeled as he lost his balance. With a thud, he landed on the ground. With his heart pounding in his chest, Tyler prepared to be thrown up against the car and smacked around.

Instead, the older man stood over him with one eyebrow cocked. "You okay, son?"

Tyler put on his best sneer. "I'm not your son." Tyler knew it wasn't smart to talk back, but he couldn't help himself. If he was going to get hit, he'd rather get in a good jibe and make it worth it.

The man, with his hawk-like face, and serious eyes, held his hand out for Tyler to help him up, but the boy could only stare at the offered hand with suspicion and disdain.

"Kid, we can have a conversation with you sitting on your ass, or you can get to your feet. Makes no difference to me. You're obviously here for a reason. You followed us. I'd like to know why."

The pounding in his chest started to ease off. Tyler didn't trust adult men much. His stepfather was an asshole who liked to kick him around whenever Tyler wasn't fast enough.

This guy was much older than his fat, drunk of a stepdad, but something about the way he moved made Tyler believe he wouldn't be easy to outrun. His stern face had interesting lines, but those grey eyes that studied him told Tyler that this guy was used to giving orders and having them obeyed.

With some reluctance, he took the hand and allowed the man to pull him up.

"My name is General Paul McAlister."

Tyler took a small step back, ready to bolt. "I didn't do anything wrong."

The General leaned up against the SUV. "Never said you did. And don't run. I might be old, but I've been at this shit far longer than you. Why'd you follow us Tyler?"

At first, Tyler wanted to just tell him to fuck off, but he stopped himself. "How do you know my name?"

The General smirked. "It was an educated guess. Talk to me Tyler. I'd like to hear about your friend Cameron."

Tyler narrowed his eyes. "Why do you give a shit?"

The General crossed his arms. "Because, when I was your age, nobody gave a shit about me. Talk to me."

Narrowing his eyes, Tyler tried to decide if he should trust the General. He gave off a no-bullshit vibe. He'd been warned to keep his mouth shut about Cam. That idiot Officer Kinney had told his stepfather, just like he'd promised to do.

If he told this old man about Cameron, and Kinney found out, his stepfather would get pissed, but who cares. He'd get pissed off about something else sooner or later, and Tyler was sure Cam was in trouble. If there was a chance this old man could help Tyler, it would be worth getting smacked around.

"Cameron lived next door to me. Foster kid. Those people have them coming and going, but Cam's mother is still in jail, so he didn't go back with her. A couple of months ago, he started acting all weird, but he wouldn't tell me what. Then he disappeared. He's not at school, he's not at home. I asked the Dubins, that's his foster family. They chased me away. Told me…" He trailed off, averting his eyes. "Doesn't matter. After a week, they told the teacher he's been reassigned, but nobody will tell me anything."

The General's face remained passive, and Tyler was ready to be dismissed until he reached into his pocket and pulled out his phone. "What's Cameron's last name?"

Tyler blinked, unsure what was happening. "Matthews. Cameron Matthews. I don't know his middle name, but his birthday is March fifth. He just turned ten."

With a nod, the General hit a couple of buttons. "Ari. I'm in Cheyanne. There's a boy. Cameron Matthews. I need to know everything you can find out, including if he was put into a different foster home. He turned ten this past March fifth. Hold on."

The General held the phone out. "Is Cameron taller

than you? Shorter?"

The question echoed in Tyler's mind for a few moments as the General relayed details. "No…he's like an inch or so short. He's a little small, but that's not his fault."

"What color hair? Eyes?"

"Um…" Tyler had to rack his brains for details. "Blond hair. Not like yellow blond, kind of like… brownish blond. Brown eyes."

Putting the phone to his ear, the General kept his eyes on Tyler. "You get that?"

"Yes, sir. I'm sending you an image now." Ari's crisp Middle Eastern accent came through the speaker on the General's cell.

Tapping the screen, the General arched an eyebrow as he studied the image that had appeared. He held the phone out to Tyler. "This Cameron?"

Tyler moved closer, lowering his guard. On the screen was a picture of Cameron right around the time they'd first met. "Yeah, yeah, that's him. Do you know where he is?"

The moment he'd said it, he wished he could take it back. Of course, they didn't. They couldn't.

"No, I'm sorry," the voice on the phone said. "I can't tell where he is, but I think we can rule out that he's home. He hasn't been to school in several weeks, and his foster parents pulled his records, but haven't had them sent anywhere. They're still cashing the checks. Should we call CPS?"

With a scowl that could freeze Hell, the General glanced at Tyler.

"No. I'll handle it. Keep digging." Without waiting for a reply, the General disconnected and made another call. "Madison, the boy we saw was looking for his buddy who's missing. I'm going to go into town, have a word with Officer Kinney. You okay in there."

He listened, and his scowl grew deeper. "I know. I got this."

Putting his phone away, the General glanced at Tyler. "Let's go see the police."

Instinctively, Tyler took a step back. "They won't believe me. I've tried."

Opening the door for Tyler, the General grinned. "Let *me* try."

And for the first time in a long time, Tyler decided that he would trust this man.

****

Lilly watched the three children huddled together, debating which movie to watch. Abbie was the new kid, but she seemed to have taken control of the pack. Jay had spent nearly twenty minutes on the phone begging his father to let him stay late. Jay's father had already texted, telling Lilly it was fine for Jay to stay, but not to say anything. Let the kid call, beg, and plead.

Cole was quiet, more so than normal. His eyes were wary, watching and waiting for Edward to come out of the shadows. It would be a long time before Cole really understood he was safe. How could he?

Thankfully, both Jay and Abbie understood that Cole didn't want to talk, so the pair of them filled the silence, argued about X-Men vs Justice League, and allowed Cole to just be there.

Whenever Lilly pictured that little boy being forced to witness such atrocities, her breath caught in her throat and her eyes stung with tears that desperately wanted to fall. Instead, she busied herself. Re-clean the kitchen, get the kids a snack, and putting the dishes away. Busy work.

When the doorbell rang, she was nearly relieved to have something different to do. Although there was another hour before Jay's father was supposed to come for him, she assumed that maybe Mr. Lancaster had come early. She wouldn't be surprised if he came to talk to Cole himself.

When Lilly opened the door, she was shocked to find two men she recognized from her days in Ember Falls High. Although she was never friends with Sam Reynolds, she knew who he was in an instant. The other, leaning heavily on crutches must be his younger brother Ethan.

Both appeared miserable, unable to initiate eye contact, and ready to collapse from exhaustion.

"Can I help you?" Now wasn't a good time for unexpected visitors, but a part of her wanted to invite them in, give them food and drink and see why they both had a desperate gleam in their eyes.

Sam stepped forward. "I need to speak with Drew Duncan. Is he here? We checked his house around the corner and…"

Drew, who hadn't left Cole's side since Brooke had left, came to the door next. He stepped past Lilly onto the porch. "Sam. Ethan. What's up?"

Ethan opened his mouth to say something, but Sam shoved a large, vanilla folder into Drew's hands. "We wanted to give you this. It's a settlement offer. It's time to try and put this behind us."

Drew didn't take the offered package. "Sam, today isn't a really good time."

Sam's jaw was set as he shoved the envelope into Drew's hand. "This won't take long. My mother is being very generous. Sign it, take the money so we can move on."

A flash of anger sparked in Drew's eyes, but he kept the explosion at bay.

Lilly stepped in front of Drew, taking the envelope from him. "Drew will want to have a lawyer look at this, read it through."

Sam towered over Lilly, his face contorted in rage. "We don't need to bring in lawyers. This is a great deal. He should take it before we pull it. It's more than what he deserves."

"What the hell do you know about what I deserve." Drew's face turned red as he threw the envelope at Sam. It fluttered in the air until Sam caught it. "You didn't sit in a fucking cell for months for a crime you didn't commit. You had your father protecting you from every crime you did. Are you still dealing, Sam?"

The color drained from Sam's face as he stepped back. His eyes darted to Ethan who was stepping in front of his brother, wincing in pain as he did. "Drew, I'm sorry for everything you and your family have been through, and I know that there's no amount of money that will ever make up for it. I'm also sorry for my brother. It's been a rough week for us."

He glanced back at his brother who wouldn't make eye contact. "The fact is, we're both really worried about our mother. She's not well. After what happened with me, and now with my father killing himself..." Ethan stopped as if remembering that moment when his father shot himself. "I know how hard it must have been for your family when everyone thought you were a killer. All of the hate and vitriol directed at them. I'm sure it was worse for you. We're getting that now. And I know it's different because my father's guilty of framing you. And more. But my mother didn't do anything. We are seriously worried about her health and we want to try to put this behind us as quickly as possible. We're just watching out for our family."

Drew blew out a breath. "I sympathize with what you're going through. I know what it's like to lose someone you love. I'm sorry for how hard it is. I haven't had time to think about that. My focus has been on my nephew. You know the story. As long as his stepfather is at large, I can't be distracted."

Lilly put her hand on Drew's arm. "It's been a difficult week for all of us, and I know Drew doesn't want to extend your family's suffering. Give me the papers. We'll read them soon. He has a friend who is a lawyer who can look them over, and I promise, we'll call. Go take care of your mom."

She held out her hand, and with an air of reluctance, Sam handed the papers over.

Ethan held his hand out for Drew, who took it.

"Ethan, I was sorry to hear what happened to you. And your family does have my sympathies. I hope your mom is okay. How is your sister doing?"

Ethan's eyes widened, freezing in place as if someone had reached into his chest and grabbed his heart. He glanced back toward his brother, who was sweating.

Ethan's eyes quickly scanned up and down the block. "She's doing fine. We should go." Ethan turned, and with excruciating effort, he started down the stairs. "I know you need to take care of your nephew. Thank you."

Sam helped his brother to their car. A moment later,

they quickly drove away.

Lilly turned to Drew. "I feel like we're missing something here."

****

Tyler had never met anyone like the General. He walked into the police station as if he owned the place. He wasn't a cop, but within minutes, he was in charge of the entire place. He demanded to see Chief Decker. He started by handing his card to the officer on duty. "Show him this. He can call and check on me. State Police, Justice Department, FBI, Homeland, CIA, Pentagon, Secret Service, or the White House if you can get through. Take your pick, but don't take long. I'm not in a patient mood today."

The young officer who had greeted them frowned as his eyes went from the card to the nearby phone, unsure of what to do.

The General leaned close. "Son, this is where you get up, find your commanding officer, and let someone with rank decide what to do."

The rookie blinked and glanced up towards the General who narrowed his eyes.

"*Now.*"

With wide eyes, the rookie stood up. "Yes, sir. I uh…" A touch of panic filled his eyes. "I'll just…" He patted his pockets as if searching for a pen. "There's coffee over there, help yourself. I'll just…go." He backed up, nearly tripping over his chair. "Sorry. Excuse me."

As the young officer scampered off, the General smirked at Tyler. "Rookies. I can smell 'em a mile away, and they piss their pants easily."

Tyler stifled a giggle as the General sat down next

to him. Tyler felt oddly at ease with the man. He didn't bullshit as most adults did. At least so far. "How did you know my name? Or Cams?"

The General clearly considering his words.

Tyler prepared for the first lie.

"The person I came in with is FBI. Have you seen the news about Edward Hunter?"

Tyler's eyes widened. It was all anyone could talk about. He was a real serial killer, like Ted Bundy or some guy who used to dress as a clown, and he lived here in town.

"We're trying to learn about him. That brought us here. I wanted to know what kind of police department this was, so we may have done a little digging. Heard the time you called. Keep that between us for now. Wasn't exactly legal. Deal?"

"Are you FBI?"

The General shook his head. "No. I'm a retired Marine general and I run a company called McAlister Security. We provide security for events and high-profile people, do private investigations and do a variety of other things. I'm running an Op out of Ember Falls, where some of his victims were from. I have a…" he pursed his lips, "personal connection to one of Hunter's victims."

The lines in the General's face tightened, hardening his face. Normally, Tyler would get frightened of someone who was that angry, but he found he still trusted the man.

Footsteps echoed from down the hallway. The General winked at Tyler and stood up. With his hand clasped behind his back, he waited for three men in uniforms to greet him. The General didn't take the offered hands of the men with five gold stars on their white collars.

"Let's not waste time." The General spoke as if he were addressing troops heading into battle. "You know who I am, or you wouldn't be here. We need to have a long-overdue conversation over a missing child named Cameron Matthews. I expect you to have your full attention and cooperation, or I'll go over your heads and you'll find that you won't even be able to wash police cars when I'm done."

The three men in uniform glanced uncomfortably at each other. The one in the center, the oldest, with the least amount of hair on his head, stepped forward. "I'm sure we can clear this up quickly General McAlister sir. Why don't we step into my office?"

****

Brooke tried to pace himself, taking small breaks every twenty minutes, going back and forth between reading notes and watching videos.

The files contained detailed information on people who had been a part of the teenage sex ring in Ember Falls. Most had retired or moved out of the small town, but there were a few that were still there including the warden of the prison where Drew had been held, as were several of his top deputy wardens. Hunter had logged and even recorded conversations with Senator Brook about cutting Drew off from any communication with his sisters, putting him with abusive cellmates. He even provided the names of the three inmates who would ambush and rape Drew, and the names of the specific guards who would ignore it while it happened.

Watching the videos tore at Brooke's soul. Seeing the depravity on display, the glee that Hunter took in the pain and suffering of these women was nauseating. He was a hardened Special Agent of the FBI's elite BAU. He'd seen cruelty in all its forms. Rescued men, women, and children who had been stripped of all dignity and reduced to pathetic souls begging for death.

How did Cole survive this?

After the last video, one that must have been taken right before Kelli had taken Cole and run, Brooke took a long break. He went outside and forced himself to breathe deeply. He called Abbie, heard her voice, laughed with her, and promised he'd peek in on her when he got home. Then he called Lilly.

"What's wrong?"

Brooke paced with the phone in his hand. "Can't I just call to see how things are going?"

He could envision her, on the other end, twirling a lock of her pretty red hair.

"I can hear something in your voice. Is it not going well in Cheyanne? Did the information Cole gave you not pan out?"

"It panned out." She didn't need the details, and putting that on her would be selfish and downright shitty. "It's just been a long day."

There was silence on the other side, and he knew she understood what he wasn't saying. "I can't imagine how hard it must be for you, but you're doing it to help Cole. To help all of his victims. To stop him."

Brooke felt some of the tension that had built within him fade. She got it.

"When you get back, we'll curl up together. Watch a comedy. We don't have to talk about it."

Brooke managed a smile. He wanted to tell her he loved her. How losing her was the worst thing that ever happened to him, and he couldn't bear the thought of losing her again.

Then he thought of how this was bound to end. She'd hate him. It was inevitable. "I'll see you later."

Disconnecting the call, Brooke put the phone away and forced himself to head back in. He was a selfish prick. He would take comfort tonight in her arms. Maybe in her bed.

All while knowing what was coming.

He made his way back to Hunter's computers, took a deep breath, and opened the next video file.

The next several files were filled with much of the same as before, absent one key ingredient. Cole. These were after Kelli had finally escaped with Cole.

Robbed of his audience, Hunter was even crueler, but something was different. He didn't seem to get the same joy out of his kills. He seemed almost bored. Had Cole's presence become part of the ritual?

Brooke felt as if he was on the precipice of an important understanding, but he wasn't quite sure what it was. He loaded the next video and waited.

It started like the others. A woman, shaking from the cold, more terrified than she'd even been in her life. She was bleeding and naked except for the chains. The door opened, and the girl's whimpering turned into sobs.

Brooke watched, sure he knew what was coming.

He was wrong.

Grabbing his cell, he called Jacob. "You need to watch the file I'm sending. Look at this now. Get it to everyone. Get it to Foster and her team. We have a new problem."

Chapter Nineteen

Cameron

The Uber pulled up in front of the police station, and Brooke was out of the car before the brake was fully engaged. He strode into the station holding a USB in his hand, and a scowl on his face. He found a fresh-faced rookie by the front desk. Flashed his FBI identification. "General McAlister. Where is he?"

Wide-eyed fear registered in the rookie's eyes, telling Brooke that the General had very much made an impression. The rookie nervously pointed down the hall. "He's in Interview Three, with the Chief, Deputy Chiefs, and Officer Kinney, questioning the Dubins on a missing child. Last door down that hallway. You um…" He swallowed hard. "You need me to take you down there?"

Brooke stormed down the hall, forced the USB into his pocket, a laptop bag slung over his shoulder, and knocked on the door of Interview Three.

When a deputy chief opened it, Brooke showed his ID again and stepped inside, not waiting for an invitation. He glanced around the room and sized up the situation.

The three chiefs were hoping they could resolve this, and placate the General. Officer Kinney was just praying he wouldn't lose his badge, knowing if they didn't work this out quickly and heads needed to roll, the Chiefs would choose to sacrifice his career over theirs.

The Dubins were scared that they were going to lose their ability to foster children, for which the state paid them. For most foster parents, the decent ones who cared, the monetary stipend didn't cover the expenses of the children they took in. However, there would always be a few who skimmed the money and ignored the kids.

In the corner was the kid that had followed them earlier. He was watching the General with an amazing amount of awe.

The General was pissed, but back in control. Of both himself and everything else.

"This is Special Agent Madison, FBI." The General glared at Mr. and Mrs. Dubin. Both sat in uncomfortable chairs, she was wearing expensive jewelry and his clothes were wrinkled. They were most likely sweating bullets before Brooke arrived. Now they were in a real panic. "They're trying to convince us that Cameron just ran away the other day, despite attendance records from school that he hasn't been in class for nearly a month."

Brooke's eyebrows went up, but he ignored the Dubins. Instead, he concentrated on the boy. "Tyler, right? You're Cameron's friend?"

The boy glanced over his shoulder toward the General. "Yeah. I tried to tell people that something was wrong."

Brooke pulled out a chair, near Tyler and across from the Dubins. "You're a good friend. I'm sorry that nobody listened to you, but I promise we'll work to find Cameron. I need you to do something for me. It could really help us find Cameron. Okay?"

Tyler once again glanced at the General.

Brooke turned to the Chief. "Could you call the

young officer at the front desk in please?"

As the chief did so, Brooke turned to face Tyler. "You need us to contact anyone at home? Let them know you're not in trouble, but you're helping us?"

As the Chief used a landline phone on the desk to call someone into the room, Tyler shrugged. "My mom died a year ago. My stepdad won't give a shit."

The General put his hand on Tyler's shoulder. "Don't worry about him."

The rookie appeared at the door. He handed the Chief a laptop.

Brooke read his nametag. "Officer Frazier. Can you take Tyler someplace quiet? Give him pen and paper. Get him something to eat and drink."

Brooke turned to Tyler. "I need you to write down everything you can remember about Cameron. What he likes. Food, snacks, drinks. Things he likes to do. Games. Anything that makes you think of him. Any detail could help."

Tyler didn't move at first. The General leaned down. "I think Officer Frazier will be okay. Go on. I'll deal with your stepdad after we're done here."

The boy slowly got up and headed towards the door. He looked back at the General one last time. "You won't just forget about him?"

The General locked eyes with the child. "Not going to happen. Marines never leave a man behind."

Tyler stepped outside with Officer Frazier.

Reaching for his laptop bag, Brooke casually turned towards the Dubins. "We'd all like to clear this up as quickly as possible. I'm on a very important case, and we can't let this distraction stretch out. Did General McAlister tell you what I'm here for?"

The General put on his best poker face. He didn't know where Brooke was going, but he was willing to let this play out.

Mrs. Dubin shook his head. "No. Alls I know is he won't believe that we took that boy in out the goodness of our hearts. Opened our home to him. But he just kept making trouble. Cutting school. I wouldn't be surprised if the kid was doing drugs. I mean, I know he's young, but he ain't innocent. Right, Warren."

Warren began to open his mouth to agree but was cut off by his wife. "I know we should have called social services right away, but he'd done this before. That's why little Tyler didn't see him."

She leaned in as if she were about to tell Brooke a secret. "Just between you and me, I think he was scared of Tyler. He's got such a mouth on him. His daddy ain't no prize either, right, Warren?"

Brooke continued to open his laptop, powering it on, all the while Mrs. Dubin kept going on and on about how wonderful they were, and how awful and challenging the children they were saddled with could be, and asking her husband to chime in, yet never letting him get a word in.

Brooke keyed in the password to give him access. "Okay, so what I'm hearing is that Cameron is a troubled kid, but you did right by him."

Mrs. Dubin smiled, clearly pleased that Brooke seemed to understand. "Oh yes. I mean, if you find him, we'll take him back. I'm sure I could get through to him in time. He just ran. I'm sure if you give it time, he'll probably return on his own. He's just being foolish, but he'll want that warm bed and a full tummy."

Brooke pulled out the USB from his pocket. "And you feel his friend Tyler was a bad influence?"

Mrs. Dubin nodded. Mr. Dubin shook his head until he received an elbow in the gut from his wife. "Yes, sir. Cameron was quiet when he came to us, but he got a mouth on him pretty soon. You ask his teachers. They'll tell you he started to act out. Get angry all the time." She leaned in again. "Started to wet his bed like a baby. I was horrified."

Fingers dancing across the keyboard, Brooke listened intently but never glanced up. "When was that? His bedwetting trouble. About a month or so ago?"

Mrs. Dubin glanced towards the ceiling as if the answer was written up there. "Yes, yes that sounds about right."

"Good," Brooke answered, his eyes locked on the computer screen. "And you think it was Tyler's influence? Who else did he spend time with? Anyone older? Rougher around the edges?"

Mrs. Dubin glanced towards her husband, who shrugged. "I don't know. Maybe."

Brooke's congenial smile melted away. "Maybe someone like Edward Hunter."

He hit a button on the laptop and positioned it so everyone could see it. An image of a young girl of seventeen, naked, sobbing, and chained up appeared. She was shaking from the cold and began to scream when the door opened.

A shadow appeared. A new cry filled the room. A small figure was thrown to the floor. It was Cameron.

Edward Hunter walked into the room, grabbed Cameron by the hair, pulled him up, and shoved him closer to the girl.

Brooke hit a key, and the image froze. "This video was from a couple of months ago. Around the same time,

Cameron started to wet the bed. My guess, based on what we know about Edward Hunter and his signature, he threatened Cameron. Told him that if he went to the police, he would slowly torture everyone he cared about. I wonder if Hunter threatened you? Or maybe just Tyler?"

Brooke rose and slammed the laptop closed. "Tyler realized Cameron was missing at the same time that we learned Hunter was a serial killer. Right at the same time he burnt his house to the ground and fled. We know that Edward Hunter enjoyed terrifying another young boy. Kept exposing him to this level of cruelty, and sadism, and threatened to kill everyone he loved. That child is safe. Hunter has now replaced him with the young boy entrusted in your care for over a month, and you haven't even reported him missing."

Brooke turned on the police chiefs and Officer Kinney. "And you ignored Tyler when he tried to tell you. Told his stepfather he was lying, knowing he'd get hit for it. Yet he kept trying. Tyler has more courage than the rest of you combined."

Brooke paused, allowing the weight of his words to sink in. He watched as the horror registered on everyone's face. Slowly, he sat down across from the Dubins. "My job with the Bureau is to sit across the table and study people like Edward Hunter. To read him so well, I can predict what he'll do next. So we're going to have a conversation about Cameron. A *real* conversation about how he was when he arrived in your home, and how he changed over the last couple of months. I want to know every detail you can remember. We're going on the record, and it is a crime to lie to the FBI during an active investigation. I look into the eyes of stone-cold killers, and I can tell when they lie even a little. Don't think for one instant that I won't see through you."

Brooke reached into the bag and pulled out a small recording device. "Interview with Warren and Mary Dubin. Present in interview, Officer Kinney. Chief Decker, Deputy Chiefs Lehman, and Pickering. Civilian Consultant Retired General Paul McAlister. Let's talk about your foster son, Cameron Matthews, and how he ended up with a serial killer on the run."

Chapter Twenty

Confession

By the time they had walked out of the Cheyanne police station, the Dubins knew their foster license was done and the agency that had placed Cameron there would be next. There should have been weekly checks, follow-ups, and people who knew what was happening. Everyone had failed Cameron over the last few weeks.

The chiefs were all ready to put in their retirement papers and Tyler was placed with a family friend. The General had located an aunt that lived out of state from his mother's side that would be happy to take in her nephew. He promised Tyler that he would check them out and only when he was satisfied, he'd see that the boy got there safely. The General and Brooke barely spoke as they drove back to Ember Falls. Brooke reviewed files on his phone and made phone calls to Agent Foster and Jacob. The General kept his face passive as he drove, but Brooke was sure his mind was working overtime.

They pulled in front of Lilly's home. Putting the car in park, the General reached into his pocket for his cell. The General tapped at his phone to open the message. His face was passive as he opened the email, his pupils moving back and forth as he began to read. "We have the results for those DNA tests."

Brooke's heart began to thud in his chest. Something

twisted in his gut.

The General handed the phone to Brooke. "You need to read this for yourself."

Accepting the cell, he saw the email had an unopened link. Taking a deep breath, Brooke opened the link and read the results.

And reread them, several times.

After a moment, he stared out through the window at the house. Now he had another reason to hate himself. What the fuck had he just done?

He handed the phone back to the General with the results open. "Read them."

The General took the phone. His eyes narrowed as he read. Shutting the phone, he killed the engine. "We have to tell them."

Brooke was ashamed to admit to himself he was tempted to leave and never come back. He wanted no part of this.

But he owed it to everyone to do the right thing. "Let's go."

Together, they walked past the beautifully tended garden, and onto the open porch. Brooke raised his hand to knock, but it fell back to his side. "Shit."

The General placed a hand gently on his shoulder. "I can tell them. I ran the tests."

Breathe. Just breathe. Don't be a fucking coward.

"No. This is my mess. Time to own it."

Before he could change his mind, Brooke knocked on the door. The door swung open, and Lilly was on the other side, smiling as she greeted them. "Have you two eaten? I could heat up some…" Her radiant green eyes narrowed as she took stock of Brooke. "What's wrong?"

"Hey, guys." Brooke stepped inside. Everyone was

around the dining room table, magazines and paperwork spread out as they planned out the upcoming nuptials. His chest tightened as Lilly reached for his hand. Her first thought was to give comfort.

Her mother had been right. Trash like him had no business touching a girl like her.

"We need to talk." Brooke took a seat at the table she had welcomed him to a few nights ago.

The room went still. With a silence that made it seem as if they were making funeral plans, everyone took a seat, except for the General who stood in the far corner, closest to Drew. The soft hue from the setting sun was fading from the bay window, and the shadows slowly stretched across the room.

"Let's start with some of the information that's about to go public." Brooke folded his hand in front of himself. "We found the place he took Cole. We found videos that documented everything."

Ashley listened with her arms tightly folded, her lips a thin blue line. Ollie sat as close as he could get. Drew's face was a mask of anger, just waiting to spill out.

Lilly sat nearest to Brooke and leaned closer. "That's good, right? If you have enough evidence, maybe you can avoid a trial?"

"Yes, but it led us to something new." Brooke sighed. There was no way to say this that could soften the blow. "A few weeks ago, a young boy went missing. He was a foster child who was placed in the home of a couple who cared more about the support check than the kid. His buddy started to see he was acting strange. Then he stopped showing up at school. Hunter has the boy now."

Lilly gasped while Drew cursed. Ashley turned and

finally looked at Brooke. "Why?"

Pulling his knees up to his chest, Cole began to roll back and forth. "I don't understand."

Brooke searched his mind for a way to explain it, one that wouldn't add to Cole's trauma more than needed. He quickly reviewed everything he'd learned about Cole, going back to the first time the file had hit his desk with the copies of the comic he and Jay had created.

"Cole, do you remember how the villain in your story, Galactor, how he fed on fear? How did you see that working?"

Cole shrugged, his eyes fixated on the simple flower display in the center of the table. "Fear was like food."

"Exactly," Brooke said. "When they were there alone, they were scared about what was happening to them. But when he introduced you, you were scared for yourself, *and* them. It gave him more to feed off of. He needed you to watch."

The rocking stopped, and Cole glanced toward Brooke, but still didn't make direct eye contact. "The way to stop him is to not be afraid. But I can't help it." Tears welled in his eyes.

Drew reached out for him. "You have nothing to be scared of. He's not getting anywhere near you."

Ashley placed one hand over her belly, as she grasped Ollie's hand with the other. "You're safe here Cole."

Lilly rose from her chair and went over. Tentatively, she placed her arms around Cole. "He can't hurt you."

Everyone chimed in, giving Cole their take on how brave he was. Drew told him about how scared he'd been while he'd been under fire. Sam talked about how scared she'd been when she had to save her Nana from a man with a gun to her head. Ollie spoke about seeing Ashley bleeding, worried that he'd lost her just as he'd gotten her.

As they spoke, Abbie remained silent, her small hands folded in front of her. She kept her soft brown eyes fixed on her fingers, but Brooke could tell she was listening intently. When everyone else had their say, Abbie turned to Cole.

"I'm still scared."

Her words hung in the air as all eyes turned her.

She ignored their watchful eyes as she continued. "When you're as scared as that, it doesn't just end because you've got a warm bed and someone to tuck you in at night. It gets better. There are days I'm still terrified that one day, Jefferey Jones is going to find me. Sometimes it's so bad I can still smell his breath. Like bad eggs. That's why I can't stand being away from Dad. I know he'll protect me."

Abbie turned to Brooke and blinked away the tears that were forming.

Brooke rose and went to her side, pulling her in a hug. "I'm sorry. I shouldn't have taken this assignment so soon."

Abbie shrugged. "You had to."

Brooke closed his eyes as he held her. She was right, he had to do this for himself. To confront his demons and prove he wasn't the throwaway. And to protect a woman he was convinced hated him. It turns out, Lilly didn't hate him.

Yet.

He stood. The time for honesty was here. "There's more to this case than I've let on. On a personal level."

He walked away from Abbie and went back to his seat, but he remained standing. His eyes wandered the table, taking in the faces of everyone around him. Lilly, who was next to Cole had placed a reassuring hand on Abbie's shoulder. Brooke didn't want to see any of their faces as he spoke, but he forced himself to face them. They deserved that much.

"The other day, I revealed that I believed Senator Brook is my biological father. Thanks to the General, and quick work from McAlister's lab, I now know that's true. Thomas Brook is my father. But that isn't all I suspected. I wasn't the only illegitimate born to Senator Brook. There are at least two more. I suspected one when I arrived. The other one I started to suspect after coming to Ember Falls, thanks to Ollie."

Ollie frowned. "Me? I don't remember saying anything about Senator Brook having…" He trailed off as his eyes moved back and forth quickly. "Jesus. You mean…*Diana*?"

Brooke nodded. "You wondered why she called out for a father that we have no record of one. We've already identified that she received money for college and grad school that came from a shell company that we now know he's behind. It also contributed to his campaign. And he used these to make payments to certain people to keep them quiet."

"Hold on." Drew held his hand up. "You've been saying that the senator was behind my sister's death, but whoever is also had Diana killed. You're telling me that you think Diana was Senator Brook's daughter? That he knew that, and he still allowed her to be killed? One he fathered illegitimately, yet chose to help financially?" His scowl told Brooke he wasn't buying it was anyone but Reynolds.

"Those might have been payments to keep her quiet." Brooke took a moment. It was time. "He did the same with me, only the money was paid to my mother, who smoked it, snorted it, or shot it up her veins. He did the same thing directly to another woman for a time, and then when she was killed, directly to her son."

Brooke took a deep breath, and one last look at Lilly, who he was sure would never see him the same way again. "A man who I now know is my half-brother. Edward Hunter."

Chapter Twenty-One

Brothers and Sisters

Brooke's words reverberated through the air, bringing a deafening silence that echoed through the room. He wasn't sure what was worse, the wide-eyed panic that had Cole turning white, the simmering anger that displayed in Drew's narrowing eyes, or the blank stare from Lilly, who absently pressed a hand to her stomach.

Cole didn't move. "I don't understand. He's your brother? You grew up together?"

Brooke shook his head. "No, I've never met Edward Hunter, or Edward Tice, his real name. I started to suspect he might be another illegitimate son of Senator Brook after the news broke about Edward Hunter being a serial killer who was responsible for Molly's death. Who would pay to have her killer protected? Senator Brook, about to become Presidential Candidate Brook, has a lot to lose, and he's got the money. The connections. The coldness to do that. He used my mother for years, paid her way knowing it would feed her addiction, and never gave a damn about me."

Brooke's lip curled as he thought of the man that had fathered him. Maybe to an extent, Drew had been right. Brooke wanted the Senator to be guilty. That didn't change the fact that he was.

"We recovered a video that Hunter made without the Senator's knowledge." Brooke folded his arms as he spoke. "It seems the Senator, back when he was running for Mayor, had an encounter with Hunter's mother that went bad. He got violent and broke the woman's arm. The Senator called Hunter to ask him to calm his mother down, but instead, Hunter killed his own mother."

Lilly gasped. "His *mother*?"

Brooke forced himself to make eye contact. "I think it was his first kill, although I'm sure we'll find evidence that…" He glanced at the two children, both of whom had seen far worse than "sexually sadistic fantasies" in their young lifetimes, but they were still children and needed to be treated that way. "Evidence that he thought about hurting people long before that."

Drew took a step around the table. "Cole, I want you and Abbie to go upstairs now."

Abbie crossed her arms. "No. He's my dad."

Brooke forced a smile. "It's okay Abbie. Go ahead."

Avoiding eye contact, Lilly reached her hand out to each of the children. "Let's go. I'll set you up with a movie."

Cole rose, but Abbie stayed in place. Her face was cemented in a frown that made it clear she wasn't happy.

"Abbie." Brooke gestured towards Lilly. "It's fine."

Slowly, she slid off her chair and followed Lilly and Cole. Brooke waited until they'd climbed the stairs and he heard the door close. "I know I should have said something sooner. I'm sorry."

"Why didn't you?" Drew jabbed an angry finger at his oldest friend. "What else are you hiding from us?"

Brooke jutted his chin out. "Nothing. I kept that to myself. I haven't told anyone, including Jacob or the rest of the Bureau. When it comes out, they'll want to pull me from the case."

"You sure that wouldn't be a good thing?" Drew stepped the rest of the way around the table to stand in front of Brooke. "You aren't being objective. Just because the Senator is a bastard, doesn't mean he set me up. We have a confession from Reynolds, right before he killed himself. He's the guy. Even his kids know it. They showed up today."

Brooke frowned. "His three kids came here?"

"Just the sons," Lilly said as she came back down the stairs. "I've got Cole and Abbie watching a movie, told them to stay in Cole's room, but knowing him, he'll still try and listen so no shouting."

She came into the dining room and placed herself between Drew and Brooke. "Sam and Ethan wanted Drew to take a settlement deal. They were desperate for him to take it. They certainly seemed to believe that their father is guilty. They got a little…" She shrugged. "Weird at the end, but they weren't protesting their father's innocence."

The General stepped out of the corner for the first time. "What do you mean weird?"

He and Brooke locked eyes for a brief moment.

Lilly paused and thought back. "When they first got here, all they cared about was getting Drew to agree to the settlement, but then all of a sudden at the end, they practically ran out of here."

Brooke leaned on the back of his chair. "Why? What changed?"

"Nothing changed." Drew pushed past Brooke and went to a nearby table. He picked up a large manilla envelope. He came back and shoved it toward Brooke who took it. "They know their father was guilty. He was the one who got me locked up. They just got a little squirrely at the end."

Brooke opened the envelope and scanned the pages. "Have you read this yet?"

Drew shook his head. "I don't want to deal with that now. I don't want to—"

Brooke held the paperwork out to him and opened to a particular page. "They're offering you twenty million, with the condition that you publicly accept that Reynolds was solely responsible for you being blamed and incarcerated for the murder of Molly Winters. Read the paragraph where they spell out what that means."

Brooke pointed to a jumble of words that followed right after the large sum of money they were willing to throw at him. His eyes quickly scanned the paragraph. "I'd have to guarantee that McAlister Security would end its investigation into the matter, and formally request that Chief Miller do so as well, leaving the apprehension of Edward Hunter to the FBI."

Ollie stood up and reached his hands out for the papers. "Mom won't agree to that. I mean, you can request it, but she wants to know what happened. If it was just Reynolds or more involved."

Drew shook his head. "It was Reynolds. I know it was. I can still remember when I was in that damn hospital bed, just having survived being ODed on whatever was slipped to me. I could see it in his eyes. Reynolds knew I was innocent; he just didn't care."

The General stepped up and took the papers next. "I can tell you that even if you take this deal, I would not call off the investigation. Not sure how they'd enforce it since it's not your decision, but I'm assuming you aren't buying whatever the fuck it is their selling."

Drew walked away. "I won't lie and say we couldn't use that kind of money, but no. I'm not going to be silenced. But it doesn't make sense that they would want us to settle and back off. We have no reason to suspect them. Even Sam Reynolds. He was an asshole drug dealer, but he didn't have anything to do with this, let alone his younger son, or their sister."

Lilly frowned but stayed silent.

"What is it?" Brooke turned to her. "You just thought of something."

Her frown only deepened as she shook her head. "I'm sure it's nothing. It's just that's when things got weird today. When I asked how their sister was doing. All of a sudden, they got antsy and disappeared."

Images flooded Brooke's mind. "Describe it. Be exact."

"What does it matter?" Drew asked.

Brooke and the General locked eyes again. It was the General who spoke. "It matters, son."

Drew's eyes darted back and forth between them. "Why? What aren't you telling us?"

That wasn't a question that Brooke wanted to answer until he figured this out. Something was wrong. He was missing something. "Tell me exactly what happened at the end."

Lilly pursed her lips as she tried to recall the memory. "Sam was a little belligerent. He just wanted Drew to sign the papers and take the money. Ethan was far more reasonable and sympathetic. He admitted his father was guilty, but told us they were worried about their mom. I got Sam to give me the papers and told them we'd call them. It seemed to calm things down. I told them how sorry I was that they had to go through this. It's not their fault. And then…" She frowned, her eyes moving, and she shook her head. "I asked about their sister. Right?" She glanced at Drew, frowning because she couldn't remember any other details.

"Yeah." Drew rubbed the bridge of his nose. "I guess. Sure. You asked that and Sam started to sweat, and he and Ethan couldn't get out of there fast enough. I just…" He shook his head. "I just wanted them gone, to be honest. I know it's not their fault. Lord knows I feel for Ethan. Sam was always an ass, but Ethan was a nice kid who got pushed around by Sam. Probably his dad. But I guess yeah, there was a change there at the end."

Brooke walked to the front porch and stepped out into the night air. He tried to picture it. The brothers were here to speak with Drew, but Ethan was used to Sam taking charge. Still, when things got heated, Ethan stepped up.

Brooke sensed more than he heard Drew, Lilly, and the General behind him. Everyone else stayed inside. He paced on the front porch. "Sam came up first but backed off when Ethan spoke. Sam got angry but seemed almost embarrassed or ashamed when Ethan spoke. We saw that when Ollie and I interviewed them. He's ashamed of what happened to his brother. Desperate to make up for it. To earn Ethan's forgiveness. Everything he's doing is to try and find absolution. But he was angry?"

Lilly nodded. "Yes. I mean, he didn't scream, but he tried to bully Drew. Not smart."

But the image worked for Brooke. Sam reverted to what was familiar when he was scared. "Sam doesn't have the tools to try and appeal to Drew the way Ethan did. He wasn't just angry…" Brooke remembered it in his eyes from the day Reynolds had shot himself. "He was panicked. He covered with anger. Ethan kept the act up better, but the fear was there. It came out…"

He pointed ahead to where he imagined Sam and Ethan stood.

Without warning, he went inside. Both the General and Drew stepped aside as Brooke moved back into the dining room. "Ollie. When we were at their house, did either of them mention their sister? Or did their mother?"

Ollie slowly rose, and a frown clouded his face. "Um…I don't think so. I mean, I can't remember them mentioning…" He paused. "Wait, *I* did. There was that painting of the family and I asked what she was studying…"

The image formed. Mrs. Reynolds' face had grown pale. Fear.

"Son of a fucking bitch." Brooke pulled out his cell. "Jacob. I know you've had a rough day, but I think we have a situation. I need you to quietly look into Tiffany Reynolds. She should be a senior." He rattled off her school, her age, and basic description. "Keep this off the radar, I don't want to chance anyone knowing we're looking, but I need to know if she's been in class for the last week or so. Anything out of the ordinary. Call me when you have it and get it fast. I'm heading there now."

He ended the call and headed for the door.

"Wait." Drew stood in front of him. "What the hell is going on?"

Brooke glanced towards the General, who gave Brooke the slightest shake of his head. Nobody saw it. Now wasn't the time for the rest of the bombshell.

"If I'm right, I need to reinterview the Reynolds. Now."

The General stepped towards them. "You should take Drew. It might throw them."

Drew headed for the door. Brooke followed but stopped when Lilly grabbed his arm. "You should have told me about Hunter."

There it was. He'd betrayed her. A son of a whore like him had no business touching a girl like Lilly.

"I'm sorry."

At least this time, he knew how he fucked it up.

****

Neither Brooke nor Drew spoke on the way to the Reynolds'. As they drove, Brooke wondered how much the Reynolds family knew.

Brooke rang the doorbell. They didn't have to wait long before the door swung open.

Mrs. Reynolds' face was bare. The classy makeup she'd worn the day her husband had killed himself was absent and had been replaced by dark bags under her reddened eyes. She looked nearly ready to collapse but stiffened at the sight of Brooke and Drew. "Mr. Duncan. Have you signed the paperwork? I can have my lawyers put everything into motion and get the money to you right away."

Brooke stepped in front of Drew. "We'd like to come in and discuss things first if it's not too much trouble. We'll try not to take up too much of your time."

Mrs. Reynolds' eyes narrowed as she studied Brooke. She turned as Ethan slowly came down the stairs. Sam stayed close to assist but never touched his brother. Mrs. Reynolds' eyes returned to Brooke, glancing past him. To Drew and then beyond as if she thought someone was right behind him.

She opened the door the rest of the way and stepped

aside. "Of course. Please, come in."

Brooke took stock of everyone as they entered. Heavy bags under the eyes. Lethargic movements, pale skin, and each appeared to have aged a year since they'd been here last. A picture started to form. He walked farther in and turned, sending a glance toward Drew.

Ethan finished limping down the stairs and came over. "Have you signed the papers yet?"

"Mr. Duncan hasn't looked at the papers yet." Brooke locked eyes with Drew, hoping that despite his anger he'd go along with the deception. "We need to have a few questions answered first."

Their response was immediate and telling. Mrs. Reynolds gasped, her hand flew to her mouth and her eyes watered as she fought back tears. Sam's fist clenched, ready to lash out. He stepped forward as if he wanted to attack, then halted in place, trembling.

Ethan maintained control the best, although his face was ghost white. He labored forward, his bad leg shaking as he stepped closer to Brooke. Sam wanted to help but seemed to know better than to touch his brother.

"I don't understand." Ethan leaned heavily on his cane. "Of course, we want to cooperate in any way we can, but we don't know anything else. You can't possibly think we're…" He winced. Brooke wasn't sure if it was the words he was about to say that hurt, or if it was the pain of just standing. They all appeared ready to collapse. "Think that any of us has any connection to Edward Hunter. I can assure you, whatever my *father* did, he wouldn't bring that man into our lives."

There was a harshness to his tone when he used the word father. His brother sneered at the same moment, and Mrs. Reynolds had closed her eyes. The hatred they felt for Bob Reynolds was pouring out of each of them, but that didn't explain the raw terror. Brooke needed to choose his words carefully, not just to control their responses, but to push them over the edge.

Brooke shook his head. "Of course not. Rest assured, nobody thinks you're conspiring with Hunter. I can only imagine how exhausting this entire ordeal has been for you. I know you're eager to put it to bed, and the last thing we want to do is hold you hostage with the manhunt. We just need to tie up a few last details, and then Drew can look at your proposal. Give him a day or two to sleep on it. But let's try and kill off any last questions with this part of the case."

It was working. They were more and more on edge with each moment. If he was alone with Mrs. Reynolds or even Sam, he'd have them by now, but Ethan was holding on. Barely. Poor kid looked ready to fall flat on his face.

Ethan hobbled a few more steps forward. "Of course, we'll answer whatever you need."

Brooke resisted the urge to help him. "Great. We're fine with everything you said. Same with your mom and brother. No questions there."

Ethan frowned. He glanced towards his mother who had lowered herself into a chair. "I don't understand. I thought you said…"

"Not you." Brooke tapped the body-cam on his tie for effect, reminding them everything was being recorded. "We just need to get a statement from your sister. Where is Tiffany?"

Sam took a step back as if slapped. Mrs. Reynolds was trying to hide the tears forming in her eyes.

Ethan was shaking, a combination of fear and agony

was overtaking him. Still, he inched forward. "Tiffany isn't here right now. I'm sure we can answer whatever—"

"I'm afraid we need to speak with her." Brooke shrugged as if he understood what a bother it was. "We promise to be sensitive. We just need to record a statement."

Taking a deep breath, Ethan turned to his mother who wasn't able to make eye contact. He swallowed hard. "I'm sorry. She's not here, but I can get her to write a statement and email it." With utter desperation shining in his eyes, he began to sweat. "Or if you need it notarized, we might be able to arrange that." He let out a short breath as if he'd just realized the answer to a tough problem in the nick of time on a test. "I hate to bother Tiff and have her come back home."

Brooke paused, letting him think that might work for just a moment. "I'm sorry, but we have to do it in person. This is too high profile. I need to have a body on camera when I take the statement." He ignored the rising tide of guilt as he watched Ethan fight to keep from hyperventilating. "But we don't want to inconvenience her. We're happy to go to her. We know she wasn't in classes today. When did she leave?"

Ethan blinked. "Umm…"

Brooke shrugged. "I'm sure she came home as she hasn't been in class all week. Again, you and your family have my sympathy. We can head up to…what is it? Syracuse?"

Drew scowled, his eyes focused on Ethan who was ready to collapse. "Brooke, maybe we should—"

"You're right." Brooke headed for the door. "We're sorry to bother you at this horrible time. We can give her a day to settle and get some sleep. We'll be up there the day after tomorrow. We'll be mindful of her classes. It won't take long. We can leave you and your family to rest. Mr. Duncan can get to the papers in a week or so after this is put to bed."

Ethan reached out and moved to stop Brooke from leaving. "Wait, I—"

His knee wobbled in an awkward direction. There was a crack and Ethan went down hard.

Mrs. Reynolds cried, no longer able to hide the tears. Sam burst past Brooke and knelt to help his brother up.

"Are you all right Mr. Reynolds?" Brooke asked, keeping his voice nonchalant and casual. He waited as Sam helped Ethan to a nearby sofa. Kid was about faint, but he was holding on. Fighting the pain with every inch of strength he had left.

Brooke turned towards Drew. "Let's go. We'll just go to the school to see her. We're sorry to bother you."

Mrs. Reynolds intercepted Brooke just as he reached for the door. "Please, Agent Madison. You can't do this."

Brooke frowned but kept a pleasant tone in his voice. "Do what, ma'am? We really only need five minutes with Tiffany, face-to-face. I can promise you, we don't want to do anything to hurt her."

Her lips formed a thin line. Tears ran down her face. She glanced at her sons, both sitting on the couch. Sam was shaking his head, but Ethan was still wincing in agony.

Brooke signaled for Drew to head out. He didn't seem to understand what was happening, but they turned to leave.

Mrs. Reynolds grabbed Drew's arm, stopping him. "Please. I'm begging you. Just sign the papers. I can get you more money. I'll give you everything. Just sign the papers."

Drew's eyes filled with compassion. He wanted to help her. He didn't yet understand.

"I'm sorry." Brooke placed his hand on the door but didn't open it. "Mr. Duncan is legally prohibited from even reading those papers until we close this out. I assure you this isn't a bargaining chip. The last thing Mr. Duncan or I want to do is hold this process hostage. We just need to do things right. We'll be in touch, maybe in a week after we speak to your daughter."

Brooke started to turn the handle. Inwardly, he gave her three seconds.

"You can't. Please, you need to…" Mrs. Reynolds began to sob, her body shaking in grief. "Please. You're her only hope. She's…"

Sam shot up from the sofa. *"Mom!"*

Mrs. Reynolds ignored him and placed her hand over Drew's chest. "You have to sign those papers and end this. I'm begging you. If you don't. She'll die. I'll lose my daughter, and you…"

She swallowed hard, gripping his shirt to hold on. Her lower lip trembled as tears welled in her eyes. "You have to help her. She's your sister."

Chapter Twenty-Two

Daddy Dearest

Drew staggered back, blinking. His eyes searched the faces around him, waiting for someone to tell him this punch to the gut was just a bad joke.

Finally, he allowed his gaze to settle on Brooke.

"I just found out as I pulled into the driveway earlier." Brooke stepped forward, keeping his arms at his sides. "I was going to tell you, but…"

Drew held up a hand to stop the rest. It was too much and he didn't have time to decide if he wanted to punch Brooke. He clenched his eyes shut and played it out in his head.

Frank Duncan wasn't his father? Bob Reynolds was? One bastard beat him senseless, tortured him and his sisters, and set him up to be raped. The other allowed him to be raised in that home and then did his damndest to frame him for the murder of Molly Winters.

He opened his eyes and jabbed a finger at Brooke. "We'll deal with this later."

Brooke just nodded.

"Mom?" Ethan tried to stand up, but his legs wobbled so badly that he fell back onto the couch again.

Mrs. Reynolds took a hesitant step towards her son, reaching out into the air. "I'm sorry Ethan. Your father told me they had gotten some drunk girl pregnant.

Several men had had sex with her. She was confused. She didn't even remember that night. Frank wasn't even there, but everyone knew he wanted her."

Brooke's eyes were moving as if reading. "We need to put that aside for now. Where is your daughter? Where's Tiffany?"

Mrs. Reynolds just wept and shook her head.

Sam stood up. "We don't know. They told us that she'd be let go after the investigation into who framed Drew was over. If you accepted it was my father acting alone." His face turned red and he clenched his fists as he spoke. "I told Dad to tell them to fuck off when they first told him to accept responsibility. They told him someone was going down and my father was top on the list. Some asshole made sure the investigation would point to him. Dad said he was toast, and that's why he…" He flinched, clearly remembering his father blowing his brains out. "We didn't know they had Tiff then. We found out the morning you came over."

Sam's face was red as his haunted eyes watered over. "I swear I wanted to demolish those assholes, but they had her. We saw…" He winced.

Ethan managed to stand. He put a comforting hand on his brother's shoulder. "They had a video. We get one every day. Proof of life they call it. She's in a dark room holding a newspaper."

"What paper?" Brooke asked.

Ethan frowned as if the words didn't make sense, but he pulled out his phone and tapped at the screen. "Um…it's a small publication. Here."

He handed the phone to Brooke who hit play on the screen. Drew walked over to watch.

Tiffany Reynolds was probably a pretty girl when

284

she didn't look terrified and exhausted beyond belief. Her dark hair was unkempt and she wore no makeup. Her hands shook as she held up a newspaper titled The Daily Journal. "I'm still alive. They haven't hurt me."

The bruise on her cheek and marks on her wrists told Drew that was a lie. She'd tried to escape and failed. They were keeping her tied up. She was scared, furious, and just devastated. "P-p-please get me out of here. All they need is some signed paperwork and they'll let me go." Her eyes closed. "I just want to come home, Mom. Ethan. Sam. Please help me." The video ended.

Drew scowled as he took the phone from Brooke. The urge to throw it against the wall was overwhelming. Bob Reynolds left him and his sisters in the care of a monster. He glared at Mrs. Reynolds. "Did your husband know I was his son when he tried to get me to take the fall for Molly?"

Mrs. Reynolds didn't answer, but she practically vibrated in place.

Her silence was all Drew needed. "Your husband tried his damndest to get me to take the fall for Molly Winters. I spent months in prison because of him. Do you have any idea what it was like in there for me? How much I've lost because of him?"

Mrs. Reynolds began to sob. "I didn't know I swear. I thought you were guilty. Maybe I wanted to believe it. I realized my husband wasn't the man I thought he was when I found out about you, but I stayed for my children."

She stepped closer, and tried to reach out, but faltered. "Hate me if you want to. I deserve it, but my daughter didn't do anything. She's innocent, and if you don't sign those papers, and get Chief Miller to shut down the investigation, Senator Brooke will have her killed."

Stalking across the room, Drew wanted to smash things. He wanted to scream. He needed to pound on something or someone.

Drew glanced at a small table that held trinkets and pictures. For a brief moment, he thought about breaking everything he saw on it. Until his eyes settled on a picture of Tiffany Reynolds.

Taken during her high school graduation, Tiffany's image smiled up at Drew. Her dark hair framed a pretty face, and she radiated hope and joy. Something nobody in his family ever had. Still, there was something about the shape of her eyes, the curve of her nose. She had blue eyes, with just a hint of sparkling grey.

Just like Kelli's.

He sighed. "I'll go get the papers and sign them now."

Drew started for the door, but Brooke stepped in his path. "Drew, if you sign those papers, you're signing Tiffany's death warrant."

Ethan struggled forward. "But... We've been promised. If you sign the paperwork and the investigation halts..." He swallowed hard. "He has no reason to kill her. She's just eighteen."

Brooke shook his head. "He won't take the chance that this gets out. If she's alive, she can talk. I wouldn't be surprised if he's got plans to take all of you out. He's desperate." He glanced toward Drew. "We can find out where she is. We'll do everything we can to get her home safely to you. He's doing this because he still thinks he has a future to protect." Brooke locked eyes with Drew. "He doesn't."

"Drew." Sam stepped hesitantly towards them. "I know I've been an ass. My brother has paid for all the stupid things I did, and now my sister..." He paused. "*Our* sister is suffering for everything my father did. Please, help her."

Forcing himself to swallow the bile rising in his throat, Drew pushed the hatred and anger down. "I'll do everything I can to find her and bring her home safely. I'm not losing another sister."

****

Tom Brook had barely stubbed out his cigarette before he was reaching for the pack he kept hidden in his desk drawer. He would have to change his suit before he left the office. It wouldn't do for him to stink like a common smoker as he pressed the flesh at a church group where he was to give a speech about taking back the streets from crime.

He read through his speech once more. It was an upper-class neighborhood, entirely white and just rich enough to make it worth his time. They wanted to hear how, when he became President, he'd keep them safe from the *wrong kind* of people. The speech never came out and said it, but they would be able to know that he understood who the wrong people were. As president, he'd let the police do the job that they were hired to do, and not be afraid of petty civil rights issues. After finishing his fifth readthrough of the speech, he closed the file and brought up another. In two days, he'd give another speech at the Baptist Church just outside of Albany. The topic was how to stop the horrible police from arresting and killing their sons, and how as their President, he'd stop the school-to-prison pipeline. Neither speech would be recorded, so it was fine if he completely contradicted himself in each. As long as he got the money from the first and the legitimacy from the second, he was happy.

As he tweaked a few words here or there, he did his best to resist clicking on the open browser he'd minimized in the bottom corner, but when he found himself rereading the same paragraph a third time, he gave in.

He breathed out smoke through his nostrils, as he flicked through the static IP addresses, each one set up on a different closed-circuit camera. He skipped one, as he didn't want to see her. He'd known her since she was a baby, and he didn't take any pleasure in the terror she must be feeling. Nor would he when he gave the okay to end her. If he stopped to think about it, it made him sick to his stomach. Which is why he didn't want to think about it. Instead, he stopped at the image of the front gate, more than a mile away from the front doors. Everything was fine.

And it would stay that way. He'd worked too hard for this. Made too many deals, stabbed too many people in the back. He couldn't lose now.

Someone gently knocked on the door. "Senator."

Smoke billowed out of his mouth as he sighed. "Yes, Bill."

The door opened. "There's someone here to see you. Said you'd want him to come right back."

Tom frowned. "Elijah isn't supposed to be here for another two hours. Is he early?" Even as he spoke, he knew it wouldn't be his chief campaign officer.

Bill shook his head. "It's an FBI agent. Brooke Madison."

Tom's heart started to slam in his chest. He felt an

icy chill in his veins and he started to sweat. "I'm not speaking to him. If the FBI wants to interview me, they can go through proper channel and speak with my lawyer. Get Elijah Bellows on the line."

Bill didn't move to do as he was told, but he shifted in place. He presented as a man worried about being the bearer of bad news. "Senator…" He ran his finger under his collar. "Agent Madison says he's not here in an official capacity. He's here as…"

Bill swallowed hard, causing Tom to rise from his chair. "Spit it out, Bill."

Stiffening, Bill managed to blurt out the rest of his message. "He says he's here as your son."

Tom Brook froze, unable to move or breathe.

Son of a fucking bitch.

"I don't have a son." Tom crashed back into the chair.

Tom wasn't worried about Bill. A little extra under the table, and he'd send his own mother up the river. "Yes sir, but that's what he said. Should I still call Elijah?"

Images flashed in his mind. Would Elijah still work with him? Not if he knew the full extent of what was going on. He needed to know what Madison wanted. God damn it, if he was his son, hopefully, he'd be open to reason. Or a fucking bribe.

"No. Just…" Tom looked around his desk. He quickly put the ashtray away in the top drawer. "Bring him in, but make sure he isn't wearing a wire. You can do that, right?"

Bill nodded, but he didn't make eye contact. "Of course, sir."

Closing his eyes, Tom willed himself to calm down.

He needed to slip into the skin of the practiced politician. Every man had their price. He was about to find out what Agent Madison's was.

Another knock at the door. Tom took a deep breath; he was the future President of the United States. He needed to exude authority. His tongue flicked out to lick his lips before he answered. "Come."

The door opened and Bill entered first. "Special Agent Brooke Madison, Senator Brook."

Inwardly, Tom cringed at the man's first name, as he entered. Madison took after his mother in many ways. That light shade of brown, with the face that could grace the cover of a magazine. But his blue eyes, the same eyes all of Tom's children had, were his.

"Thank you, Bill. How can I help you, Agent Madison?"

Brooke entered the room, holding eye contact with the Senator until Tom looked away. Bill quickly retreated from the room.

Tom gestured towards a chair in front of his enormous desk. "Please, Agent Madison, sit down."

The hint of a smile played across Brooke's face for just a moment. "Thank you, but I'd rather stand. Is it normal procedure to have your men confiscate cell phones and scan FBI agents for wires?"

Tom felt weak in the knees, but he'd be damned if he'd sit while Madison stood above him. "As you know, I'm running for president. I need to control the narrative of everything that comes out."

"So, you would do that to any member of the bureau coming to see you, not just the son you've never acknowledged."

Tom stiffened. Should he deny it? Act surprised?

"Don't bother." Brooke pulled out an envelope and tossed it on the gigantic desk that stood between them. "Those are the DNA results. You really shouldn't leave pens behind after putting them in your mouth. Funny, isn't it? I never see you or any politician smoking in public, but clearly, you're a pack-a-day smoker. Smells like you were chain-smoking in here before. You'll have a fresh suit to put on, that's kept in another room, but it only masks the scent a little. You reek of it, but you've gotten so used to the smell, you don't notice it. Your staff...Bill was it?" Brooke glanced momentarily at the door. "He's too used to the money and too fearful of you to tell you differently, but his bought loyalty is wearing thin."

Tom narrowed his eyes. "Everyone has a vice, but it doesn't make good copy to allow people to see it. As for Bill, he's loyal. I pay him more than enough to ensure that."

"Every man has his price?" Brooke grinned, almost amused. "But does that purchased loyalty have a limit? When the shit hits the fan, will he go down by your side? Or turn on you?"

Tom refused to allow the images of Bill, Elijah, or any of his other staff turning state's evidence against him to enter his mind. "What makes you think the shit is going to hit the fan?"

Sighing as if he were tired of explaining himself to a simpleton, Brooke reached into his pants pocket and pulled out a USB drive. "Because I don't know how much longer I can keep this from the bumbling Ember Falls Police Department, let alone the bureau." He held the drive dangling on a string out to Tom, who stared at it as if were a snake about to bite. "You'll want to see this. Relive a father-son bonding moment."

Tom reached out his hand but didn't take the drive. "I don't have any sons. Just two daughters."

Brooke arched an eyebrow and pulled the drive away. "You had *three* daughters until Diana Lakeland met an untimely death in the courtroom. Did you know her last word was 'father'? Even though she was raised by a single mother. As far as sons go, I wasn't talking about myself, but I suspect you know that." He held the drive up once more.

Brooke leaned forward, allowing Tom to study his eyes.

He wasn't going to stop now. "I'm assuming this isn't the only copy."

Brooke spread his hands out. "You would assume correctly. It's also not the only bit of information I was able to get off of Edward's computer up at the old Tice warehouse. It took me fucking all day to download it all, and then wipe the servers. The bureau arrives tomorrow to go over that place, unearth all of Edward's victims and go through that place with a fine-tooth comb."

Tom was livid, but there was a part of him that was proud that Brooke was taking his time, laying it out. There was evidence, that much was clear. Still, he should have sent it all to his superiors the moment he discovered it, and clearly, that hadn't happened.

Brooke started to stroll about the office, examining plaques on the wall, books on his shelves, and knickknacks all around. He moved as if he'd been in this place a thousand times before, and he and Tom were thick as thieves. "I thought of just pulling out the stuff relating to you, but decided that would have been too time-consuming, and suspicious. This way, it looks like

Edward wiped his drives before he left. I've been going over it myself. I imagine I've just scratched the surface of all the crap he has on you. Why in the world did you let him set up those shell companies?"

Tom frowned but allowed himself to relax. Madison was here to deal. "In retrospect, that had been a mistake, but Edward was so good with that sort of thing. By the time I realized how much of a menace he was, it was too late."

Brooke nodded casually as he made his way to the front of the desk. "He didn't bleed you dry. You gave nearly as much over the years to Diana as you did to Edward. Did she have something on you, or was that just you trying to be a good dad?"

And here we go. Hurt feelings, and an empty pocket. "At first, it was just because I wanted to do the right thing. I tried to be there for her, but it was difficult. She wanted me to acknowledge her, and I couldn't do that. Every once in a while, she'd comment on what a shame it would be if she had to sell her story to get through college. I realized she was just like all women. They'd screw you to keep you paying. So, I paid."

Brooke didn't appear offended or surprised. If anything, he seemed amused. "She paid in the end, though. I am curious why you didn't have Edward tie up that particular loose end. Did you think he'd balk at the idea of killing his half-sister?"

Tom scoffed. "Please. He didn't need any incentive to murder his mother. I never asked for that, even if it did solve a big issue for me. I just didn't think it was a good idea to put him back into Ember Falls. Not while Cole Duncan was there. There's something about that kid that just gets Edward going."

Tom sat back in the chair, feeling more at ease. This was his element. "Please. Sit. You've gone to a lot of trouble to help me, and I appreciate it. I'm sure we can come to an understanding. I'd like to know what you'd like to get from me."

Brooke didn't sit. Crossing his arms, he scowled. "What I'd like is to know why you decided to have a relationship with two of your illegitimate children, and not me? You connected yourself with Diana who kidnapped a child and played a hand in murdering Kelly. You've got some sort of relationship with your son Edward Hunter, a serial killer. But I had to work out on my own that you were my father. It was more of a hunch before I came back to Ember Falls, but as it turns out, it was correct. I get not wanting to announce me to the world, but you didn't publicly embrace Diana or Edward. Was it just because of my skin color?"

Without missing a beat, Tom shook his head. "Of course not, Brooke. Can I call you Brooke?"

Brooke gave him a nonchalant, half-shrug. "It's the name my mother gave me. She figured since I couldn't share your last name, she'd claim it as my first."

Not knowing what to say to that, Tom opened his desk drawer and pulled out a pack of cigarettes and an ashtray. He offered one to Brooke who shook his head.

Tom lit one and took a drag. "You need understand that your mother was intoxicating to be with, but she has her demons. She'd get crazy when she was high. Threaten me. And she'd get angry whenever I came around and then left, so it was smarter to not be around her. I know I should have done more for you, but she assured me she would take care of you with the money I gave her."

Brooke leaned on his desk. "Well, she smoked most of what you gave her. She barely had enough to make rent on that shithole of a trailer. I was working to buy food by the time I was fourteen. She went downhill just as I turned nine."

Tom forced a sympathetic look onto his face. "That would have been just about the time when I stopped coming around. It was selfish of me, but I'd hoped she was taking good care of you. I hadn't realized how bad she'd gotten." He closed his eyes and counted to three, which seemed long enough to emulate caring. "I'm truly sorry Brooke. I should have checked up on you. It was selfish, and I'd like to make it up to you. I can't acknowledge you as my son, but that doesn't mean you and I can't have some sort of relationship. And of course, I feel as if I owe you for all the years I wasn't there. May I ask, when did you figure all of this out?" He took a long drag.

Brooke pursed his lips as he considered. "That you were my father? It first occurred to me when I was still in high school. Mom had disappeared for a few days. It had happened before, but this was longer than normal. When she finally showed up, she was…" Brooke winced at the memory, "amused that I was so concerned. Until she realized I'd bothered some of her favorite guys that she hung with. A couple were married and it didn't go over well. I asked if any of them were my father, and she said no. 'I gave your father's name to you the only way I could.' " Brooke shrugged. "I wrestled with that for a few months, until I saw you get elected to Senator. That's when it clicked. I wasn't sure. Never asked because I knew she'd lie. Then I left Ember Falls and left it all behind me."

Brooke finally sat down. Glancing off to the side, he took in a deep breath, letting it out slowly. "I still didn't know. I had no way of really knowing if it was right or just some crazy idea. Then when the old sheriff of Ember Falls died in bed, handcuffed to two underage male prostitutes, the rumors about an underage sex club for the rich and powerful started."

Senator Brooke wagged a finger at Brooke. "Those were quashed."

Brook smirked. "Yes, they were. Very quickly. Too quickly. It was enough to make me revisit the idea and do the math."

Tom sat back, his lit cigarette hovering an inch from his lips. "Math?"

Brooke glanced over and Tom could see his own eyes in the young agent's face. "When my mom was young, she would have been just around the right age for you as a local politician to have been," Brooke made imaginary quotation marks in the air, "*introduced* to my mother. I guessed that at the time the club wasn't as organized as it was in later years. It occurred to me that someone like yourself might have seen an opportunity. Introduce up-and-coming elected politicians to a few girls or boys who were willing to entertain them. Prostitution was already illegal, but if someone failed to mention that a few of the participants weren't quite of legal age, that would really help you keep everyone in line. You did have a reputation for getting by bi-partisan cooperation on important bills."

Tom took a long drag, studying Brooke through the billows of smoke. "I suppose that would be smart for anyone who might have been a part of that. To build that sort of black market sex ring." He kept his face passive as he spoke, choosing his words carefully.

"Very smart." Brooke leaned forward, a small grin tugging at the corners of his mouth. "Smart enough to bring this very divided country together. A person who may have made a few questionable choices, but used them to do a lot of good."

Locking eyes with Brooke, Tom felt the knots in his stomach unravel. "You do understand the position I'm in. I was in a situation I hadn't asked for, but I did the best I could with it."

Brooke nodded. "Senator, I need to be honest with you. I'm vulnerable in this myself now. If it were to come out that you were my father, and that I knew about it, it would be the end of my career with the bureau. Let alone what will happen to me once they find out that Edward Hunter is my half-brother." Brooke let out a hollow laugh. "I'm in the same position you were when Hunter killed his mother, clearly without your knowledge. I fucked up, and now I'm in some trouble myself."

Tom's eyebrows raised. *Maybe he had a little leverage here.* "Oh? In what way?"

Brooke slouched in his chair. "I was obligated to turn in everything I know. I should have called my superiors and taken myself off the case, but I didn't. I just thought, he *should* be nothing to me, but dammit, he *is* my father. And now, there's no going back for me, so I need to make sure this doesn't blow up. I can deal with the investigation into who framed Drew. Talk Drew through accepting that Reynolds acted on his own. Blame a little on the old Police Chief. The hitman Jericho has to be put on Reynolds." Brooke paused. "That component we recovered from Jericho's laptop made it out to be Reynolds. I knew there was a reason a professional like Jericho was so sloppy that he left parts of the motherboard undamaged. What we need to talk about is Reynolds' family. Specifically, Tiffany. Where is she and what are your plans with her."

Tom narrowed his eyes. "Why would you think anything has happened to Tiffany?"

Brooke exchanged a knowing look with Tom as if they were both in on a private joke. "I've had to earn my way through the world. I'm very good at what I do. I'm not some country bumpkin cop who's used to writing tickets for hunting out of season. Do I need to spell it out for you?"

With a smile that could easily win a presidential race, Tom spread his hands out in an inviting gesture. "Please."

Rolling his eyes, Brooke continued. "Fine. I guess it's not a bad idea for you to see what an ally I can be. I've profiled Edward Hunter, formally Edward Tice. He's transitioning to a spree killer. He knows there's no way he's going to get away, and he's prepared to go down in a blaze of glory. I wouldn't be surprised if he told you that. He had his systems set up to upload all of his files, videos of him killing dozens of women, including Molly Winters, to several press outlets. He has it set so it will send if he doesn't remotely change the time, this way if he gets killed you go down."

Tom scowled. Edward had been the one wildcard that Tom hadn't figured out how to control. He had someone on the manhunt who was supposed to try and take him down, but there was always the possibility that someone would capture him first.

Brooke continued. "I watched her being killed on

video. She told him how she was blackmailing you, among a few others. She gave him the location of a recording she made of you and her indulging in some behavior that would not go down well on the campaign trail. I guess Mrs. Brooks is only into traditional sex?"

Tom remained calm, outwardly. Inside, he wanted to start tearing his office apart and kill Brooke Madison. But the son of a bitch was dead on, and he wasn't even threatening blackmail outright. *Yet.*

"She's not much into sex." Tom shrugged. "A man has needs, but what I did with Molly was cruel."

Brooke held his hands up. "Hey, I'm not judging. Everything you did with her I imagine she did with plenty of other guys. Nothing that's not a healthy indulgence between two adults. Of course, technically speaking, Molly wasn't a legal adult when you two started, but she was hardly innocent."

Gesturing with authority, as if he were on a debate stage, Tom shook his head. "I had no way of knowing how old she was the first time. After that, well…"

Brooke shrugged. "I get it. She was making you pay; you might as well enjoy the ride. No worries. I don't have a lot of sympathy for Molly. Not after what she put Drew through. I do want to make sure that Drew and Cole are taken care of. Just like you, I want something positive to come out of all of this. Are you sure the Reynolds family can afford the terms of the settlement? Will you make sure they actually pay him?"

With his hands flat on the desk, Tom nodded. "I'll make sure he'll get what he's due. I meant what I said to him. It's time for healing."

Brooke seemed to relax. "I know you've probably got more than six degrees of separation between you and

Tiffany, but they know. She'll go public, and that will end your political career. Even if she can't prove it for prosecution reasons, that mud will stick. And I'm not telling you anything you haven't already thought of. But taking out an entire family is going to be much harder than taking out my sister Diana. Much stickier. Unless you've got a plan in place, I think I know a way to help."

Tom relaxed as he took a long drag. "Oh? How's that?"

Brooke leaned forward. "You remember the guys who worked over Ethan Reynolds?"

Tom closed his eyes for a moment, trying to project sympathy and pity. "It breaks my heart what he went through."

As smoke billowed between them, Brooke sat back. "James and Joseph Sullivan who Sam had screwed over in a drug deal, grabbed the wrong brother to torture. Imagine if the both of them somehow escaped and decided to find Sam, the brother they *meant* to get. Of course, Sam's at home with his family, so this time they end up taking them all out. Somehow, the police will come and of course kill James and Joseph, because we can't have any survivors. I've done my homework. You have connections in the Capital Region Penitentiary? How hard would for the pair of them to..." Brooke smiled, "escape?"

Tom took a long drag as he considered. "Warden Brasswell owes me a few favors, plus he knows if this blows up it will take him down too." He blew out smoke. "I might be able to convince him, but he'll want to know what's in it for him. I'm sure I could grease his palm a little."

"Brasswell...Brasswell..." Brooke scowled as he

rubbed his chin. "I'm pretty sure I saw his name in Edward's files. What was his type?"

Tom laughed out more smoke. "He didn't have one. Not really. It was more about what he could do with them."

Staring off into the corner, Brooke squinted his eyes as if he were trying to read very small print. "Oh, that's right. He was more into degradation than anything else. Some of the crap he did even Edward found disgusting. Not the stuff where the good warden hurt the girls, Edward far surpassed him there. It was more of the…" His lip curled in disgust. "Ways he used natural body functions to humiliate them. To say he was into some nasty shit would be not only an understatement but also rather accurate."

Tom took one last drag before snuffing out the cigarette. "Yeah. I never got any of that stuff. He'd brag about it." Tom shrugged. "We'll need to protect him too."

Brooke pressed his lips together. "I remember his videos. Couldn't watch them. Jesus, he did a number on some of those girls. He's obsessed and he's not going to stop unless someone stops him. He's in a position of power over a lot of people. You know a personality like that, he's abusing them."

Tom leaned forward. "They're not all innocent like your buddy Drew Duncan."

Brooke stood and paced. "But they're still people. I don't have much use for privileged assholes like the Reynolds. They got it coming, but most of the people in his custody don't. I just…" Brooke closed his eyes.

Tom could see the internal struggle. Brooke wasn't quite as ready to let go of morals to do what needed to be done. He needed a push. "We could tell him part of the deal to get rid of those files is to resign. He retires on his nice, comfy pension, and then if he continues, you'll deal with him. Think about what kind of good we can do, son. Especially if I'm in the White House."

Shaking his head, Brooke walked back to the desk. He stood with his arms folded, a scowl etched on his face. "He'll need to be dealt with. Harshly. I can give him a few months, but he won't stop. He might even be worse. But yeah, we can lose those files. We'll have to if we want his help."

Heaving out a breath, Brooke sat back down. "We need to move quickly. Edward is still a wild card, so we have to get everything else in place before he's caught. We need to keep those recordings as leverage until his part is done. We have to rush this through so he, or anyone else, doesn't have time to piece it together. Everyone will just be interested in covering their own asses. Where is Tiffany? We need to have her ready. We should do this today or tomorrow."

"She's close." Tom glanced at his computer screen. He still had the window with the live feed minimized. "Shouldn't we get Brasswell onboard first?" He studied Brooke, searching for signs of deception.

"Makes sense." Brooke pulled out a small USB. He held it up by a string. "I've got the files here. You can send it to him so he sees he doesn't have a choice."

Tom reached forward and took the device. Holding it, his eyes met Brooke's. A surge of power channeled through him as if this tiny, black USB gave him control over his fate.

Edward had boasted about how he had dirt on powerful people, even joking once that eventually at least one of them would probably end up in the White House. It wouldn't surprise him if there was something on some of the other candidates who were throwing their hats in the ring.

Brooke Madison had just handed him the keys to 1600 Pennsylvania Ave.

Unable to suppress his grin, Tom plugged the USB into his computer and opened up the files inside. He glanced up at Brooke, wondering if the idiot realized that once he was no longer useful, he'd have to be eliminated.

Something about the way Brooke was watching him made Tom's blood run cold. The young agent studied him. His deep blue eyes felt as if they could read his mind and see into his soul. Despite wearing a very expensive suit reeking of cigarette smoke, Tom felt naked in his son's gaze.

Something beeped on his laptop, and Tom's eyes went to the screen. A single text popped open.

"You have the right to remain silent. Anything you say can and will be used against you in a court of law. You have the right to an attorney. If you cannot afford an attorney, one will be provided for you. Do you understand the rights I have just read to you? With these rights in mind, do you wish to speak to me?"

Brooke rose from his seat. Reaching into his pocket, he pulled out a warrant that gave them the right to search the Senator's Electronics. He repeated the Miranda Warning as he tossed it on Tom's desk.

Tom didn't glance up. His face had gone pale, and his eyes moved back and forth as if he were reading the screen over and over again. His head started to shake as if he were saying no, but he remained mute.

"Senator Brook, do you understand what I've just

told you? I need you to answer." Brooke took a step closer.

Tom's hand ripped out the USB. His breath came out in heaves as he reached for the keyboard and typed in a code. He waited. Did it again. "What the hell?"

Brooke picked up the string of the USB. "Don't bother. That thing took about five seconds to switch off any auto-delete program you had. What it needed to do, it did. My colleague is currently looking through your files. It won't take him long to find out where you've been keeping Tiffany Reynolds. You could tell us now, and maybe try and spin that you cooperated with us, but I'd say you don't have more than a minute or two."

With a shaking hand, Tom loosened his tie. "We can make a deal. If I go down, everyone at the Bureau will know you investigated your own father. They won't believe that it wasn't for personal reasons. You'll lose your shield."

Brooke nodded. "Probably. I made my peace with that fact. I already filed the report. So yes, this might end my career. It *will* end yours. That works for me. Now, where is Tiffany Reynolds?"

Tom jumped up from his chair. "Do you know who I am?" His face went red as he leaned on his desk. "Do you know the people I'm friends with?"

Brooke shrugged. "I don't think *you* know who you're friends with. You have people who might owe you favors, but friends? Your buddy Bill? He knew what I was here for. He didn't warn you because he knew you were done for. You don't have any friends. You have accomplices. You have 'yes men,' and henchmen, and all sorts of people who will do your bidding. But how many people do you think are going to stand by your side when they know you orchestrated the murder of a single mother who had escaped an abusive home with her young child? That you helped frame her brother years ago for murder to cover up a teen girl who was blackmailing you? That you killed Diana, your own daughter, just to keep her quiet?"

Brooke leaned down on the desk, putting himself right in the senator's face. "You're going to watch all of your so-called friends scurry off and pretend like they never liked you much. Me? I'll be okay. One way or the other."

Brooke and Tom glared at each other, hatred pouring out of their eyes. "I should have made your mother abort you. I just didn't think you'd matter."

A small grin spread over Brooke's face. "Sucks for you that at least today, I did matter."

The door behind them opened. Ollie stepped in. "Jacob has the location of Tiffany. He's got a live feed of her location up on his computer."

Brooke reached over to turn the laptop around. He touched the screen on one of the minimized windows and a new screen popped up, showing a home on a long road. A few seconds later, the scene changed to a pair of guards playing cards. He watched as it continued to cycle through live images from static IP Addresses, until it finally shifted to one of a young woman, curled up on a bed, crying.

Tom Brook collapsed into the chair, took a deep breath, and closed his eyes. He knew it was over.

"You should go." Ollie pointed to the door. "Jacob already has the location of the house. It's down by the lake, past the cliffs where those idiots dive off of. Someone needs to stay with the Senator until State shows up to take him into custody. It should be me."

Brooke frowned as he headed to the door. He knew that Ollie meant it shouldn't be the Senator's illegitimate son and it sure couldn't be Drew who was likely to tear Ember Fall's former mayor to pieces for destroying his life.

"Just sit tight and keep an eye on the monitor." Brooke opened the door. "Oh, and Senator?"

He waited until Tom glanced up, defeat reflected in his eyes.

"I hope you don't mind, but I don't think I'll be able to visit you in prison this Father's Day."

Chapter Twenty-Three

No Good Deed

Peter Criscuola took the turn on Fall's Creek Road a little too fast, but it felt good. He was pissed. He had a right to be pissed. He'd been working the same stupid job for over a decade now, and his managers got on his back because he was five minutes late coming back from break. It was the first time in years he'd been late, and they knew it because they would have chewed him out each time. He made his numbers, month after month, and they couldn't cut him some slack because his upset stomach had caused him not to be able to get back to his desk in exactly fifteen minutes? They were half the reason he had an upset stomach half the time.

His red Buick careened another corner, the tires squealing in protest.

The speed of the drive felt good. So did the hard and heavy guitar that wailed through his speakers, while his dashboard shook with the pounding of the drums. He had his favorite playlist ripping out so loud that he jumped when the phone rang through his Bluetooth. The name Beth appeared on his dash.

"Peter, where are you?"

Peter sighed as he blasted down the highway. "I'm just driving. I got written up at work today. Late from break by one and a half minutes. Pissed me off. They started to do the same thing to Tony last year, remember? They got rid of him. They want us all out cause we're union and they want to hire nonunion."

The was a pause from the other end of the phone. "I hate your job, and what it does to you. Just try to calm down. I hate to think you're going to get into an accident because you're going eighty miles per hour just because you're angry."

Glancing at the speedometer, Peter saw he was actually at eighty-five. His foot eased off the gas and his speed started to reduce. "I'll be fine. I thought you were still at your mom's, or I would have come straight home."

Peter took a right, thankful that his speed had decreased enough not to cause the tires to squeal again. He was in the area just north of Ember Falls where the super-large homes sat on acres of land. His second-hand Buick was very out of place.

"I just got home. I can't even think about cooking, so maybe you could pick something up for dinner?"

Peter tensed. Beth loved to cook. "Is something wrong?"

"Nothing except the fact that I have a really strong craving for Lasagna from Mario's. Along with a nice, big slice of their chocolate fudge cake. I don't suppose you could pick that up for us. I know little Andrew or Christina wants it too, as the little punk is kicking at my bladder every five minutes."

The picture of Beth with her hand on her stomach eating lasagna forced the last remnants of tension to melt away. He slowed down deliberately to match the speed limit and laughed. "I'll be there as soon as possible. Might take me a bit. I made it all the way to the Heights.

Why don't you call in two orders of that, and I'll… *Shit*!"

Peter slammed on the breaks. His heart jumped into his throat, as the tires protested the sudden stop. The smell of burnt rubber filled the car as Peter's breath heaved, knowing that had he not slowed down because of Beth's call, he never would have stopped on time.

"Peter, what is it? Are you okay?"

Peter reversed the car up slowly, so he could survey the scene better. "I'm fine. I had to stop short. Someone is lying on the road. I didn't hit them. I better go check on them, maybe call an ambulance. Shit, I think it's just a kid."

"Oh my God, should I call the police?" Beth's voice crackled with fear as Peter shut the engine off.

With the Bluetooth connection disconnected, Peter reached for his phone which was clipped to a holder on the dashboard. "He hasn't moved. I'm sure I didn't hit him, but something must be wrong. Yeah, call for an ambulance. I'm going to go check on him."

With shaking hands, Peter wrestled with his seatbelt until he managed to hit release. He opened the door and approached, taking his phone with him. He could hear Beth using the landline at the house to speak with a 911 operator.

At first, it appeared as if the kid might have simply dropped dead in the middle of the street, but Peter was even more certain now that he hadn't hit him. His clothes were wrinkled, filthy, and torn. There was no blood. And there was movement.

The boy's chest was rising and falling in panicked short breaths. His limbs were trembling from adrenaline shooting through him. Kid was scared. Peter couldn't blame him. Was he just screwing around and didn't expect to have a car nearly hit him? Now he was simply frozen in fear? If so, Peter might just strangle the kid himself after he hugged him, grateful that he was okay. Why would a boy of, what was he? Nine or ten? Shit, what did he know? Either way, it was too young to have a death wish.

Inching his way forward, part of Peter expected the boy to leap up and bolt. If that happened, Peter wouldn't chase him. He'd wait for the police. "Hey, kid, you're okay. I didn't hit you."

The boy didn't respond or even open his eyes, but the trembling increased. He wasn't just rattled from a prank that went bad, this kid was terrified. There was also something odd about the way he was lying, with his feet close together, his hands folded on his chest.

"Peter." Beth's voice coming from his cell made him jump. "What's going on? Is he all right?"

Peter didn't answer right away. His eyes focused on the kid's hands. They were bound with plastic ties. Peter's gaze traveled down to the boy's ankles, where another plastic tie kept him immobile. The kid's eyes weren't just closed, but clenched shut, tears still managing to escape from beneath his eyelids.

"Peter! What's happening?" Beth's voice crackled with desperation.

Peter knelt by the kid.

The child whimpered in fear as his tear-filled eyes burst open. His bottle lip trembled madly as the boy glanced first at Peter, then over his shoulder. "I'm s-s-sorry."

Peter frowned in confusion.

Pain cracked into Peter's skull. Something had hit him from behind, knocking him forward. He fell face-first onto the boy's chest. The kid was begging someone to stop as a hand grabbed Peter's hair and pulled his head back.

"Peter, what's going on." Beth's voice screamed from the cell which was now on the ground. "The police will be there in less than five minutes. Peter? *Peter*!"

A voice carried by hot breath that reeked of cigarettes whispered in his ear. "We need to take your car. I'm going to need your help with something… Peter is it?"

Peter wanted to fight, but he was too disoriented to move. "Take the car. Leave the kid."

The desperate pleas from the mother of his unborn child were the last thing Peter heard as he felt someone wrap their arm around their neck and twist so fast his neck snapped.

Chapter Twenty-Four

The Man with the Happy Face Shirt

Tiffany Reynolds pulled her knees up to her chest and tried to ignore the growing stabs of hunger in her stomach. It wasn't as if they'd been starving her, but they often took their damn time bringing her food.

When she'd woken up in this room, she'd been so groggy that she was sure she'd been drugged. She always heard about college guys slipping something into your drink, but the male students she hung out with would never do something like that, nor would they let someone take advantage of her. It wasn't until her mind cleared that she realized she wasn't even at the college anymore.

She hadn't been allowed to leave the small room since. There was no window. The only light source was a lamp without a lampshade with a dim bulb. She couldn't tell if the sheets were white or grey, but they were stale and dusty. There was a small bathroom, but the door had been removed. There was no TV, books, or magazine to read or much of anything to do.

There was a camera, placed in the high corner of the room, opposite the cot where she slept. On her first day, she threatened whoever was watching her from the other side of that camera to set her free. Threatening soon turned into pleading, which quickly devolved into begging. After the first few days, she'd just ignored it.

Mostly, she'd slept. Sometimes she'd paced. Once in a while, she'd try to get some exercise, but since there was no shower, just a small sink in the bathroom with no door, she didn't want to get too sweaty.

When they brought her food, it was simple, barely edible, and just enough to keep her alive. A single scrambled egg in the morning, a small ham sandwich with no condiments for lunch, and four nuked chicken nuggets for dinner. They had forgotten lunch twice and dinner three times, but never breakfast.

Since there was no clock in the room, it was impossible to know if it was lunchtime or not, but she was so hungry that she hoped that a sandwich would be coming anytime now. It would be delivered by a large man wearing a ski mask and a black suit.

She knew there were different men. She could tell by their build, hands, and eyes. She'd been sure there had been at least seven different men: three White, two Black, one of mixed race, and one Hispanic. Most said nothing. They simply pointed a gun at her with one hand and handed her a plate with the other. One of the men stayed on her second night, watched her eat, then after she'd finished, reached down as if he was going to take the plate. Instead, he groped her and offered to entertain her for a while.

She'd scrambled away. The masked creep had shrugged, laughed, and left. She'd barely made it to the toilet before she'd thrown up the meager meal she'd just eaten.

The masked creep had returned several times since. Sometimes, Masked Creep didn't bother her. Once he came in and exposed his ugly dick to her, stroking it. Another time, he brought her a small rose. She flushed it down the toilet the moment he'd left.

The door handle jiggled. Someone was unlocking it. When it swung open, she knew it was him. She froze, praying he would just give her the food and leave.

"Sorry, we're late, sweetheart." Masked Creep kicked the door shut and closed the distance to her. Holding out the plate, he grinned from beneath the mask. He held the gun in his right hand and a plate in his left.

Tiffany took the plate and placed it on the small table close to the bed. She wouldn't eat with him in the room while tidal waves of nausea threatened to overtake her. She didn't want to waste a meal by purging it from her system.

Masked Creep moved closer and her eyes moved down to see his fly was open. She could tell he was partially erect, but he hadn't pulled himself out.

Yet.

"I so much want to give you just a little bit of joy in your last few days. If only you'd let me." His left hand pressed hard against his crotch for a moment. "Sooner or later, you're not going to have a choice. But I've got a poker game to get back to. Try not to miss me too much sweetheart."

With a laugh, Masked Creep backed away, opened the door, and left.

The moment the door clicked closed, a strangled sob escaped. She'd known for some time they were most likely going to kill her.

She concentrated on her breathing, trying to stop herself from shaking. She was so hungry, but if she scarfed down that sandwich now, she'd probably retch.

Just as the tremors started to subside, she heard the doorknob jingle again.

What the fuck? He's never come back in so quickly before. No, she wasn't going to let him.

The door swung open and Masked Creep stepped in, walking backward. Only now Masked Creep was unmasked and not laughing.

Another man followed wearing a white t-shirt with a giant yellow happy face on it. He was large, with cruel eyes and a nasty grin that contrasted with the one on his shirt. In his right hand, he held a gun which was aimed at the now unmasked man's chest. In his left hand, he held a long chain that stretched out to the hallway.

Was he here to rescue her?

Something about the way his deep blue eyes looked at her as if she was a meal he was about to tear into, told her the situation had just gotten worse. "Hello, Tiffany. You've been the guest of my father, Senator Brook, for the last several weeks. I'm sorry that it's taken me this long to get here, but it'll be worth it."

With a sneer, he pulled the trigger. Tiffany screamed as Masked Creep crashed back into the small table. He fell to the floor, blood gushing out of his throat where the bullet had ripped through him. His eyes stared, pleading with Tiffany to do something for a moment before the life drained out of him.

The man who killed him yanked the chain he held and a small boy who was shaking even more than Tiffany stumbled into the room. "My name is Edward Hunter. Perhaps you've heard of me?"

****

Brooke kept his eyes on the road and didn't glance at his passenger as he navigated through the streets. Chief Miller had contacted a friend of hers in the nearby town and arraigned for a police team to meet them at

Senator Brook's home, but they wouldn't leave until the warrant came in. Jacob was working on it, and it should be any moment now.

Drew sighed as they passed a group of kids playing tag football. "I hope this doesn't become a shooting match. Those guys in there have to all know they're screwed the moment we show up. If they try to fight their way out, Tiffany could get hurt."

Brooke winced as he saw two of the kids try to catch the ball and smash into each other. They hit the ground and sat up a moment later laughing. "We'll take care. We're not going to let anything happen to…" Brooke frowned. "I almost said your sister, but I'm not sure how you feel about that."

Drew shook his head. "Yeah, neither am I. Probably a lot better about that than knowing that Sam Reynolds is my brother." He closed his eyes. "He was an ass in high school, and I assumed he'd be the same throughout the rest of his life, but all he wants is to make things right with Ethan, and get his sister back. Ollie cut me a break and forgave me for being an ass to him when we were kids. Maybe I should do the same for Sam?"

Brooke was about to offer words of encouragement when the blue tooth in the car signaled an incoming call from Jacob. Brooke pressed the phone key on the steering wheel. "Jacob. I'm assuming you've got my no-knock warrant and my backup is on their way to the Reynolds place?"

"Yes, to both, but we've got a problem." There was just enough tension in Jacob's voice to tell Brooke it was big. "It's Hunter. He's there in the house."

Brooke slammed on the gas. The car surged forward. "What? How the fuck…He was last seen near the Ohio border." Brooke's eyes moved back and forth as he did some quick calculations in his head. "He must have driven nearly all night. Fuck? Why head to his father's place? What…" He put the car in drive and slammed on the gas. "He wants Tiffany. Jacob, we're less than three minutes out. How long until my backup arrives?"

"They're on the way. Thirty minutes."

Brooke took a turn so fast that the tires squealed. "We're not waiting."

****

Tiffany winced as she heard more gunshots from within the house. She ran to the door, but it was locked. She knew there was a thick padlock on the other side. Turning she saw the small boy curled up in a fetal position on the ground. He had his thumb in his mouth and was trembling like a leaf.

Her hunger forgotten, she knelt by the small child. Gently she reached out to touch him. He jumped. The whimper he let out broke her heart. "Hey. I'm not going to hurt you. My name is Tiffany. What's your name?"

She softly stroked his hair and waited.

"C-C-Cameron." He slowly sat up. His face was streaked with tears. "I'm sorry."

Tiffany tried to untangle the chain from around his wrists. "You didn't do anything."

Cameron winced as the thin metal chain cut into his skin. "He's going to kill you. Badly. He'll make me watch. I won't be able to stop him." He closed his eyes tightly.

Tiffany examined the way the chains wrapped around his wrists. His hands were so small, and the chain wasn't very thick. If she had something, it would bend.

317

Cameron choked back a sob. "I-I can't stop him. He's gonna k-k-kill me too. It's my fault."

"Hey." Tiffany's tone was sharp. "Listen to me. I can't imagine what it's been like with him, but whatever has happened isn't your fault. And I'm telling you right now if he kills me, and you survive, you find my mom and brothers and tell them I love them. You don't blame yourself. Do you understand?"

Cameron's face had gone even more ghostly white.

"Now you and I are going to work to try and get out of this. I've been held here for too long. I've got an idea of how to get these chains off of you. It might hurt, but we're going to need you free if we have a chance. Are you with me?"

Slowly, Cameron held his trembling hands up to her.

Tiffany put her hand on his. "I think we're going to make a great team, Cameron."

****

From a distance, the secluded house appeared picture-perfect. Tucked off of the road, the off-white home sat back on over three acres of property. The stone-front three-story home was protected by a steel gate and a small security station which was just becoming visible as Drew gunned the car towards the house.

Brooke scanned the area. Nothing seemed out of place, but Hunter would be inside. "We need to have that guard open that gate."

Drew watched for the guard. "We don't have the warrant in hand yet."

Brooke reached into his pocket to pull out his ID. "We just got word a known killer is onsite. If that isn't exigent circumstances, then I'm a choirboy."

The car raced down the road, and Drew took a hard

right to enter the driveway. The gate was open, and the small shed seemed empty. "No guard?"

As they got closer, Brooke was able to see a smear of dark red on the glass of the guard shack. "Shit. Stop the car by the security post."

As soon as the car came to a stop, Brooke jumped out and ran around to check. If there was any chance that someone was still alive, they had to check.

A young man in his late twenties lay on the floor. He'd been shot twice. First in the chest, the second time in the head. Brooke pulled out his weapon as he ran back to the car. "Can't do anything for him. Let's go."

Less than a minute later, they were by the front door, right behind a red Buick with the trunk popped open.

Both men exited the car. Using hand signals, they approached the front door which was slightly ajar.

Standing on either side, Brooke used his fingers to count. On three, he swung the door open and they entered as one. Quickly, they did a sweep. No sign of Hunter, but there was another body. Male, dressed in a dark suit, not a security guard.

Brooke checked for a pulse. A moment later, he shook his head.

A loud gunshot echoed down the hallway. Drew and Brooke took positions against the wall, as Brooke pulled his cell out. "Jacob, we've got an active shooter situation. How far away is our backup?"

Jacob's answer was accompanied by the sound of him typing furiously on his keyboard. "I'm following their progress. They left three minutes ago. ETA fifteen to twenty minutes. There's some heavy traffic."

Drew shook his head. "I'm not waiting. We've got to find Tiffany and Cameron."

Brooke nodded. "Agreed. Jacob what can you tell us?"

There was a pause. "I'm into the security cameras but they don't have much to go on. I can see Tiffany and Cameron, but not where they are. The Senator has other security cams, but they're not turned on. I could access them from here, guide you, but you have to turn them on. Where are you?"

Brooke did a quick glance down the hallway. The problem with a house this big and this empty is that every noise echoes. "Main foyer. I see a security cam by the front door, but there's no light."

More tapping on keys. "I'm sure the Senator didn't want a live feed for the rest of the home. Based on the plans for the house and where the most energy is used, I'd say if you go down the hall in front of you, you'll find the control room."

"I'll call back when we find it." Brook shoved the cell back into his pocket. He and Drew started to move down the hall.

Methodically, they checked each corner, covering each other's blind spots. They passed a dining room where a woman in a smart-looking business suit was lying dead in a pool of her own blood. Drew quickly checked for a pulse before they continued.

They moved towards the plain white door at the end of the hall. Above the door, another camera sat lifelessly. They did a fast check of a small library to clear it and returned to the hall.

As they started to edge forward, Brooke realized something was off. He held a hand out to halt Drew. "Look." He pointed to the camera.

A small red light blinked at the base of the camera

mounted to the ceiling. Brooke reached into his pocket for his cell. The sound of keys being clicked came through the other end. "Jacob, did you manage to get the cameras on remotely?"

The clicking stopped. "No. I've been trying, but you need to physically flip the switch. Let me see..." The keyboard tapping increased and the blinking red light turned to a solid green. "Brooke! Move!"

The white door started to open. The barrel of an M-15 poked its way out held by Hunter, wearing a smile that was matched by his shirt. Brooke jumped to grab Drew and together they landed on the floor of the library just as the hall lit up with the rumble of automatic gunfire.

Brooke rolled off of Drew and trained his weapon on the entrance to the library.

"Guys, you need to get out of that house." Jacob's voice came from Brooke's phone which was lying on the floor near Drew.

Drew got up. Once he was in position, Brooke rolled to his feet and grabbed the phone. "He's staying in the room with the cameras."

"Brooke listen to me." Jacob's voice was tenser than Brooke had ever heard, and he'd never called Brooke by his first name. "He's setting up some sort of bomb in there. You guys need to haul ass."

Drew grabbed the phone. "I'm not leaving Tiffany or Cameron."

Brooke locked eyes with Drew. "Jacob, can you direct us? Where are they?"

"Hold on." Jacob started to type furiously. "I'm running a program to compare what I'm seeing on the screen to the floor plans so I can tell...wait...that's not on the plans, but it has to be in the basement. Two ways there, but you have to go back down that hallway."

Drew handed the phone to Brooke and headed towards the door.

Brooke followed. "We'll contact you when we're back in the foyer."

"No, go back to the dining room." Jacob kept tapping. "I can see Hunter. He's got that door barricaded now. He's got C-4 explosives. It won't take long before he's done so you should move. This could be his final stand."

Brooke and Drew backed into the hallway. As they moved in reverse, keeping their guns trained on the door, Brooke replayed Jacob's last words in his mind. *Hunter might like to go out, taking innocent people with him, but would he plan it knowing the only innocent people were Tiffany and Cameron?*

They made it to the dining room. Brooke called Jacob again. "We're in the dining room. Jacob, I don't think he's going to blow that thing with himself that close."

"Maybe, but he might do it by accident. The dining room opens up on both sides. Go through the far end, down that hall. You'll find the kitchen. There's a stairway to the bottom."

Both men took off, confident that Jacob was keeping an eye on Hunter.

"He's up to something," Brooke said.

Drew led the way. "Probably, but who cares? Let's get them and we can wait him out with tactical. If he manages to blow himself to kingdom come, then oh well."

While Brooke agreed with the sentiment, something

bugged him about this.

They found the kitchen with a messy sink. Someone had started to make a sandwich before the shit hit the fan. Brooke spotted the door to the basement in the far corner. Just as they opened it, Jacob came back on the line. "I'm blind. He just shut the cameras. You better hurry."

They thundered down the stairs and worked their way forward. There was a trail of blood that led down the hall. There were three locks on it. "This has to be the place."

Brooke holstered his weapon as Drew spun around to cover him. The two top locks were turn bolts, the third needed a key. Brooke scowled. "Stand back."

They moved a few feet away. Pulling his Glock, he aimed at the door. Squeezing the trigger, the lock blasted to pieces.

Drew pushed past Brooke and burst into the room. As he entered, a chain looped over Drew's head.

Tiffany yanked the chain back, screaming. "Cameron, run!"

In the corner, a small, terrified boy shook in fear before he launched himself forward. Tiny fists pounded into Drew as he struggled for air.

"FBI!" Brooke came in, pulling his ID. "Let him go."

Tiffany's eyes went wide as she let go of the chain. Cameron didn't stop his flurry of aggression.

Drew dropped down to one knee, grabbing Cameron. "Hey. *Hey*! My name is Drew. We're not going to hurt you. We need to get out of here."

Brooke's phone chirped. "Yeah, we got them."

"I scanned the images of the house from when the cameras were on. I didn't pay attention to the empty rooms before, but he's got at least two more of those bombs in the house. I think they're rigged to go off together. Move."

Brooke held the door open. "You two, stay between me and Drew. Move with us and if we say run, you don't look back. Let's go."

They made their way up the stairs, through the kitchen. Brooke went to open the back door and found it was rigged to blow. "Shit. Head to the front. We know that's clear."

They moved down the hallway, Brooke in front, Drew in the rear. As they neared the foyer, Brooke's cell chimed. "I'm monitoring their Wi-Fi IP activity. Some wireless devices came online and linked. I think he's going to blow it."

The front door was still open, left ajar from their entrance. "Let's move. Now!"

Drew grabbed Cameron, hoisting him over his shoulder. They bolted for the door. The squeal of sirens filled the air. They burst through the front doors as three black vans came to a stop, and heavily armed police piled out. Many aimed their guns at Brooke and the others. He kept running. "Bomb!"

Just as they cleared the front steps, a blast erupted from behind. The house exploded as flames burst through the windows and front door. Brooke and Drew dove to the ground, using their bodies to cover Cameron and Tiffany.

As the dust settled, they moved to allow Tiffany and Cameron to breathe. Tiffany grabbed a hold of Cameron and pulled him into a hug. "I told you we'd make a great team."

Chapter Twenty-Five

Picking Up the Pieces

The police command center was a semi-truck, all black with the local police insignia boldly painted on the side, adorned with a giant golden badge. It was armor plated, with the customary blue and red lights in a small strip on top. In the back, a dense metal rod went straight up with a thick chord wrapping around it as it snaked upwards to a rectangular antenna.

The vehicle was in the open position, with an awning extended over the left side, giving shade to a pair of ranking officers near the metal stairs in the middle of the massive truck.

The two officers saw him coming, gave a curt nod, and left without a word. They knew who he was, and they didn't want to interact with him.

Brooke stopped by the stairs and took a deep breath before stepping inside.

The inside cabin was well-lit, with a bank of computers against the far wall. Two stations were manned, one by someone wearing headphones and deep into whatever he was doing, the other pretending to be working, but not doing much of anything. Three officers huddled with someone in a grey suit over the conference table, listening intently to someone on the monitor on the wall at the back of the PMCV.

Even before Brooke saw the face, he knew who it was just by the gravelly sound of his voice. "I understand that our profile was off, but no profile can be a guarantee. We'll have to look closely to see what we missed. The investigation into what happened today remains in your capable hands. We'll start wrapping up the manhunt since there seems to be very little point to it. I want to thank you and your team for your professionalism. I see my agent has arrived."

The three men turned away from the image of Director Burkhardt to glare at Brooke. None of them were happy. They had one hell of a mess to clean up.

"Gentlemen," Director Burkhardt said. "We'll make sure everyone knows about your department's valuable contribution to this. I do need to hear my agent's report in private please."

Reluctantly, the men headed for the door. None of them bothered to introduce themselves. The man in the grey suit, most likely a lawyer, tapped on the cop's shoulder who was wearing headgear. The other officer had beat them all to the door.

The moment the door clicked shut, Brooke stepped towards the screen. "Sir."

Burkhardt folded his hands. "I've been reading your reports as they come in. As expected, you've done exceptional work getting Cole Duncan to open up to you. The information you've recovered will be very valuable. Agent Foster and I both believed that Edward Hunter would make his way to the border. You were on record in your belief that he'd want to come for Cole. Since he was leaving a trail of bodies to the border, it appeared like he'd gone from an organized serial to a spree killer who was going to take as many people out as possible before he made it to Mexico. What changed?"

On the outside, Brooke remained calm and analytical. Inside, he could hear his heart thump so hard he was surprised it wasn't bursting out of his chest. "Nothing, sir. I think that this was his plan all along. Make us think he was just trying to get away, when in fact his goal was to get to Cole. His signature evolved once Cole was old enough to understand what was happening. Remember, he was abusive to Kelli Duncan, but to Hunter, her main function was to make him look like a well-adjusted member of society. His abuse of her and Cole probably escalated over time. At some point, the idea of making Cole watch as he hurt a stranger occurred to him."

Brooke closed his eyes and tried to put himself into Hunter's head. A part of him wanted to vomit.

Knowing full well he'd be sick later, he let the scene play out. "At some point, Cole didn't just hide. He tried to stop Hunter, but couldn't. Still, the effort amused Hunter. At the same time, we'll see with the tapes we got that right before Cole starts appearing in them, they'll be more sadistic, but shorter. It just wasn't as fun as it used to be for him, and at first, he couldn't figure out why. He wanted that audience; someone he could share the experience with. So, he brought Cole in to watch. Made him helpless to stop. And he threatened Cole that he would do the same to his mother if Cole told. The more Cole fought; the more excited Hunter got. And Hunter wanted Cole to fight."

Burkhardt raised his hand to pause Brooke. "I agree that his signature evolved. We assumed that being exposed would be enough of a stressor to trigger him to spiral. But you correctly deduced that he'd go after Cole.

While we may never know since he killed himself in that explosion, it seems more likely you were right. Would you say that his obsession with Cole is the reason he didn't make a beeline for the border?"

Inhaling slowly, Brooke steeled himself to do what he needed to. "I think that played a major role in it, but it wasn't the only thing that factored in. Hunter wanted to strike back at Senator Brook. When you see all the tapes, you'll realize how deep the cover-up in Ember Falls went. The former mayor, DA, police chief, and many of their cronies used their power and money to abuse and exploit the vulnerable. We now know that Linda Duncan was probably drugged by someone and raped by then Ember Falls DA Bob Reynolds, Frank Duncan, and possibly others. When she found out she was pregnant, Frank wanted her so he assumed responsibility for the children. Frank Duncan always had a thing for her. He pretended as if they'd hooked up and Linda agreed to marry him. He thought it was a bargain, but he resented having to be a father to three children who weren't his. Resentment turned to hatred. We also know Reynolds wasn't the only one to have fathered illegitimate children. Senator Brook did as well.

"Edward Hunter, whose real name is Edward Tice, was one of those children," Brooke continued, unable to stop himself now. "Based on Hunter's age, he was probably one of the first from before he was even Mayor. Tom Brook would never claim Hunter as his own, but Hunter himself became a sort of morbid curiosity. Plus, he got to continue to screw with Edward's mother, Maureen Tice. At some point, we know Tom Brook got angry enough to strike out and injure Maureen Tice. He called Edward to try and calm his mother down. Instead,

Edward killed her. A serial killer was born, and the relationship between Hunter and Thomas Brook took on a whole new dimension. If Edward was caught, it would end Thomas Brook's political ambitions, but keeping his secret allowed him to use Hunter to clean up his messes. Molly Winters, a high school girl who was blackmailing several of the men she'd had sex with, being one of them. You should also be aware that Edward Hunter isn't Tom Brook's only illegitimate offspring. Diana Lakeland, Kelli's counselor who was a co-conspirator in her murder was another. We've found that Tom Brook paid for her college tuition at least in part after she confronted him, soon after her mother's death."

Burkhardt nodded casually. "Anyone else?"

Brooke realized he was nearly standing at attention. He tried to relax, but it just wouldn't work. "Yes, sir. I never had any confirmation of this, but I'd wondered if Thomas Brook might also be my biological father. We'd never met until earlier this week, but well..." Brooke sighed. "You know my background. My mother was an addict. She'd slipped once about how she named me after my father. Took me a few years after that, but certain pieces fit. It'll all be in my report, but I did get confirmation of that. I also used that today when I spoke to him. I played the part of a son who wanted to be something to his father. He was desperate enough to believe it. It gave us the edge we needed. However, I should have reported that I suspected this before I accepted this assignment. I also should have reported it the moment I had confirmation of my lineage. I can assure you, the case against him is solid. I wouldn't have risked it otherwise, but that doesn't change the fact that I broke protocol."

And with that, it was out. Brooke felt a little lighter for not having to carry that secret any longer. Now he had to just see what the consequences were.

Burkhardt sat with his hands folded. His dark eyes, shielded behind glasses, remained calm and passive as if nothing Brooke had said fazed him.

He wasn't reacting at all as he should.

"Agent Madison, I'm glad you did tell me. It will make the investigation into this next part much smoother. We received a signal from the Brook estate before the explosion. It was scrambled, but it didn't take us long to decipher it. I'd like to play that for you now."

The screen went black. Two seconds later, the FBI logo came on, to be replaced by an image of Edward Hunter. He was dressed in the same white t-shirt with the happy face he wore today. He was sitting at a desk in what appeared to be a control room. In front of him, were six stacks of what Brooke assumed was C-4, wrapped with black tape. Wires were coming out of the homemade device, and Hunter was holding a phone.

"Well now, how is the good old FBI? I'm guessing you're getting a good workout trying to catch me. It's been a fun ride for me, especially dealing with Alice and her pathetic husband. Man, you'd think the FBI would teach their agents how not to scream when a guy is drilling them?" He paused to offer the camera a cold, cruel grin and Brooke felt his blood boil. "Even if that guy is using an actual drill. But enough nostalgia. I'm getting a little bored going after people connected with Drew Duncan. Besides, it's pretty clear he and that old boss of his figured that out, so it's just not practical anymore. Today, as they say, is a new day."

He stopped speaking as he played with the circuitry,

tucking it into the bomb, and then began to attach the cell phone. The setup was simple enough. Once at a safe distance, Hunter would call the cell which would trigger the bomb. "I need to pay a visit to my dear old dad, who helped me on my journey. You guys know him as Senator Thomas Brook. He's been a bad boy. He fucked Molly Winters, and a bunch of other chicks in that stupid hick town, Ember Falls. While having a killer for an illegitimate son is not great for the campaign, he did help me out financially here and there, so I want to go on record as endorsing his candidacy for the White House. I was a little pissed that he had my half-sister killed, but it's not that Diana wanted anything to do with me, so..." He shrugged. "As far as my half-brother Brooke Madison..." He smirked. "You gotta hand it to Destiny Madison, naming her boy with Dad's last name, just as a way of saying fuck you. But anyway, I don't know good ol' Brooke as we've never met. I do believe he's the one who tracked down my little hidey-hole. Good for him. I wouldn't be surprised if Brooke and I have a lot in common. I don't want to kill him, so if you could reassign him so he and I don't cross paths, I'd appreciate it. Of course, if you don't, then I'm not going to hesitate to blow him away if I have to. I have no intention of spending my life in a cage, so consider this fair warning to shoot on sight. Once I'm done here, my next step is—"

The screen went to snow.

The buzzing swarm of black and white was replaced by the face of Director Burkhardt. "I appreciate the fact that you came clean with me before you were confronted with this. And I'm not unsympathetic to not wishing for us to know this, but you should have disclosed it as soon as you knew. I never should have sent you to Ember Falls. So far, it appears as if you've done a good job documenting things so our case against Thomas Brook won't be in jeopardy, but this is potentially a serious breach of ethics. I'm placing you on administrative leave for now. Spend some time with your daughter, and we'll talk in a few days once we've had a chance to review everything. Do you understand Agent Madison?"

Brooke couldn't speak at first. He wasn't even sure he was breathing.

"Agent Madison? Please acknowledge."

Slowly, Brooke nodded. Numbness spread through his body. "Yes sir. I understand."

He didn't pay attention to the last few words Director Burkhardt said about getting representation. He just waited for the video call to end, before he stumbled out of the trailer. Black smoke billowed from the house as emergency workers carefully walked over shattered glass carrying out a stretcher with a body. Brooke marched over, flashed his badge, and had them unzip the body bag. There was no face, and the body was missing an arm and leg, but the remnants of that stupid happy face t-shirt were there.

Brooke walked away, secure in the knowledge that just like his lifelong dream of being a profiler for the FBI, Edward Hunter was dead.

****

Brooke parked a few houses down from Lilly's house and walked over. He should go inside, to check on both of the kids. Cole deserved to know that Hunter had blown himself to kingdom come. The monster was dead. Cole's nightmare was over.

Brooke's was just beginning.

Fuck it. Drew probably told him. If not, Ollie would have. And even if nobody has, a few more minutes of not knowing wouldn't kill him. Brooke needed a moment alone.

As he snuck past the house, he could hear voices coming out through the kitchen window. He paused; hearing Cole say something along the lines of oops. Whatever had happened, it set Abbie off on a long tirade about *boys*, *messes*, and *neatness*.

"Not all girls are that neat. I told you about that time Aunt Ash tried to make cookies, right?"

Ashley groaned. "Thanks, kid. Threw me right under the bus."

"How hard is it to clean as you go? It makes it *soooo* much easier to clean afterward. Right, Lilly?" Brooke could just see Abbie with her arms crossed, tapping one toe.

"Right, Abbie," Lilly said.

"Oh, you like things *super* clean," Cole said. "No wonder Lilly likes you so much. Now there are two of you."

Laughter erupted.

"That's not the reason I like Abbie." Lilly's voice held that tone of playful offense. "Well…It's not the *only* reason. But hey, us girls have to stick together."

That spurred on another wave of hearty laughter.

It made Brooke yearn to go inside and just hold her. Something he knew he had no right to do.

He made his way to the upstairs apartment. Let them laugh without him.

He slipped inside and avoided turning on the lights. He wasn't ready to be found. He should pack. Get out of Lilly's hair. Abbie wouldn't want to go, and Lord knows that girl could use someone like Lilly in her life, but Brooke needed to figure out what to do with the rest of his life.

He'd been willing to sacrifice his career to keep Lilly. If he had to make the same choice again, he would. But it was for nothing. Edward Hunter had managed to screw him.

Could that have been his plan all along?

Lilly would never let the half-brother of the man who had tortured Cole be anywhere near the boy. Brooke had lost Lilly, once and for all. And this time, he had nobody to blame but himself.

"Fuck!" Brooke smashed his fist into the punching bag. He wore no protective gear, but the pain felt good. "Son of a bitch!" He hit the bag, again and again, losing himself in the fury, ignoring the stabs of pain. Brooke wasn't sure how long he stood there, pummeling the bag, but when he was done, his knuckles had started to bleed.

Brooke glared down at them in disgust. He'd have to clean up before he talked to Cole, but for now, let them throb. He deserved it.

"Oh my God, Brooke. What happened?"

Lilly appeared at the door.

Brooke desperately wanted to go to her, to take comfort in her touch and embrace, but he couldn't even make eye contact.

"Ashley is with the kids, probably wrecking the kitchen." Lilly strode over and took his hands to examine them. Her eyes scanned the smears of blood on the punching bag, and she understood. "Drew called. He's at the hospital. Said that it was over, but didn't want to go into more detail over the phone. Told me to keep Cole away from electronics and the TV off until he had a chance to talk to Cole."

As she spoke, she pulled Brooke to the small sink to run his hands under cold water. "Is it really over? I mean, I know there's going to be a trial, but…"

"No, there won't be a trial." Brooke pulled his hands away and stalked across the room. "We found out that Senator Brook, my father, was holding Tiffany Reynolds hostage. Drew and I were going to meet a police team to rescue her while Ollie babysat my father. Just before we got there, Hunter arrived. He had the kid Cameron with him. He planned on blowing up the house with everyone in it, then coming for Cole. His bomb must have gone off as he was setting it up. He blew himself to smithereens."

Lilly's hand went to her mouth. "Are you okay? Drew? Was anyone hurt besides Hunter?"

Brooke almost answered no, but that wasn't true. The men in the house deserved to see the inside of a jail cell for their part in the kidnapping and holding of Tiffany Reynolds, but they didn't deserve to die. Hunter had no right to kill them. "Hunter killed all the guards who were keeping Tiffany prisoner, but that was before we arrived. Drew and I got Tiffany and Cameron out on time. Barely, but we made it."

Lilly paused, considering what she was being told. "So what's wrong? There's something you're not telling me."

Brooke scowled. He had no right to say this to Lilly. No business in taking any comfort from her. "Hunter made a recording just before the bomb went off. It was set to go to the FBI an hour after he planned on being out of there. He talked about how Tom Brook was his father, and I was his half-brother. I had just told the Director myself anyway."

Lilly furrowed her brow as she walked over to him. "I don't understand. You didn't have anything to do with either of them until today. You worked hard to bring them down. They can't hold this against you."

Brooke let out a hallow laugh. "Sure, they can. I should have disclosed this the moment I suspected I might be related to either Senator Brook or Hunter. The FBI would have never sent me here. But Goddammit, I needed to be here. I needed to..."

Lilly placed her hand on his. "You wanted to come back to protect me."

"My coming back made no fucking difference." Brooke stalked away. "No matter what, he would have ended up in that same house, blowing himself up. I didn't stop him, I just got to be there when they started to pick up to pieces. Now my career is probably over, and you would have been better off without me coming back."

Lilly folded her arms. "Why would you say that? Brooke, do you have any idea the difference you've made for Cole? He's going to have a long road to recovery, but he can start on that road now that he's told us..." She walked over. "Told *you*."

She pulled out a chair by the table and sat down. Pointed to the other chair, she waited for Brooke to join her. "You told me you figured out that Tom Brooke had Tiffany Reynolds. You were going to get her out of that awful place. If you hadn't, would either her or that poor child even be alive?"

Brooke didn't respond, but her words rolled around in his head.

"You're not the same kid whose mother was more interested in a fix than she was in making sure you had a full stomach. Look at what you've made of yourself."

Brooke shook his head. Was he not allowed to grieve for what he'd lost? "You don't understand. I came from nothing. I *was* nothing. Then I was yours. And I lost that. I pushed myself even harder to get into the academy. To make myself a special agent who could profile the monsters of the world. And now that's gone. I'm nothing again."

Lilly laid her hand on his. "That's what you don't get. You were never nothing. And you're certainly not nothing now. You're a good man. You're a great father. I've seen you with Abbie. She adores you. You took that frightened little girl, who nobody wanted, and made her yours. The FBI can't take that away from you."

She reached over with her free hand, and gently touched his face. "Was I upset that you didn't tell me about your connection with Hunter? Of course, I was. You could have trusted me, but I get it wasn't really about trust, was it."

Brooke shut his eyes. "No. I was ashamed. Edward Hunter is a monster. I don't use that term lightly. I've sat across from people who have done horrible things, but they were damaged. They knew what they did was wrong and they regretted it. There was just something broken in them. Maybe with the right help, it could be fixed." He leaned back in his chair. "Hunter is one of those guys who truly enjoys hurting people. He needs to control, to manipulate, to torture. He had a truly anti-social personality disorder. He didn't just torture and kill. He blackmailed powerful people to keep himself safe. He has reams of files on the people who used to run Ember Falls, and who run Cheyenne. He was a fucking cancer. And I'm his brother."

His eyes burned from the need to cry, but he fought

it. "How could you stand to touch me, to be near me when the man who put Cole through so much has the same blood that runs in my veins? How can you even stand to look at me?"

Lilly put her hands gently on his cheeks, but Brooke still avoided eye contact. "I am looking at you, and I see you. Brooke, you and Hunter shared a sperm donor. Tom Brook was no father to you. A father isn't someone who knocks up your addict of a mother and then lets her raise you. You grew up, mistakenly believing that you're nothing. But in reality, they're nothing. They're certainly nothing to you."

Brooke tried to pull away. "Do you realize we all have the same eyes?"

Lilly wouldn't let him move. "I don't see either Tom Brook or Edward Hunter when I look into your eyes. I see a kind soul, a gentle heart. I see a man who *had* nothing and made himself into an extraordinary man." She took his hands. "I see the man that I never stopped loving, and the man that I want to try and rebuild a life with. I know it's fast, but Brooke, we were meant to be together. You haven't lost me. You just need to let me be there for you."

Finally, Brooke looked into her eyes. There was no sign of disgust at the sight of him. He knew his world was broken, but something about Lilly telling him that she wanted a future with him made him feel whole again.

He leaned forward and kissed her. For a brief moment, he was afraid she'd pull back, but she returned the kiss. He lost himself in her embrace, and felt the final walls start to fall. She was his safe space. Suddenly the weight of it all, knowing his biological father never gave a shit, that he would now be known as having a monster

338

as a brother, the horror of everything he'd seen during this investigation, and that everything he'd worked his entire life was lost came crashing down on him.

Lilly gently wiped his tears away. "I'm not going anywhere."

Chapter Twenty-Six

Party Pooper

Jacob shifted in bed.

"What time is it?" Brandon asked, his face still buried in a pillow.

Jacob didn't need to check the clock to know since he'd been watching the minutes tick away for over an hour now. Jacob hadn't gotten back to the hotel until nearly 3:00 a.m., and Brandon had been there waiting for him, knowing how difficult a day it had been. "Almost a quarter after eight. We're supposed to be at the park for Cole's birthday by noon."

"Then why are you awake?" Brandon rolled over. His normally neat hair fell haphazardly over his eyes. "Something bothering you? About what we talked about last night?"

Jacob shook his head, making eye contact to make sure Brandon could see his eyes. "No. I already sent the request to transfer to the Albany unit."

Brandon leaned in and kissed Jacob. "I know this thing between us kind of moved quickly, but it means something to me. I'd like you to meet my family next weekend. Maybe you'll introduce me to yours?"

Jacob almost sneered at the idea of introducing Brandon to his father, but realized he had family that was far more accepting. "I'd like that."

Brandon sat up in bed and stretched. "Then what's on your mind? You were restless all night."

Rolling into a sitting position, Jacob sat next to Brandon. "I just feel like something's off. Edward Hunter engineered so well. He targeted powerful people, blackmailed them on their secret vices, and played the long game. He laid enough breadcrumbs to make some of the Bureau's best chase him cross country, even though he planned on returning just to go after Cole. Then he ends up blowing himself up, taking out nobody of importance to him."

Brandon shrugged. "He meant to take out Tiffany Reynolds and that kid Cameron."

Jacob grabbed a pair of pants as he got up, and pulled them on. "Yeah, okay. But so what? He'd never met Tiffany. She didn't matter to him." Jacob stood and began to pace. "I've been trying to play out what would have happened in my head. Hunter plans on blowing up one of his father's homes. Not one where his dad actually is at the time. Okay, maybe if he knew about the senator holding Tiffany—"

"Which we can assume he did, based on what little Tiffany told us," Brandon interjected.

Jacob nuzzled into the crook of Brandon's arm. He tried to relax, but the more he spoke the more uptight he felt. "Right. So, if things had gone as he'd hoped, he'd have sent that call outing both Senator Brook as his biological father and Agent Madison as his half-brother. Then what? Plans to go for Cole? Kid is never alone. Sheriff Miller has had a police presence by the school. His uncle, Officer Rossi, and Detective Miller are with him at home. And that was all in place as Hunter is, to the best of our knowledge, moving farther away. Now he announces in a huge way he's one town over from Cole. People were careful with Cole when the official word was that Hunter was fleeing away from Ember Falls. What happens when everyone knows he's less than a half hour away? If he hadn't blown himself to bits, his uncle might have grabbed the kid and absconded to an underground bunker in Brazil."

Brandon tilted his head. "Why Brazil?"

Jacob blinked. "What?"

Brandon shrugged. "Why Brazil and not Europe, or Australia, or somewhere here in the US like Hawaii. Hawaii is nice."

Jacob rolled his eyes. "Hawaii is no more or less nice than any other place from an underground bunker. My point is, he just made getting to Cole harder, not easier."

Leaning back on the bed, Brandon contemplated the question. "I don't know. You're right, it wasn't the brightest move, but he may have been unraveling. Isn't that a thing?"

Jacob thought about it. "De-evolving. From an organized killer to an unorganized killer. But this wasn't really unorganized. It was just…" He shrugged. "*Badly* organized. Especially when you compare it to everything else he did."

Brandon got up himself. "What does it matter? Someone is lying in three separate drawers at the coroner's office. And if that's not Hunter, then who the hell is it? All of Senator Brook's henchmen were accounted for. Some mystery guest of the same body type, wearing the same stupid shirt he wore in that video?"

The question rolled around in his head. Jacob knew

it made no sense. There was no possible way some random person who met that description would just happen to be there.

Unless…

Jacob sat up, pulled on a pair of pants, and sat down by his laptop. Firing it up, he began tapping his fingers as he waited for it to boot up.

"I don't like that look you have Jacob."

As the FBI logo and login page displayed, Jacob saw his reflection on the screen. "Neither do I."

****

Cole quickly got dressed. He sat on the edge of the bed, slowly breathing in and out as Brooke had shown him. Today was his first birthday party ever. He should be able to simply enjoy himself, not be looking over his shoulder for a man who was probably dead.

But somehow, Cole couldn't convince himself that Edward had really been killed. He'd asked Uncle Drew last night. Uncle Drew wouldn't lie to him, so Cole had told himself that if Uncle Drew said Edward was dead, he was.

Uncle Drew, after taking a moment to mull it over, hadn't said yes. "We don't have confirmation, but it looks like he is. But since I didn't see him, I can't promise you. Not yet."

Cole could tell Uncle Drew wanted very much to say "yes," but he refused to unless he was absolutely sure.

So how could Cole not still be afraid?

There was a small knock. Cole jumped and turned to see Abbie standing in his doorway. She was in a brand-new outfit that Lilly bought her for the party. Soft-pink stretchy pants and a white t-shirt that read *Relax, the cool kid just got here.* She eyed him casually. "You

343

okay?"

Cole took a slow, deep breath. "Yeah, why?"

Walking into his room, she plopped down on the bed next to him. "You're jumpy."

Cole's face burned red.

"Relax. It's nothing to be embarrassed about and I'm not going to tell anyone." Abbie scooted a bit closer. "I still get them from time to time. Dad walks me through the breathing like what you were just doing."

Cole was able to somewhat relax, knowing Abbie understood better than most would. "He taught me how to do it. And it's not the party. I'm just..." He sighed. "I want to know he's dead. I mean, really know it."

Abbie slid off the bed and walked towards the window. "It'll help, I'm sure. But knowing he's dead, that it's over forever, isn't going to make all the nightmares go away. At least, it didn't with me."

Cole rose to join her. He wondered what she was gazing at. "What did?"

With a shrug, Abbie stared out at the street. "Mostly time. Talking about it with Dad. It's still there. Maybe it always will be, but it does get better."

Together, they watched the street from Cole's window. It was quiet, with very few people walking by. A small yellow VW Bug passed by, and a white van with tinted windows was parked down the block. This was where he'd gotten his first glimpse of Uncle Drew. Strong, solid, and determined to get Cole to trust him. "It's not *just* a birthday party, y'know. It's my first. I never had one before."

Abbie smirked. "Then we best get going. Let's head down the back stairs. Maybe we can each steal a cupcake if Lilly hasn't put them all in the cases yet."

Together, they made their way to the back stairs and quietly descended to the landing that would open one way to the kitchen, and the other way to the backyard. Opening the kitchen door, they spotted that there were three cupcakes not packed up. Probably just wouldn't fit. Lilly had made enough to feed Cole's entire school. They exchanged mischievous grins and got ready to pounce when they heard something crash.

Lilly screamed. A chair was knocked down and skidded across the table.

A familiar deep voice grunted. "*Bitch*!"

Cole froze. He had to still be asleep and this was just another nightmare. It couldn't be him.

Lilly came into view, struggling against someone three times her size. She was slamming her foot down on his, reaching for his eyes and trying to smash her fist into his balls, but he was too big. He held a white cloth over her mouth. Her eyes found Cole's before they rolled back. She collapsed on the floor.

Edward Hunter came into view. He walked over to the oven and grabbed one of the cupcakes. Shoving the entire thing into his mouth, he helped himself to milk from the fridge to wash it down. "You put up one hell of a fight for a girl your size, but fuck if that isn't one of the best cupcakes I've ever had. You stay put. Let's go see if Cole is upstairs."

He headed into the living room and began to stomp his way up the stairs.

Cole and Abbie ran to Lilly's side. She was alive, but out cold. Abbie reached for the small cloth, but Charlie grabbed her hand. He couldn't remember the name, but it must have that stuff on it that makes you pass out.

"Cole, you up here?" Edward called from the second floor. "Come on out Cole, it's time to have some fun again."

Both Cole and Abbie tried to pull at Lilly, but she was too heavy for them to budge. When Edward started to stomp down the stairs, Cole grabbed Abbie and pulled her to the back door. There was a white van with tinted windows in the driveway. The side door was open. As the back door crashed open, Cole and Abbie hid in the bushes.

Edward came out, carrying Lilly over his shoulder. He threw her into the back and grabbed a roll of duct tape to bind her wrists and ankles. When done, he started to close the door, then stopped himself. He turned around and headed back to the house.

Cole knew there was no way to get Lilly out of the van and hide her before he came out. He was going to take Lilly, and there was nothing he could do about it.

Cole reached for his phone, but realized he'd left it charging in his room. He turned to Abbie. "Do you have your phone?"

Abbie stared blankly at him.

"Abbie, give it to me, quick."

Abbie fumbled into her pocket, pulled out her phone and handed it to Cole who checked to make sure it was on.

Cole shoved it in his pocket. "As soon as he's gone, get my cell. It's on my dresser. Use the code 1-2-3-4."

Abbie scowled. "That's a stupid password."

Cole ignored her. "There's an app. It's got an M on it. Press it. Tell whoever talks to you what happened. They'll find us." He stood up. "I know they will. For now, just hide!"

As he got up, she grabbed at him. "*What*?"

Cole yanked his arm away and ran to the van, where he climbed on board and hid under a blanket in the back.

He was able to see through a small hole in the blanket as Edward returned with two trays of cupcakes. He tossed them in the passenger seat and slammed the backdoor shut. Edward climbed in, helped himself to another cupcake, and backed out of the driveway.

Chapter Twenty-Seven

Guess Who's Back?

Although he was on paid leave, Brooke had felt the need to go to the Ember Falls Police Station to give his report directly to Chief Miller. She deserved to know exactly what had happened. To his surprise, she was gracious about what he'd held back. Part of him wondered if she wasn't simply grateful that Hunter was dead. Besides, as they walked together into an interrogation room, Brooke could see her mind was on other upcoming events.

"Whoa." Brooke's eyebrows went up as he took in the impressive stack of gifts. "Kid's going to make off like a bandit."

Ann grinned as she picked up a hand-held gaming system and began to expertly wrap it. "We can't help it. Cops have a soft spot for kids. And Cole has had one hell of a life."

"Not to mention, this department has had one hell of a year." Polansky had his glasses on the tip of his nose as he tied a ribbon around a gift.

Ann reached for another gift, a giant set of Legos that would build a Death Star. "And we have a way to go before we're through with it. The wrap-up of this case is going to take forever. How many more people who were Ember Fall's officials are we going to have to slap cuffs on? I'm sure our old Deputy Mayor is in on it. Plus, even once Duncan signs on officially, we'll still need to find more detectives." She selected birthday paper covered in popular superheroes. "I don't suppose you'd consider applying for the job?"

Brooke wasn't sure if he wanted to laugh or cry. "I'll keep it in mind."

He said goodbye and left as Polansky, his bulldog face as serious as ever, used a pair of scissors to curl the end of a ribbon.

Climbing into his car, Brooke started to wonder what it would be like to work here as a detective in Ember Falls. Once the current mess was over, he doubted he'd have anywhere near the same sort of cases. Ember Falls had a relatively low crime rate. While it would make it a great place to raise Abbie, it wouldn't be somewhere his skills were needed.

As he pulled into traffic, he thought about working for the General again. There he could probably do what he was trained to do, just not as an agent.

His cell signaled an incoming call and Brooke activated the Bluetooth speaker on the car. "Jacob. You ready for the party."

"What? Um…no, not yet. Listen, Agent Madison, I've been doing a little digging, and…"

"Jacob, we're off the case." Brooke hated saying that. It was probably a blow to Jacob just as he was starting to gain confidence but it was important to Brooke that none of this blew back on him. "You didn't do anything wrong, and I'm sure you're not going to get jammed up, but they wanted us hands-off until our debriefing with Agent Foster on Monday. Don't get yourself in trouble now."

"Yeah, I know, but this is important. I think Hunter is alive."

The car squealed in protest as Brooke made a sharp turn and pulled into a parking lot. "What are you talking about Jacob."

"It just didn't sit right with me, that after all that planning, Hunter would announce to everyone where he was right before he made a try for Cole. I started to do some scans of known pictures, to get body dimensions. Then I hacked into the file that has pictures of the body they pulled out."

"You did what?" Brooke gripped the wheel tightly. "Dammit, Jacob if that gets out…"

"Forget about that. I didn't have access and I needed it." Jacob's voice was firm and determined. "It's not an exact science, but what I'm seeing isn't a match. Hunter is a little bigger than the torso we pulled out. Then I thought about how weird it was that the body had no teeth or fingers. And yeah, since he took a bomb in the face, maybe not so weird, but maybe that's what we were supposed to believe."

As Jacob spoke, Brooke ran through things in his mind. Edward was an organized killer who planned things out well in advance. It was part of his signature. The planning, the execution of the design, was part of the excitement. Tipping his hand that he was near Ember Falls would be stupid. If they hadn't thought Edward was dead, they would have put Cole on lockdown. Brooke put the car back into drive and started to head for Lilly's house. He cut off a slow-moving Volkswagen whose driver rolled the window down to curse him out.

"There's more," Jacob said. "I started to check missing person reports. A woman reported her husband missing. Peter Criscuola. Cops didn't want to make it a missing person at first. It hasn't been forty-eight hours and they speculated since she was pregnant with their first child, he might have just gotten cold feet, but she said she was on the phone with him when something happened. He stopped because of a young boy lying on the road. Call got cut off, and there was nothing found when cops searched the area."

As Jacob spoke about digging up social media and using the same techniques to analyze probable height and body dimensions, Brooke put the pieces together. Part of the reason why Edward had remained at large for so long was that he knew how to blend in. In the video, he'd worn a bright, white shirt with a yellow happy face on it.

Jacob hesitated. "Maybe I'm crazy, but what I'm thinking is…"

Brooke cut in. "Edward used the kid as bait. Some poor Samaritan stopped to help, and Edward killed him, put him in that shirt, and brought him there. Smashed his teeth in, ripped off his fingers as if they were blown off in the explosion. Not cut. Nothing that would send up a red flag. Placed the damaged body in a place we'd expect to find him. He knows he only has a small window. We're rushing the DNA through. I'm heading to get Cole. We need to find Cameron. Three-way call to Drew, he might know where the kid is."

****

Drew stood back and studied what they'd done. A giant bounce house that would allow ten kids in at a time sat ready to his left, while a giant clown's head filled with balloons to pop with throwable darts to win prizes was to his right. A pair of workers were currently inflating half-dozen things called bubble balls. The kids would put them on over their heads and bodies, leaving just their lower legs free. This would allow the kids to smash into one another as if they were human bumper cars. Ashley was just putting the final touches on an auction game, where each kid would get fake money to bid on toys that were wrapped. They would have no idea what they were bidding on, but everyone would walk away with something.

This was going to be one hell of a birthday party.

"You think we got carried away?" Ashley walked over after she placed the last wrapped gift on display.

Drew grinned. "Maybe a tad, but Cole deserves it. Still, it's going to be hard to top all of this next year when he turns ten."

Ollie came trotting over. "Hey, where do you want to hold the nerf-gun war?"

Drew glanced around, and for the life of him, he couldn't find a location that was open. "Yeah, we definitely went overboard. Maybe right behind the bounce house? Is there room? Or will the nerf pellets find their way into the bounce house?"

Ollie scanned the area. "We've got some folding tables left. What if I set them up on their sides? Kids could use them as shields. That way, we know which way everything is being fired. Each team has to send each member through and try to protect them. Make a game out of it."

Drew wasn't quite sure what Ollie had in mind, but was quite positive he didn't want to know. "Sounds like you're in charge of that."

Ollie gave a fist bump, thrilled with the assignment. "This is going to be great. Cole is going to be the star of his class. Hey, look whose here." Ollie pointed.

The Reynolds came walking towards them. Although her ordeal had ended only the other day, Tiffany walked briskly in their direction, holding hands with Cameron Matthews. Cameron seemed cautious as he walked in, his eyes darting back and forth, searching for danger. It reminded Drew of Cole. They were followed by Sam and Ethan. Ethan was limping, but didn't seem quite as physically stressed. Sam carried a small stack of presents.

While Ollie went to set up the nerf war, Drew and Ashley went to greet their first guests.

Tiffany went straight to them. Cameron stayed close, glued to her side. Tiffany offered her free hand. "I hope you don't mind us showing up early. I wanted to see if we could help."

"Not at all." Ashley took the offered hand.

Tiffany waited until both of her brothers were by her side, each flanking Cameron to give him a sense of safety. "I've been brought up to speed on our..." She paused, searching for the right words, "relationship. It's a little unnerving for us to know we have a brother and sister. My mom said you were open to us getting to know each other. My brothers and I all agreed that we'd like that. I know that my father..." She winced. "*Our* father, did some horrible things. We're all very angry with him. I don't know if I can hate him like you must."

Ashley stepped forward. "You don't need to. You had a life with him as your dad. I'm sure there were some great moments. I hope in time, you can still find joy in those memories. You don't owe us giving that up. We'd just like the chance to get to know you guys."

A wave of relief washed over all of the Reynolds. Tiffany responded by putting her hand over Cameron's shoulder. "My mom couldn't make it today, and figured you'd prefer she stay away. However, we're trying to get custody of Cameron. His old foster family is under investigation thanks to someone named General McAlister. He spoke to Cameron yesterday and Cam asked if he could stay with me. He said he'd see what he could do."

Drew gazed at the small boy. "If the General said that, you can count on him moving mountains. He should be here any minute now." Drew bent to address Cameron. Noticed the kid flinch, moving back a step. Sam was the first to come up behind Cam and place a reassuring hand on the kid's shoulder. That one gesture told Drew that Sam wasn't the same person anymore.

As Tiffany and Ashely started to gently draw Cameron out of his shell, Drew's cell chimed. Pulling it out of his pocket, he saw it was Brooke. "Hey, how much longer until you get the birthday boy over here? Cole is going to flip when he sees this place."

"Drew, I've got Jacob on the line." Brooke's tone, more than his words had Drew's blood running cold. He could see that Sam spotted his change in demeanor, and he gently pulled Cameron to the side and started to point out all of the things they'd set up for the party.

Drew stepped back from everyone. "What's going on?"

"We think Hunter is still alive, and he may have set things up to make us think he was dead." The sound of an engine going full throttle could be heard in the background. "Jacob found someone who he thinks is the body we found."

"Sending it now," Jacob said just as Drew's phone pinged.

The picture of a man in his late twenties appeared. At first glance, he appeared nothing like Hunter. His light brown eyes shined with amusement, and he wore an infectious grin at whatever gathering where this picture was taken. Even the way he carried himself spoke of a genuine, nice guy.

But erase the face, punch in the teeth, make him nothing but a bloody stump pulled out of the rubble wearing the same t-shirt that Hunter had been wearing. "Yeah, that could be our DB. But if so…"

"If so," Brooke interjected, "it means that that Hunter planned for us to think that was him, but he has to know we're going to run his DNA. He has to know we have it, he left plenty of it inside of Agent Mills. Something he's never done before. That means he knows he's got a short time frame."

"Fuck." Drew spotted Ollie and Sam shooting each other with nerf rifles. He signaled them, but neither was seeing him. "Ash, go get Ollie and Sam. Now."

Her eyes wanted to ask questions, but she'd learned to trust Drew. She ran to her fiancé.

"I've got to get to Cole."

"I'm almost there," Brooke said. "Listen, right now this is just a theory. We could all just be so unsure of Hunter being dead that we're spinning out of control. I need you to find that kid Cameron and show him the picture that Jacob sent. Any idea where he is."

Drew took three long strides forward. "He's right here. Give me a moment."

Cameron eyed him wearily. Kid was still in a fragile place, and Drew didn't want to do any more damage, but he needed to know.

As Drew approached, Sam put a hand over

Cameron's shoulder, intent on protecting him. "What's going on, Drew?"

Smiling as best he could, Drew lowered himself to one knee so he'd be on the same level as the kid. "Cameron, I need your help. I want you to know you're not in trouble. I just need to show you a picture of someone. Tell me if you recognize him. Can you do that?"

The only answer Cameron gave was to start to shake.

Sam tried to calm him down, but Cameron cowered away from his touch and ran to Tiffany.

"What the hell are you doing?" Sam asked.

"Sam, this is important. I hate it, but I have to do it."

Cameron just kept his face buried in Tiffany's side, shaking his head and crying. He was repeating how sorry he was over and over again. Drew's stomach turned thinking of how Cole apologized for things beyond his control.

Sam was ready to argue when Tiffany reached her hand out. "Let me see the picture please."

Drew rose up and went over. He handed the phone over to Tiffany. She frowned, not understanding, but crouched down near Cameron. "Sweetie, I know you're scared, but Drew wouldn't ask if it weren't important. I promise, you're not in trouble, right, Drew?"

Drew knelt down, once again. "Absolutely not. Cameron, we know what Edward did. What he made you watch. We know he used you to trick some people, but *he* was in control. Not you. Now you do have control. I need you to look at this picture. Please."

Drew was desperate, but he wasn't sure that Cameron could even hear him. He'd dropped to the ground and was rocking back and forth. With his thumb stuck in his mouth, he kept muttering. "He'll know, he'll know…He'll always know."

Tiffany crouched down next to him, took his face in his hands. "Cameron. I know you can hear me. We're never going to let that man hurt you again. You trust me, right? You'll trust that I'll do whatever needs to be done to protect you?"

With glassy eyes, Cameron managed a nod.

Tiffany held her hand out for Ethan. "And Ethan? Sam? They're my brothers. You trust them, right? If I say you're family and need to be protected, they'll do that too, right? None of us blame you for what that man did. We know you couldn't stop him. It's not your fault."

Cameron didn't say anything, but his eyes glanced at both of her brothers. Somehow, the bond he'd formed with Tiffany had been transferred to them as well.

Now how the hell do I get the kid to trust me? Even if just long enough to look at that damn picture?

As if she'd read Drew's mind, Tiffany reached her other hand out to Drew who clasped it tightly. "This is Drew. Drew is also my brother."

Her eyes made contact with his, and all the confusion and turmoil of what he was dealing with having new siblings seemed insignificant. This was *his* sister.

Cameron's breathing was labored. He was trembling as if he were freezing, but he glanced towards Drew.

"I know how evil that man is." Drew kept his voice soft, his eyes locked on Cameron's. "What he did to you, he did to my nephew. I've told Cole a million times; it wasn't his fault. I'll tell you too. I just need you to look

357

at this picture and tell me if you know who this is. It's not Edward Hunter, I swear."

Slowly, with a shaking hand, Cameron took the phone. He studied the picture for a brief moment before his eyes widened in shock, then shut tight.

"He made me. I didn't want to, I swear." Once again, Cameron began to rock back and forth. "I couldn't mm...m...move. I was tied up. Edward made me lie in the road so this man would stop. Edward usually wanted girls, but he wa...wa...wanted a guy. He said this one would do. The man was trying to help me. I didn't..." He pressed his small face against Tiffany's chest. "I should have told him to run, but I was scared. And then..." He trailed off, his eyes shutting as the tears flowed.

"Did Edward take him with you?" Drew asked.

Cameron's face grew paler by the moment. "Put him in the trunk. We went somewhere nobody could see. He put a shirt on him. Then he put the same shirt on too. I don't know why. I'm sorry."

Drew gently took his phone back. He needed to call Brooke back, but he couldn't just leave this child in this state. "Cameron, you have nothing to be sorry for. And thank you. You just helped save lives. Today, you helped beat Edward. Don't forget that."

Drew rose up and started to walk away. Ashley and Tiffany's brother Sam were by his side in an instant. Ollie and his fiancée Sam came running over.

As they gathered around, Drew got Brooke on the line and put him on speaker. "Cameron just confirmed. That guy Jacob found the report on was killed by Hunter. Fucker picked out some guy who was alone and his basic shape and size. Then put him in that damn t-shirt so when we found the body, we'd think it was him. Hunter is alive."

Ashley gasped and turned to Ollie. Both Sams cursed.

"He has to know we'd put a rush on the DNA," Brooke said from the other side of the phone. "Which means he's going to make his move on Cole sooner, not later. I'm heading there right now. Until Hunter is in custody or confirmed dead, we need eyes on him at all times."

"I'm on my way." Drew ended the call and moved towards the parking lot, his fiancée, Ollie, and Ashley by his side.

"Drew," Sam Reynolds called out. Drew paused for just a moment to turn. "Be careful. I do want to make things right with you."

Drew nodded and took off for his car. Hunter was alive, but if Drew got to him first, that would change.

Just as he reached his car, Drew went to call the General who was en route to the party, when his phone chimed. Drew hit the accept button. "I was just about to call you. Hunter is alive, and he's probably going to make a move on Cole soon."

"I think he already has." The General's voice was grim. It sent a shiver down Drew's spine. "Cole activated his McAlister App on his phone. We're not hearing anything except crying. We're triangulating, but it's coming from somewhere in your home. Could be he's there. Move now."

Drew slammed the car into drive. The smell of burnt rubber mixed with the sound of squealing tires as Drew bulleted home.

****

Brooke entered the house with his gun drawn. The McAlister people didn't know if Hunter was searching for Cole, so they didn't want to attempt to talk to him. Which meant Hunter could be around any corner.

Silently, Brooke cleared the living room, then entered the kitchen.

Signs of a struggle. An overturned chair. Items on the table knocked off. A white cloth on the floor. Brooke picked it up, took a small sniff. *Chloroform.*

A creak came from the ceiling. Swiftly and silently, Brooke headed to the stairs and ascended. Moving like a ghost, he went to Cole's room. He heard heavy breathing, and a faint whimper from the closet. "FBI."

"Dad!"

Abbie bolted out of the closet and into Brooke's arms. Her sobs came out in heaves and mixed with her words as she attempted to tell Brooke what had happened.

"I've got Abbie, but she's alone." Brooke announced into the phone as he lowered himself to one knee. "You're safe. He can't hurt you. Abbie, I need you to tell me where Lilly and Cole are."

Tears streamed down Abbie's face. "He took her. He did something and took her. Then Cole...I didn't know he was going to do it. I couldn't stop him."

Brooke scowled, mustering all of his ability to restrain himself as he spoke. "What did Cole do?"

Abbie pointed as if Brooke would be able to see through the wall, and into the past. "He got in the van. He took my phone and got into the van with her."

Brooke held Cole's phone up to his mouth. "McAlister, Hunter has Lilly Danvers and Cole Duncan stowed away. Cole has my daughter's phone." He rattled off the cell number as he heard the front door smash open downstairs. "Drew, upstairs, now! McAlister, you need to start triangulating the signal from Abbie's phone. If Hunter realizes Cole is there, both of them are dead."

"We're on it," a voice tinged with a Middle-Eastern accent said from the phone.

Drew came into the room, his eyes searching for Cole.

Brooke held his daughter as she wept. "Hunter was here. He took Lilly. And Cole snuck onboard. He's got them both, but he doesn't know it yet."

Chapter Twenty-Eight

Come and Get Me If You Can

Cole couldn't tell where they were going. From underneath the smelly blanket, he could barely see. Lilly was still out, although every now and then, she'd move. Not much, but enough to know she was alive. Cole prayed she didn't wake up soon. Edward wouldn't start until she woke up.

He had no idea where they were or were going. He could hear the cars go by. Feel the bumps on the road. He tried to stay still and didn't cry out when Edward hit a bump hard enough that he bounced on the metal floor.

Did Abbie know how to use his phone? As long as she entered the dummy code, McAlister would be alerted, but would they talk to her? She'd call her dad. Brooke would make sure someone was coming, if not for him, then for Lilly.

The van turned and Lilly moaned slightly.

No, don't wake up. He'll just tie you up if you're still out, he won't hurt you until you're awake.

Edward glanced down at Lilly's still form, but when she didn't stir, his eyes went back to the road.

Cole tried to be as still as possible. If Edward saw the blanket start to shake, he'd know he was here. He gripped Abbie's cell so tightly he thought it would break. Terror poured out of him in sweat. Slowly, he reached over and put his other hand on the cell, afraid that it would pop out of his grip.

Still. Stay perfectly still.

Edward reached over with his right hand and flipped open the center console. Pulling out a pack of cigarettes, he yanked one out with his lips. Using a lighter from his pocket, he lit it and took a long drag.

That first scent of nicotine was always the strongest. Smoke billowed out of Edward's mouth as he navigated through the streets of Ember Falls.

Cole's hand moved to his nose to attempt to quell the twitching in his nostrils as his heart began to pound in his chest. He squeezed his nose and breathed out of his mouth. He could feel the involuntary spasm fight to escape.

Edward thought it was funny when Cole went into sneezing fits. Blew smoke right into his face and laugh. It was far from the cruelest thing he'd done, but any complaints from him or his mother would end with a beating for them both.

Cole held his nose so tight it hurt. He clamped his mouth shut, praying that he could hold the sneeze in.

Lilly stirred again, and Edward glanced at her as he breathed out smoke. He took a long drag, watching to see if Lilly would wake up, but a moment later, Lilly was still again. Taking one last pull on his cigarette, Edward rolled the window down and flicked the butt outside. Much of the smoke escaped before the glass slide back up as if it were running away from the devil himself.

Laughing, Edward took a sharp right. Cole fought to stay in place and not tumble with the sudden turn.

The shadows reflecting through the window changed. The solid grey turned to a mish-mash pattern of intertwining shapes and lines. The sound of the road became muted, while the surrounding traffic sounded more distant. The roughness of a dirt road reverberated through the floor of the van.

They had left the busy streets of the city of Ember Falls and were on a backroad. Somewhere private and secluded. Cole knew what that meant.

Edward liked his privacy when he hurt people.

The van turned again, slowed down. Edward whistled to himself as he pulled near an old house. The brakes squeaked as the van came to a stop. Edward glanced over Lilly's still form, and just waited for a moment.

Cole found himself holding his breath, afraid to move an inch. He just needed Edward to get out. He'd call Uncle Drew. They'd all come. Edward wouldn't hurt Lilly until she was awake and able to really be terrified.

Edward began to whistle again as he turned in his seat. Unbuckling himself, he got out of the van. Cole allowed himself to take a few short breaths but wouldn't move. He could still hear the whistle. The side of the van opened, and Edward reached in and pulled Lilly's limp form out. Throwing her over his shoulder like a sack of potatoes, Edward walked away, leaving the side door open.

Now was his chance. He wanted to slip out and run. Lilly would tell him to run. If she knew where he was, she'd be begging him to run. But Cole didn't move. Part of it was that he didn't want to leave Lilly, but he was just too scared to budge.

Alone, with the sound of Edward's whistling gone, Cole slowly allowed himself to breathe. He was gripping Abbie's phone so tightly in his sweaty hand that it nearly slipped out.

Stay still just a little longer. One more minute.

Cole tried to imagine the seconds ticking down, convinced if he moved before the full minute had passed, he'd be caught.

The blanket pulled away from him, and Cole blinked from the stream of sunlight penetrating the van. Edward grinned at him. "Hello, Cole. Did you think I wouldn't see you hiding back here?"

****

Brooke held onto his daughter tightly, as if he let her go for just a moment, Edward Hunter would slither out from the shadows and drag Abbie away to never be seen again. She trembled as she held onto him, her tough girl exterior gone.

Drew slammed in through the front door, Ollie, Ashley and Sam right on his heels. Drew's eyes were narrow slits of hate and Brooke assumed the fist that his childhood friend had clenched at his side was headed his way. If so, Brooke deserved it.

Drew glanced towards Abbie. "Are you all right, sweetie?"

Abbie buried her face in Brook's side. "I'm sorry. I'm sorry. Cole just…"

Drew placed a hand softly on her shoulder. "It's not your fault. I'm glad you're okay. I need to talk with your father so we can find Cole and Lilly. Can you go with Ashley?"

With downcast eyes, Abbie meekly stepped forward.

Ashley took her hand and pulled her into an embrace. "We'll go the garage apartment so we're out of your way." She began to lead Abbie through the kitchen, pausing once she saw the overturned table and chairs. Instinctively, she shifted so Abbie wouldn't see it, but turned to her brother. "Drew. Find them. *Finish* this."

Drew locked eyes with her and Brooke recognized the silent promise between them. When they found Hunter, they wouldn't bring him in for a trial.

As soon as Ashley and Abbie left the house, Brooke turned to Drew. "I'm sorry. I should have—"

"Save it," Drew snapped. "He fucking played all of us. Let's find him and put him down."

Brooke ran his hand over his head. "Best I can piece together, Abbie went to get Cole. They were going to try and sneak a cupcake and Cole didn't have his phone with him. They hid when Hunter attacked and incapacitated Lilly. They both would have been safe, except Cole snuck into the van. He took my daughter's phone with him and McAlister is working to try and trace it. Abbie didn't get a plate number, but she told us it was a white van. Sheriff Miller has a BOLO out on it and every cop in Ember Falls is looking for it."

Drew scoffed. "A white van? Yeah, not too many of those out there."

Ollie took a step closer. "Mom will have every single car on the road pulled over and searched. She's calling in every favor she has to the surrounding jurisdictions. He won't get far."

Brooke turned to examine the wreckage in the kitchen. "No, and he knows that. This is his last play, his final game. He's been plotting this since he was outed. Going by the book, the smart play would have been to switch cars and make a beeline for Mexico and not make any stops along the way, but he zigzagged and killed along the way. He left bodies for us to follow so we wouldn't realize he'd double back."

He paced from the kitchen to the living room and back again, picturing the struggle in his mind. He hated that he could see it so clearly, visualize Lilly fighting him with every ounce of strength she had. Her instinct would have been to protect the kids. Nothing else would have mattered.

He stopped short, shook his head. "He had to know we'd do a DNA test. Small window before we realized he was alive. If he just wanted to get away, he had better chances. He's had this planned out, each move, each counter move. He's not playing by our rules. He's not trying to escape. Not yet. Maybe not at all."

Drew scowled. "Why Lilly? He barely knew her. If he wanted to hurt me, he'd have gone for Ashley or Sam."

Brooke shook his head. "This isn't about hurting you. It didn't matter to him that it was Lilly. He would have grabbed whoever was here, as long as they're connected to Cole."

If Hunter realized he had Cole, that might just be the end of the game for him. But Brooke felt there was more. Something else was driving Hunter.

"He's not making a run for the border and he'd have gotten off the street as soon as he could. He already has a place ready." Brooke pulled out his cell. "Jacob, I need you to search for properties in or around Ember Falls. Someplace secluded that has been either rented or bought over the last few months. Probably a few weeks. It won't be under Hunter's name, but it'll be a name that means something to him."

"On it." Jacob disconnected.

"What now?" Ollie asked. "Stay here and wait, or

go out and search?"

Brooke knew it was smarter to stay put until they had someplace to go, but he also understood Ollie's desire to want to do something. They needed to wait until they had direction. But dammit if he didn't want to go door to door himself.

Brooke glared at his phone, trying to will it to signal an incoming call or a text. Something that told him Jacob was making progress.

A text from a familiar number displayed on his screen and for the briefest of moments, Brooke saw a glimmer of hope. Then the words coming from his daughter's phone registered in his mind.

My brother from another mother. Don't let those two assholes and that bitch know I'm texting you, or you'll find pieces of Cole through all of Ember Falls.

Brooke's eyes narrowed as he reread the text.

Duncan is pacing, and the bitch he's fucking is trying to calm him down. Now get them out of the fucking room. No more talk about my final game.

"Brooke." Drew's voice snapped him away from reading his texts. "We have to do something. Maybe we can..." He trailed off, knowing there was nothing to do.

But Brooke needed them out of the room. "Ollie, Sam. I probably didn't do a great job talking to Abbie. I was just barely holding it together. Maybe the two of you can take another pass at her."

Sam placed a reassuring hand on Brooke's arm. "Sure. We'll be gentle."

As the pair of them left, Brooke turned to Drew. "Jacob is researching places that Hunter might be connected to, but he's constrained by legalities. As a private company, maybe McAlister could get around them a little faster. And maybe you can talk to one of McAlister's profilers. I know they have them. Maybe I'm misreading this."

Drew frowned. Clearly, this wasn't the "something" he was hoping for. "Why the self-doubt on your profiling? You don't half-ass things."

Brooke grimaced. "I just…I need to be sure."

With a scowl, Drew pulled out his cell and walked through the door to the back porch.

Brooke glanced back at the phone.

Very good. Now put your phone and gun down and go to the mailbox. Get the phone I left in there, and get in your car. I'll bring you right to me. I think it's time for you and me to finally meet, bro.

Brooke scanned the room. Somehow, Hunter must have left a camera. One with an illegal audio component. Brooke didn't have time to continue to search. He needed to leave while everyone was out of the room.

Quietly pulling out his sidearm, he placed it and the phone down on a table and silently left through the front door.

He moved quickly to the mailbox and reached in. His fingers found another phone. Taking it, he moved to the car, started the engine, and pulled away.

The burner cell rang the moment he turned the corner, making Brooke's stomach jolt. Brooke answered. "If you hurt them, I'll fucking tear you limb from limb."

Hunter laughed from the other end. "Of course, you will, brother. And I'm sure it'll be brutal. Maybe you and I have more in common than you think. Head down to Milton Oaks Road, make a right onto Meadowlark Lane. About a mile and a half down the road, there's an old barn with an American flag painted on the side. Half the stripes are missing, you can't miss it. Pull in on the left side, close the doors and call me. It'll be the only number in the contacts. It's almost noon. If you're not there by a quarter after, the next call is to hear how loud one of them screams when I cut off their fingers. Your daughter's phone is going off, now."

The line went dead.

****

Drew stood by the backdoor, his eyes fixed on the window into the apartment over the garage. He'd gotten a glimpse of Sam settling across from Abbie to question her, and the silhouette of Ollie was visible. While they talked, Drew waited.

He had called in to McAlister, and had asked to speak to one of the profilers they employed. He was still, refusing to pace. If someone passed by, they'd just see a man on the phone. Inside, the anger was surging within him, quivering in his muscles. He was aching to take action, not make phone calls.

The hold music stopped, replaced by a single ring that let Drew know his call was about to be picked up. Drew wasn't at all surprised when the voice on the other end didn't belong to anyone in the division that worked on profiles.

"Report, Marine." The General's barked order was dripping with hostility and held as much warmth as a blizzard. It gave Drew an odd sense of comfort.

"Sir, Hunter is still alive." The very thought had Drew clenching his fist. "He planned the whole thing out just to buy him time to circle back here to grab Cole. He has Lilly too. We thought it was over. I thought Cole was safe and…"

"Don't finish that last sentence. You need to be at

the top of your game, not bogged down by blaming yourself. This isn't over. Cole is smart and tough. He's survived worse."

Drew paused, forcing himself to breathe. Cole had survived being kidnapped by corrupt killer cops, and a psycho hit man, but this was different. Edward Hunter was the monster that terrified Cole's nightmares in the flesh. Even if they got Cole back, how was he going to recover from this?

He closed his eyes to try and center himself, and regretted it as the picture of Cole, helpless at the hands of a monster, filled his mind. It took every ounce of self-restraint to stop himself from breaking down and crying.

Instead, Drew gave his report, explaining what they knew. He hated himself for how impersonal he sounded as he rattled off the pertinent details. "They don't have a big head start, and Jacob is already trying to run a trace on Abbie's phone."

"He's good, so I'm not going to waste time having Ari duplicate his efforts. Which leads me to my next question. Why are you calling in for a profile on Hunter? Our people did that. So did Madison, and his was probably the best I've seen. Why the second-guessing?"

Drew scowled. "I don't know. I thought it was a waste of time, but Brooke…" Drew shook his head. "Maybe he's doubting himself."

There was a pause while the General contemplated what he was being told. "I'm not buying that. Madison was the only one who was sure Hunter planned on coming for Cole. He just got proven right. Find him."

Drew instantly opened the back door to the house and went inside. "Brooke," he called, but there was no answer. He scanned the room. His gut told Drew he was missing something. He moved towards the front door, to see if Brooke went outside. He stopped at the sight of Brooke's phone, badge, and sidearm on the small table near the door.

Drew was through the door in an instant, where he found the spot where Brooke had parked his black FBI SUV empty.

There was no way Brooke would leave with Lilly and Cole missing. And even if he did, he wouldn't leave behind his sidearm. Drew raced back to the front door, reached for the handle, and stopped dead.

Something Cameron said echoed in his head. It was the same thing Cole had said over and over again.

He'll know. He always knows.

Drew put the phone to his ear. "I think we have a new problem."

****

Blurry shadows swirled as Lilly fought to open eyelids that felt weighted down. Pain stabbed at the base of her head, and a panicked thought occurred to her. If she didn't get the cupcakes out soon, they'd burn.

No. Cupcakes weren't the reason to panic.

There was something nearby. Something small and fragile. It moved within the silhouettes and darkness danced with each other, slowly taking shape. Instinct made her want to reach out to the tiny shape that was forming, but her arms would not move.

The only sound was quick, shallow breaths. Not her own. Lilly wasn't even sure if she was breathing, but something was. What was it?

So small. So frightened.

The shadows and shapes coalesced.

"Cole." The child she loved as if he were her own

flesh and blood sat a few feet away, but there might as well have been miles separating them. He was chained to a support beam in whatever dusty old warehouse they were in. Metal wrapped around his tiny body, crisscrossing on top of his chest. *"Cole."*

She kept her voice in a whisper type of shout, but it was no use. Cole's eyes were glassy and wide with terror. He was trapped back in his most horrific nightmare, and there was nothing she could do to protect him.

Lilly tried to move, only to discover she was chained in the same way. The old-fashioned lock lying over her heart, sealing her fate.

Son of bitch planned on torturing her to death, slowly and painfully. And he would make Cole watch.

"Cole, if you can hear me, we're going to get out of here. It's going to be okay."

A hoarse, low laugh came from the shadows. "I don't think Cole is with us right now, but he'll tune in. Once the screaming starts."

Edward Hunter stepped into the light, smoking a cigarette and munching on a cupcake. "Punk's gotten bigger since I've seen him last. Of course, if you've been cooking for him, it's no wonder." He held up the cupcake. "These are freaking awesome. I've had four already."

Lilly narrowed her eyes. "I hope you choke on them."

Edward shoved the remaining half into his mouth.

Lilly had seen pictures of him before, knew he was over six feet tall, and built like a brick wall, but something was off. His skin hung on him like an oversized rubber coat, as if he'd lost a lot of weight in a short amount of time. His eyes seemed sunken, and his skin had a yellowish gleam to it. This wasn't just a man on the run, fearing for his freedom.

Lilly narrowed her eyes and decided to take a shot. "You're sick."

Edward snorted as he licked his fingers. "I've been called sick, depraved, and a monster." He leaned on a nearby table that had a layer of dust so thick Lilly could see it from across the room. Part of her wanted to beg Hunter to let her have a dust rag and some pledge. "All of which is correct. Cole here will tell you just how sick I am."

Lilly forced herself to stay calm. "I don't mean your need to hurt helpless people to make yourself feel powerful. You're physically ill, aren't you?"

His grin faded as he took a long drag before tossing the spent butt away.

Lilly decided to take a shot in the dark. "Cancer?"

Hunter simply stared dully at her as he threw the paper from the now-devoured cupcake on the floor. The careless littering when there was a trash can not five feet away made her cringe. "Yup. The big *C*." He reached into his back pocket and pulled out a half-empty pack of cigarettes and a lighter. He pulled one out and lit it. The tip of the cigarette glowed eerily as he took a drag. "I got the trifecta. Lung, pancreatic, and liver." Smoke escaped as he spoke. "I'm fucked, so I decided to go out with a bang. That's the funny part."

He took another long drag. The smoke billowed out as he laughed. "Everyone thinks that I started on the sojourn because I got outed by Duncan and the EFPD. I was already planning this. One last round of murder and mayhem."

Lilly's nose twitched from the smell of burning

tobacco and nicotine. "Some people when faced with death try for atonement. They might see this as their last chance to make things right before standing before God. I suppose you don't believe in any deity except yourself."

He shrugged as he took one last drag. "I don't know. I've had fun with a few bitches that were avowed atheists until I got a hold of them. They begged God to spare them. I've seen some decide there was no God because he didn't save them." He flicked the cigarette away carelessly. "Best was this one who was convinced I was the devil in the flesh." He chuckled. "Man, I had fun with her."

Lilly really didn't care, but she wanted to keep him talking. She knew Brooke and the others were searching for them. She just needed to keep Cole alive long enough for them to arrive.

"So, you're not worried about going out on a murder spree? No last-ditch effort to make peace?"

Hunter rolled his eyes. "Really? I can't even count the number of women I've murdered. A few guys too, but that was more out of convenience. If there is a God, you really think there's anything I can do to wipe that slate clean?"

Lilly had to admit, he had her there.

Hunter glanced over to where Cole sat, his eyes wide as saucers, staring out into nowhere.

Hunter's face grew dark, as he walked toward Lilly. "I ain't got nothin' to say to God, but I still have one more thing to do." He reached down with his meaty hand, grabbed Lilly by her long red hair and yanked her close to his face.

Lilly turned her head away. His sour breath nearly

made her retch.

"One more game to play, and you and Cole are going to help me."

"Leave her alone!"

Lilly strained her neck to see Cole, fighting against his restraints. His small frame rocked back and forth. With a red face of fury, he locked eyes on Hunter.

Hunter let go of Lilly and stormed over.

Hatred emanated from every pore of Cole's body.

Despite being sick, Hunter was enormous and towered over Cole.

"Please, don't hurt him." Lilly's voice broke. "Please, do what you want with me, leave Cole alone."

Hunter never bothered to look at Lilly. He simply stormed out and slammed the door behind him.

****

Brooke passed by the empty shell of a burnt-out farmhouse. The old Pitney place had burned to the ground when he was twelve. Brooke could recall riding his bike over with Drew and a few buddies, and watching the flames do battle with the local fire department. Days later, they heard it was arson, but nobody had ever been arrested.

Now he wondered if it was a young man then named Edward Tice who was responsible.

The Pitney place faded from view and Brooke spotted the barn with the fading American flag on the side. Pulling up in front, he glanced at the clock. He had two minutes.

Brooke studied the barn. It was barely standing. Hunter would want privacy. He would want to make Lilly scream where nobody would hear her. Someone passing by the barn could hear a sneeze from inside.

Brooke wasn't sure what he'd find in there, but it wasn't going to be Hunter. Hitting the button to open the rear hatch, Brooke jumped out and quickly went to the back, grabbing a pair of small handcuffs, and a small roll of crime scene tape which he shoved in his jacket pocket. Finally, he pulled out an assault rifle, entered a clip and clicked off the safety.

Brooke had less than thirty seconds. He reached in to grab the burner phone, trotted over to the barn door, and pulled the left side open.

There wasn't much to see in the sprawling skeleton of a barn. The dirt floor had dried up leaves scattered about. It was dark, save for the holes in the roof that allowed light to shine in as narrow beams. There was more than enough space to pull the SUV in right next to the brown sedan sitting next to it with the keys waiting in the ignition.

Brooke started to glance around when the burner phone chimed. "Where are you, Hunter?"

Hunter chuckled. "Not too far. Not too close. I need you inside the Buick now. Stop looking for a way to send a message to Duncan. Drop that assault rifle. Now."

Brooke tensed, his eyes scanning the dark corners of the room. He picked up a spec of red from one corner, another from directly ahead. "Get in the car. You're not leaving any messages."

Grimacing, Brooke dropped the rifle, yanked the door open, and got in. He turned the key and heard the ignition start. "Now what?"

Another chuckle. "Now, you back out." His voice sounded strange, as if he was stuffing his face. "Get back on the road, this time head south. Make the first right. Drive until you see the rock quarry. Text here. I'll send the next marker. You have ten minutes."

Damn, Hunter wanted me to go back in the direction I came in to throw everyone off the moment they realized I was missing. He had to stall.

"How do I know Cole and Lilly are alive?"

"Mphwhamht?" There was a pause. "Sorry, but that bitch makes the best cupcakes I've ever had. So, you want what? What is it they call it? Proof of life? Yeah, sure. I guess that's fair." The shuffle of Hunter getting up was followed by a mixture of creaks and heavy footfalls. "One second."

Brooke moved the phone closer to his ear, listening to each sound. Hoping he'd hear something that might help him.

If he puts Lilly or Cole on the line, try and get them talking. Keep them talking. Stall, delay.

The squeak of a large, old door opening echoed faintly in his ear. "Hold on."

The sound of a gunshot had Brooke jumping. The boom faded replaced by the sounds of Cole screaming.

"Son of a bitch!" Images of Lilly shot, blood pouring out of her, flooded Brooke's mind.

Underneath the echoing blast and Hunter's laughter, Brooke heard another voice. It was distant but strong.

"Cole, we're okay. I'm not hurt. Sweetie—"

The voice stopped with the bang of a door.

"Man, I bet Cole wet his pants. I miss terrifying that kid." The amusement in Hunter's voice faded. "Okay, that's your proof of life. You now have eight minutes. I'd get going. I can promise you I'll keep them alive until you get here, but I won't promise they'll be whole."

The line went dead. Brooke revved the engine hard, scorching the ground beneath the vehicle before he pulled out and made a hard left.

He came to a screeching stop. Getting out, Brooke ran to a stop sign, pulled out the crime scene tape, and tied a decent amount to the top into a tight knot.

He rushed back to the still running car.

Tires screeched as he raced down the road and made an absurdly fast right. His heart pounded in his chest as if it wanted to explode like a cannon aimed at Hunter's head.

Just hang in there, Lilly. I'm coming.

****

Drew ignored the horns from motorists as he blasted down the roads of Ember Falls, gunning for the direction where Brooke had gone. He burst through red lights, and took a turn so fast, Sam had been bounced around in the back seat. None of that mattered. Getting to Hunter, saving Cole and Lilly, that's all that existed for him.

Brooke had left his gun and badge right out in the open, knowing that someone would spot it quickly enough and put two and two together. Brooke had to have known that Jacob would not only be able to get them into his phone to see the texts, but also track his FBI vehicle to wherever Hunter was sending him.

The bastard thought he was setting Brooke up to face him alone, but Brooke wouldn't be alone for long. They were closing in on him. They'd hang back, let Brooke take the lead, but in the end, they were all going in.

And Hunter was *not* coming out. Drew didn't care if he spent the rest of his life in a cage. Hunter was going to die, and this time, he'd stay dead.

"Shit." Jacob's voice came through the cell that Ollie held.

"What's wrong?" Ollie asked, holding the phone close to the middle of the car.

"Brooke stopped, not far from you. I suppose that could be where they are, but I'm seeing an abandoned barn. Records show the house burned down a few years ago. Not a great place to hold a couple of hostages."

Ollie frowned. "That's the old Pitney farm. It's still owned by the grandkids, who plan on selling it."

Sam leaned forward in her seat. "Why would he send Brooke there if he weren't there waiting for him?"

"We'll find out when we get there," Drew snapped, worried that he knew the answer. "How much farther, Jacob?"

A few quick clicks. "Two minutes."

Dammit, this isn't going to be as easy as I thought. "You still working on where properties that Hunter might have purchased?"

"Yeah, I'm narrowing it down. Barn or the land it sits on still in the name of Scott, Janet, and Mark Pitney. No potential buyers that I could find. The house itself burned down a few decades ago. Edward Tice lived near here when he was younger. He'd know the area."

"We're fucked." Drew made a sharp right and pulled off the road. He came to a quick stop right by Brooke's black SUV. Drew pulled his sidearm as he got out of the car. He was aware of Ollie coming from the other side of him, while Sam was right behind. Training had him cautiously approach the barn, even though he knew what he'd find.

The door was ajar, so he pulled it open. The afternoon sun lit up the barn, empty except for the assault rifle on the ground. Drew dropped to one knee and placed a flat hand on the dirt, feeling the warmth of the soil. "Hunter had him pull up, switch cars. He knew Brooke's would be tracked."

"Drew." Ollie tapped his shoulder.

Drew looked up. Ollie motioned forward. A small camera stared at them.

"Shit. Back out." Drew grabbed the assault rifle and got up. He and Ollie backed out of the barn, closing the door behind them so Hunter couldn't see what they were doing. "If he was watching, he knows we got this far."

"Over here," Sam called. She was pointing at the ground. She waited until Drew and Ollie were by her side. "You can see the tracks of where the SUV came from, but look at this. This track is deep and fresh."

Drew knelt down. Felt the dirt. "Warm." He stood up. Forced himself to let the scene play out in his head.

"Brooke left his SUV outside, knowing we'd see it. He took a left, hard. Harder than needed. Maybe hit the brakes, while pushing the gas. He's trying to signal us. Let's go."

They piled back into Drew's car. He put it in reverse and pulled out so fast that an old VW Beatle had to swerve. Changing gears, he started forward, but not as quickly as before. Ollie relayed everything to Jacob.

"There aren't going to be any traffic cams in that area, but I'll focus on finding someplace tied to Hunter. Some property."

Sam pointed ahead. "Drew."

Drew hit his signal, made a hard right near a stop sign with crime scene tape tied in a knot over it. "Brooke is leaving us a trail of breadcrumbs with crime scene tape."

****

The Buick sounded like it was about to fall apart.

The piece of junk was older than Brooke, and definitely on its last legs. Brooke had to floor it to make it to each spot Hunter was sending him. Each time, it left him at a road where he could turn right or left. Brooke would text

—*Here*—and Hunter would text which way, where to stop, and give an amount of time to get there. Each time, it seemed the time allotted was getting shorter.

It didn't help that at each stop, Brooke would jump out as soon as he knew which way they were going, and use the crime scene tape to indicate which direction he was headed. The last stop, a simple fork in the road, was the biggest challenge. The only signpost was right where the road split, so Brooke had tied one end of the tape to it, pulled out a decent amount, and put it on the ground with a small stone on top. It wasn't pretty, but hopefully, if Drew saw it, he'd understand that was the way he went. That was if the wind didn't free the tape from the stone to the left.

Glancing at his watch—the Buick was so old, it didn't even have a clock on the dashboard—he saw he had less than two minutes to get to the latest designated spot. The parking lot of an abandoned group of warehouses. He gunned it, then skidded to a stop in the parking lot. He grabbed the phone and texted one word.

—*Here*—

He waited, and nothing happened. "C'mon. I made it on time. Don't do this you fucker."

Still nothing.

His heart raced. A sharp knife of pain split into his skull as he waited. "You didn't play this game to shoot your load early. You wanted me out here. Let's do this."

Still, nothing happened. The silence was deafening. Brooke wanted to smash the phone on the dashboard of the Buick.

Nothing.

"God fucking dammit!"

He beat his fist on the steering wheel, cursed, and felt a wave of nausea rise in his gut.

The phone chimed with an incoming text.

—Wow, and I thought I had a temper. Almost there, bro. Almost there. Hit the unlock button three times to be safe, and get out.—

Brooke had to read the text three times before the full meaning sunk in. This was still on. There was still a chance he could save them.

And Hunter was still watching. Somehow, from somewhere, he still had eyes on him.

Pushing back the darkness that had nearly taken over his thoughts, Brooke hit the unlock button three times and slowly slide out of the driver's seat. He slammed the door closed and felt the phone buzz again.

—Throw the key. Hard.—

Brooke gripped the key, and considered trying to palm it, but didn't want to get caught. Instead, he chucked the keys as far as he could.

—Good. Go to the trunk. There's something waiting for you. I'll tell you just where I am. You're not that far. You have five minutes. Oh, and I got you a present bro.—

Brooke pocketed the phone and circled back to the trunk. That was the reason Hunter had him hit the unlock button. Grasping the grip, he pulled the trunk open and saw a letter sitting on a thick drop cloth. His eyes scanned the handwritten note.

Yo, bro,

There's a warehouse nearby with the same street address of your passenger. See you soon.

Frowning, Brooke read the note again. Passenger?

Understanding set in as he gazed at the dark, heavy drop cloth. There was someone under it. Brooke grabbed the corner. He yanked it away.

Seeing his mother's eyes, frozen in terror and agony, her skin bloodied and bruised from a long, hard death, Brooke fell to his knees and began to scream.

Chapter Twenty-Nine

Electrifying

Brooke had only five minutes to find the warehouse marked four, but that meant leaving his mother's body here. He couldn't just close the trunk on her.

Gently, he scooped her out. She was always thin, but now in death, there seemed to be a heaviness to her slender, wiry frame. He placed her down on the ground, wincing as she settled into the gravel. He softly closed her eyes, leaving traces of his tears on her face.

Standing up, he grabbed the blanket that she had been wrapped in and used it to cover her. His chest was heavy with grief, with images of how he'd yelled at her when he'd last seen her.

She was far from the perfect mother. She was broken, and weak, a victim of her vices. But he'd come from her, and through years of abuse and neglect, were moments of tenderness. She loved him as best as she could.

Brooke forced himself to turn to the warehouses. There were seven, but he just needed to reach number four. And he had less than three minutes to do it.

With gritted teeth, he began to sprint towards the large, abandoned buildings. Each looked ready to fall if you sneezed on them. Broken windows, missing bricks, uneven roofs, and badly spelled graffiti seemed to be the common motif.

The first building had a giant lopsided 1 hanging on its side, ready to fall at any moment. The one across from it was blank. The one to the left of 1 was marked with a 3, although it was currently upside down.

Brooke skidded to a stop and scanned the building across from it. The number four was the first one standing straight up. With balled fists, Brooke entered.

****

Drew came to a stop, spotting another piece of crime scene tape fluttering in the breeze. It was tied to a post that indicated warehouses to the left, and a school to the right. There was no way to know which way Brooke had gone.

"Shit." Drew smacked the steering wheel. "What the hell?"

Sam leaned forward from the backseat. "Brooke must have tried to get it to go one way, but the tape came loose. He's probably doing these in a rush. Hunter must be giving him time limits."

Drew glanced down in both directions. There was nobody around to question. "Which way?"

Ollie had his phone out, googling something. "That school is the old St. James School. It closed about seven years ago. Lots of privacy. That could be it."

Drew's hand hovered above the gear shift. "Maybe, but that's with the assumption that's where Hunter is. It could just be one more stop along this ride. If we go right, and Brooke went left…"

Sam looked out through the side window. "Maybe Ollie and I can flag someone down, go one way. You go the other."

The anger and frustration were vibrating in Drew's

bones. "It's a Sunday. There's not a lot of traffic. Hunter chose this area in part because there's nobody around. You could be there for twenty minutes."

Make a choice. Go for the gut feeling.

But Drew's gut was too busy twisting in the wind like that piece of crime scene tape. He was holding on by his fingertips.

He felt Sam's hand gently touch his shoulder, centering him. "We'll find them. Brooke won't let anything happen to Cole or Lilly."

Drew needed to believe it. He had to because losing Cole would destroy him.

He glanced at Ollie, who shrugged. Nobody wanted to make a guess and be wrong. They needed to move, but they were frozen in place. They needed a sign.

They needed a fucking miracle.

Drew's phone buzzed with an incoming call. It was Jacob. Drew hit accept. "Tell me you got something."

Jacob's voice sounded exhausted but steady. "I see you on my monitor. You're at the fork in the road by Route 80. Make the left. The warehouses. Someone bought the land six weeks ago. Put it under Cole's name."

Tires squealed as Drew hit the gas, and slammed the car into gear.

Hang on, Cole. Uncle Drew is coming.

****

It was like walking into death itself. The building stank of mold and decay, like flesh decomposing. The electrical wires were like exposed veins. If there was still power to this place, Brooke was sure they'd be bleeding sparks all over the place. There was a hum, somewhere in the distance. A generator, giving power to wherever

Hunter lurked and waited for him.

There had been more than a few parties here by whoever wanted a place to drink, smoke, and shoot whatever illicit substances into their bodies. Broken bottles, syringes, and used condoms were scattered amid the rest of the filth on the cold concrete floor.

A crunching of leaves that had blown in through the open windows had Brooke's hand instinctively go for his gun before he remembered he was unarmed. Movement in the shadows told him that the culprit was an animal.

But Brooke was sure he was being watched. He could feel it in his bones. Hunter must have prepared this place. He'd have eyes on him.

Resisting the urge to run through the building until he found Hunter, Brooke began to move forward slowly, methodically. He kept close to the wall, his eyes scanning his surroundings as he went.

A high-pitched wail of feedback pierced the silence, followed by the crunch of static.

Brooke came to a halt and prepared himself for a fight.

"Well, hello, bro. It's about time we got to meet each other, don't you think?" Hunter's voice boomed through the old PA system.

"Where are you?" Brooke yelled. "Come on out and let's finish this. Let Cole and Lilly go."

There was a moment of silence before the scream of feedback returned. "Bro, I see you're yelling something, but I can't hear you. This thing only goes one way. You look like an idiot. Just come down the hallway to your left. The piss-yellow door. We'll chat. Compare family history. Cole and Red are waiting."

The room was dark, with jagged shadows stabbing

out of the edges of the room. Brooke started to make his way to the left, but slowly. He wanted to race to save Lilly, but every instinct had him moving cautiously.

Hunter didn't plot and plan this out just to kill him from behind, but who knows what the man intended. He wouldn't do Lilly any good if he were dead.

As Brooke proceeded into the darkness, he felt as if he was being swallowed by the shadows. His skin felt electrified and blood pulsed through him like jet fuel. He was desperate to get his hands on Hunter.

The yellow door lay ahead. It might have once been a bright, happy yellow, but just as Hunter said, it now resembled the piss of someone with a severe urinary tract infection.

Taking a deep breath, Brooke grabbed the door handle.

A wave of electric heat surged up his arm as if he were exploding from the inside. He fell back, and the world went black.

Chapter Thirty

Nice to Meet You

Reality was a vortex of sensations that made no sense. Twisting shadows mixed with the scent of burnt flesh. Images of his mother's lifeless eyes combined with the sound of someone calling his name. A distant feeling of pain underlined with the pull of falling back into unconsciousness. Sobbing, laughing, and the taste of copper.

His mother's voice echoed in the back of his head.

I didn't give you much, but I taught you how to fight.

Brooke was drowning, black water filling his lungs. A monster was pulling him deeper... deeper...deeper.

You hearing me? Fight this bastard who killed me. Don't let the fucker win.

Sharp pain radiated through him. His lungs were on fire and he willed his eyes open. Swirling shapes were accentuated by the sound of Lilly screaming his name.

Edward Hunter's face came into focus, just as his fist made contact with Brooke's gut.

Edward grabbed the back of Brooke's neck. "I think he's finally coming to."

Laughing, Hunter swung again. Instinct had Brooke trying to block, but agony radiated through his arm that wouldn't move. Hunter's fist connected with his face, knocking him off of his feet, where he hung like a slaughtered cow waiting to be butchered. Brooke forced his eyes to open and glanced. He was handcuffed to a pipe.

His arm felt like it was being twisted off, but Brooke ignored the pain. He slumped in place, his body drooping down to the floor. His eyes fluttered and then closed all the way, but his feet remained planted firmly on the floor.

"Oh, no you don't, brother." Hunter reached down to grab Brooke by his shirt, pulling him up. "You ain't checking out on me yet. I've waited all this time to meet you. Don't let me think you're just a—"

Brooke threw his head forward and his legs to ram himself up. His forehead smashed into Hunter's nose. Hunter toppled back several inches and blood spurted from his face. Brooke twisted around and kicked into Hunter's chest.

Losing his balance, Hunter went down hard. *"Fuck!"*

Brooke attempted to stomp down on Hunter's leg, but the killer rolled out of range. Brooke's foot came down hard and he nearly lost his balance.

Trapped in a chair a few feet away, Lilly struggled against a set of chains with the lock resting over her heart.

Shackled against a support beam, Cole's face was pale white, eyes wide and trembling. The same sort of chains went around him, and the lock was identical to the one that was on Lilly's heart.

Hunter didn't plan on killing Cole. That was the final piece Brooke needed. Things fell into place. Brooke understood Hunter's endgame.

Now all he needed was to figure out a countermove.

Vincent Morrone

"Jesus, that hurts." Hunter slowly got up. He wiped the blood from his face, laughing as he did. "Well, all right. Glad to see you're not a complete pussy."

Control your breathing. Conserve your energy. Wait for your chance. Be ready to strike, but give nothing away.

"You wanted me here. Let them go." Brooke positioned himself so his weight was supported by the metal beam that the pipe ran down. He gave his arm a small tug, testing the strength of the old copper. It was sturdier than Brooke had hoped, but with enough fighting, it might give.

Not that Hunter would give him the chance.

Hunter grabbed an old towel and used it to wipe his face. "You haven't thanked me for the present I left you. My mom and yours don't look the same, but after hearing her mouth, I'm starting to think our old man had a type."

Lilly stopped fighting for a moment. "What is he talking about?"

Brooke didn't answer. He watched. He waited.

Edward turned to Lilly. "Oh, I took care of his mom for him." He made a slicing motion with his finger across his neck and shrugged. "I didn't have the time to really make her scream, but still…" He shrugged.

Lilly's eyes widened. "Oh, Brooke, I'm sorry."

Brooke remained mute.

Hunter studied him. "Bro, you are a cold-blooded son of a bitch. Maybe we have more in common than we thought."

Brooke jutted his chin out. "Why don't you undo these cuffs, and we'll see how much we have in common."

Hunter, clearly enjoying himself, shook his head. "I don't think so. We've got a lot to do and probably not too much time to get to it. I suppose you're wondering why I wanted you here."

Brooke considered Hunter. *Get him off balance. Delay so Drew could find you.*

"You know your days are numbered." Brooke kept his voice neutral. "You're not just a serial killer, you killed an FBI agent and her husband, which means the chances of you being taken alive are low. Judging from the pallor of your skin, you're sick. You have no wish to live out your time in pain and suffering, hiding from everyone. You wanted to meet me. We came from similar places. Abusive, neglectful mothers, knocked up by a man who couldn't keep his dick in his pants. You wanted to see for yourself that Senator Brook would fall from grace before you went down. I believe I helped with that."

Hunter blinked in surprise but grinned. "Yeah, that was sweet."

Brooke ignored the remark. "You can't help but wonder why you turned out as someone who needs to cause pain, while I didn't. Maybe I was faking it. Maybe I was just as cruel as you. You hate me for not being you. You don't want to face the fact that there is something broken in you."

Brooke turned towards Cole. The boy wasn't looking at Brooke, but he was sure he was listening. Waiting. Praying.

"That's one of the reasons you started to make Cole watch as you tortured women. He was a sweet child. Despite how his life started, his mother managed to make sure he felt loved. Kelli passed on her kindness, just like he got a huge dose of bravery from his aunt and uncle."

Hunter snorted. "You think Cole is brave? You have any idea how many times he pissed himself?"

Brooke locked eyes with Hunter, but these words were intended for the frightened child who had somehow stopped shaking. "Cole is something you can't begin to understand. He still tries to protect. He can see the beauty in others. He hates seeing someone in pain. After everything he's been through, it takes more courage than you or I can fathom for him to love, but he manages it. And that's why you're not going to win."

Hunter frowned, his eyes going back and forth between Brooke and Cole. "I'm not? Cause right now, I kind of feel like I'm in control."

Brooke nodded. "Yeah, I suppose right now you are. But killing Cole isn't what you want. You don't win by killing him. It was never about that. It was about the most basic, albeit in your case, twisted instinct someone can have."

Hunter sneered. "Yeah? Do tell."

Watching Cole from the corner of his eye, Brooke kept his tone casual. "You want him to carry on. You want to turn him into you. You won't kill him. You'll make him do something. More than watch this time. You'll want to break him by making him a murderer like you, but you can't. As you said, *you're* in control. He'll be traumatized. He already is, but Drew, Ashley, and the others? Even if Lilly and I never walk out of here, they will make sure he understands it wasn't his fault. They'll love him. And the fact is, you may have a real hard time hurting Lilly."

Brooke was treading on dangerous territory, but if there was even a chance he could save both Lilly and

Cole, he had to take it.

Hunter strode over to Lilly and grabbed her by the hair, making her scream. "You think I can't kill her?" He pulled a knife and put it to Lilly's throat. "I could split her wide open and there's not a fucking thing you can do."

It took every ounce of control to not scream, but if this was going to work, he had to stay calm. "You can, but you won't. You changed when Cole came into your life. You probably didn't get much out of whatever kills you scored after he left. That's why you grabbed another kid. Cameron's going to be okay too. He's got a family that will be there for him. But you've realized that you don't enjoy killing when you don't have someone like Cole or Cameron watching. Terrified, and begging for you to stop. So, all Cole has to do is close his eyes. He doesn't need to fight. He doesn't need to get away and find help. He just needs to ignore you."

Brooke shrugged. "You might still manage to kill Lilly and me. You won't enjoy it. You won't get that rush. You'll do it out of frustration. And you'll never recover, 'cause Cole will win, by simply shutting his eyes."

Hunter was turning red, and his grip on Lilly's hair tightened. He was shaking in fury. "Yeah, let's just see what the punk can and can't ignore." He let go of Lilly and jabbed his hand into his pocket. He crossed the room towards Cole, pulling out an old-fashioned key. "Let's get this fucking show on the road."

Cole froze, his eyes squeezing shut.

Hunter smacked him across the face.

"Leave him alone, you bastard!" Lilly once again struggled against her constraints.

Hunter ignored her as he fumbled with the key. He jammed the key into the lock and began to turn it. The chains started to fall away.

Cole stayed frozen in place. He didn't fight. He didn't resist. He just kept his eyes closed tight.

"Get up, you little shit!" Hunter grabbed Cole. "You're going to help me. Time to pop your cherry."

Cole didn't move. He didn't make a sound.

Pulling him to his feet, Hunter got right into Cole's face. "Listen you little—"

Cole opened his mouth and bit down on Hunter's face, drawing blood.

Hunter screamed. He ripped Cole off of him and threw him to the side.

Scampering up, Cole planted his feet as his uncle had taught him. Cole slammed a quick one-two punch into his stepfather's bleeding nose. Hunter's head snapped back. He toppled over and dropped the key.

"Cole!" Brooke looked towards the key.

Grabbing the key off the floor, Cole started to move towards Lilly, but Hunter grabbed at him from the floor. Squirming out of the way, Cole glanced up to where Brooke and Lilly were. There was no way for him to get to their side without Hunter grabbing him.

Hunter began to rise, cursing out threats as he felt the ripped skin on his face. His voice was a low, dangerous growl.

Brooke desperately tried to free himself, but the pipe was too strong.

"Cole!" Lilly screamed from the floor. "Run!"

Gripping the key tightly, Cole saw Hunter rise from the floor, his face covered in blood and murder dancing in his eyes.

As Hunter stumbled forward, Cole turned around and ran.

Chapter Thirty-One

Standing Behind Cole

Cole ran through the shadows of the building, holding the key in his hand so tightly it hurt. Sweat poured from his face and he searched the bowels of the warehouse.

Which way is out?

Cole could barely remember being dragged down here. Edward had thrown Cole over his shoulder and carried him like a kicking and screaming ragdoll.

The place was a maze of dirty walls, broken drywall, and metal doors.

He needed to get out. He needed to find Uncle Drew.

And then tell Uncle Drew how I ran and left Lilly behind.

He was a coward. Useless and weak. Edward was killing Lilly now. She was bleeding, knowing that he'd run away.

But Brooke told him to run. Why did he do that?

Lilly was going to die, screaming and in pain, and like always, Cole couldn't stop it.

"Cole!"

His stepfather's voice screaming his name had Cole freezing in place. He couldn't run, but his heart pounded as if it knew it needed to escape his chest.

"I'm going to find you, you little fucker!" Edward's

voice was getting closer. "I'll find you, and you'll hold the knife while we slice that red-headed bitch up."

Cole collapsed into a dark corner and began to shake.

"You're going to watch as we make her scream Cole! You'll be the last thing she sees when we *cut out her fucking heart!*"

Cole felt as if he were drowning as Edward's words echoed in his mind. He was going to find him and make him watch.

Make him watch as he hurt Lilly.

Make him watch…

Brooke was talking about how Hunter wanted Cole to watch. He didn't hurt Lilly because Cole ran away. He didn't kill her… *Wouldn't* kill her unless he got Cole. If Cole could get away…

A sharp pain snapped him back to reality. He'd gripped the key so hard that he'd drawn blood.

Staring at the key, he thought how it was what was needed to free Lilly.

"I'm going to find you, Cole! I know where you are! *I always know!*"

Slowly, Cole got to his feet. *Bullshit. He didn't always know.* If Edward knew where he was, he'd have come already and dragged Cole back to that room by his hair.

Edward was getting closer, but Cole knew what he had to do. Ever since he'd come to Ember Falls, he'd been protected. Uncle Drew, Aunt Ashley. Ollie and Sam.

Lilly.

She'd die to protect him.

It was time Cole protected them.

Heavy pounding from Edward running down the hall told Cole he was getting closer, but Cole was done being so terrified he couldn't move.

Spotting an opening in the wall, Cole scampered across the floor and squeezed through the hole in the sheetrock. It was tight, but he could move. The darkness was so thick it was like moving through a river of shadows, but Cole didn't need to be able to see to move.

Right now, all Cole needed to know was that he couldn't be seen by his stepfather.

Cole moved quietly, pushing his way through the hollow between the walls as silently as possible. He'd stop, listen, and hear Edward slamming around in the distance. The more he cursed, the safer Cole felt.

Years of Edward telling him he would always know, but he didn't know where Cole was now. He didn't know Cole was going to fight back.

He didn't know everything.

Edward crashed into the room on one side of the wall. He grunted as he labored to breathe, and Cole could swear he heard him snarl. "Where the fuck are you, Cole? You think you're so tough? C'mon out and let's see how tough you are! I bet you'll fuckin' piss your pants when I make you slice up that little redhead." There was silence, broken only by the scrape of his shoes as he moved back and forth. *"Cole!"*

Cole jolted from the primal scream of his name, but he stayed quiet. He waited until he heard the trail of cursing that told him Edward was leaving to search somewhere else.

Cole pushed his way through the wall a little farther. He saw an opening in the back and decided to peek his head out. Long, jagged shadows pierced the floor, and trash littered the floor. Across the room, he saw another hole that would allow him to get in between the walls.

Listening intently, he waited for the next curse from Edward.

He didn't have to wait long.

"Fuck!"

Cole slid out of his hidey hole and padded his way over to the new opening. He squeezed in and started to look around. It was dark but like before there was some light coming through holes. Cole had to walk sideways to move, but he made his way down to where he saw some broken drywall that was almost at eye level.

He took one step at a time. Slowly. Lightly. Careful to be as silent as possible. After each step, he'd pause. Listen. Wait.

Making it to the end, he could see the drywall was rotted. Probably not the healthiest to breathe, but better than allowing Edward to find him. He had to duck down a couple of inches to peek through, but he was able to see.

One of the lights running off the generator that Edward had hooked up was in the perfect position for him to see down the hall. Peering out, he watched.

Edward stomped through the hallway. He'd gone into a room that Cole had been in before, one covered in old boxes and spare drywall. Cole could hear him curse as he tore the room to pieces.

Cole allowed himself to relax just a bit. Edward was several rooms away.

Pain began to radiate up his knees from the awkward way he was bent. Cole straightened up and regretted it the moment he did. A loose nail pierced his scalp. "Shit."

The moment he said it, he clapped his hand over his

mouth.

Stupid. Keep your mouth shut, idiot. Be quiet.

He listened intently, and the silence terrified him. But when the cursing and throwing of objects returned, Cole released the breath he hadn't been aware he'd been holding.

Cole probed the wound with his fingers. A stream of blood trickled down his face. He felt the nail and pulled it out. He recalled Jay telling him how he'd stepped on a nail and needed to get a shot from the doctor. Cole hated doctors almost as much as he hated needles.

The image of Doctor Pulaski coming toward Cole with a needle sent a shiver down his spine, which was followed by a nearly uncontrollable urge to laugh.

He was inside a wall, hiding from his killer stepfather and he was thinking needles were scary.

Right now, he needed to figure out what to do next.

As he thought, he listened.

And heard nothing.

He waited.

Still nothing.

For some reason, the silence seemed darker than before.

Slowly, he lowered himself back down and peered through the hole in the wall.

And saw Edward's hungry eyes glaring right back at him.

Edward's meaty fist punched through the wall, sending dust into Cole's mouth as his head slammed backward from the blow. Cole felt Edward's hand grip him by the throat.

"I've got you, you little—"

Cole stabbed Edward's hand with the nail he was

holding. It pierced his skin, and Cole twisted it. Howling in agony, Edward let go. Cole pushed back, crashed through the rotted drywall, and tumbled to the floor.

Hearing Edward scream, Cole scampered to his feet and ran.

****

Drew came to a skidding halt in the parking lot right near the old sedan with the trunk popped open. All eyes fell on the still form hidden beneath a drop cloth lying on the gravel floor by the rear of the vehicle.

Drew froze in place.

Too big to be Cole. That means...

"Oh, God." Sam's hand went to her mouth. "Lilly?"

Ollie was the first one out of the car. He stepped over the body, knelt, and gripped the drop cloth. Taking a deep breath and holding it, he slowly lifted it and peered underneath.

Seeing the unfamiliar face, Ollie exhaled. "It's not her." He pulled the drop cloth farther off, exposing her face to the sun as Sam and Drew came over. "It's not Lilly. I don't know who it is, but..."

"Son of a bitch." Drew cursed as he saw the body. "That's Brooke's mom."

In death, Destiny Madison appeared to have found the peace that had eluded her throughout her life. She seemed almost angelic lying on the bed of white gravel, despite the bruising on her face.

Drew pulled the drop cloth completely off. There were burns on her body, broken fingers and ribs, and puncture wounds on the soles of her feet. Eyeing the open trunk, Drew put things together. "Son of a bitch hid her body in the trunk, had Brooke drive around town with her in the back. He made sure Brooke found her."

Gently, Drew pulled the drop cloth back over her, covering her up from the sun before standing. "They're in one of those buildings."

Sam stood by his side. "How can you be sure? Couldn't he have made Brooke switch cars again?"

Reaching into the trunk, Drew pulled out the note that indicated they were in warehouse number four. Throwing it at Ollie, Drew pulled out his sidearm, pulled back the slide, and released it, loading one in the chamber. "Hunter did this to throw Brooke off right before they came face to face. He's here."

Drew marched towards the building, gun at the ready.

Hang on, Cole. I'm almost there.

****

Brooke managed to get the cuff over the elbow of the copper pipe. He was now using his full weight to try and separate the pipe from the wall. It was starting to work. It was bending. His arm felt like it was on fire, but given a few minutes more, he'd be free.

Obscenities echoed from down the hall.

Brooke glanced at Lilly who had heard them too. "That's a good thing. That's his 'I haven't caught Cole yet' curse."

"But *if* he catches him…"

Cole came bursting into the room. He was filthy, and blood stained the side of his face, but otherwise, unharmed. "He's coming."

Cole slid next to Lilly and pulled the key to the lock out of his pocket. Inserting it, he jiggled it until it turned and the lock clicked open. "I'm going to get you out of here Lilly." He began to unwrap the chain that bound her to the thick, metal beam. He glanced over his shoulder to

Brooke. "You too."

Brooke shook his head. "Just get Lilly and get out. Don't worry about—"

The door slammed open.

Bloodied and bruised, Edward Hunter entered the room. He held a gun at the ready, aiming it right at Lilly. His face was a furious mask of insanity. "Let's play."

****

Edward gave Brooke a wide berth, staying out of reach as he crossed the room. His blood-soaked hand gripped the gun. His laughter was almost manic. "Oh, we're going to have us some fun now. You're going to learn to love the way we'll make her scream."

Lilly tried to move; the chain that bound her started to unravel.

Hunter aimed the gun directly at Cole's head, pressing the barrel right between his eyes. With his other hand, he wagged his finger at her. "Uh-uh."

Lilly stopped moving.

Grinning like a madman, Hunter leaned closer to Cole. "Wrap that chain back around her, nice and tight. It's time to break your cherry."

Cole didn't move from his spot. Hunter decided he was too terrified. Kid was ready to piss himself. Trembling, tears welling in his eyes. But Hunter was in control. The way it was supposed to be. He ignored Brooke who was still attempting to free himself. His brother was helpless. He'd watch as the bitch was slaughtered. He refused to listen to Lilly as she urged Cole to do as he was told. She didn't matter.

But Cole didn't move. He didn't blink.

And his eyes weren't filled with fear.

Just loathsome hatred.

405

The humor started to drain out of Hunter's face. "Do it!"

Cole didn't budge.

Edward shook in rage.

The rest of the world ceased to exist. There was nothing else that mattered.

This little shit isn't going to fucking ignore me.

"Cole, wrap that bitch up! Do what I tell you! Do you know what I'm going to do? Do you remember who I am? I own you! *I fucking own you!*"

Hunter got louder, and Cole seemed to get calmer. His eyes were full of contempt as he lifted his chin.

"No." Cole closed his eyes.

Hunter took a step back, stunned at the defiance. Nearly dropping the gun out of shock, he raised his hand. It was as if he couldn't decide if he wanted to slap, punch, or grab at Cole. He ignored the banging from behind him and the screams from Brooke.

Lilly leaped at Hunter, wrapping the chain she'd managed to slip out of around Hunter's neck. She put all of her weight into trying to pull it back. Cole ran to help.

Hunter was too big, too strong, and far too enraged to allow himself to be stopped by a puny woman, and a punk kid he should have killed years ago.

Grabbing the chain, he shifted his weight, pulled Cole off his feet, and knocked Lilly off her balance. His fist connected with Lilly, sending her flying back into the metal beam that she'd just escaped from.

Cole landed hard, and Hunter grabbed him by his throat. Lifting him so they were eye to eye, Hunter snarled as Cole started to turn blue from lack of air. "I'm done with you."

He brought the gun up, determined to end Cole for

good.

Metal snapped and steam exploded. Hunter spun around. He narrowed his eyes, but couldn't see anything.

A primal scream shattered the hiss of the mist, followed by Brooke crashing into Hunter.

Cole was freed, dropping to the floor where Hunter couldn't see him. Brooke wrestled for the gun with his brother. With both of their hands on the weapon, a shot rang out. It went wild, hitting one of the lights above.

Brooke's fist slammed into Hunter's face, and the room began to spin. Together they toppled to the floor. Brooke grabbed at Hunter's hand that held the gun and slammed it into the concrete basement floor.

Hunter wrapped his other meaty hand on Brooke's throat. He began to squeeze.

Brooke slammed the gun down again. The weapon went off and skidded across the cement floor.

Like a wounded beast, Hunter pounded on Brooke's head. He rolled, getting Brooke under him. Hunter slammed his brother's head down.

Hunter's face was dripping red. The white of his eye had been erased by blood. His rotted teeth bared as he began to strangle Brooke. "Say goodbye, brother."

"Get off him!"

Through the mist, a small figure emerged.

Cole held the gun just as Brooke had shown him. He stood with his feet planted and grim determination displayed on his face. His small eyes were slits of hatred.

Hunter laughed manically. "You ain't got the balls to pull—"

Cole squeezed the trigger, and a chunk of flesh was ripped from Hunter's arm. Another shot grazed Hunter's ear.

"You little prick." Hunter snarled through the pain of the flesh wounds. "You can't even aim for shit!"

Soft hands reached through the dark, steadying Cole's hands and moving less than half an inch to the left. All traces of fear and doubt melted away from Cole's face.

Lilly's face came into view above Cole's shoulder. Her eyes were locked on Hunter's.

"No, but I can, you son of a bitch."

Lilly aimed the weapon and Cole pulled the trigger.

Blood poured out of the center of Hunter's chest. He stumbled back, falling off of Brooke.

Together, Lilly and Cole pulled the trigger again.

Hunter felt the trickle of blood roll from the center of his head. It filled his eyes with dark red before the world went blank and he fell over.

Chapter Thirty-Two

Putting The Pieces Back Together

Drew burst through the doors, his gun at the ready, his eyes sweeping the room. His heart had nearly stopped when he'd heard the first gunshot, but it took less than a second for his training to kick in. He didn't pause for the second shot, and he tried to ignore the images of Cole being killed that flooded his mind.

Steam still filled the air, but Drew could make out movement in the center of the room. Shadows within the mist, but without a distinctive form.

He moved closer and saw the hint of metal in someone's hand. "Drop it."

"Uncle Drew!"

Cole burst through the fog and launched himself into Drew's arms. The small child buried his head in Drew's chest. Drew held him, felt him tremble, and tried to make out what Cole was saying.

"H-he...H-h-he...he's dead..."

Drew swallowed hard, as an icy grip tightened around his heart. "Brooke?"

Cole shook his head. "Edward. I...w-we...k-k-killed..." Cole's voice broke first, followed by Cole himself as he began to sob.

Drew held Cole tightly, taking a moment to holster his sidearm.

"Brooke needs help!"

Exchanging glances with Sam, they stepped into the mist and followed the sound of Lilly's voice. They found her kneeling by Brooke's side. She'd ripped a piece of his shirt off, and was pressing it against the back of his head. As Drew knelt, Brooke forced himself to sit up.

"I'm fine." Brooke scowled, motioning to the side. "It's over."

A few feet away was Edward. Eyes open, staring into nothingness. Blood pooled around him like a demonic halo dripping from the hole in his head.

This time there was no doubt. He was dead.

Drew stiffened as he stared into the face of the man who had terrified Cole for his entire life. The monster who plagued Cole's nightmares and lurked in every shadow. An almost irresistible urge to stomp on Hunter's face and erase him from existence flowed through Drew, burning like lava in his veins.

He'd wanted to be the one to kill Hunter. He wanted it to be slow, painful, and final. Drew's heart pounded as if it were trying to blast out of his chest like a missile.

A sob escaped from Cole, snapping Drew out of his haze of fury.

Sam knelt by Hunter's body and felt for a pulse as they were trained to do. With a quick shake of her head, she holstered her weapon and pulled out her cell. "Chief Miller, we're in the old Warehouse District near Greensville. Fourth warehouse. We need medical." She paused as she listened. "Brooke is hurt but appears stable. Lilly and Cole are safe." Her eyes narrowed as she took a breath. "I've got eyes on Edward Hunter. He's dead."

The hiss went silent and the mist began to dissipate.

Ollie came through the remainder of the fog. "Got the boiler shut off. Steam should clear." He began securing Hunter's body, per procedure.

Sam put her phone away, knelt by Brooke, and assisted Lilly in tending to his wounds. "Lilly, are you hurt?'

She shook her head. "Bruised. Sore as hell. He batted Cole around more than me, but I think we're fine."

Drew gave Cole a visual examination. He had blood on him, but Drew wasn't sure if it was his or Hunter's. His neck was bruised and he'd probably have a black eye before long, but there didn't appear to be anything life-threatening.

But the kid was in shock. He was white as a sheet. His eyes were glassy and he was trembling while sucking on this thumb.

"I'm going to take Cole out of here. We'll wait for Chief Miller to show up with the medics. Make it easier on them to find us. Someone call my sister and let her know."

Without waiting for an answer, Drew stalked out of the dark, misty room. The scent of the musty steam grew weaker the farther away he went. He cradled Cole like he would a newborn, whispering in his ear that everything was going to be okay.

Hunter was dead. The nightmare was over.

And Cole had a hand in killing him. Healing was going to be a long, hard road.

****

Brooke pulled out the plastic bag that had been stowed under the hospital bed and started to yank out his clothes. Ripping off the blue hospital gown they made him wear, he dressed, determined to leave as quickly as possible.

"Brooke."

A cold chill swept through Brooke, mixed with the nearly overwhelming urge to run to Lilly and hold her close.

Slowly, he turned.

Lilly entered the room, shutting the door behind her. "You're okay? I was so worried. There was so much blood."

Brooke's hand went to the back of his head, as the memory of Hunter slamming his skull onto the ground came flooding back. "Head wounds tend to bleed a lot. I've got a thick skull. I'm fine. Small concussion. A few stitches. No lasting damage."

She nodded but didn't move closer. "I ran into Jacob. He told me he was here to pick you up, but that you were headed back to the hotel. Not back home."

Brooke nearly broke at the way she used the word home as if it were a place that belonged to the two of them. "I was staying there to keep you and Cole safe." The irony of how badly he failed at that made the room seem dimmer. "I didn't think you'd want—"

"Stop." Lilly held up her hand, her quiet voice filled with as much authority as the barks of command he'd heard from the General. "If you wanted to know what I'd wanted, you should have asked me. You didn't."

Taking a deep breath, Lilly took a step forward. "Brooke, talk to me. We failed years ago for a lot of reasons, and not talking to each other was a big one. You walking away from me, and me not knowing why will kill me." She swallowed hard. "If you can't forgive me for that, then just…"

"No." Now it was Brooke who moved forwards.

"Lilly, this is nothing to do with you. With my not wanting you. God, I fucked up. I came here, thinking…" He closed his eyes and fought for control. "Believing that years ago you finally saw me for what I was. The son of a whore. The unwanted child of an unknown father." He opened his eyes and cursed himself for the tears he saw welling in her eyes. "I was nothing more than that. And by this time tomorrow, I will be again."

With a furrowed brow, Lilly took another step closer. "What are you talking about? How will you be nothing?"

Brooke averted his eyes. The shame of having to spell it out made him feel naked. "My father was complicit in protecting a known serial killer. My brother *was* the killer. I didn't tell anyone. If I had, they would have barred me from coming anywhere near Ember Falls. They would have never assigned me to be here. Never let me near Cole." He didn't wipe away the tear that rolled down his cheek, but he made eye contact with Lilly again. Shuffled a step closer, yearning with every fiber to hold her. To be held by her. Knowing at her core that she deserved better than him.

"I was ready for that. I was prepared to take leave. To quit." Anger surged within him, radiating up his spine. He scowled and clenched his fist. "I couldn't let him hurt you. I wouldn't…" He broke off, closing his eyes. "I couldn't even get that right. God damn it, Lilly, he took you and your son. I couldn't even keep my fucking family from putting you in chains. From hurting you. I couldn't see…" He winced. "I'm supposed to be able to see twelve steps ahead, and Hunter played me. He…"

He felt her hands gently touch him. Softly, she

wiped away the tears. She pulled him to her and held him close. "They aren't your family. No more than DA Reynolds is Drew's father. Hell, as far as I'm concerned, Frank Duncan wasn't Drew's father. That title belongs to the General. Edward Hunter was Cole's stepfather for years. Would you tell him to let Hunter define who Cole calls family? Or his self-worth."

Brooke didn't answer, because she was making too much sense. And his dark and twisted world was being lit up.

"Do you know where we went wrong last time?" She asked.

Brooke closed his eyes. "You blamed yourself for losing our baby. I let myself believe a lie."

Lilly took his face in her hands, forcing him to see her. "We didn't fight for us. We belonged with each other. We loved each other, but we had so much shame from years of emotional abuse that we didn't fight for it. Fight for our love. Because we were so convinced that we were unlovable."

There was a defiant gleam in Lilly's eyes as she spoke. "I'm done with that. I know I deserve love. I love Cole. And despite every hell that boy has been through, he loves me. I've only known Abbie for a few days, but I'm already falling in love with her. And I love you, Brooke. If you don't feel the same, then say so and walk away. It'll hurt, but I'll survive. But if you love me, and I think you do, then fight. Face the Bureau and fight for the life you built. Maybe you'll win. If not, fight to build another life. You came from nothing, but Brooke *you* were never nothing. Not to me. Not to Drew. And not to Cole. He's asked about you. He needs to know you're okay."

Brooke shook his head. "I'm the brother of the monster that hides in his closet. I'd be a reminder of his worst nightmare."

"No." Lilly's voice was firm. "The monster has been slain. He needs you to show him that being connected to that monster doesn't define him. He needs to see you fight. To see that kindness, that gentleness." She smiled. "That fierceness that you always had when you loved me. Just like Abbie does. Just like I do."

Brooke stared into her eyes and saw the hope and dreams he'd always had shining in them. He was ready to fall into a dark hole of depression and despair, and here she was, his warrior, pulling him out.

All he had to do, was climb.

Brooke gave in and resolved to fight for what was his. He crushed his mouth down on hers. Standing there, embracing her, kissing the woman he'd loved for as long as he could remember, he felt whole and ready to take on the world.

The kiss ended, and he breathed in her scent. "God, I love you, Lilly. Let's go home."

Chapter Thirty-Three

Welcome Home

The fact that Brooke was sitting in an Ember Fall's Police Interrogation room did not, in Brooke's mind, bode well for the conversation that he was about to have with the Unit Chief of the Behavioral Analysis Unit.

Brooke doubted that there was no other room available for his official debrief. Nothing Burkhardt did was by accident. The man rarely asked a question without knowing the answer. Burkhardt had forgotten more about reading people since he'd had his first cup of coffee this morning than most people would understand in their lifetime. Brooke included.

He made Brooke sit in there, waiting for him, for nearly an hour. When he entered, there'd been no pleasantries, no polite inquiries as to his injuries. He simply sat, opened a file, and began to read in silence for a good five minutes. Finally, he hit record on a small digital recorder, settled back in his chair, and as casually as he would ask a waitress for a second cup of coffee, he nodded towards Brooke. "Let's hear it."

Slowly, methodically, Brooke took him through the events. He left nothing out, but he framed it to give his reasons for doing what he did. He made it clear, in no uncertain terms, that he never even considered protecting the two men who shared his blood.

Burkhardt listened, making a few stray notes here and there, giving nothing away as Brooke spoke. When it was done, Burkhardt skimmed his notes, then reached over and switched the digital recorder off.

Each moment was long, drawn out, and methodical. From the way he closed the file, to how he took off his glasses. The way he pulled out a small, soft cloth from his jacket pocket and used it to clean his glasses before placing them in a hard, plastic case and snapping it shut.

"Do I strike you as an idiot, Agent Madison?"

Blinking rapidly, Brooke started to respond, then realized that he had no idea what to say. "I'm sorry, sir, but...*What*?"

Casually, he placed his hand over the file. "I'm asking if I strike you as an idiot. Because I'm fairly sure someone in this room is not as smart as the other person always thought. I'd just like to know if it's me, or you."

Certain that he appeared almost comical with his mouth hanging open, Brooke did his best to recover. "Sir, you have never struck me as anything but the most intelligent and capable agent I've ever worked with. If I've given you any offense, or reason to believe I thought otherwise..." He trailed off as Burkhardt raised his hand.

"Madison, you're sharp. Sharper than three-quarters of the agents that have passed through the BAU since its inception." He wagged his finger at Brooke as a warning. "I'll deny that if you ever repeat it. I know you're smart, but that doesn't preclude the fact that you can also be a complete idiot at times. And underestimating me is one of those times."

Brooke wasn't quite sure what was happening, but he was starting to believe this was one of those times where you should say as little as possible. "Sir?"

Burkhardt sighed. "You think I didn't make the possible connections? Somebody used Duncan to cover shit up. He got screwed, driven out of town. During that decade, the one sister…" He opened the file, and glanced through the notes. "Ashley. She was pissed at him. No chance of her asking him to come back. Then the other one, Kelli comes back. Lo and behold, Diana Lakeland 'volunteers' to be her counselor." Burkhardt made quotation marks in the air as he spoke. "That wasn't a coincidence. They wanted to see if she would do what the other Duncan sister wouldn't do. Ask her brother to come back. The entire town had accepted the narrative that Duncan had killed the Winter's girl. It would have worked much better had he been put away, especially if he'd taken a plea, but the SOB wouldn't so keeping him away and keeping that lie alive was important. But to who? Who had something to gain, or more importantly, something to lose, if people started to question that narrative? It wasn't the old police chief. He was dead. It had to be someone who was still in a position of power. There are only so many people who fit that bill. Reynolds was one. That was the backup plan. You realize who hatched that, right?"

Brooke allowed himself to relax just a bit. "Jericho. He'd realized he'd failed to throw them off track by blaming Duncan's father. He put information on that laptop that would point to Reynolds, made it appear like he was destroying it, but in reality, he was leading the cops right where he wanted them to go."

Burkhardt's right eyebrow twitched. "See? Sharp. When I sent you here, I had Reynolds on my shortlist. So was the old city comptroller, although he was low on my list. The coroner had to be bought for the frame-up of

Duncan to work as well. We have two FBI agents, one of whom is in line for a promotion to head an office out of Maryland that came from Ember Falls. Problem is, I didn't think any of them had the money to pull this off. To me, it came down to either Bob Reynolds or Thomas Brook. And the Senator had the most to lose.

"Now did I 'know' that he was your biological father?" He made the air quotation marks again. "No. But did I *suspect*?" He rolled his eyes. "I knew what your life was like here in Ember Falls. I knew your mom was being fed money by someone, besides you. The question was who. The little name game? Brooke with an E versus Brooke without one? That was just a tad too on the nose to ignore. The problem is, there was no way to know it. And if I was right about Senator Brook, any official investigation into him would be flagged. Who the hell knows who he had to warn him? Well..." He flipped the folder open again, quickly opening it to one of the pages towards the end. "Thanks to those files you found and turned over, we do now. He had three moles within the Bureau. One of whom would have easily let him in on what we were doing."

Brooke examined the names. *Gary fucking Wilkes. The same guy who liked to bully Jacob. Son of a bitch.*

Burkhardt pulled the file back, and flipped it closed. "Point is, I'm not surprised by the whole family angle. I wouldn't have sent you here if I wasn't sure you'd do what was right. Did I believe you were right that Hunter was going to try and make an end-run-around us to get back to Cole Duncan? No, I'll admit I missed that. You didn't. And none of us saw through his plan to play the decoy with the dead body thing. At least you clued into it before it was too late."

Not soon enough to keep Lilly and Cole safe.

"That part was all Agent Rivers." Brooke's world was too focused on how he'd used his connection to the former and now-indicted Senator Brook in trapping him to find Tiffany Reynolds. "He realized something was off. Did the work on it. He deserves a commendation."

Burkhardt began to rise. "He'll get one. And a promotion with his transfer."

Furrowing his brow, Brooke rose as well. "Transfer sir?"

Once again, Burkhardt covered his mouth as he coughed. "Yeah, Rivers is being put in Foster's new team. I'm assuming you don't have any problems with that, as you'll be headed there as well. You'll be Foster's second in command. Her request."

Brooke's eyebrows squished together as something fluttered in his stomach. "I'm…What?"

Burkhardt scowled, but Brooke could see the amusement dancing in his eyes. "Foster is leaving Quantico and getting her own unit. She figures she's tired of you being right and her not being able to use that so she wants you to be right for her. That's after all the paperwork on this mess is done, and you need to be cleared by the boys in the white coats, but that shouldn't be an issue. In the meanwhile, could you maybe call off General McAlister and the Duncan kid." Burkhardt shook his head. "McAlister going to bat for you was one thing, but I had to interview Cole and that kid really kicked my ass. I hate when that happens."

Without waiting for a response, Burkhardt left, leaving Brooke to collapse back in his chair as he blinked slowly in disbelief.

He pictured telling Lilly that he came in here, ready

to fight for his career, and then it wasn't needed. He just got…

His eyes shot open as adrenaline shot through his veins. His chest tightened as he launched himself out of the chair and through the door. "Agent Burkhardt, *where* am I going?"

****

Lilly paced back and forth, stopping every few moments to glance at the kitchen, or living room rug, or the giant bay window in the front of the house. It was as if the invisible dust and dirt were calling her name, begging her to do battle.

The only battle she was waging was inside of herself. For the last two days, she had Brooke in her bed. She felt whole as if the pieces of her that had been ripped away for years were sewn back on.

Now, forces beyond her control were tugging at those bits of her, threatening to rip them away forever, leaving her in a tattered mess on the floor.

No, whatever happened, she and Brooke were going to make this work. Or they wouldn't, and she'd go on without him. She'd have Cole, she had her store, she had her entire life to look forward to. It was time to start living it. Even if she had to do it without…

Her face flushed at the memory of Brooke's hands on her, the weight of him on top of her, the electric shock rippling through her as that magical mouth of his found her every sensitive spot.

She groaned, the thought of not having him in her bed for the rest of her life was horrifying. She closed her eyes and forced herself to let it go. There are some things that you can't control. Tilting her head back, she practiced her breathing.

In. Out. Center yourself. Feel the rug with her bare feet. Flex your toes through the soft fibers of the carpet. Don't think about the fact that it's been almost a month since you last shampooed it. Feel the breeze from the ceiling fan above you.

Opening one eye, she studied the fan, leisurely spinning around, blissfully unaware of the turmoil right beneath it. The fan that she hadn't cleaned in... *How long had it been?*

"We are not getting the ladder out to clean the ceiling fan."

Lilly turned to see Ashley coming in the back door with Sam. A knot in her stomach loosened. She'd never be alone. She had sisters.

"Relax. I'm..." She sighed. "Okay, I was thinking it, but I'm not going to let Brooke come home and find me up on a ladder with a dust rag. He was nervous about today."

Sam steered Lilly into the kitchen, sitting her down at the table.

Ashley went and poured them all cups of coffee. "It'll work itself out. Ollie says Chief Miller would love to get her hands on Brooke. I mean, not in the same way you've been doing..." She wiggled her eyebrows at Lilly who turned red. "But having a former FBI profiler under her command would really fill out her ranks. And think about it, all our men, working in the same place. They could carpool with Sam."

Lilly accepted the coffee and took a sip. "While I like the idea, Brooke worked his entire life to be a profiler for the FBI. I don't want that taken from him. I mean, it'll be simpler if he works for Chief Miller since that'll be local, but I just don't want him to feel as if that's been stripped away from him."

Sam placed her hand over Lilly's. "It'll work out. Drew told me the General planned on speaking to FBI Director...Burkhardt was it? He said he planned on pulling out the big guns, whatever that means."

Lilly wondered herself, but if anyone had "big guns" that could be used against the Director of the BAU, it was General McAlister.

Tiny feet came stomping down the stairs. "You're wrong. You couldn't be more wrong. In the history of wrongness, that is the most wrong wrongness to ever be wrong about." Abbie came into the kitchen from the back staircase, throwing her hands in the air in frustration.

"No, no, no." Jay followed behind her, pushing his glasses up on his nose as he spoke. "You just don't get it. We're talking about death and life here. You just don't get it. Dead is dead and you're dead wrong."

Cole scampered down last. He was quietly listening to each of them, but he didn't interrupt as Jay and Abbie continued to throw out words like blood, monster, death, and killing.

They had brought Jay over to try and help keep Cole's mind off of what happened, not get bogged down in a debate over how he'd nearly been murdered. "Hey, guys, maybe you guys could talk about something else?"

Jay spun around, his eyes darting from Lilly to Ashley, to Sam, and back to Ashley. "Hi, Ms. Duncan. Ms. Danvers. Ms. Rossi. Ms. Duncan."

Abbie and Cole both rolled their eyes.

"This is important." Abbie came over to stand near Lilly. "If there were a war between zombies and vampires, who would win?"

Lilly frowned. "I'm sorry...What?"

Leaning on the kitchen counter, Jay rubbed his hands together. "Imagine that the zombie apocalypse started. We know humans would have no real chance, not if we're assuming the zombies are the new, fast ones. The old-style ones that shamble could be beat by the three of us." He gestured to himself, Abbie and Cole. "But the new zombies are really hard to kill. They never get tired. They can attack in the day or night, while the vamps have to take a dirt nap during the day. They have a lot of weaknesses that can be exploited too. Holy water. Crucifixes. Garlic. Daylight." He ticked each point off on his fingers. "See? Zombies rule."

Abbie crossed her arms and practically snarled at Jay. "Oh. My. God. You're as braindead as the zombies. Zombies can't think! They won't know to use garlic, holy water, or any of those other things. They see you, they want to eat you. Vampires are fast, strong, and would simply smash their heads in. I'm hungry."

Hiding her snicker, Ashley pointed to the counter behind Abbie. "There are fresh cookies over there."

Abbie reached out for one until Jay stopped her casually. "Oh, you baked cookies Ms. Duncan?"

Lilly was studying Cole, how he stood silent in the corner. Something was going through his mind, but she wasn't sure what. "No, I made those earlier. Oatmeal raisin. Cole's favorite."

Relief washed over Jay's face as he handed Abbie a cookie and helped himself to one. "Oh, I love oatmeal raisin." He handed one to Cole.

The grin melted off of Ashley's face as she watched Jay happily munch on Lilly's cookies.

"Cole?" Lilly frowned, concerned that he seemed to be studying his cookie, not scarfing it down. "Is everything okay?"

Turning the cookie over in his fingers, Cole bit his lower lip. "Food."

Lilly stood up, ready to bust out her pots and pans and make Cole whatever he wanted. He'd gone back to just pecking at his food for the last few days like he had when he first arrived but seemed better since hanging out with both Jay and Abbie. "I was planning on a roast for dinner, but if you're hungry now…"

Cole glanced up. "No, food. We've been talking about zombies and vampires fighting, but zombies could probably eat vampires. Vampires need living humans to survive. If the vampires have nothing to eat, they'll get weak. They won't be able to fight."

Abbie scowled while Jay pumped his fist. "Yes! See, zombies would totally kick vamp *as*—" Jay's eyes darted to the adults in the room, "butt. Yeah, totally. Right, Cole."

Cole pursed his lips. "No. Vampires would win."

Now Jay's mouth dropped open into a perfect *O* while Abbie smirked.

"How so?" Jay demanded. "You just said—"

"No, listen." Cole held up a finger, making him resemble a tiny professor explaining a confusing problem to a befuddled student. Cole was in his element, plotting stories and creating worlds. "So, vampires need humans to live, but zombies have to kill humans. If they don't, they lose. Vampires can feed off humans and not kill them. They *just* need their blood. So, if I were a vampire, I'd work with humans."

Jay frowned. "A human/vampire alliance?"

A small grin spread on Cole's face. "Yeah. The humans would guard the vamps during the day, and the

425

vamps would go out and kill the zombies at night. They'd work out a system of keeping the vamps fed. I mean, the vampires can't feed off zombies and if the world becomes just zombies, they'd all die out. So yeah...A vampire/human alliance would totally happen. There'd be tension, and fear that the bloodsucking vampires would turn on the humans. And what if a human was bit by a zombie, just as a vampire tried to turn him?"

Jay blinked, exchanging a blank stare with Abbie who shrugged. "I got no idea. What would happen?"

Cole's eyes lit up. "You'd get a new creature. One that could control the zombies, but has the speed, strength, and intelligence of the vampires. A Vampire/Zombie King. That would be the bad guy to defeat." Immensely pleased with himself, Cole took a bite of his cookie as Jay began describing what a Vampire/Zombie King would look like.

Abbie put her cookie on the counter and concentrated on the front window. "Hey...Dad's home." She raced to the front door.

Lilly stood, aware of how hard her heart was beating in her chest. She ignored Jay's chattering and realized Cole was watching for Brooke to come in. Together, they walked into the living room to the big bay window.

Brooke was just getting out of the car. Abbie was on the front lawn, bouncing on her heels, waiting for her father.

Brooke's face gave nothing away as he walked over, and spoke to her. After a few moments, Abbie hugged her father. Was she thrilled for him, or trying to give him comfort? Lilly wasn't sure, but she stopped breathing as the pair made their way to the front door.

Time seemed to stand still as she waited. If Brooke's career was ended, he'd be devastated, but maybe she could help him rebuild his life here in Ember Falls. She couldn't wish for that, but if everything was fine, he'd be packing up and taking Abbie back to Virginia. He'd want her to come, and she'd want that too, but she couldn't. She couldn't leave Cole, and she couldn't take him away from his aunt and uncle.

Somehow, tears would be shed and somebody's heart was about to get broken.

The door opened and Brooke came in, holding Abbie's hand. His face was almost unreadable, but Lilly knew him. Even after all this time, she could see the joy in his eyes.

Her heart both ached and broke at the same time, but the delight she felt for Brooke outweighed the worry about what happened next. "You're still with the FBI. Everything worked out."

Brooke smiled. "Yeah. Burkhardt worked out a lot of what I did on his own. He decided it was better to send me in with the possible connection because any official report could be intercepted. He may have been right. So, yeah I'm still a profiler with the BAU. In fact…"

Brooke knelt by Cole. "I understand both you and General McAlister spoke to him?"

Cole grinned. "I heard you talking about it with Uncle Drew. I asked if I could help. He set me up to speak with him so I could tell him what happened. Did it help?"

"Yes, it did." Brooke held out his hand. This time when Cole took it, it was without hesitation. "He said you scared him worse than the General."

Cole's grin widened. "So, he's going to let you stay

here in Ember Falls?"

Lilly gently placed her hand on Cole's shoulder. "Cole, Brooke was assigned here because of this case. His unit is stationed out of Quantico, Virginia."

Furrowing his brow, Cole glanced up at Lilly and then back to Brooke. "But I thought...I told him..." The smile faded from his face. "I wanted you to stay."

Brooke met his eyes and winked. "That means the world to me, Cole. It really does. However, as it turns out I'm not headed back to Quantico."

Now it was Lilly who frowned, but something in his voice had her heart trembling. "Wait, you're not? But isn't that where..."

Brooke stood up and took her hand. "He promoted me. Agent Foster, who was the lead on the Manhunt, is getting her own unit. I've been assigned as her second in command. Which isn't in Quantico."

Lilly's mouth went dry. "Where?"

Placing his hand on the small of her back, he pulled her closer. "Albany. Less than an hour's drive from here. I need to be cleared by medical, and psych. Standard after what happened. In the meanwhile, Abbie and I need to move someplace close."

His face was less than an inch from hers, making her feel as if she could melt into him.

"So," Brooke said. "You know someplace where there's room for us?"

Radiating with bliss, Lilly pulled him down into a kiss. She felt Cole squirm away, muttering the word "yuck" under his breath, and could feel Abbie rolling her eyes at them. The kids ran upstairs to begin plotting their vampire/zombie war. Ashley and Sam headed back to the kitchen, giving them space.

Lilly just held Brooke tight. She had the life she'd always wanted. She had the man to whom she'd given her heart back and had children she could love. She finally felt complete.

Chapter Thirty-Four

Paying It Forward
15 Years Later

Cole smiled as he parked the car behind the small bookstore that Lilly and Aunt Ash owned. Somehow, through the expansion of online stores, and E-readers, the tiny little shop had survived and even thrived. They did far more than just sell books, which they still did. Not just the current bestsellers, but also rare, hard-to-find gems.

They also sold the idea of reading. Everything one could need to lose yourself in stories. They hosted book clubs, some of which streamed around the world. And many authors came over time to one of the last of the brick-and-mortar stores, to host signing events. A few were beginners, just starting on their journey, while others were bestselling authors with lines stretched around the block.

This would be Cole's third book signing event here. And as usual, the place was packed. He spent the day signing copies of his novel which wrapped up the three-book arc filled with demons, dragons, wizards and witches, and tons of magic. There were children present, as his books were most popular with the young crowd, but there were adults who had come for themselves.

Cole made it a point to speak to each person, and

tried to write something special to all of them. He then sent them to the next table to get the book signed by the man who drew all his covers, and the artwork that began each chapter. Jay chatted with them, sitting beside his book of original art.

Even though they'd seen each other just last night, everyone in the family came by to see Cole during his event.

Of course, Abbie was there. She practically ran the partnership between Cole and Jay. They weren't her only clients, but they were her most important ones. Abbie was, to all intents and purposes, Cole's sister. And she was much more to Jay. Even now, she was waddling around, making sure each detail was perfect. Jay had to practically beg Abbie to sit down and eat something. She was, after all, eating for two.

Cameron showed up, holding hands with a young man he introduced as Aaron. Cole had only met him once before, but Aaron seemed to be able to draw Cameron out of his shy shell. In the years since Cole and Cameron first met, Cameron had begun to heal from his early life. The Reynolds family had managed to become his guardians, and together they became a family.

A few years ago, Tiffany had come over just before Cameron was due to graduate high school. She and Cole talked about how they had gone to family therapy. Their father had loved them as best he could, but he'd put up walls around them. Each felt alone, isolated. Sam thought he needed to be his father, Tiffany pretended her family didn't exist, and Ethan was just lost. But they had come together, for each other and Cameron. He represented a new beginning.

Mrs. Reynolds passed two years after her husband's

suicide. She never fully felt connected to her family again, nor did she ever acknowledge the fact that Uncle Drew and Aunt Ashley were half-siblings to her children. The three of them had grieved, but they found comfort with each other. Each of Cole's Reynolds family members came in, hugged him, and congratulated him. They had once been nothing but strangers, but now, they were family.

Uncle Drew and Sam came early in the morning. Sam had made detective within two years of getting married, just after returning from maternity leave. The twins were now almost eight. Paul and Matthew walked in, holding hands with their little sister Mary named after Sam's mom.

Ollie managed to bring his brood in, who ran throughout the store like the little heathens they were, skidding to a halt under the deathly stare of one of the bookstore owners, their mom Ashley. Kelli, their oldest daughter, sighed as she tried to help her mom wrangle her younger siblings, all four of them, into some sort of order so they could say hi to their Uncle Cole, Uncle Jay, and Aunt Abbie. Thankfully, their youngest sibling Lauren was still trapped in her stroller, but something told Cole she was going to be the wildest of them all.

Of course, Lilly was with Cole all day. This wasn't just her store that she owned and ran with Aunt Ash, but the event was completely her doing. She breezed around the store, often hand in hand with Abbie, seeing that everyone was happy and every need of their customers was met. She only took a break from her role as event planner when Brooke came by.

Three years after they'd tied the knot, they had adopted Mia. She was a mixed-race foster child that everyone in the system had given up on. Between her traumatic past, and troubling behavior, not to mention that she was thirteen, they said they knew it was too late for a girl with a learning disability, ADHD, and autism to find a forever home. Everyone knew that, Mia most of all.

Brooke and Lilly had proven them all wrong. For years, it was rough sailing. Mia fought, battled, and did everything she could to give her new parents an excuse to reject her. They never did. They dug in, they worked harder, and they loved her with every fiber of their being.

One night, Cole found her on the back porch. He recognized that glint in her eye. She was ready to run. Instead, he took her out for a milkshake and a long conversation. She'd tried almost everything she could think of to be treated how she expected to be treated. How she felt she deserved to be treated. Maybe it was time to try something new.

Things weren't all roses and sunshine from that moment on, but they did slowly change. Lilly and Brooke had done everything they could think of before that night, but the one thing they hadn't done was talk to Mia about where they had come from. Where they all came from.

The unlovable, who became a family that loved.

It planted the seed. Mia understood, she wasn't alone.

A lot had changed over the years. The General had retired from heading McAlister Security but left it in the capable hands of Stephanie. He had married Nana Rose, and the two of them argued as much as they acted like teenagers.

Ollie was now chief of police in Ember Falls, with

Drew as his head detective. Every once in a while, Drew would take a leave to work on a case for McAlister, but those were few and far between. He always came home, to Ember Falls, where he belonged.

After the signing was over, the store closed its doors and Cole helped Lilly clean up. They chatted as they worked, Cole telling her about his next book that was ready to come out soon. Within a few months, he wanted to have a launch party from right here. It was the best thing Cole had ever written. It was filled with heroes and monsters and magical fantasy, but in its own way, it was more real than anything else he'd written. Lilly had presented early copies to his family the night before. Press hadn't even begun, and the ink was barely dry, but there was something about this book that Cole felt was special.

It was *his* story, wrapped up in superheroes and galactic villains.

There was a knock on the door and Lilly smiled. "That must be them. Go sit. I'll bring them to you. You remember what I told you?"

Cole's heart froze the moment she'd spoken to him about the special favor she wanted from him, and the conditions that went along with it. "Yeah. No touching. Don't expect eye contact or take it personally if he doesn't say a word to me. Stay in my seat, and don't tower." He rolled his eyes for effect. "I don't tower over anyone but you."

She smirked but ran off to open the front door.

From the back, Cole could hear Lilly make small talk with a man and woman she'd met through a support group for adoptive parents. The young couple thanked Lilly profusely for allowing them to come now after everyone else had left.

Cole wanted to go to the front to greet them. To see the faces associated with the voices he was hearing, but he stayed in his spot and waited. He understood, better than almost anyone, how important this went right for the one person whose voice he didn't hear.

After a few more moments, Lilly let the family forward.

The father was big, not unlike Uncle Drew. Mike worked construction but with the build of a pro wrestler. Still, there was a kindness in his eyes that spoke volumes. The mother was tall, thin with thick black hair and a face that told Cole she ruled in the board room of her small company. Lauren had her hand clasped with her husband but seemed hesitant to touch her son. Lilly had told him they'd been married almost five years and had just adopted the small boy who currently held Cole's book and had his eyes glued to his sneakers.

Seth had seen way too much for a child of eight. What he'd seen, nobody was sure. He still wouldn't talk about it, even though both of his very abusive parents would never see him for the rest of his life.

He saw a phycologist three times a week, but wouldn't speak of whatever he'd witnessed. He'd been in his new home for six months but barely spoke a word. The only time he seemed at peace is when he could lose himself in a story where the monsters were fought and slain with magic.

For the briefest of moments, Seth peeked up and Cole saw his eyes. It was like staring into a mirror of his past.

With much urging, Seth shuffled forward to present the first book in Cole's debut series for an autograph. He

Vincent Morrone

got much more.

Cole signed the book and asked if he'd read the sequels. Seth managed a small nod.

Lauren stepped forward. "We didn't want you to have to sign all three of them. Just giving him the chance to get to meet you is so wonderful."

Cole reached over to a pile of books he had near him. He quickly signed books two and three in the series and pushed them forward. "They should be in a set. Seth, your mom and dad told Lilly how much you love reading. I can't tell you how much it means to me to meet you. I mean, I get it. I get how important it is to be able to retreat into a world of fiction when the world is scary. After all, monsters…Real monsters, are scary, even when they can't hurt you anymore."

Seth didn't respond, but he did lift his eyes just a fraction of an inch.

"I also heard you like to write stories. Handwriting them can be a pain."

That earned him a small shrug.

Cole reached down beneath the table, pulling up a fabric bag that had a picture of his three-book trilogy on it. An idea had occurred to him last night, one he wasn't sure was a great idea at the time, but now that he'd met Seth who was doing his best not to tremble, he knew it was the right move.

"I want to give you a couple of things." Cole kept his voice soft, as he hunched down as much as he could to be small. He saw the involuntary flinch that Seth gave with almost any sound. That haunted look in Seth's eyes made the darkness in Cole's soul threaten to storm forward, but he pushed it back. He'd have a good cry later.

"When I was just about your age, I came to live with my aunt, uncle, and Lilly here." He gestured toward the red-headed woman who was watching him from a few feet away, pride beaming in her eyes. "She really indulged my love of books. And my Aunt Ash? She got me this."

From the bag, he pulled out a small laptop. It was old, and out of date, but for what it was needed, it would work. "It's got word on there. No internet," he glanced at his parents, making sure they were okay with what he was doing, "but your mom and dad can use a USB to transfer files, and print them off. Even email them. I wrote my first stories on this. Worked on the comic book I did with Jay Lancaster."

Cole pushed it forward, next to the pile of books he'd just signed. "I even wrote the first draft of Magic's Fire on it. There are a lot of little stories I created on this thing. Might even put them into an anthology at some point. I found that creating a new world, it helped me deal with everything that terrified me in the real one."

Cole sat back, and waited.

Slowly, Seth put out his hand. It touched the laptop lightly as if he were afraid it might be so hot it would burn. "You don't mean…"

Lauren's hand shot to her mouth. Clearly, she never expected her son to speak tonight.

Cole smiled. "Yes. I want you to have it. I want you to use it to write. See, authors, we need to write. It's inside of us. Getting those words out, telling those stories that happen in our minds…" He gently pushed the laptop forward another inch. "It's what we do. And you'll be surprised at what you can say with a story set in another universe, or in a land full of dragons."

He leaned forward just a touch. "It helped me, when the monsters that terrified me felt like they were just lurking in the shadows. So, I want you to write. And I'm going to give you my email address. My personal one. I want to read whatever you write. I will read anything you send me. Because stories are *meant* to be read. Okay?"

Seth's fingers traced the old stickers of dragons, zombies, and superheroes he'd stuck on the laptop years ago. For the first time since coming into the store, the little boy made eye contact with Cole. It didn't last for more than an instant, but it happened.

"Oh, and one more thing." Once again, he reached into the bag and pulled out a book. It featured colorful artwork with a mighty superhero glowing with power, ready to do battle. "I first wrote this story for the first comic book my buddy Jay and I created back when I was eight. It was a moment of such pride until I realized that I let a little too much truth into it. I ended up throwing it out. I never wanted to see it again."

Reaching into the bag again, Cole pulled out the old amateur comic book. The paper was yellowed, and a few pages were torn in the corners, but it was whole. "My uncle kept it. He gave it to me a little after I turned eleven. I'd been in counseling. It took a while for me to learn it was okay to talk about what happened. Longer to learn it wasn't my fault. Uncle Drew saved this until he thought I was ready. I cried for an hour." He handed the comic to Seth. "That's okay too. Crying. My tough ex-marine uncle taught me that. But this time, I didn't throw it out. I read it. I kept it. And promised myself that someday, I'd finish the full story."

Cole tapped the new novel. "And here it is. This won't be released for another six months. I just got these copies for my family two days ago. And I need a favor from you."

Seth, who had been mesmerized by the new book and old comic, glanced up. Suspicion whirled in his small, narrowing eyes. "What?"

Cole folded his hands. Seth was looking at him, right in the eye. The concept was probably petrifying, but the kid was managing to do it.

"I'd like you to tell me what you think after you read it." Cole sat back. "This story is complete fiction, but it has a lot of truth in it. *My* truth. And it's a little scary to put it out there. I'd like to hear what you have to say. You can call me, or you can write to me. Whatever is easier. Read my story Seth, and then at the end, there's something called an afterword. It's a little bit where the writer talks directly to the reader. I put that in there, knowing it needed to be said. But until now, I didn't realize I might have been writing it for you. Now, don't cheat." He allowed himself to smile just a little. "Story first. Then, read that part. Okay."

Seth nodded and for the briefest of moments, he smiled back.

Cole stayed at his place until the family had left. Mike shook his hand. Lauren leaned down and kissed him gently on his cheek. But it was the small wave that Seth sent him that told him that just maybe, he'd made a difference tonight.

****

It took Seth two days to read the book. He read it slowly, not because he couldn't plow through it, but because he wanted to savor every word. Picture every battle. Feel every emotion from the safety of the page.

In the story, a boy named Charlie lost his mother.

She was an astronaut, searching for a new home for the people of Earth. In reality, she wasn't dead. And Charlie would have to be drafted into an interstellar law enforcement group called the Nova Corps and become a superhero named Captain Nova to save her.

The bad guy was named Saeva, and he was downright evil. He seemed super powerful, more powerful than even Captain Nova. But Charlie would learn that his power was based on the fear of others.

In the end, Captain Nova didn't defeat Saeva alone, but with the help of his friends. Interstellar heroes who would become his family.

When the story was done, Seth turned to the afterword.

This was the story I created when I was being haunted by my own Saeva. That name means Cruel in Latin. It's what my stepfather was. By now, most of you reading this know about the man who killed sixty-three women. Many know how my family defeated him. What they don't know is how I managed to heal.

My stepfather did everything he could to make himself into the personification of hate, but he was just a pathetic coward.

My family healed me. They loved me. They listened. They let me know I was never alone. And I wasn't.

The biggest battle I ever faced wasn't against Edward Hunter, but with the fear in my mind. He'd told me to never tell anyone. That he'd know. He'd always know.

But in fact, talking would take away his power. And helped give me mine.

So, if you're reading this know that the secret that haunts you is also what holds you back. Find that person who loves you, and tell them. Reach out. Take your power back. Be your own hero.

Real heroes are afraid. They cry. But they rise and find their voice. Their power comes from love. Embrace it. And remember, it was never your fault.

Seth reread it twice before closing the book. Slowly, he slipped out of his bed. It was late. Only five minutes until he was supposed to turn out the lights and go to sleep, where Seth would be alone with the demons in the dark.

He crept downstairs to where his new parents sat. They were probably talking about him because they got quiet the moment he appeared.

Mike smiled at him. "Hey, buddy. It's almost time for bed. We were going to come up in a minute."

Seth walked over and sat down. He wiped the tears away that he hadn't realized he'd shed. His new mom started to reach forward but was afraid to touch him. Afraid to scare him.

Seth held out the book, opened to the afterword that Cole Duncan had written just for him, before ever meeting him, and took a deep breath. "I want to talk."

A word about the author...

Vincent Morrone is an eclectic author of dark stories filled with broken souls that find healing through laughter and love. Born in Brooklyn, he now lives in Upstate New York with his family. Their home is operated for the comfort of their four dogs. Vincent runs a local critique group and has conducted workshops for his local RWA chapter. He is the author of nine published novels, including the award-winning Torn series, the Vision series, and Just Breathe, plus one novella and three short stories.

As they say in Brooklyn: Yo, you got something to say? Vincent would love to hear from you at Vincent@vincentmorrone.com

www.ingramcontent.com/pod-product-compliance
Lightning Source LLC
Chambersburg PA
CBHW060805030726
47503CB00002B/347